SHATTERED PEACE

VIGILES URBANI CHRONICLES BOOK 4

KEN LANGE

Shattered Peace
Ken Lange

Published by Ken Lange
Copyright © 2020, Ken Lange
Edited by Lisa Miller
Cover Art by Natania Barron

This is a work of fiction. Names, characters, places, and incidents are products of the author's imagination or are used fictitiously and are not to be construed as real. Any resemblance to actual events, locales, organizations, or persons, living or dead, is entirely coincidental.
All rights reserved. No part of this book may be used or reproduced electronically or in print without written permission, except in the case of brief quotations embodied in reviews.

To anyone I've let down, mistreated, or hurt during the course of my life, I'm sorry. All I can say is I'm a work in progress and I'm trying to be better than the person I used to be.

I cannot change what happened, but be assured, I've learned and grown from the person I was.

1

August 15th

The scent of magnolias lilted in from one of the nearby neighborhoods as ancient oaks swayed gently in the breeze. Lights kicked on, highlighting the edges of the perfectly manicured grass along the asphalt walkways that ran throughout Audubon park. With the last vestiges of sun beyond the horizon, night gripped the city.

The patrons—okay, the rich pricks living around the park—paid a fee to ensure there was plenty of lighting here. A harsh white glow kept the long shadows at bay, allowing those still milling about a measure of safety they wouldn't otherwise have.

When photographers, film crews, and writers wrote about New Orleans, they painted scenes like the one before me. These were always too sterile, too clean…too fake. Postcards, movies, and TV shows portrayed the city as being full of charm, gentile folk, and exceptionally romantic, or a party city where you didn't have to care about tomorrow.

They sold a lie. Not really their fault; someone spun that tale long ago. All they did was perpetuate it.

If these people knew the truth—darkness surrounded them, and monsters were real—they'd hide in their homes, or better still, move. Yet, somehow, they didn't notice it or the war that constantly raged in the shadows.

Couldn't blame them completely...violence and death were commonplace here. Always had been, probably always would be. It was as if the land was corrupted by an ancient darkness.

One day, if we weren't careful, it'd devour us all.

Terrible shit I assure you, but that was later, and this was now. And the now wasn't exactly rosy.

On a global level, we were screwed.

How?

Let's start with the Black Circle, a group of nut job necromancers who aspired to...well I wasn't exactly sure what their endgame was. Last year I found and wiped out enough zombies in New Mexico to overtake a small country. By their own admission, they murdered my predecessor, and generally meant me personally—and the Archive as a whole—harm.

Next up to bat were the Gotteskinder, a group of fanatic mortals who wanted to exterminate everyone with power. For a touch of cosmic irony, they were the unwitting puppets of the lich lords. You heard that right. The insane fanatics who'd rather cave in their own skulls than dirty themselves by being in the presence of those of us with power actually worked for the Black Circle...a bunch of people of power...corrupted as it may be.

The icing on this massive shit-cake came in the form of the vampire Courts and their current situation.

A little over a month ago, the strigoi, a strain of vampirism, perished in an instant. One moment they were alive, killing folks, and generally being assholes. The next they were extinct. Took a minute for that to sink in since they were bound exclusively to Romania, but when it did, shockwaves rippled throughout the supernatural community. For the first time in recorded history, one of the royals was killed. With very few exceptions, vampires around the globe closed their doors, shut down their businesses, and vanished from sight within the week.

Those few exceptions came in the form of those who worked for the Archive directly, i.e. a governor, prefects, triumvirate members, and a couple of businesses whose only client was the Archive.

War was coming and there wasn't anything I could do to stop it. It wasn't a matter of if any longer. Now it boiled down to when.

Lazarus, being the wise and gracious leader he'd always been, called a meeting of the governors…minus me and the vigiles…because that made perfect sense. I mean, why would you invite those of us who were bound to uphold the law and defend those under our protection?

Oh, did I mention that this roundtable of experts was meeting in his home?

Not sure how he'd managed it, but he built his house around one of the two gates in Rome then cut access to it with complex enchantments. Only way through it was with an invitation that could be revoked at any time.

That being said, Andrew and Kimberly, Heather's mother, opted for the second gate three days ago to assess things. Judging by Kim's call to her daughter, they felt a need to ask for an additional set of eyes and hands.

I wasn't a fan of the idea, but she felt a need to go. If it were up to me, they'd just come back tonight. That, however, was off the table.

Heather nudged my arm. "You okay?"

"Not even a little bit."

She sighed. "Me neither."

At least she had sense. "Still think you should convince Andrew and your mom to come home tonight. Barring that, I should come along, unofficially of course, to lend moral support."

"You know as well as I do that's a bad idea. Over the last month, what little relationship you had with Lazarus has gone straight to hell." She gestured at me. "If I go, it won't raise any eyebrows. You showing up, however, will."

Goddamn it. Hated it when she was right. "Fine, but keep your phone on while you're there."

She placed her hand on her hip and turned to face me. "You know damned good and well that Lazarus has forbidden them at the conference."

Crap.

"Actually, I'd forgotten…again."

Heather grinned. "Don't fret."

What the hell was she so happy about?

"Why not? You're going to be cut off while you're there."

She opened her bag, her fingertips glowed slightly, and she ran them along the seam of her purse then pulled it open. The inside of which was much larger than it should've been. "Is that a pocket reality?"

Her eyes sparkled. "Yep."

"Didn't realize they were portable."

A small laugh escaped her lips. "They're not supposed to be, but you know Pépère always finds a way."

Pépère, Henri Fabre, was Heather's grandfather and extremely clever. "For you…and his house."

She bumped her shoulder into mine. "You can't blame him for the latter."

True. Nearly thirty years ago, a necromancer named Ruth attacked him in his own home. Due to a healthy dose of blood magic, a hole opened inside the pocket reality in his office, imprisoning him in Muspelheim. It was sheer stupid luck he'd escaped a few months ago. Since then, he'd upped his home security system. To be specific, he created a ton of realistic looking insects, birds, squirrels, etcetera, and filled them with varying types of magic from Talbis, Gabriel, and himself, making them all extremely lethal.

"No, but he's bordering on paranoia if you ask me."

She glided up the steps of the Pavilion and paused. "It's only paranoia if no one is trying to kill you. In his case, he's got cause."

I frowned. "I know. But this is…well…pushing it."

"Perhaps." She shrugged and waved her hand in front of the pillar. "Got to run. Talk soon."

Kissing her on the cheek, I said, "Be safe. Call when you can."

"I will." She paused. "Oh, and don't forget to check on Andrew's place." Pulling her keys out of her purse, she said, "Would you drop my car off at the shop while you're out? They're expecting it tomorrow."

How could I forget? Andrew had sent me a dozen messages about it this evening. One of the sigils around his house went off about an hour ago and he'd been pushing me to look into it ever since. "I'll take care of it."

A second later, she stepped through the moving picture and it vanished behind her.

For the first time in months, I actually had a little alone time. Gabriel, Alexander, and Heather hadn't let me out of their sight for more than a few minutes since I uncovered the Gotteskinder. I appreciated their concern, but having them hover around me every second of every day got old, fast.

Still, this was golden. It didn't last long as the trip back to the house took a grand total of three minutes.

I strode through the metal archway leading out my side yard... technically still part of the park...and onto the sidewalk leading up to my driveway in front of our three-car garage. I used the extra space to house my gear.

As I approached Heather's SUV, I thumbed the key fob and hit the button to unlock it. Opening the door, I slid into the driver's seat and adjusted it. Heather was tall, but at six-six, I still had several inches on her. After buckling in, I started the vehicle, pulled out my phone, and waited for it to sync. Her taste in music differed significantly from mine. She enjoyed opera for instance, my knowledge of which began and ended with Bugs Bunny.

I changed the radio to media, scrolled through my lists, stopped at the one I'd aptly named, *A Playlist*, and pushed play. Super creative of me I know. With the music handled, I stuffed the phone back into my shirt pocket.

With luck, I could drop the keys in the slot, check on Andrew's place, and be back home within the hour. That'd give me about eight to ten hours on my own before the others figured it out and showed up on my doorstep. Might even sneak a call in to Cain…if he was back from whatever walkabout he was on in the mountains. I needed to figure out which vampire strain was next on his hitlist.

Sighing, I turned on the air conditioner and backed out of the drive. At the stop sign, I wheeled out onto Calhoun. Dark clouds rolled in out of the gulf to obscure the moon. Rain was on the way. Just what this city needed…more moisture in the air, because it wasn't thick enough already.

Suddenly, at Pitt Street, a set of brights cut through the passenger window. Time seemed to slow as they rapidly approached to reveal an older model F150. Shattering glass filled the quiet, not to mention the entire cabin. Metal tore, screeched, and crumpled as the entire right side of the vehicle lurched inward. The F150's engine continued to rev at full tilt. Screeching tires, theirs and mine, dominated the night. Heather's SUV lurched and stuttered sideways.

My armor snapped into place as my head whipped to the side, breaking the driver's side window. A dull thud sounded in my head as it impacted the interior of my helmet. It hurt, but my skull wasn't splattered on the sidewalk.

We weren't at a complete stop when the roar of a powerful diesel cut through the night. Then a beat-up dump truck barreled into view as it flipped on its headlights a half second before slamming into the front bumper. A nasty metallic crack sounded, the SUV listed to one side, and one of my tires shot across someone's lawn.

My head rushed forward into the steering wheel. Stars flashed in front of my eyes, a faint pop sounded as my nose broke, and blood ran freely down my face. The seatbelt jerked me back and held me in place.

In an instant, time resumed its natural course and we came to a stop. Putting their vehicles in reverse, metal and plastic pulled away from the SUV, which limply sat there quite dead. This was some bullshit. Grabbing hold of the door, I forced it open, made a blade of ice and sliced through the seatbelt then staggered out onto the street.

The F150's engine sputtered then died as a person on each side stepped out of the cab and moved in front of their high beams. Someone switched off the dump truck then two people scrambled out of the passenger side and one out of the driver's. Thanks to the fucking brights, all I got of my assailants were silhouettes. Still, I guessed the two from the F150 were male. Our other guests included two more males and a small woman in front.

Someone on the passenger side of the F150 spoke. "Is he dead?"

The outline of the woman in front of the dump truck was off slightly, then again, I did just slam my face into the steering wheel. When she spoke, she had a heavy Irish accent, her words carried power, and everything about her chilled me to my soul. "No, but he will be momentarily."

A thick column of darkness slammed down over my head, encasing me in onyx. My armor dug into my flesh as the inky thing around me pressed inward. Sweat poured down me, my body trembled, and every inch of my skin felt as if it was on fire. I hadn't the breath in my lungs to scream, but that didn't stop me from trying.

The weird energy pressed inward as it seeped into my flesh. I couldn't see it, but my armor began to change, morphing into something entirely new. All the while, my nerve endings writhed in agony as my body betrayed me, keeping me upright. Every muscle in my body was locked. I was unable to move...hell, I couldn't even fall to my knees and beg for mercy.

Darkness ringed my vision as unconsciousness threatened to take me. The black that surrounded me thinned and...someone...a woman...shrieked in pain as the spell broke.

I collapsed to my knees, still unable to breathe, move, or do anything but remain where I was. The Irish woman lay whimpering on the asphalt. One of her people stayed at her side while the others marched my way.

A massive bright light shone behind me.

This was how I died. Unable to move or use my powers. I was trapped in my own flesh and that'd be the end of me.

The four men in front stopped. Then an instant later, four massive shards of golden light protruded from their chests.

Whoever was by the truck grabbed the Irish woman and vanished on the spot.

Four wings made of light and shadow passed over me as the back of someone wearing a long, raggedy, heavy coat with a hood came into view. They touched down between me and the dead, held their hand out, and pulled the four souls from the aether.

My eyes rolled back and I collapsed into oblivion.

2

August 16th

Aww...goddamn it...I was awake.

Every single part of my anatomy hated me. I ached. Odd spasms of pain shot through me for fun, causing my breath to hitch. Whatever torture device I was laying on made things worse. The thing beneath me was hard, jagged, and thin cords ran at weird angles across my back. And the fun was just starting.

My heart thudded against my chest, amping up my misery with each beat. Then there was my breathing. Every breath caused my torso to expand and contract. The muscles around my ribcage stretched, pulling on the bruised and likely fractured bones there. Not a single fiber of my mind, body, or spirit was pleased at this bout of consciousness.

Sadly, though, my suffering wasn't great enough to cause me to blackout again.

I opened my eyes to find myself in a dark bedroom. My vision changed spectrums...the room wasn't mine...nor anyone I knew...an unusual smell hung in the air...was that fall? Where in the hell was I? Certainly not New Orleans as it was still full tilt summer with more heat and humidity than you could shake a stick at. There were birds outside. On the wind was a multitude of scents; spruce, pine, oak... along with many others.

A soft voice floated in from the other room. "Good, you're awake."

It sounded familiar but I couldn't place it. Opening my mouth, I tried to respond. My mouth was dry, and my tongue didn't want to work properly. The sudden intake of breath caused me to choke then cough, which turned into a vicious cycle, thoroughly pissing off my entire being due to the misery it brought me. It took maybe a matter of seconds for the fit to stop but it felt longer.

The door cracked open. A woman with short black and purple hair pushed in backwards carrying a tray. She turned—it was Jessica Grant, now Jade Baker. She held up a hand. "Don't try to speak again. I've got some water."

A few sips later and I could breathe without choking on my own spit. "Thanks."

She grinned and helped me into a sitting position. "Not sure how you're alive...shouldn't be, but here you are looking barely the worse for wear."

The glass was overly heavy, but I managed to hold it on my own. "Magic and I...have a special relationship."

Jade arched an eyebrow. "Magic I'd understand...you were hit with pure necromancy from Deheune."

"Who is that and what makes them so special?" I took a sip of water. "Isn't one necromancer like another?"

She paled. "First off, have a little respect for the enemy. Deheune is a lich lord. She may not be as powerful as Seth or Osiris, but she's never met a person she didn't want to kill." Her expression faltered. "Until last night, she'd never failed doing just that when it suited her."

Oh, uh, okay. "One day, I'll have to make a list of these assholes."

She flicked up a finger as she started counting them off. "Seth, Osiris, Ashur, Sargon, Ambrosio, Osha, Nu Gui, Deheune, and Ke'lets. The latter of which is dead."

Hope to god Kur took note of them, because I wasn't going to remember their names in T minus five seconds. "It isn't that I'm not grateful, but why were you in New Orleans?"

She motioned for me to keep drinking. "To warn you. But I was too late...which is why you're here instead of dead."

"Thank you." Emptying the glass, I set it aside. "Where are we, anyway?"

She shrugged. "Canada. Been holed up here while I collect things needed to start my life over."

Awfully vague, but she'd just saved my ass, so I wasn't going to pry. "How'd you figure out they were after me?"

"It wasn't just you." Her gaze hit the floor. "They came for the Archive as a whole, targeting specific individuals... I haven't a clue how they picked them." She paused. "Thought I had enough time to warn you...but I didn't."

I moved to the edge of the bed and placed my feet on the floor. "Need to let the others know."

She placed a hand on my chest and forced me back down. "You don't understand. It was to be a coordinated attack. They hit you, the governors, two triumvirates, a vigil named Vasile, and several others all in the same moment." Her voice hardened. "Other than you, they had a specific ax to grind with Alfred Monet, your uncle Andrew, and Gabriella Medina."

Either I was a lot weaker than I thought or she was much stronger than she appeared. "Mind letting me up? I need to see if I can stop this. Maybe they weren't able to coordinate things properly."

She gave me a look like I was the dumbest bastard on the planet. "Really? You seem to think that the Black Circle and the Courts, two of the world's most clandestine organizations, can't pull off a simple coordinated attack on an unsuspecting Archive. You're kidding, right?"

Someone ate their Sarcastic-O's this morning. "If that's the case, they're going to need me sooner rather than later...how long was I out?"

She blew out a long breath. "Four hours...it's barely midnight. At the rate you're healing, you'll need another hour or so."

I gestured at her. "Maybe if you did that thing you did when the Grants tried to kill me that'd speed things up."

She chewed her lower lip. "Already tried. Nothing. You're bruised from head to toe, meaning you're hurt, and my ability should heal you." Her voice dropped to a near whisper. "But no matter how hard I try, my powers cannot touch you." Glancing up, she said, "Whatever is happening to you is beyond my ability to help with…I'm sorry."

"Sorry?"

Jade shivered. "Yes…the only people I've ever met I cannot heal are the lich lords. While I know you're not one, something within you is the same, and for that, I'm sorry."

What did you say to something like that?

Simply nodding, I said, "I should go."

Jade pulled several pieces of paper out of her back pocket and handed them to me. "You need to wait till you're healed or you're going to wind up like Alfred and the others."

Unfolding them, I found multiple news reports fresh off the printer. Headline of the first read, *Man Mutilated on the Steps of Notre Dame.*

A photo followed, showing a covered body and dark blood running down the stairs.

Reports are still coming in about prominent businessman and philanthropist, Alfred Monet. From what the police have pieced together from camera footage at the church, Mr. Monet entered the restricted zone at 1:58 a.m. pursued by nine masked assailants. They tackled him to the ground, stabbed him several times, and cut out at least one of his internal organs while he was still alive.

Alfred was a governor due in Rome later today…not sure why he sought sanctuary at a burned-out church.

The editorial continued but I moved to the next.

An article out of Hong Kong.

Woman Burned at the Stake.

A photo of a blurred-out body and scorch marks around the base came next.

Local restaurant owner, Van Hang, was tied to a post, doused in petrol, and set afire outside her home in broad daylight around nine this morning.

While the motives are unclear, there is some speculation that the Triad is involved.

Van Hang was a triumvirate out of Asia.

Flipping to the next, I found a clipping from Cape Town.

Severed Head of a Woman Found on Spike.

Photo of a beheaded corpse with spike followed.

Local artist Aitan Kaya was found brutally murdered in her driveway at two this morning. Neighbors complained to the police of shouts and screaming. By the time they arrived, Ms. Kaya was already dead.

A triumvirate out of southern Africa.

On to the next.

House Fire in Covington.

Photo of a burning house followed.

Local city official's house was set ablaze…neighbors called the fire department shortly after eight p.m. No body has been found yet.

Ms. Dodd was a prefect for the southern territories of North America.

So far, all the hits were on those of the vampiric persuasion.

Next.

Three Abandoned Vehicles Found in the Garden District.

A photo of the dump truck, F150, and Heather's destroyed vehicle, along with three tarps covering what I assumed were bodies, followed.

The incident was called into police around eight p.m. after a neighbor had a tire crash through their front window. NOPD has sent a special investigations unit, the Uncommon Crimes Department (UCD), to check into what happened. Officer Jeremy Riggs was first on the scene.

According to what we know, there was a multiple car accident involving a black SUV and two other vehicles resulting in four fatalities. At least one of the drivers is unaccounted for.

Next

Building Collapses Near Vatican.

Photo of an ancient three-story stone building that'd caved in followed.

Shortly after one a.m., a small fire broke out in the residence, causing the gas line to explode. At the time, the owners, who have been unavailable for comment, were throwing a party of some sort. We can confirm at least eighteen people are dead. Several of the guests escaped the blaze but haven't been seen since. The police are currently looking for them so they can be questioned as to what happened.

My heart sank. "Do you know if Andrew and the other governors were amongst the living?" I glanced through the pages again. "I don't see anything about Vasile."

Her eyes glowed slightly in the darkness. "If the texts on your phone are any indication, they're alive."

My phone, fuck. "Where is it? I'll need to contact them."

She handed it to me. "There's no signal out here so you'll have to wait...but I thought you'd want whatever information you could get."

And she was right. "Thanks."

I scrolled through the messages.

Baptist was first up.

Found Heather's vehicle smashed to bits and several dead bodies impaled with golden spears. Either you've developed a new ability, or you had help. Get in touch.

Andrew via Heather's phone.

Things have gone to shit here. On the move. Contact you shortly. Andrew.

Gabriel was next.

Are you okay? Baptist called, said there was a mess.

Where are you? We're all checking our symbols every few seconds to make sure you're alive.

Alexander followed.

My people have combed the area. As far as we can tell you didn't personally teleport out. Get in touch.

• • •

Finally came Vasile Ciocan.

Had some unpleasant visitors while I was in town tending to a situation. They were vampire and necromancer. I've handled things. My current concern is you. From what I understand, you're missing. As soon as you can send a message, do so. If I don't hear from you by dawn, I'll come looking.

Dozens of others like it followed.

Christ, I knew we were seriously unprepared for this war, but this…this wasn't what I'd imagined it'd be.

"I've got to go before dawn."

She frowned. "Why?"

Holding my phone out, I pointed to Vasile's text. "Because I've got a strong suspicion you don't want to be found. The moment he decides to find me, he will."

Jade shifted on the spot. "Good point." She pointed at the far end of the room. "There's a shower in there and your clothes will be ready shortly. They're in the dryer now."

Huh? I glanced down. Shit, I was naked. "Uh…why am I undressed?"

She scrunched up her nose. "You were covered in your own blood. Thought you'd appreciate being clean before returning."

Fuck that, I wanted to go now. But being naked would raise more questions than I'd like to answer. "Thank you, again."

Twenty minutes later, I was clean and wearing freshly laundered clothes. The shower returned a portion of my strength and it was time for me to leave. "If it's all the same to you, I'm going to head out now."

"I'm not quite ready to take you back yet." She frowned. "Rather you didn't know where I lived. Sorry, it isn't like I don't trust you, but an overabundance of caution is never a bad thing."

Couldn't blame her for being careful. "That's all right, I can leave from here."

Jade gave me a curious look. "You can?"

Pausing, I asked, "Do you have a cell? Some way for me to contact you other than email?"

She shook her head. "No, but with the way things are going, I suspect we'll be talking sooner rather than later."

Well, that wasn't promising. "So, you're not going to interject yourself into the current mess?"

She lowered her voice to a near whisper. "It isn't time yet. The only reason I intervened now was to save your life. There are four of us... You, me, the Star Born, and the Plague Bearer."

I froze. "Do you know who the others are?"

She nodded. "Viktor Warden is the Star Born. And since the strigoi are no more, I suspect Cain is awake."

Well that was specific. "I can see how you figured out Viktor...but Cain?"

A small laugh escaped her. "Seth's been obsessed with him since well before I was born. He tasked Inna, my former handler, to find him after Ke'lets death. It was my understanding that she was getting close over the last few years." She smiled. "By the sound of things, you know the man."

My meeting with Cain and Nid wasn't what you'd call unpleasant, but it wasn't fun either. It was more like a necessary evil. "We've met."

Her eyes glowed again. "What'd you think of him?"

That was a good question. "He...he's not what you'd expect. That's not to imply he's a nice guy or a cruel one, for that matter." Frustrated, I sighed. "The man has a job to do. It isn't pleasant, but it has to be done. That takes a special type of dedication...and he's perfect for the job."

She snickered. "Informative yet extremely vague."

I shrugged. "When you meet him, you can decide for yourself."

"When?" She cocked her head to the side. "What makes you think we'll meet?"

"Like you said, there are four of us. Eventually, we'll cross each other's path...it can't be helped." Seriously, it was as if someone were orchestrating things, giving us each just enough information to keep us alive but nothing more. "There are other powers at work here that make it impossible for it not to happen."

She nodded. "Speaking of other powers at work...did you know all the diviners have gone blind? Not literally, but in the sense they can no longer see the future with any accuracy?"

"I didn't. Are you sure about this?"

She rubbed the back of her neck. "Absolutely positive. It's my understanding that over the last fifteen months or so, their ability to foresee what's next has gotten worse and worse. Then a few months ago, everything went dark."

I blinked. "Do you know specifically when that happened?"

Jade chuckled. "I can give you an exact date."

"Oh?"

She nodded. "The day the strigoi were killed. That was when things went dark."

Wasn't that some shit. It'd also explain why Lazarus hadn't seen the attack coming. "Good to know. Thanks."

She held out a hand. "Before you go, I offer you a warning. The Archive has been compromised in multiple ways. Be very careful who you trust...especially Lazarus."

Curious. "Why especially?"

She shook her head. "Nothing solid...just rumors within the inner workings of the Black Circle claim that Lazarus was compromised before the Archive's inception."

Interesting. If that was true, what was their—Lazarus and whoever he was working with—endgame? "Good to know, thanks." I waved. "Might want to step back a bit."

She arched an eyebrow. "Why?"

"Not sure how the outer bubble works, but it is made of fire so... your choice if you want to get scorched or not."

She took two large steps back. "Okay."

"I'll be out of your hair in a second." Lowering my gaze to hers, I said, "Cannot express to you how much I appreciate you saving my ass...again."

She waved. "You're welcome."

With a thought, indigo flames enveloped me.

Materializing next to my desk, I deeply considered another shower, some food, and a few aspirin. All that would do was piss folks off enough to have them finish what Deheune started. This sucked, but there was no way around it. Easing into my chair, I slowly pulled out my phone and set up a group text for Andrew, Gabriel, Baptist, Alexander, and Talbis.

My thumb hovered over the keypad on the screen.

Damn it.

If Jade was correct, and I had no reason to doubt her, Lazarus was a security risk. That meant our entire system was likely compromised.

I still needed to let everyone know I was fine though. I'd have to keep it brief. With that thought in mind, I pecked out a text.

Sorry for the delay in getting back with you all, had a rough/long night. While it's unfortunate about Heather's SUV being totaled, you should be aware, I'm fine.

Exercise extreme caution with all lines of communication. Do not put yourself at any unnecessary risk by moving if you don't have to.

More shortly.

Vasile rated a private text.

I'm safe, contact you soon by alternate means.
Need to talk and your help.

Setting the phone aside, I leaned forward and hit the power button on the computer. The welcome screen popped just as the doorbell rang. Great. I closed my eyes, took a deep breath, and stood. No way I'd make three flights of stairs before they either started pounding on the door or left. Three flights of stairs weren't going to happen in my current condition. Flames wrapped around me. Hobbling over to the front window, I pulled back the curtain to find a very tired and grumpy looking Captain Baptist.

This was going to be a fun conversation.

Opening the door, I said, "Morning. Come on in, we've got a lot to go over."

His thick Russian accent made him sound angrier than I hoped he was. "How the hell do you know I'm not a shifter?"

Honestly, it was a fair question. "Because you don't stink of jasmine. Now, do you want to come in or take a chance on someone shooting us in the head?"

Baptist frowned as he strode over the threshold. "You really need to get this place warded soon."

He wasn't wrong. As a housewarming gift, Andrew placed a few sigils around the house. If someone made it inside the place without having their gray matter splattered across the walls, they were safe. When things slowed down, he'd finish. "What's the worry? The work Alyosha did on the place should keep me safe."

"Aly's craftmanship is amazing, but if they found a way inside…all that armor on the outside wouldn't do anything to help."

Andrew was paranoid enough for all three of us, which was why he'd done the quick and dirty enchantments. "True…sure, we'll finish up the wards soon. For now, we have adequate protection."

He didn't appear convinced. "We'll see." His tone lightened. "You okay? Heather's vehicle is trashed…not sure how you're upright after such a collision."

"Let's find a comfortable place to sit. This whole being vertical thing is overrated." I gestured for him to follow. In the living room, I gingerly hobbled over to the nearest recliner. While I had the information Jade gave me, I needed to know what was happening within the official channels. "How bad is it?"

His expression hardened. "There's a whirlwind of shit out there. Someone attacked Lazarus, the six governors in Rome, and they managed to murder Alfred Monet." He shook his head. "There for a few I thought they'd gotten to you as well. But your ties to the house weren't cut and the centurions were still marked, so we knew you were breathing."

Thanks to Jade. "What about Heather and Kimberly?"

"My understanding is Heather was injured." He held out his hand to stop me. "But they're somewhere safe and treating her wounds."

Not great news. "Anything else?"

Baptist raised his gaze to mine. "A few triumvirates died and loads of vampires who worked for the Archive were killed. At this point, what we know is more or less status updates with each one landing one blow after the other." He paused. "My main concern is where you've been since the attack."

Truth was always best. "Teleported…not sure where. At which point I proceeded to be unconscious for several hours. You heard from me the moment I had a signal."

He was quiet for several seconds. "And your mysterious helper?"

"I'm nearly as clueless about them as you are." I didn't lie. Jade was truly an unknown factor. "Thing is, if they'd meant me harm, I'd be dead. Simple as that."

"That's true." He scratched his beard. "I…well…I'd like to ask them a question or three…hell more than that."

I frowned. "What's got you so bothered?"

Wonder shone in his eyes. "The golden shards…they're unlike anything I've ever seen."

Last I recalled, they were little more than light. "You say that like they're literal gold."

Baptist pulled air in through his teeth. "More golden than gold." His voice trailed off. "We could cut through gold." He gave me a dismissive wave. "Whatever it is, we've sent it over to Warden Global for analysis."

That was some shit. "How'd you remove the bodies?"

"Pulled the first one out by hand." His gaze hit the floor. "Then people started coming out of their homes…too many witnesses around, so the others had to wait for the crane to arrive."

"Huh?"

He chewed on his cheek. "Each spike weighs in at fifteen hundred pounds. Didn't want people wagging their tongues about me pulling the others free."

What the...he can manhandle that much weight on his own? That was insane. "Wow...okay." I blew out a breath. "This probably won't help you figure out what it's made out of, but it might be important."

"What's that?"

Best just to say it. "It wasn't like I got a good look at what was happening...I'd just gotten bitch slapped by Deheune—who happens to be a lich lord. Anyway...those spikes started off as what looked to be shards of golden light."

All the color left Baptist's face. "Wait. You were attacked by Deheune...and she's a lich lord?"

Guess he didn't have a list either. "Yep."

"She's powerful." His shoulders slumped forward. "And vile as they come."

Someone needed to share. "You've heard of her?"

"Only in whispers." He gave me a dismissive wave. "They made her out to be some sort of goddess." A derisive snort escaped him. "It never ceases to amaze me how some people of power, or in this case a lich lord, have made themselves into some sort of deity in the hopes of being worshiped...talk about being vain. I'd hoped she was myth."

The thought of being encased in that onyx pillar made me wince. "She's definitely real. And she packs a mean punch as well."

He frowned. "I'm sure she does. The important thing is you survived."

A point we could both agree on. I opened my mouth to speak when my phone rang.

Alexander.

Damn.

I raised a finger. "Hold on a sec, people are checking in."

Answering the phone, I said, "Hello."

He let out a low growl. "That's it? All you've got to say?"

"All I'm going to say over the phone. I'll be checking in with the others shortly. You going to be there?"

He paused. "Already here. How long will you be?"

Shrugging, I said, "Not long. Speaking with Baptist now."

Alexander grumbled. "Should've guessed he'd be there. He's been dealing with that mess you made around the corner."

"Great, talk soon."

Lowering the phone, I ended the call.

Baptist blinked. "That was…well…impolite."

"It wasn't meant to be." I sighed. "We have to consider our communication system may've been hacked."

He pulled out his phone. "Someone would need access to some sensitive information to make that a reality."

Leaning forward, I placed my elbows on my knees. "Yes, they would. The number of people I trust at the moment are few and far between. Anyone outside my immediate circle is suspect up to and including Lazarus."

His voice dropped. "Do you have reason to suspect him?"

Wish I didn't, but I did. "Several. Over the last six months or so, our relationship has been…strained." That was an outright lie. The man barely spoke to me and when he did, he wasn't pleasant about it. "Rumors have it he isn't thrilled with me freeing the weres…among other things."

Baptist shifted in his seat. "Heard them…hoped they weren't true."

My gut said that the weres were only part of the issue. "Me too. For now, we've got to figure out who we can trust, move forward, and fix things as we go."

"Da, that'd be best." He sighed. "What can I do?"

"Just focus on getting the new building up and running. Speaking of which, with that crew that Viktor sent over…how's that coming along?"

A big smile crossed his lips. "We've actually moved into a small section on the first floor. With the tech upgrades Warden Global is supplying—"

Cutting in, I said, "Make sure they don't hook into the UCD network. I want to keep you offline until we can ensure the system is safe. Last thing we need to do is compromise you guys out the gate."

His expression hardened. "Then you're fairly certain there's a problem."

"Well…I can't say with one hundred percent accuracy." Shaking my head, I closed my eyes for a moment. "But the odds are high it is. In this case, it's best to err on the side of caution."

He got to his feet. "I'll see to it. I suspect you have other things to tend to."

Unfortunately, I did. "Thanks. As soon as I figure out a safer way to communicate, I'll let you know."

Baptist paused. "I could ask the tech guys from Warden Global. I'm sure they'd be happy to get us some new equipment…unless you think they're compromised as well."

Why hadn't I thought of that. "Doubt anyone would live long enough to infiltrate their organization. Do it. Worst they can say is no."

"Doubt that'll happen." He got to his feet and waved. "Talk soon."

With that, he was out the door.

That took care of one of my obligations. Now to check in with the others then form a rescue plan for the governors. Easy.

3

The first rays of light were peeking over the horizon when I arrived outside the perimeter of Henri's property. His recent upgrades took offense to my sudden appearance. They did their best to murder me and thankfully failed. The main issue came in the form of the destruction of the tinker toy after it expended its energy on me. Since their introduction, I decided it best to walk through the gate to prevent their demise. With the way things were going at the moment, he, along with everyone else, could use the added protection.

I barely had the gate open when Gabriel lumbered out onto the porch.

"Morning." He cocked his head to the side. "You all right?"

Everything hurt, my body ached, and I couldn't get past the fact everything felt off as a whole. "Well enough. Are you the welcome committee?"

He stepped off the porch to meet me about halfway. Towering over me, he dropped his voice to a near whisper. "I'm thrilled to see you're okay…the others will be too…right now though, they're frightened and angry." He cut his gaze toward the house. "They're going to come at you wrong, especially considering the night you've had." Gesturing at me, he said, "All I ask is that you don't lose your temper. I've got a feeling that we'll need everyone above ground for the fight ahead."

It was times like this that exemplified what most people would consider to be his angelic nature. After what I'd learned about angels, I'd disagree. What was on display now came from his late mother, Martha O'Neill.

"I'll do my best." I patted him on the shoulder. "Where are they?"

He thumbed over at the door. "In the dining room."

Time to get this over with so I could move on with the whole rescuing Heather and the governors' part of my day.

"Who's here?"

Gabriel grinned. "Family only; Talbis, Alexander, and Henri." His expression faltered. "Sent for Isidore but haven't heard back yet."

Isidore was Andrew's personal guard. Normally, he'd be with him, but Lazarus specifically forbade Isidore from coming. As such, he went on a retreat in the bayou out past New Iberia with the pack he led. Had to wonder how pissed off he'd be when he got the news.

As it stood, the people inside were trustworthy; a commodity currently in short supply.

I waved him ahead. "After you."

Gabriel chewed on his bottom lip as he nodded. Pivoting on the spot, he walked up the stairs and pulled open the door with me right on his heels. We trekked down the hall and turned right into the dining room. Henri sat at the head of the table with Alexander on his right and Talbis on his left.

He forced a smile onto his face. "Told you, he's fine."

I pulled out the chair opposite Henri and plopped into the seat.

Let the inquest begin.

Alexander's expression soured. He leaned toward me sniffing the air. "You smell different."

Weird, but not totally unexpected. I showered at Jade's, so that was bound to change my scent.

Kur wriggled in my mind. *"It's more than that. There've been changes...not sure how deep things go, but that bolt of pure necromancy has altered you on a fundamental level."*

Wasn't that special. *"How damaged am I?"*

He flitted around the interior of my skull. *"You're not. If anything, it's a major upgrade. Need to look into it more to figure out exactly what it's done."*

"Get back with me."

I shrugged. "New soap."

Alexander shook his head. "No, it's something else."

A cautious smile crossed Henri's lips. "Alexander's right. There's something off about you."

Gabriel stood next to me facing the others. "If the pictures we saw of Heather's car is any indication, he's had a rough night."

"It's okay." Taking a deep breath, I let it out slowly. "Here's the deal. I got T-boned by an F150 then a dump truck plowed into the SUV for shits and giggles. Once we came to a stop and I stumbled out of the vehicle, Deheune, a lich lord, proceeded to bitch slap me." I shivered. "Apparently, she showed up personally to put me in the ground."

Talbis blinked. "Wait…you're sure it was Deheune?"

Somehow doubted Jade would get that wrong. "Ninety-nine percent."

His mouth fell open slightly. "Uh…hmm."

"What?"

His gaze tracked up and down me again. "Don't take this the wrong way, but you're a lot tougher than I'd guessed and that's saying something."

High praise coming from the former jinni. "Care to be a bit more specific?"

"If Elbis's memories serve me properly, her name is well known in Muspelheim." He shook his head in disbelief. "A being of such extreme power…many believe she is a goddess. Even Surtr recognized her as a capable ally."

Not sure why, but the thought of everyone thinking she was some kind of deity grated against my last nerve. "Unless lich lord is code for god, that's not the case."

He grinned. "True, but the fact you fought one and survived is shocking."

Wish there'd been a fight...then I would've done something other than stand there waiting to die. "Wasn't quite like that. After they finished playing demolition derby, Deheune hit me with a bolt of pure necromancy. Neither of us did well as a result."

Concern etched itself across his face. "How did you survive?"

Honesty up to a point was best here. "Had help...thus the whole golden spike thing. They kept me safe until I was able to travel on my own."

Alexander leaned his elbows on the table. "Care to share exactly who they are?"

"Nope. This is one you're going to have to take on faith." No way I was going to betray Jade after she helped me. "They're on our side, but they're not ready to bubble to the surface just yet."

He flopped back in his chair. "Romania all over again, isn't it?"

Damn, he was still harboring a grudge that I hadn't told him about Cain yet. "Maybe...but you've got to admit the world is a better place without the strigoi in it."

His tone hardened. "While I can't argue the point, it makes me feel like we're working with one hand tied behind our backs."

I glanced around the room. "You all feel this way?" Most of their gazes hit the floor. "Sorry to hear that." Leaning forward, I placed my forearms on the table. "Here's the deal. There are two major players who've surfaced in the last six months to a year. One is the Plague Bearer, the other is the child of light and darkness, both of which I've spoken to you about."

Alexander's expression faltered. "Oh...uh—"

I cut him off. "They both play important roles in the war that's coming. So, if my silence buys them the time they need to prepare themselves, I'm all about doing that." I paused. "How would any of you have felt had someone spilled my secrets for the sake of keeping everyone up to date?"

He held out his hand. "Yeah, okay, I get it. Doesn't mean I like it."

"Neither do I, but for right now, these are the cards we've been dealt." I ran my hand over the top of my head. "I won't purposely put any of us in danger. Please don't ask me to do less for others, particularly when one of them saved my life."

Henri nodded. "We understand. Sorry."

I shook my head. "No need to be. I get why you're concerned and why you'd want to know. But believe me, neither of them will be invisible much longer. When that happens, I'm sure we're going to have an entirely different conversation…especially about the Plague Bearer."

Gabriel chuckled. "Doubtful."

"I'll remind you about saying that." I rubbed my forehead. "That is something we can address later, though."

Henri nodded. "Fair. What do you need from us?"

"Collect all your mobile devices and toss them on the table." They did. "Anything important on them?" Everyone shook their heads as they mumbled. "Great." I scooped them up and slagged them. Standing, I strode into the kitchen and tossed them in the garbage. Upon returning to the dining room, I gestured at the stairs. "Henri, would you be so kind as to give us a tour of your lab?"

Alexander sighed. "Shit. Things are way worse than I expected."

I cut my eyes at him and he went silent. Two minutes later, we were comfortably seated around Henri's worktable in the pocket dimension behind the bookshelf in his office.

Gabriel fidgeted in his seat. "This place weirds me out."

It didn't make me feel great either, but it was safe. "We won't be here long." Turning to the others, I said, "I need intel and lots of it. What do you know? And how much of it was gathered over the UCD's computers?"

"Don't know as much as I'd like…but none of it came through official channels." Alexander grinned. "We weren't sure who was compromised, so I reached out to the weres in the affected areas."

That was promising. "Let's hear what you've got."

Fifteen minutes later, he'd only confirmed what Jade told me. Vampires and necromancers worked together to pull off a simultaneous attack on me, Alfred Monet, Vasile, Cole, the two dead triumvirates, Lazarus, and the governors. Only a few of which accomplished its goal.

I grimaced. "Just what in the fuck was Alfred thinking? By all accounts, he was running toward Notre Dame and away from the gate."

Henri closed his eyes and clasped his hands over his face. "I actually have an answer to that."

Curious. "Okay, please share with the rest of the class, because it doesn't make sense to me."

He made a *meh* sound. "It does if you have all the facts…which none of you do."

Something about the way he said that made me very uncomfortable. "Then please fill in the blanks."

Henri walked over to a bookshelf, pulled a large leather-bound tome out, and laid it on the table. "Alfred approached me in 975." Flipping the monstrous thing open, he pointed at a sketch of a pocket reality unlike anything I'd seen. "He asked me to help him with a project, which if discovered, would've gotten us both killed."

Kur wriggled in my mind. *"I wouldn't have thought such a place possible…yet here we are looking at blueprints for a world inside a world."*

"Huh?"

He shushed me. *"Quiet, I need to know how he did this."*

Henri sighed. "At that point I said no…but he persisted…eventually explaining what he wanted to do."

I gestured at the ancient page. "What was that, exactly?"

He collapsed into his seat. "To create a safe haven for vampires who wished to leave their clan. Back then, it was a death sentence. There were some who just weren't cut out for the murdering, agenda driven culture that is the vampire world." His voice dropped to a near whisper. "Told him I'd like to help, but what he was asking was beyond my skills." He pointed at the book. "That's when he gave me this. It opened my eyes to the other realms, and taught me how to create pocket realities beyond anything I thought possible. I shiver to think what it could do in the wrong hands. Until this very moment, I've never shared it or its contents with another living soul."

Without hearing Kur's question, I knew what he wanted. "Is the book Alfred's creation or someone else's?"

Henri shook his head. "As far as I can tell, it predates this world's conception."

Gabriel snorted. "How's that possible?"

After speaking with Cain, I understood that nearly anything was plausible. "Better question is, what makes you think that?"

Henri leafed through the pages to the front cover. "Because the only thing made from this planet is the false cover. If you'll look here, you'll see that the text, ink…even the paper is alien in nature." He jabbed his finger against the page. "Then there's this." Right above his finger in flowing gold script was Lilith, Eden Outpost, the Rim. "As far as I can tell, Lilith is a myth. There's never been an outpost called Eden and I've only heard references to the Rim in my studies…it's the literal rim between the nine realms. There's no way anyone at that time, in that place, could've had access to such information."

Holy shit, that was Cain's mother, and after our talk, I was familiar with Eden and the Rim…it wasn't a great place. "I'm inclined to agree with your assessment."

Alexander cut his eyes at me. "Are you kidding me? That sounds like pure science fiction."

Talbis leaned forward, suddenly looking older than the body he inhabited. "I've been to the Rim…it was long ago and the only thing there was an onyx plate. There were tales that it'd once been a harsh world where the last remnants of an ancient civilization reached out to the stars." Irritation flashed in his eyes. "As for Lilith, she was real… the first of your kind to reach out to the other realms."

His issue with Lilith seemed personal and I didn't feel like digging into that. "We've gotten off track. But if I understand you correctly, you created a super advanced pocket reality to save vampires…what's that got to do with Alfred getting murdered on the steps of Notre Dame?"

Henri closed the book. "Because a few decades after I finished the project, they built Notre Dame on top of the entrance…at Alfred's insistence."

"You think he was trying to flee into the pocket dimension?"

He slowly bobbed his head up and down. "Yes."

That'd be suicide. "Wouldn't they just follow him in and murder him and everyone else as well?"

He raised his gaze to mine. "No. You need a key to enter."

Talbis grinned. "Possible allies."

Henri rolled his shoulders. "Perhaps…but they fled this world to keep from shedding blood needlessly. Not sure they'll want to join our cause."

We needed to try. "Maybe if you spoke to them? I mean there's got to be some people who remember you…from what you said, it took nearly a century for you to complete the place."

Henri shook his head. "That's not possible. As part of the deal, the entrance was made so only vampires could enter. So, unless you have a vampire willing to go talk to them…that you trust…then it's unlikely we'll be able to get in touch."

Cain, Gabriella, and Vasile were all good candidates…but my money was on Vasile. "But even they'd need a key…right?"

Henri gave me a curious look. "Yes, but—"

I held out my hand. "No buts…there are a couple who are trustworthy that I can ask. Can you make the key?"

He sat up in his chair. "Absolutely."

"Good. Please do so." Turning to Alexander, I said, "I need someone to track down Ms. Dodd. She's the only vampire working directly for the Archive that hasn't shown up on a casualty list. Talbis, you and Gabriel piece together whatever we've got on Andrew's location. While I can pop in on them…I'd feel a lot better about getting everyone out alive if I had people nearby."

They nodded.

I got to my feet. "Meeting adjourned."

Alexander held out his hands. "What are you going to do?"

Smiling, I said, "Recruit some additional help and speak to a vampire about running an errand."

He frowned. "How are we going to keep in touch?"

Shit, forgot. "Hopefully, Baptist will have a fix for us by the afternoon. If not, send someone to buy a fuck ton of burners."

He sighed. "Okay, I'll be in touch with smoke signals until then."

"Drop by the station before heading out." I shrugged. "That's what I'm about to do."

His shoulders slumped forward. "I can do that."

I patted him on the shoulder. "Good man. Look, I've got to get going. I'll be in touch one way or another by nightfall at the very latest. It's my hope it'll be in the next few hours…but given the places I'm headed, that might not be possible."

He nodded. "In other words, don't freak out until after the sun goes down."

"Right." I gave him a thumbs up. "Oh, Alexander, I need you to do one more thing."

He paused. "What's that?"

This wasn't going to go over well. "As soon as you have a secure line, reach out to every centurion around the globe. Have them set up weres as protection at the local gates for each of the governors. Then have Isidore and your people on hand to secure the gate here and in Rome."

Alexander stood stock still. "We'll be moving them then?"

"That's the plan." I sighed. "As I get more information, I'll let you know. In the meantime, start the ball rolling."

Waving, I allowed indigo flames to envelope me.

4

With a bag full of goodies from Warden Global, I materialized in the tiny park at the corner of W De Vargas St and Galisteo. Okay, so park was a bit of an exaggeration. It had a few trees, a place to sit, and a restricted area for the drainage system. Thankfully, rush hour was still an hour or two away. It wouldn't do to have too many prying eyes to acknowledge my arrival.

Shifting the duffle around on my shoulder, I paused as an uneasy sensation snaked its way up my spine. In the far reaches of my mind, the Grim fixated on the intrusion and marked it as necromancy. I hadn't been attacked, there wasn't a spell in the works…no outward signs at all to give me this disquieting perception, yet it called out to me like a beacon.

Hopefully, Cole and Danielle were somewhere safe. Only one way to find out. I straightened upright then set off at a steady pace and turned onto Alameda to cross the street. The sensation continued to grow as I reached the corner and the front door of Del Charro.

The shades were pulled, lights off, and the door locked.

There was, however, one positive sign in the form of a note stuck to the glass.

. . .

To all our valued customers,

We're sorry to say that we'll be closed for the next few days due to a family emergency. It's our hope that we'll be able to reopen soon. In the meantime, we appreciate your understanding during this trying time.

Thank you again,

Management

I stood there reading and rereading it, hoping they'd left a clue. They hadn't.

None of the reports said anything about an attack here. I mean, it wouldn't surprise me. Atsidi gave me the books we were using to uncover the secrets of the Black Circle. On top of that, Cole stood with me as we lay waste to a horde of undead and helped bury the Grants.

That uneasy feeling surged to the forefront of my mind. Turning my head, I watched as a well-built middle-aged man with salt and pepper hair strolled across the street with a big smile. He wore black slacks and a white long-sleeved button up shirt with the cuffs rolled back onto his pale, muscular forearms.

Holding out his hands for calm, he spoke with a slight Scottish accent. "Easy now, I've come in peace." He gestured at himself. "My name is Dermot Campbell and you're the infamous Gavin Randall." Clucking his tongue, he gave me an appraising look. "With the stories about you, I thought you'd be…bigger." He chuckled. "Size isn't always a determining factor in lethality though, is it."

Obviously not. The man was five-eight…maybe nine with the boots. I didn't need to look around for additional support; he'd come on his own. That uneasy feeling I'd gotten earlier was coming from him.

"No, it's not."

Dermot gestured at the door. "Mind if I pick the lock? There's no need for us to have this conversation on the street." He paused. "As an FYI, no harm has befallen Cole or his lovely wife."

I stepped back. "What makes you think I want to talk?"

"Curiosity." He touched the door, and there was a click of the deadbolt sliding back. Pushing it open, he placed his hand on the keypad and the countdown stopped. "Excellent, come on in. Care for a drink?"

This guy was seriously making himself at home. "I'm good." I closed the door. "If you fix yourself one though, make sure to leave cash and a tip."

Dermot strode behind the bar and picked up a particularly nice bottle of Irish whiskey. After pouring himself a glass, he pulled three one hundred-dollar bills and placed them on the counter. "You sure about that drink?"

"I am." Sitting at the far end of the bar, I drummed my fingers against the counter. "You wanted to talk?"

He carried the bottle with him as he came around to sit catty-corner to me. "I did." He sipped a bit of the amber fluid. "You're an anomaly to me…you have no idea how rare that is." Running his finger around the edge of his glass, he said, "Technically, I should've heard about you shortly after your birth. For whatever reason, that didn't happen. Can't say why…maybe due to the fact you were on the reservation or perhaps the whole lack of power thing until your arrival in New Orleans last year." He leaned forward. "How'd you manage that? Sure, some kids don't show any abilities till their teens, but with the hormones—and general arrogance—they always give themselves away. But not you. Why?"

Honestly, I didn't have a clue.

"Couldn't say."

Dermot grinned. "Keeping secrets, are we?"

I wish. "Wouldn't be the first time."

"It wouldn't, would it." His tone remained casual. "Took a lot of digging to find next to nothing about you. There are rumors you worked for the US government as some sort of enforcer, but there's nothing official in your file." He pulled a thumb drive out of his pocket and slid it to me. "According to that, you're nobody special… unable to hold a job for more than a year or so at a time…some mental issues…and a real shitty opinion of authority figures. Then in

May of last year you arrive in New Orleans, kill Walter Percy, and take over Naevius's old position like it's nothing."

I placed an empty tumbler over the drive. "I'm not sure what you're looking for here. Maybe if you explained how either of those things are a big deal, it'd help me understand."

"I like you." The corner of his mouth twitched up. "Walter was powerful. In a few more years, he would've taken his place next to Inna as one of my seconds."

Flicking up a finger, I asked, "Inna, as in the lady who runs the Onyx Mind."

Dermot shrugged as he took a drink of whiskey. "Technically, she does the day to day grunt work." He pointed at himself. "The actual running of our entire organization falls on me." Rolling his shoulders, he sighed. "Unimportant though." He lifted his gaze to mine. "As to Naevius…the fact you assumed that position with such ease is what intrigues me."

"Mind if I ask why?"

Laughing, he said, "It'd hurt my feelings if you didn't." He poured himself a second round. "You see, it took a lot of work to trick the coin into accepting him." His eyes glazed over slightly as he lost himself to his thoughts. "Using blood magic, we put Naevius through hell trying to graft enough power into his pathetic form in order for the coin to take hold and allow for the foundations of what would one day become the Archive."

I blinked. "Sorry, what?"

He gave me a dismissive wave. "It wasn't like he had a clue who we were…the man was dumb as a rock. Not to mention greedy. When we offered him a chance at power, he didn't bother to ask questions as to why."

"If that's the case, why have Chandra kill him?"

Holding his glass, he pointed at me. "Oh, you're well informed. Excellent. That makes this so much simpler." He took another sip. "His greed and arrogance got the better of him. At some point, he began to believe the power that'd been leant to him was his." Downing the drink, he poured another. "That's when his usefulness came to an end. Then shortly after, so did he."

This made my head hurt. "Still not sure what you're looking for here."

"Neither am I." He leaned back in his chair, slightly perplexed. "You're something new. My masters are unsure what to do with you… well, until last night. Deheune tired of the bickering concerning your continued existence and decided to kill you herself." Awe worked its way into his tone. "Yet, here you are unharmed, while she remains in a comatose state since her return. A few hours ago, Osiris and Seth approached me and asked me to speak with you."

"For what purpose, exactly?"

Dermot set his glass down. "To ask you to step aside." He paused. "Allow the war to play itself out between Dvalinn and Heidr. As far as we can tell, you don't have a stake in the matter."

I pulled air in through my teeth. "So, let you guys kill each other off…along with countless others, while I…what exactly?"

Capping the bottle, he said, "Live." He got to his feet and placed a business card on the bar. "Reach out when you're ready." His tone turned solemn. "Until you do, we'll consider you a hostile and act accordingly. I have to say, there are a lot of people within the Archive, Black Circle, and the Courts who want you dead. You've survived this long on sheer luck…that'll run out one day. What's the old saying?… You have to be great all the time…and all we have to do is get lucky, once." He tapped the card. "Think about my offer."

Dermot pulled a coin out of his pocket, clasped it to his chest, and vanished on the spot.

Kur whispered, *"That explains a lot."*

"How so?"

He sighed. *"The use of blood magic would damage my systems and cause black spots in my memory. If any of the vigiles after him were exposed further…it'd erase or corrupt those files beyond repair."*

Damn. "Meaning there's no chance to recover the files concerning Martha's death, among others."

"Likely, true." Anger tinged his tone. *"I'll need to create a scan to run*

through our system. *If there's anyone in the network that's contaminated, we'll know in a few days. At which point, you'll need to remove them from service in order to set things right."*

Given the scope of the scan, a few days seemed quick. "We'll do what needs to be done if it comes to that. Right now, I've got to find Cole."

Kur wriggled in my head then he was gone.

Guess I should check on Atsidi to ensure he was still amongst the living. Maybe he'd know where Cole and Danielle were holed up.

I walked over and locked the door then indigo flames enveloped me.

When they dissipated, I stood outside Atsidi's home.

Cole pushed open the door with one hand and wrapped fire around the other. He paused, the fire died out, and relief swept over his features. "Hey, uh, sorry for the warm welcome."

Keeping my mouth shut, I handed him my phone with a text on the screen which read: *Gather your mobiles, pull out the sim cards, and destroy them.*

They did, and I handed them three replacements.

"Here, use these."

Atsidi frowned. "I assume the old ones were compromised?"

"Can't be sure but it's very likely." I shrugged. "In this case, better safe than dead."

Danielle waved me in. "Come, let's talk."

I couldn't recall a time in my life when those words ever turned into a fun or even remotely pleasant conversation. "I don't have long, but sure, why not."

Atsidi's place was cozy…small…but there was enough room for us to sit without being on top of one another…barely.

She gestured at me. "You look pretty good for a dead guy."

"Who said I was dead?"

Cole held out his hands for calm. "No one said it as much as implied it."

Like that made things better.

"The question stands."

Atsidi sighed. "Amelia…she's been trying to commandeer everyone since things went south last night."

Anger flashed in Danielle's eyes. "Amazing how fast she shut up when you sent that text this morning."

Cole nodded. "Yeah, not a peep from her."

At no point had she bothered to contact me, so that was weird. "Okay…was she the only issue?"

Danielle folded her arms and leaned back in her seat. "Hardly. That bitch Chala Tren out of Southern Africa was right there with her."

That made two big mouths who hadn't bothered to get in touch with me yet and they'd obviously been spouting a ton of shit prior. Interesting. Not really, it was really fucking annoying. "And just what were they saying?"

Cole shrugged. "Mostly that in your absence and likely death, they'd be assuming control until things were settled. The new chain of command was to work with Amelia and Chala at the top with Carlos as their second."

Glad they divvied shit up in my absence. "First off, they're in charge of shit. Secondly, Carlos isn't even a goddamn vigil these days."

Danielle grimaced. "I know. Just what in the fuck were they thinking?"

"That's unimportant at the moment." It was, but I'd have to figure it out another time. "I'll deal with their bullshit later. Right now, I was hoping you'd let Cole come out and play."

She gave me a sad smile. "Thanks for making it sound like I have a choice in the matter." She nodded. "Yes, you can borrow him for a bit."

That was a relief. "Thanks."

Apprehension worked its way across Cole's face. "Where are we going?"

It wasn't as if I didn't trust the others, but the less they knew, the better. "Meeting another vigil then saving the governor's collective asses."

Atsidi got to his feet. "Anything we can do while you're out galivanting?"

Well… "Actually, there is. Make a list of people you'd trust your lives with. In this case, I mean that literally. I'm not sure who is with us and who isn't at the moment. So, any help in that department would be greatly appreciated."

Danielle's gaze hit the floor. "That'll be a short list."

Atsidi nodded. "Agreed."

I knew the feeling.

"That's fine. Back soon." Turning to Cole, I asked, "You ready?"

His knuckles turned white as he gripped the arms of the chair. "No…but that's not going to stop me." He got to his feet and walked over. "Let's do this."

We waved as indigo flames enveloped us. There was a weird sensation in my stomach then a half second later, we appeared deep in the midst of a forest. Cole staggered to the side and propped himself up against a thick spruce.

He gritted his teeth. "Goddamn it, I hate that fucking thing."

"You're not even blue…you'll be fine." It was the truth; he looked way better than he did the last time. "Shake it off and let's see if we can find Vasile."

Cole straightened and rubbed his hands against his arms. "Is that who you're searching for?"

"Yeah. Other than you, he's the only vigil I implicitly trust." That was an unfortunate statement. "The rest of them…well…let's just say that they've yet to prove themselves to be the right people for the job…then again, they haven't done anything that warrants me removing them either."

That comment alone hammered home the fact there was need for change on a grand scale. Scrapping the old and building something new would be tough, but it had to happen.

"You might be waiting a long time for them to show their true colors." He grimaced. "Some of these assholes have had centuries to hide their less desirable qualities."

Obviously, he had something to say. "Don't be shy. If you've got something on your mind, let's hear it."

Cole was quiet for several seconds. "Amelia."

Ah, the woman who'd gone to great lengths to avoid me. We'd met exactly once since I joined the Archive, and that was more of an accident than anything.

"What about her?"

His voice dropped. "Know much about her personally or professionally?"

Other than her being an unhelpful shit during the Archive's time of need? "Not a lot...we haven't exactly spoken face to face for more than a few minutes. There are the basics of course...born in Quebec back in the fifteen hundreds...sorcerer...not the easiest person to deal with. But if you're looking for something else, I don't have it. If you do, please, enlighten me."

"Hard to get along with...that's kind of you." A small chuckle escaped his lips. "She's arrogant, purposely obstinate, and more than a little cruel to those she thinks are beneath her station." He raised his gaze to mine. "Until you came along, she was the unofficial head of the vigiles. No idea why, but that's the way it'd worked out."

I'd heard the rumors over the last year, but this was the first time someone had come out and said it to my face. "Okay, a pain in the ass...but loads of people think I'm way worse. We going somewhere specific?"

Anger crept into his voice. "Just demonstrating the type of person she is." He took a deep breath. "Not long after the Grants arrived, we reached out to the Archive for help...Amelia showed up, took one look at the Grants, and threw her full support behind them. She spoke to the chief, telling him that, as simple savages, we should accept the Grants and their help and not fight it. She was also quite clear on the fact she wouldn't be back." Hanging his head, he sighed. "When Martha showed up, we had hope once more...then Amelia said something to her... and she never spoke with the tribe again... instead, conducting her investigations through outside sources only."

As much as I wanted to be surprised, I wasn't. "Sorry you guys had to deal with that type of shit."

"We got used to it." He locked his gaze onto mine. "It's good to see things are changing."

Unfortunately, most were fighting me every step of the way. "That's coming a lot slower than I'd like."

"But it's happening, and that's what's important." He stood up straight and glanced around. "Where's Vasile?" He glanced over at me. "Is your teleport thing on the fritz."

Pivoting on the spot, I frowned. "No idea. I mean, if we weren't connected, we wouldn't have left New Mexico…yet, here we stand…elsewhere."

It wasn't as if I could be specific.

Cole bumped my arm. "Tried calling him?"

Actually, I had. "It went straight to voicemail. Doubt he's answering random numbers after people tried to kill him."

"Good point." He cocked his head to the side. "You sure that you're not glitchy after getting your bell rung?"

While it was possible, that didn't feel right. "Be a weird thing for it to suddenly act up here after going home, Henri's, your place, and Atsidi's."

"Guess you have a point." He swept his gaze across the landscape. "Suppose we should look around before calling it. I'm not exactly keen on getting back inside that bubble."

Funny man. "Fine, let's go for a hike."

Cole shivered. "Good plan."

Someone cleared their throat above us.

A choir of demons screaming in the distance sounded in my ears as my armor snapped into place and the scythe materialized in my hand. Jumping back, I hovered in the air as I looked up at…Vasile.

Wait…I should've hit the ground by now…but… I glanced down to find myself about ten feet up. Then, just like that, I plummeted downward as the armor and weapon vaporized. The earth was rather unforgiving, but I didn't really feel the impact as my mind was busy trying to wrap itself around the whole levitation thing.

Vasile touched down next to me. "You all right?"

"Think so…did you see that?"

He paled. "Way clearer than I'd like."

Huh? "Was my ability to hover that bad?"

"Oh, that's what's got you so worked up?" He snorted. "It wasn't graceful and the landing left a lot to be desired, but you did fine."

Confused, I asked, "What the hell were you talking about?"

Vasile glanced over at Cole. "You saw it, right?"

Cole didn't look well. His voice trembled. "Wish I hadn't."

This whole vague thing annoyed me. "Did I miss something?"

Vasile's expression hardened. "Your armor…its different."

"That all?" Talk about making a big deal out of nothing. "Cole's seen me go full Grim, so whatever it is with the armor can't be that bad."

Cole held out a hand. "That's where you're wrong. It's way worse."

"I'll take your word for it."

Vasile gestured toward a small hill to our right. "For now, let's go somewhere more private."

Anything to change the subject was good with me. The current topic was a little uncomfortable. "Sounds good. How far we going?"

He pointed. "Just over the hill there."

Curious, I asked, "Were you home when we arrived?"

Vasile's expression hardened. "Yes."

I waved a hand in front of us. "Please lead the way."

By over the hill, he meant way over. About ten minutes later, we were standing in front of his cabin. It was a simple thing. One story, made of logs, wood frame windows, and old. Vasile obviously kept the place up, but it'd been here at least a few hundred years.

Gesturing at the place, I asked, "Come over on the Mayflower?"

Without missing a beat, he chuckled. "Much earlier, but that's a story for another day."

"Awesome place." Cole stepped to the side. "It's bigger than it looks. Is it built into the rocks there?"

Vasile puffed out his chest. "It is. Took me a few decades to get it right, but it's all set up just the way I like it now."

"Good to hear." Cole patted him on the shoulder. "So, with you being a vampire and everything…do we need an invitation to enter?"

He didn't really go there, did he? Hopefully, Vasile had a sense of humor.

Vasile cut his eyes at Cole and grinned. "Seeing how it's my home, it'd probably be smart to get an invitation."

The man had a point. "Mind if we come into your home? Discussing shit out here probably isn't the best idea."

He chuckled and waved for us to follow. "Come on." He paused. "After we're inside, don't touch anything without asking first. I'd hate for you to wind up dead."

Someone was awfully protective of their belongings.

Cole huffed out a laugh. "Sure thing."

When I stepped over the threshold, I came to an abrupt halt. He wasn't kidding when he said the two didn't go together. The exterior looked ancient, but everything inside was straight out of the future. Cold gray metal lined the walls and holographic screens were peppered along its surface throughout the house. My mind screeched to a halt when my gaze fell onto the only antique thing in the room…a painting of a woman. She was dark skinned with short cropped hair and was absolutely stunning. Thing was, I'd seen her or her doppelganger before.

I nodded at the painting. "Who's that?"

Please don't be who I think you are.

Vasile hesitated slightly. "That's my mother."

Not exactly informative. "Does she have a name?"

His body tensed. "Not important." He gave her a dismissive wave. "She's been gone a long time." Gesturing around the room, he sighed. "Most of this was hers. She was—maybe still is—a brilliant woman."

Cole arched an eyebrow. "You don't know?"

He pulled out two chairs at the nearest table before sitting at the head. "No. She raised me through my trying times then when she knew I was safe, she told me that people were looking for her and her presence would put me in danger. She picked up and left in the middle of the night. Two days later, war came in the name of a man who claimed to be my father." Anger burned in his tone. "He did his best to imprison me, but that didn't work out so well for him. I commandeered his things—which turned out to be my mother's—and moved about until I settled here."

Christ, it was Lilith. And the man claiming to be his father had to be Adam. "What makes you think this man wasn't your father?"

He sighed. "Eventually, he came out and said so. Of course, that took me nearly killing the man." Disgust fixed itself onto his face. "His crazy wife stopped me from finishing the job."

Yeah, that sounded like Adam and Eve all right.

"Did he know who your father is or was?"

He snorted. "He gave me some bullshit answer about the Star Born. As far as I can tell, there's no such person. Never has been, never will be." He sighed. "Finished grilling me about my parentage?"

Viktor was his father? Holy fuck. Unable to speak, I nodded my head.

Cole meandered over to his seat and plopped down. "This is a super cool place."

Finally finding my voice, I added. "It is."

He and I were going to have to talk about his mom…soon.

Vasile pressed his thumb against the edge of the table and a globe appeared in the center. "You'll notice there are several areas marked with different tags. Each one corresponds with what I consider a major incident." He tapped Europe and Alfred's image appeared. "Murder of one of the governor's qualifies."

Interesting. "Guess you were able to check in after they came for you?"

Vasile wobbled his hand back and forth. "Not officially…been around long enough to have back doors into the pertinent information. It isn't like Amelia and Chala can be trusted. Especially after they were claiming you were dead or, at the very least, compromised due to being captured."

It would seem that Amelia has another fan. "Before we delve into those two…where did they find you last night?"

He folded his arms. "Had an alert about an elemental moving part of the mountain…when I arrived, they jumped me."

Well shit. "Who is they?"

Vasile pulled out his phone, touched the screen, and handed it to me. "By my count, six necromancers and eight vampires."

Holy shit. They hadn't come to play.

Cole arched an eyebrow. "No offense, but all that for you?"

I flicked through a few pictures to see the carnage and passed it over to Cole. "Obviously, they came underpowered."

"Holy shit." He picked up the phone and skipped through a few more pictures. "You did this? On your own?"

Vasile shrugged. "Smelled them before they hit…so it wasn't a fair fight."

Okay, good to know. "How'd this elemental business wind up on your desk?"

"Email…looks like it came from official sources." He paused. "We could've been hacked, or we have a mole inside. Either is bad."

No shit. "True. But you're fine…right? No lasting damage?"

A dark smile crossed his lips. "Oh, I haven't felt better in years. But that's an entirely different subject."

Sure it was. "I get the feeling you don't trust Amelia…or Chala for that matter."

"I don't." His voice was flat. "Hard to trust racists."

Couldn't argue the point. "And they hate…?"

Cole and Vasile spoke at the same time. "Weres."

Why didn't that surprise me. "I see."

Vasile gave me a dismissive wave. "That's not why you're here though, is it?"

"No, but it's all good to know." I sighed. "Need some help rescuing the governors…was hoping you'd lend a hand."

He glanced at Cole. "The three of us then?"

"Nope. Lined up some help through the centurions—"

Cole cut in. "Weres and Henri."

That was redundant since they were the only one's volunteering. "Right…anyway. We'll have all the appropriate gates covered for the returning governors along with the public gate in Rome."

"Not tending to Lazarus's personal one?" Disgust coated Vasile's tone. "Can't believe that asshole's managed to keep it to himself all these years."

Me neither. "No need to worry. His was buried in the attack…most of his home collapsed in on itself during the fight."

Vasile snickered. "Well that's a plus."

Probably was. "Anyway, you in?"

He smiled. "As if there was any doubt."

There was one thing that bugged me. "Before we head out…mind if I ask a question?"

He leaned back in his chair. "Of course not."

"If you were home…I should've been able to teleport directly to you…instead I was nearly a fifteen-minute walk away." I had a guess, but I needed his input to make it a reality. "Any idea why that might be?"

"None." Vasile grinned. "We should be on our way."

That wasn't helpful. "Give me a few minutes to make sure everything is in place."

Thirty minutes later, we were ready to move. Henri and the others out of New Orleans were going through the main gate in Rome as Lazarus's was still blocked. Vasile, Cole, and I were going to pop in on the others in twenty minutes. At that point, the chips would fall wherever they landed. One way or another, people were going home today.

5

As the flames vanished, I was hit with multiple scents; antiseptic, stale air, and dust. Necromancy filled the room, making it hard for me to breathe. The single swaying lightbulb cast shadows across the speckled terrazzo tile. There weren't any windows and the old brick walls screamed basement of some sort.

Silver light wrapped around Cole. His form stretched out along a long, thin, gray line that shot across the room, coming to a halt next to the hospital bed holding a sleeping Heather. Vasile blurred across to the opposite side, stopping near the incinerator there.

Chione and Lazarus stood a few feet in front of me. The other governors were congregated around Kimberly, who was patching up Attila's arm, who, upon seeing me, jumped to his feet. Green light wrapped around his injured arm as he stepped my way.

By the look on his face, he wanted to end me. I didn't take it personally, as popping in on folks unannounced brought out the worst in people.

Andrew held out his hand. "Calm, this is Gavin, my nephew and vigil for the Archive."

He remained focused on me as suspicion crossed his features. "Word was you were killed or, at the very least, severely injured."

There was that persistent rumor that needed to die. "Not sure who you heard that from, but as you can see, I'm golden."

Now that I had a minute to take in the others, most everyone looked rough.

Other than Attila's injured arm, there were bruises around his face and neck. Ian, from Northern Africa, was in only slightly better shape. Kylie, from Australia and the surrounding island countries, had a black eye, dried blood matted her blond hair, and she had a bit of a limp. Gabriella appeared tired, her clothes and hands stained with gore. Kimberly had several cuts along her face and neck. Heather was covered in one large bruise, as if she'd been hit by something very large. Andrew's shirt was torn, spattered stains covered him from head to toe, and he was pissed.

The only two who looked fine were Lazarus and Chione. Neither had a scratch or a stain on them.

Unable to stand any longer, Attila stumbled back into his seat. "Apparently." He winced. "It's been a long day...hopefully, with you here, things will get better."

The bandages around his arm turned bright red. Glancing over, I said, "Kimberly."

"Yes?"

I gestured at Attila. "I think he tore something."

She put her hand on her hip. "Let me see what I can do to fix you up."

Andrew stepped to the side and waved me over. "Gavin."

Scanning the room, I found Cole had put as much distance between him and Lazarus as possible. He'd mentioned a few times that he wasn't exactly a fan. Vasile was eyeing Gabriella with interest. Hopefully, he wouldn't blow her cover, since no one else knew she was a vampire.

I strode over to Andrew and lowered my voice. "What's up?"

He shook his head. "Not sure...everyone is super tense...please tell me you've got a plan."

"I do—"

That uneasy feeling I had with Dermot magnified itself several hundred times as Lazarus stomped into view.

"—Where the hell have you been?" He wagged a finger at me. "You were off grid for nearly five hours before any of us heard from you."

Kur growled. *"If he continues to be impudent, kill him."*

A sentiment the Grim wholeheartedly endorsed.

I locked my jaw, chewing back my anger and their impulses. "Been a bit busy putting myself back together after the incident last night."

"You mean having your vehicle turned into scrap?" He gave me a dismissive wave. "That's old news. What concerns me is where you were during those missing hours? Did someone help you and if so, who was it? I need to know."

The fuck he need to know for? "That's none of your concern."

He puffed out his chest. "As Caesar, everything is my concern."

Well, shit, thought I'd cleared up this situation last year.

I gave him a quick once over to see if I'd missed any obvious injuries. Nope, he looked the picture of health. Couldn't hurt to make sure though.

"Did you get hit in the head or something?"

Confusion worked its way across his face. "What's that supposed to mean?"

Cole stepped into my peripheral vision and Vasile ended his conversation with Gabriella to do the same. I made a slight gesture and they stopped moving. Lazarus seemed none the wiser… or didn't care.

"It means that I don't work for you. I work with you. Simple as that."

Anger flared in his eyes. "Watch your tone, boy." Necromancy in the form of black mist wrapped itself around his hands. "Or I'll be forced to put you in your place."

"My place?" A hardness I hadn't intended sounded in my voice. "How long has it been since anyone has told you how full of shit you are?" I stepped forward, placed my hand in the darkness, and grabbed hold of the power. "Do you really think this parlor trick scares me?" Lazarus's body trembled as he paled and struggled to breathe. "Others might fear you." Twisting my hand, I pulled more power out of him, causing him to yelp and hit his knees. "I don't."

He swayed on the spot as he choked out. "Insubordinate welp."

As I spoke again, power coated my voice and my words slammed into his face with enough force to break his nose. "If you challenge me again, this conversation will end very differently." I jerked my hand back to sever the connection between us. "Am I clear?"

Lazarus's body gave out and he lay shaking on the floor.

Everyone stood around silently watching the exchange, no one daring to move.

Sweat poured off him as he slowly got to his trembling legs. "This isn't over." He glanced around at the others. "We'll take this up again in a more private setting."

That'd be a no.

"Sorry to hear we haven't come to an understanding." I sighed. "Realize this, however, it won't matter when or where it takes place. The tune I'm singing won't change a beat."

Hate and resentment warred for dominance on his face. "We'll see about that."

The desire to finish this conversation permanently burned inside my soul with both the Grim and Kur's blessing. That, however, was me having a bad day and would likely make things worse. "Fine, let's table it for now. What I need to know is where we are and how do we get out of here?"

He snorted. "Thought you had some sort of plan to save us."

Unable to stop myself, I slammed my fist into his face, knocking him to the floor. "Unless you've got something helpful to say, shut your mouth and let me do my job."

Ian glanced at me then Lazarus and put a few steps between them. "I'm with Gavin on this." He shook his head. "Not sure what's crawled up your ass, but you really need to get that sorted."

Atilla, Gabriella, Andrew, and Kylie all edged closer to me.

"You've always had a stick lodged up your ass." Kylie shook her head in disgust. "But you've gotten significantly worse over the last year."

Chione glared at me as she helped Lazarus to his feet. "That's no way to treat Caesar."

"The moment he starts acting like one, I'll treat him as such." Cold filled the room. "I've got work to do, so either help or stay out of my way."

Lazarus wiped blood off his lip but remained silent.

Chione spat on the floor at my feet. "You have no respect for your elders."

Wrapping her arm under Lazarus's shoulder, she helped him across the room, where they sat whispering while giving me dirty looks.

Andrew stepped forward. "We're in the basement of the children's hospital not far from Lazarus's home. From here to the gate at The Gianicolo Lighthouse is about a half mile's walk."

Of course it was.

To top things off, the building was surrounded. Didn't need to step outside to verify it either. Multiple sources of low-grade necromancy ringed the block. Something else was with them. If I had to guess, I'd say the others were vampires. That would be something I'd have to see to confirm. While an exact number didn't come to mind, a lot covered it nicely.

"Thanks."

I pulled out my new mobile and typed out a message to Gabriel.

We're at some children's hospital about a half mile from the gate.

A few seconds later, it dinged.

We've secured the area. Do you need assistance?

Their arrival would only complicate matters.

No. I'm good. Still have to get everyone ready to move here. Be there within the hour. At which point, we may or may not have company.

His reply came an instant later.

Understood.

Tucking my phone into my pocket, I pulled a bag off my shoulder. "All right, I'm going to need you guys to destroy your old phones and line up for a new one."

Lazarus jumped to his feet. "Those aren't Archive issue."

"No, they're not." I shrugged. "You're welcome to keep your old one…but rest assured, no one will be calling you until you get a secure line."

Arrogance dripped from his tone. "It is secure. I've seen to it myself." He glared at the others. "Who are you going to trust, me or this newcomer?"

Attila dropped his phone onto the floor and crushed it underfoot. Andrew threw his across the room, where it shattered against the incinerator.

Kylie grimaced and held out her hand. "Stop making a goddamn mess. Someone has to clean this shit up. Hand me your phones and I'll dispose of them properly."

Everyone who still had a mobile, save for Lazarus and Chione, turned them over to Kylie; she vaporized them, leaving nothing in their wake. "See, that's better." She strolled over to me with a big smile. "I'll take my upgrade please."

I snickered. "Here ya go."

After handing out the new sat phones, I stepped over to Heather, who'd awoken during the whole throwing shit against the wall fiasco.

She smiled. "Hey there. You okay?"

"Should be asking you that question." I held her hand. "What happened?"

She grimaced. "According to Mom, a wall fell on me during the attack."

Damn.

"You able to walk?"

Heather pushed herself up into a sitting position. "Yes…slowly, but I can manage. How far do we need to go?"

I sat on the edge of the bed. "A half mile…that's the easy part."

"Says you." She winced when she laughed. "I'm sore as shit."

Kimberly leaned into view. "What's the hard part?"

Ah, yes, that.

I gestured all around us. "They're waiting for us outside." Holding out my hand to stop her, I said, "Thanks to Talbis, I've got a solution that'll protect her during the fight."

Talbis and I had sparred often over the last few months. During one of our sessions, I created a cone of ice that surrounded him. Every time he hammered away at it with a spell, it gave me a boost of power while increasing the thickness of the walls, ensuring he remained trapped.

Lazarus stalked over. "Apparently, I'm not needed here."

Someone was sulking.

"You're welcome to help—"

His tone turned catty. "—I did help." Gesturing at the others, he said, "I kept them safe while you were...what did you say...putting yourself back together...whatever that means." He snatched Chione's arm. "We'll leave you to your rescue." Arrogance worked its way across his features. "Of course, if you'd done your job in the first place, no one would need it."

Lazarus stepped back as he and Chione vanished.

"Lovely. He bailed on us." Shaking my head, I sighed. "Wish his actions surprised me."

Pulling my phone out of my pocket, I hammered out a quick text to Alexander.

Please send the weres meant to accompany Chione through the gate to secure her home and business. She and Lazarus have vacated the premises.

My phone dinged in reply.

What an asshole...and on it.

I glanced up at the others. "Guess we're about as ready as we're going to be." Pointing at the door across the way, I asked, "This the way out?"

Andrew nodded. "It is."

"Kimberly, stay close to Heather." I stepped toward the exit. "The rest of you, let's find out what awaits us outside."

Our footsteps echoed, squeaked, and clicked through the poorly lit corridor. At the end, I took the stairs two at a time, pulled open the door, and stepped inside. Green marble flooring spilled out before me, giving the impression of grass covering the lobby. The information desk dominated the center of the room and the woman there gave me a nasty look. The others quickly followed with Heather, Kimberly, and Vasile bringing up the rear.

Her pace could turn into an issue, but teleporting her—wounded as she was—could prove fatal.

Giving the unhappy woman a curt wave, I escorted everyone out the ornate brass doors. Surprisingly, there wasn't any traffic…at all. I glanced down the street to see a police barricade there and one at the opposite end. Cute trick.

Casually, I strolled down the steps. When my feet were firmly planted on the sidewalk, three vampires, two males and a female, meandered out of the shadows of the building across the street. Necromancers and more vampires followed to create a grim line to define the boundaries of what was ours and what they perceived as theirs.

A weird sheen of power waivered in the sunlight around each of the vampires.

The two males held their position as the female stepped forward. She was maybe five- three, brunette, and not hard to look at. Impossible to tell how old she was, but considering the reverence the other two gave her, old to ancient was my bet.

Her gaze tracked up and down me. "You're Gavin Randall?"

"Yep." Clenching my hand, my knuckles popped. "And you are?"

Her features turned haughty. "Phoebe, but you may address me as mistress or ma'am."

Uh-huh.

I gestured around us. "We really going to do this in broad daylight?"

"Of course, my darling." A wicked smile crossed her lips. "This is a movie set after all…or so the mortals believe."

"Since when did you guys start giving a shit about what they think?"

She brushed her brown hair back over her shoulder. "Since the beginning…but that's neither here nor there." Biting her lip, she shook her head. "For the life of me, I cannot figure out why you have the others so worked up. I mean, you're hardly a spec of a thing energetically." She leaned to one side then the other. "Not a single magic aura around you…yet, you've got the others nervous."

Dermot didn't seem worried at all. "I do?"

Phoebe pulled air in between her lips. "Yes…but I don't see the issue." Her hand twitched. "Rufus."

The stocky man on her left stepped forward. "Ma'am?"

Never taking her gaze off me, she said, "Think you could take him?"

"Absolutely." Sunlight glinted in his gray eyes. "Is that what you wish?"

A big smile crossed her lips. "It is."

Gabriella eased forward. "Rufus, it'd be in your best interest to step back and allow us to pass. Otherwise, things will get very ugly."

"Gabriella isn't it?"

She nodded.

He cut his eyes at her. "Wait your turn. I'll be with you momentarily."

Power radiated from Gabriella. "I've had about enough of all of you."

Seems like someone has a temper. Not that I blamed her. Plus, I was betting by the looks of her, she'd taken out more than her fair share of the attackers last night…so I wasn't about to stop her from killing these assholes.

Phoebe pointed at her. "Change of plans, Rufus. Kill her first."

Rufus turned his focus onto Gabriella as he charged her. She lifted her hand and an arc of white light shot across the distance to catch him in the chest. That weird sheen I'd spotted earlier flickered then exploded. The backlash hit Gabriella in the side of the face, spinning her to the ground. Rufus, however, wasn't as lucky. The blast tore him in half, immolated his skin, and he died in an instant.

Several screams cut through the silence as the shielding dropped around the others, leaving them vulnerable.

Gabriella got to her feet and glared at Phoebe. "Cute trick." She eyed the other man. "Think it'll work twice?"

Phoebe's confidence faltered. "You'll pay for that, sorcerer."

Without looking back, I placed a cone of ice around Andrew, Kimberly, and Heather. Andrew would be pissed, but I wanted to make sure that if anyone got inside, they wouldn't live long enough to do anything about it.

I held out my hand for calm. "Phoebe—"

Her tone hardened. "—I told you—"

Cutting her off, I said, "That's not going to happen, lady. Here's a counteroffer to whatever is supposed to happen...You step aside and let us go on our way." I placed my hand over my heart. "In return, I'll tell everyone how hard you guys tried to kill us and how we narrowly escaped with our lives." My tone turned hard. "This is your only chance to walk away from this with minimal losses. To be perfectly honest, I'm tired and want nothing more than to cut through each and every one of you to satiate my desire for your deaths. It's all I can do to resist my baser nature." Indigo flames wrapped around my left hand. "And I'm losing. Walk away, I'm begging you."

Her gaze tracked down to my hand and back up to my face as arrogance sounded in her voice. "That's all you've got?" She laughed. "We're not going anywhere, little man."

Rage consumed me and my armor instantly wrapped itself around me with that same creepy screech from earlier. The woman stumbled back as audible gasps from the others filled the sudden silence.

"Kill him." Panic filled her voice as she motioned the others toward me. "Do it...now."

My voice came out as a multilayered thing; deep in places, screechy in others. "You should've taken me up on the offer."

Taking my time, I stomped toward her. Her remaining bodyguard darted forward. I grabbed him by the throat. Chains made of shadow, fire, and the souls of the damned wrapped around him. He struggled against them. Smiling, I turned to face him then removed his soul and every last drop of energy left inside his hollowed-out form. Releasing him, his corpse hit the ground and turned to dust.

Phoebe paled as she scrambled back mouthing something I could not hear.

Twin vampires rushed up between us. They were tall, heavily

muscled, dark skinned, and wore dreadlocks down to their waist. On any other day, I'd be concerned, but the boost of power from the one I'd just killed surged through my veins in ways I hadn't expected.

Mirroring each other, they cracked their knuckles as they stalked toward me. Unlike the others, these two didn't fear me. They stopped a few feet away.

The one on the left huffed out a breath. "My name is Daouda." He thumbed over at his brother. "This is Brahima."

Brahima gestured at me. "Pleasure to meet you, Gavin."

What the hell was wrong with these two? "We swapping emails and addresses so we can keep up with one another?"

Dauda sighed. "No, we just want to let you know that this is business, not personal. Your death will herald a greater good. You seem like a decent man, and we're sorry to have to take your life needlessly. If the others would listen to us, we'd sit you down and talk this out. Unfortunately, we're now in a position where that's no longer an option."

"You serious?" They genuinely sounded as if they were telling the truth. "It'd be shame for you both to die here today. Walk away…survive…maybe then we can have that talk. If you persist—"

A bolt of necromantic energy appeared in my periphery a moment before it slammed into my temple. Shock, horror, and anger swept across the brothers' faces as they turned to see who'd sent the spell.

For my part, the energy felt familiar—this was one of Deheune's people. In that moment, I worked it out. Necromancers were made. The blood rite utilized to create them used a small amount of blood from a lich lord. As the newly minted necromancer gained rank, they took in a bit more of the lich lord. Whoever hit me contained a great deal of Deheune's essence.

I turned to the brothers. "We'll speak again."

Black mist wrapped around me to create massive bat-like wings made of shadows, fire, and the souls of the damned. I flexed them and took flight. I followed the trail of darkness back to its source, a frail looking man about halfway down the street.

"And you are?"

The man puffed out his chest. "Quinn, a humble servant of the true god, Deheune."

Several things happened in that moment. The vampires shot forward as a whole, attacking the group. Most of the necromancers focused their attacks on myself, unleashing one spell after the other. I raised my arms to cover my face and chest while wrapping my wings around my core.

I kicked my leg out behind me and pressed forward in an attempt to stop the backward progress. Each of the necromantic spells seeped through my armor and dug into my flesh, further empowering me. It was odd to feel stronger while still being pushed. The asphalt under my boots buckled and I came to a halt as the onslaught stopped.

Before I could lower my arms, two vampires slammed into me, one in the front and one to my side at knee level. The ground came up fast and hard, knocking the wind out of me. Claws raked against my legs, chest, and face. I flexed, causing my wings to unfurl, which tossed both the vampires off me and halfway down the street in either direction. With a move straight up out of a horror flick, I practically levitated to my feet.

Before Quinn and his choir of necromancers could unleash their second volley, I extended my claws and ribbons of power emanated from me. Taking flight, I slammed into Quinn. My talons tore through his chest, turning him to dust before anyone could react. The weird chains extended themselves, tearing through three more necromancers, turning their corpses to dust.

Not far away stood Phoebe, who quickly turned and ran. That wasn't going to help. I was on her in an instant. I tore off her head and tossed her corpse away as I consumed her soul.

The world around me slowed to a standstill as a new volley of necromancy hit me. This one was different…it belonged to multiple lich lords…including Deheune. One moment it pressed against me, the next it was gone. I sprinted toward the source, but whoever had been here vacated the area in a cloud of darkness. Ah, this was how they shadow walked—their ability to teleport by expending a captured soul. The area appeared contaminated, but it'd return to its natural state in a few hours.

Everything remained suspended for a few more seconds then time resumed its course.

Pivoting on the spot, I readied myself for the attack that didn't come due to most everyone else being dead. The few vampires and necromancers that remained upright gave me a wide birth, hoping to find easier prey amongst the others. That was a mistake.

Vasile moved with such speed and efficiency that I could barely track the man's movements. By the time he slowed, he'd wiped out his attackers. Gabriella was dusting folks left and right. Silver threads spread out from Cole to instantly slaughter the three vampires coming for him.

It took another fifteen seconds before the street was filled with the blood of the dead.

With a wave of my hand, the ice barrier vanished. I stepped toward the group. Everyone save for Gabriella, Vasile, and Cole took a step back.

I flicked my wrist to crate the scythe and whirled around to face whatever was there to find nothing. Pivoting, I scanned the area for possible attackers.

There were none.

I turned to Vasile. "Am I missing something?"

Gabriella frowned as she waved her hand up and down at me. "Uh…might want to take that down a notch."

No one was fond of the scythe, so I let it and the armor fade away. "Okay, we should move."

By the time we reached the greenspace around the Gianicolo Lighthouse it was filled with at least a hundred weres. Henri, Gabriel, Talbis, and Alexander stood at the gate.

Alexander jogged forward. "You okay?"

I thumbed over my shoulder. "Yeah, but they could use some help."

Gabriella pulled Vasile to the side and whispered something in his ear before walking over to me. "Thanks for the help."

Not that she appeared to need any. The woman was a walking, talking, death machine.

"No problem."

Alexander gestured at a group of lithe, deeply tanned young men with dark hair who instantly jumped to their feet. "Madam Governor, I'd like to present your guards for the foreseeable future."

She gave me a questioning look. "Guards?"

I sighed. "Yeah, everyone is getting some extra help. They'll shadow you and make sure you're safe."

Concern etched itself across her face. "Not sure I need that."

Translation, she wasn't sure her secret would remain safe. "They're centurions. Meaning they report to me only. They're to keep you safe, not spy on you."

Reluctantly, she nodded. "Okay."

Alexander smiled. "They're familiar with the area as they're the local werepanthers."

Her eyes twinkled. "I've never met a werepanther before."

Alexander grinned. "They'll happily introduce themselves when you're safely back home."

She waved. "Fair enough."

Gabriella and her escorts headed through the gate.

I turned to Alexander. "Get the others home. Once they're safe, we'll do the same."

It took another half hour before we made it through the gate in New Orleans. The park was clear…like oddly empty save for Alexander's clan, Isidore, and what I suspected was the massive werewolf pack he belonged to.

6

August 17th

Opening my eyes, I rolled over to check the time...3:30 a.m. Wonderful. Sighing, I sat up and placed my feet on the floor. I rubbed my eyes and headed for the shower. Over the last year, my body regulated my sleep patterns in such a way that I get up stupid early and crash around eight whenever possible. At this time of the day, the world was quiet. Night owls were crawling into bed and morning people hadn't gotten up yet. And while this schedule worked for me most days, some it didn't...such as today. After tucking Heather in at Henri's, I got home around eleven and crashed almost immediately.

Four and a half hours sucked no matter how you sliced it.

I glanced out the window; dark clouds covered the sky. A flash of white highlighted the roiling mess and thunder rolled out in the distance, heralding a new storm. For the record, art is supposed to mimic life or vice versa...not the damn weather. Grimacing, I strode into the bath and turned on the water.

Twenty minutes later, I was clean, dressed, and sitting in my chair.

Time to see what sort of shitstorm awaited me.

According to the text I received last night, all the governors made it back to their secure locations by ten p.m. central. Meaning, they, along with the centurions, were where they were supposed to be and where they'd remain for the duration.

For me, that meant Alexander, along with a healthy portion of his clan, were sacked out downstairs. Kimberly, Isidore, and his pack were at Andrew's. Vasile was in China sorting out Attila's defenses... the list of assets I trusted was scattered around the globe. That'd change, but for now, I was on my own.

Warden Global was helping with logistics, sorting through our databases, and generally converting one trustworthy Archive member at a time to the new network. As for Viktor...he was sorting through some recent physical changes and preparing for a visit from a lady named Xiwangmu.

Hayden was busy coordinating the Ulfr around the globe. They were having to quell the numerous skirmishes that'd broken out over the last month in general and the last forty-eight hours specifically.

The new laptop was unbelievably fast. I'd no more hit the power button and it was on. That was when the fun began. Retinal scan, fingerprint, password, and finally pin number. You'd think they would've been happy with one or maybe two...but no. The scary part was the tech guy said that they'd opted out of a few security features to speed things along.

Please Wait...

Portal being secured...entering UCD network.

Password. ***********

Welcome back, Gavin. You have one hundred and ninety-three messages, fifty-two alerts, and twenty-one critical issues. Which would you like to address first?

This new system needed a personality overhaul...or maybe just a personality in general. Not exactly realistic, but maybe one day.

As it stood, I had choices. Thankfully, I could rule out the *critical issues*. According to the tech guy, they were packets of malware designed to breach our new security features. Warden Global kept them in the system, feeding on itself while they searched for more. Once they cleaned and secured the data inside, they'd port it over into a clean system. Everything thus far amounted to gaping holes in our old defenses allowing someone, likely the Black Circle, unfettered access to our records.

Until we were clear, I had to go through multiple levels of security to get to a middle ground where messages and other pertinent information from the corrupted files were scrubbed for viewing. Next generation servers with a new wireless system were coming online in a few days, courtesy of Warden Global. At that point, we'd be in the clear as the nanotechnology involved would prove difficult to hack. It'd be fast, efficient, and even duller than the system currently in use…but it'd be secure.

The alerts…that was shit that'd gone wrong and elevated to my desk. All of which I was sure were related to the attacks against the Archive.

Taking a deep breath, I clicked the messages icon.

From: Amelia Eckerd, vigil for North America
Subject: Thanks for keeping me in the dark.
Greetings Mr. Randall,
No one could be happier to hear that Andrew made it out of Rome than me, but I have questions that you NEED to answer, immediately.

First, I'd like to know why you neglected to come to me with your plan.

Second, why were two of my subordinates brought along without consulting me first?

In the future, it'd be best to consult with me prior to doing anything as brash as what happened in Rome. It's my opinion that you've overstepped your authority and as such, I'll be filing a grievance with Lazarus.

Over the last fifteen months, you've made a number of questionable decisions without bothering to come to me or the other vigils first. One of the biggest blunders being freeing the weres. While you are technically in charge of things, you'd be better served speaking to your elders so we can advise you when you're making a monumental mistake.

While it won't stop me from filing my complaints, an apology would do wonders for you in my book.

After that, it'd be in your best interest to rethink your position on the *weres, especially in these trying times. They cannot be trusted and allowing them off their leash for too long could lead to more trouble for the Archive in the future.*

I'll be expecting a written note expressing the proper amount of regret for your breach of protocol regarding Vasile Ciocan and Cole Pahe. That should be quickly followed with some sort of plan to contain the were problem.

Today would be best. I'm a busy woman with a lot of things on my plate.

Yours truly,
   Amelia Eckerd

The skin under my eye twitched. Taking a deep breath, I pushed back from my desk to keep from hurling the computer out the window. Amelia was officially out of her goddamn mind. What the fuck did she mean by technically? It took a second, but I got my heartrate and breathing under control. I wouldn't take her bait. If she wanted to play, I'd happily set the rules. I hit the reply button.

Pleasure to hear from you as always, Amelia. As to your concerns, I'll be only too happy to address them in person. It seems I have questions of my own. If you're dead set on today being the day we have a proper conversation, I'll clear my schedule for you.

If I don't hear from you within the hour, I'll assume your schedule suddenly filled up. Either way, though, we will be speaking, in person, within the next ten days. That's nonnegotiable. I strongly advise you not to force me to track you down, because that won't end well. (I don't care if you take that as a threat or not.)

Feel free to lodge any complaint you wish with Lazarus. I don't work for him, nor do I work for you...that last bit is something you need to come to terms with immediately. If that's a problem, please let me know and I'll happily replace you by the end of business.

In addition, overstep again, refuse to acknowledge my presence or author-

ity, and include someone no longer within the Archive hierarchy, and I will remove you from office.

Due to last night's incident and your poor response to it, my patience for any sort of bullshit is at an end.

Sincerely,

Gavin Randal

If it was possible to reach through the computer and strangle the woman, she'd be dead. Instead, I had to satisfy myself with clicking the send button super hard.

Time to see who was next.

From: Paul Koenig, vigil for Europe
Subject: Sorry in advance
Good day to you Mr. Randall,

It's my hope we can speak in the near future. I'm finding it difficult to contain the narrative here in Paris concerning Alfred's death. While he didn't have any family to speak of...or friends, other than myself...and it's my understanding he wasn't close with his clan...not even sure which he belonged to...he was still a high-profile official.

As such, different governments have been reaching out asking questions I'm not sure how to answer. Lazarus isn't responding to my emails or calls, so I'm forced to dump this on you. Sorry, I'm sure this is the last thing you need.

Due to Alfred's unique situation—former governor, ancient vampire, and a loner—the responsibility for his remains have fallen to me. I've also been alerted by a local law firm that I'm the executor of his will.

Fielding calls, wrapping up his estate, and burying the man will consume the foreseeable future. That's my long-winded way of saying, you've got time.

With Lazarus out of the loop, I've got zero idea who will be taking Alfred's place. Hopefully, they'll be as kind and wise as he was.

If there is anything you need from me in the meantime, please don't hesitate to reach out.

All the best,

Paul Koenig

Goddamn Lazarus. He was making things so much harder than they had to be by acting like a prick. My thoughts ground to a halt as two silver coins and one larger gold materialized a few inches above my desk then thudded against the hardwood.

Kur swam to the forefront of my thoughts. *"Interesting."*

"What are they?"

Wonder sounded in his tone. *"The two silver coins belonged to the prefects who were slain...and the gold one is from Alfred."*

Confused, I asked, "Why are they here? Shouldn't they be in Lazarus's possession?"

"They should...unless..." His voice trailed off. *"No...maybe."*

A sharp pain shot through my skull, and I slapped my hand over my forehead. "What the hell's going on?" Gritting my teeth, I grumbled. "Is that you?"

It eased up a moment later.

Kur suddenly sounded apologetic. *"Sorry, didn't realize the feedback was going to do that."*

Rubbing my temples, I sighed. "It's fine...care to tell me what's going on?"

"I cannot say with any certainty but...do you recall the scan I'm running due to the use of blood magic to empower Naevius?"

Dermot's visit and subsequent revelation about the man set that in motion. "Yes. What's that got to do with the coins?" I leaned back in my chair. "The headache I get...the other, not so much."

He paused. *"I think the two are connected. While I can't readily identify the inhabitants of the other coins...they've got to be closely related."*

"Slow down." I turned my chair to look out at the park. "You're rambling and making zero sense."

He stopped swishing back and forth through my brain. *"Right... okay. Here's my theory. The scan was supposed to track down and isolate anyone who might be compromised through blood magic, telepathy, etcetera."*

Excitement tinged his voice. *"I'm going over the data now...fascinating stuff."*

"Please focus."

Clearing his throat, he said, "Right...due to your biological connection to Andrew, the failsafe program in the nanites he possesses triggered a similar scan...due to his telepathy, it went from him to Kimberly and Heather, setting off the same program in their nanites."

A headache developed right behind my eyes that had nothing to do with the scan. "So, you're telling me this...virus detector was suddenly triggered throughout the entire Archive?" I reached out and picked up the golden coin. "I can see that...what I don't understand is why these are here and not with Lazarus."

Several seconds passed before Kur spoke again. *"You seriously don't see a correlation?"*

Oh...oh god.

"You're saying Lazarus has been deemed a hazard?" Shaking my head, I asked, "Wouldn't his coin be here instead of Alfred's?"

He sighed. "Sorry, it doesn't work that way. His coin, along with any others that've been infected, will need to be forcefully removed."

Crap. "Good to know."

Placing the coin to the side, I hit the reply button.

Hey there Paul,

Sorry about Alfred. By all accounts, he was a good man. As you can probably guess, I'm neck deep in issues here. I'll do my best to get to you within the week. If it's okay with you, I'll talk to Henri Fabre about coming out to help with the official calls.

Wish I could say things were going to get better in the near future, but I honestly don't know that to be true. As to who will be taking Alfred's place, I'll do my best to make sure it's the best person for the job.

In the interim, though, I'll have Alexander reach out to the local weres and centurions to see what assistance they can be until things get sorted.

. . .

Sorry for your loss,
   Gavin Randall

Next.

From: Heng Song, vigil for Asia
   Subject: My eternal gratitude.
   Salutations Master Randall.
   The safe return of Attila was and is most appreciated. Once he and I speak, I'll be in touch. There's a lot going on, but his safety is my top priority.
   Heng Song

Woohoo, something I didn't need to fix.

I absolutely understand. Looking forward to speaking with you again soon.

Next.

From: Aiden Wen, vigil for North Africa
   Subject: Thank you.

Most grateful for Ian's return. Expect to hear from me soon. Hopefully, I'll have news.

And the roll continued. No idea what type of news he'd have, but on the upside, it wasn't someone being pissy with me.

. . .

Hope it's good or at least helpful. Even if it isn't, hope to hear from you shortly.

From: Chala Tren, vigil for Southern Africa
Subject: You should've checked with me first.

While I suppose a thank you is in order for returning my governor in one piece...which if you'd been on top of things wouldn't have been necessary...I'm less than thrilled with your decision-making capabilities. I doubt I'm alone in this.

Considering how little you know about the Archive, our history, and who we are as a community, it'd be in your best interest to check with people who've been here longer than you. We have a certain way of doing things and you've come in and fucked it up with these filthy weres being allowed to roam freely.

You only compounded the problem by tasking them to guard the governors around the globe. I assure you no one, other than perhaps yourself, is happy with this arrangement. Every move you've made since becoming a vigil has been one bungling misstep after another.

All I can currently hope for is that the weres you sent out are housebroken. If not, I'll be forced to put them down. In the future, speak to myself or Amelia before making any other inept decisions.

Thanks to your latest act of ignorance, I'll be unable to assist you in cleaning up this mess you've gotten us into due to having to babysit and possibly house train these...things.

Email me immediately and let me know when these filthy creatures will be removed from my territory.

Chala Tren

At this point, I no longer cared if Amelia or Chala were contaminated/infected; they had to go. My current preference would be subsequent execution of both.

. . .

Greetings Ms. Tren,

Please understand the centurions work directly for me, as do you, and they are there at my direction. You will assist them with anything they need. If you attempt to interfere with their work, they've been instructed to use lethal force against anyone or anything that gets in the way of them doing their job...in case you missed it, that includes you.

I've already taken the liberty of informing Amelia we'd be meeting in the next ten days...given the current issues, I'll need to see you within that timeframe as well. As soon as I have a date and time figured out, I'll let you know. Your presence will be required at that point. Failure to show is not an option.

Have a wonderful day,
  Gavin Randall

Next.

From: Alinta Daku, vigil for Australia and the surrounding island nations
  Subject: I'm very grateful for Kylie's safe return.

Most grateful for Kylie's return. I'll get with her and the centurions for a briefing after which we'll need to speak.

And back on track.

Let me or them know what you need, and we'll see about tending to your request as quickly as possible.

. . .

Nineteen similar emails crowded my inbox from the other vigiles from around the globe. Their general tone was less than ecstatic. I'd say about half of them were butthurt that I hadn't consulted them or asked their permission before flooding the field with weres.

Fuck them.

If they'd been doing their job all these years, we wouldn't be in this situation.

Maybe a quarter of the rest didn't care one way or the other, while the remaining were grateful for the bolstered line of defense.

This was tiring.

The remaining emails seemed to be from UCD chiefs from other countries looking for some sort of guidance. I took a few minutes to create a filter and sent them to Baptist, as he was my point person with Interpol. After I found out he was a Domovoi, I pressed for a promotion. He wasn't exactly thrilled with the idea, but it'd worked out so far. This was something he could handle.

Right now, I needed to check in with Henri and Heather.

The rest of the emails could wait.

The computer dinged, alerting me to yet another message.

Christ.

I clicked on it and froze.

Sender: John Smith

Subject: Pacis Gladius...it's time we spoke.

Hello Gavin,

While we haven't formerly met, I know you very well, as you've learned over the last several months. That wasn't the way I'd wanted to come into your life, but there's nothing to be done about that now.

Know that I've done my best to prepare you for this moment. If you want to know more, hit reply...no need to enter anything...and I'll call you.

Your friend,
John Smith, HR

. . .

Hitting reply, I sent back a blank message. Apparently, someone had my number…in this case, in more ways than one. He was right. It was time we spoke. I leaned back in my chair and stared at my mobile. After a short eternity, it rang.

I hit the answer button and put it on speaker. "Hello."

Mr. Smith blew out a breath. "No yelling?"

"Not yet." Asshole kept pushing my buttons, it might come to that. "What's on your mind and why are you contacting me now?"

He let out a small groan. "Everything except the last bit is stupidly complicated."

Seriously? The guy spied on me most of my life and now *it's complicated*? "Look, if you've got something to say then say it. If not, I'm fucking busy."

Defeated, he sighed. "I deserve that. In short, I can help you with your current situation."

That was highly unlikely. "Which one? I've got several fires burning at the moment."

"Figured we'd start with the Black Circle and the Courts then work our way down from there." He paused. "Maybe cut me some slack and allow me to give you a hand."

If he was on the level, I couldn't pass up the offer. "How are you connected to Pacis Gladius?"

Mr. Smith cleared his throat. "It's my baby. I've spent the last fifty plus years putting it together…making sure the Black Circle, Gotteskinder, Courts, and others were kept in the dark about it."

How in the hell had he managed that?

"To do that, you would've needed to know about those things first…and if you did, why didn't you tell someone?"

"Who exactly would you like me to tell?" Irritation coated his tone. "It isn't like Lazarus is trustworthy."

He had me there. "Okay, so somehow you figured out they existed decades ago, kept it to yourself, and built another secret organization to combat them. That about right?"

Mr. Smith made a *meh* sound. "Broad strokes, yes. The details, however, is where all the important bits are."

"Fine." My shoulders slumped forward. "What is it you have to offer that'd get us out of this mess?"

He was quiet for several seconds. "A way to strike back. To hurt them in a way they'd never expect. If you're able to pull it off, they'll back off and you can keep the peace while you prepare for what will eventually turn into a full-scale war."

What a cheerful thought. "Okay, I'm listening."

"Not over the phone." He chuckled. "And with the way your last few days have gone, you're not going to be trusting. So, how about this. You tend to your business. I'll be in touch when I have everything together for you. At that point, you pick the meeting spot anywhere in the world and I'll be there. Sound fair?"

That was awfully trusting of him. "What's the catch?"

He suddenly sounded tired. "None…I'd appreciate it if we weren't on full display for the world, but if that's what it takes to make you feel safe, then do it."

Either he was super confident in his abilities or on the level. "Deal." Even as I said it, I knew something big was about to happen. "How long before you contact me again?"

"Give me a couple days. I need to make sure my intel is correct." His tone perked up. "Thank you for this."

Weird but okay. "Sure…whatever." I paused. "Will you tell me why you've been so involved with my life up to this point?"

He sighed. "It'll be made clear…yes."

"Hope to hear from you soon."

Sadness filled his tone. "You will, and I'm sorry for how all this has turned out."

Without another word, the call ended.

7

Shortly after five, I picked up my phone and stuffed it in my pocket. Couldn't see delaying my trip to Henri's to check on Heather any longer. Plus, it'd give me an opportunity to speak to Alexander and Gabriel at the same time. No way I was meeting the mysterious Mr. Smith on my own. Granted, it was more cautionary than anything else. For some weird reason, I trusted the man. Something I had a hard time doing with most of my associates within the Archive.

Perhaps if I gave it a few hours, ran some errands, and generally gave the situation some thought, I'd be in a better frame of mind to be properly suspicious of him once more.

Turning off the light, I closed the door behind me and walked toward the stairs. I disliked teleporting from place to place as it took precious minutes away from me to think without distractions. Yet, taking the Tucker out seemed like a poor choice…I wasn't worried someone would squash me like a bug again…given the enchantments on the vehicle, it'd likely survive a direct hit from a nuke.

No, my problem was this…they'd know where I was going and how long I stayed. The Tucker was easy to track, watch, and even if they lost me for a minute…all they'd need to do was keep an eye on social media for pictures from random people on the street.

Porting was the only option left.

Trekking down the stairs, I found Alexander on the first floor in the living room talking on the phone.

He spotted me and gave me a thumbs up as he remained on the line. "You did?... Excellent. How far away are you? ... Not a problem." He rolled his eyes. "Really. ... Never would've guessed. ... If she gets too far out of hand, feel free to gag her or simply knock her out. Either way, get her back here a soon as possible. ... Thanks. ... Take care Sam."

I waited till he tucked his mobile away.

"Everything all right?"

"Great." He pointed at his cell. "Guess you heard that."

Duh. "Yeah. Not sure what it was about, though."

Beaming, he said, "Sam and Dean found Ms. Dodd." He snickered. "They're on their way back with her now to speak with you."

"Woah." That'd be counterproductive. "Uh, maybe have her brought over to Henri's? Got to check on Heather anyway." I gestured around the room. "And I'd rather not have to repaint the place after her head explodes if it's all the same to you."

He blinked. "What's that last bit got to do with anything?"

"I don't trust her and if she intends me harm, the walls will turn into a Jackson Pollock piece." My voice hardened. "I think we can both agree we don't need that right now."

He winced. "Oh, forgot about that. Let me text them back." Hammering out a quick message, he asked, "You driving?"

"Sorry, but no." I chewed on the inside of my cheek. "And I need you with me."

Alexander tucked his phone into his pocket. "Figured." He steadied himself. "Let's do this."

All the weres in the room took several steps back.

I chuckled. "Not sure why you get so worked up about it...Cole I get, he comes out the other side like a popsicle...you, however, are fine."

"It gives me the creeps." He grimaced. "Everything about if feels...wrong."

Alexander, along with every other were, could sense my teleportation flame bubble. None of us were sure why, but it didn't negate the reality of it. Cole and others hated it due to him nearly freezing to death the first time I used it. Since then, Heather and a few others were teleported with minor complaints. To date, Vasile seemed to be the only person who didn't care one way or another about it.

"Sorry, but there's nothing I can do about it." I paused. "Ready to do this?"

He nodded and stepped toward me. I put my hand on his shoulder. Flames wrapped around us and an instant later, we were outside Henri's Gate.

Alexander retched as he stumbled to the side. "God, that's awful."

Hanging my head, I patted him on the back. "Ah...at least you're not cold?"

"No, but I might vomit." He shivered. "Come, let's go in. Sam will be here with Ms. Dodd shortly."

Poor guy. Wish there was more I could do for him. But for now, this was it.

Gabriel stepped out onto the porch. "Morning gentlemen, come on in. Breakfast is nearly ready."

"Morning. Thanks, but I'm good." I gestured at Alexander. "He, on the other hand, could probably eat."

Alexander rolled his shoulders. "It's true, I could." He sighed. "Thing is, we've got company on the way."

Gabriel opened the gate and stopped short. "Who?"

"Ms. Dodd." I shrugged. "Didn't feel like having her brains splattered all over my new walls, so this was the safest place." Smiling, I said, "And by safer, I mean for the paint. If she fucks up here, she'll be just as dead, and the house will clean itself."

Gabriel shivered. "Pleasant thought." He gestured for us to follow. "Come, I'll make the arrangements for her arrival."

I held up a hand. "Wait...uh...look, I'm going to need to ask you both for a favor in the very near future. There won't be any prep time, no explanation, and we'll be traveling via the indigo express. Oh, and absolutely no one can know about this. You okay with that?"

Without a moment's hesitation they both said, "Yes." In unison.

Alexander puffed up. "I'll be fine. Promise."

"After about thirty seconds." Gabriel snorted. "It'll take me a full minute to stop being a popsicle, but it's a small price to pay."

"Good, it's settled." I gestured ahead of us. "Let's get things ready for Ms. Dodd's arrival."

Henri, Heather, and Talbis were sitting around the table eating.

Heather glanced up. "Morning, sunshine. How are you feeling?"

Tired, aggravated, and absolutely peeved at the current situation, but I didn't have a wall drop on me like she had. "Okay, and you?"

She held out her forearm, which was nearly clear of the bruising. "Good. Be up and running in no time."

I leaned in and kissed her on the cheek. "Glad to hear it." Turning to Henri, I asked, "Think we could use your lab this morning?"

He paused mid bite. "What's going on?"

Hated to repeat myself, but… "Need to question Ms. Dodd and I'd very much like to make sure she was properly confined until we're finished with her."

"Oh." He set his fork aside. "We won't use the lab for that."

"But—"

Cutting me off, he continued, "No buts." He sighed. "I've got another pocket reality that's better for such things." His voice dropped to a near whisper. "I've done my best to put the place out of my head since I acquired it…never thought I'd have a use for it, but destroying it would've been wasteful." Getting to his feet, he chewed on his lip. "I need to check it and make sure it's suitable for the living…it's been sealed for the better part of a thousand years."

A chill ran up my spine. "Don't tell me you've got a dungeon hidden around here somewhere."

"Okay, I won't." He waved for me to follow. "Come on, it's just under the staircase in the hall."

"Uh, okay…sure."

Henri pushed open the door to the hall, moved about halfway down, and placed his hand against a blank section of wall. Silver light emanated from his palm stretching out into a sheet about three feet wide and eight feet tall. It glowed for a moment then vanished to reveal an ancient, thick metal door. He reached into his pocket to produce a large iron key that he fitted into the lock and turned.

A massive clank sounded throughout the house.

Grabbing hold of the handle, he placed his foot against the baseboard and pulled back. For a moment, nothing happened. Then it moved the metal hinges, groaning and squeaking as it opened. A waft of cold stagnant air rushed over me then, nothing. Where there should've been a room...hall...something...there wasn't. Instead, it was just a rectangular bit of black on the wall.

He turned. "Wait here. Need to disarm a few things before it's safe for visitors."

With that, he strode into the darkness and vanished. Several clanks, clicks, and choice curse words followed over the next two minutes.

Eventually, Henri called out. "All clear."

My stomach churned and every fiber in my being didn't want to step through the opening. Still, it had to be done. All I had to do was step through that weird coalesced bit of inky black. It really shouldn't be a problem...I mean, I had this...I think. Stepping up to the spot, I took a deep breath and pushed through. In an instant, the darkness was gone. Soft white light emanated from basketball sized crystals suspended from bronze chains in the carved stone ceiling. Reaching out, I touched the wall...limestone, cold, and slightly damp.

An uneasy feeling settled in my gut. A flash of knowledge not my own spoke of sacrifice...then it was gone.

The passage was barely wide enough to accommodate my shoulders. Obviously, this wasn't from Louisiana. Hell, I couldn't be sure it was from earth. From my understanding, pocket realities took on certain attributes from the place they were created. While the limestone seemed natural enough, the massive glowing crystals did not. The gradual gradation to the floor gave me the impression I was moving deep underground.

About a hundred yards later, the passageway gave way to a massive bubble shaped cavern. Speleothems, stalagmites, and stalactites—with thick veins of silver, gold, and gems— were erratically spaced throughout. An artificial stone wall with different metallic gates dominated the right side of the cavern.

In the center, a silver chair created for the sadistic was ringed by a few dozen tables. The grotesque recliner came with a cruel looking headrest, smooth silver arms, and a gynecologist type footrest, all equipped with thick flexible metallic straps for when you absolutely had to hold a motherfucker down. On the far side seemed to be some sort of living quarters. Hanging overhead in a gyroscope was a jagged bit of what appeared to be quartz that bathed the entire area in a harsh white light.

Kur squirmed in my head. *"Sigils the like I haven't seen since before my banishment are carved into the cells."* He paused. *"Look, the chair and the straps contain multiple enchantments as well."*

I frowned. *"Any idea what they're for?"*

"To contain, strip away power, and compel any in their charge to tell the truth." His voice trembled. *"I'd heard about these during the war...but I've never born witness to such a place until now."*

None of this made any sense. *"I get that there was a massive war prior...with the Loki and others...but why would such a place exist here...in this world?"*

"Don't know...maybe ask Henri where he found it."

I pivoted on the spot. "Uh, Henri…what the hell is this place…and where are we?"

He paused. "Those are both very complicated questions."

"Short version then." I sighed. "We don't have a lot of time."

Henri chewed on his lip. "Okay, so…when I was excavating the area in Paris where the pocket reality was going to go, I found these cells."

"Wait, thought the whole point of a pocket reality was to be outside of our own and not take up space here."

He leaned against the table. "Normally, that's true. Thing was that the area Alfred chose used to belong to a powerful sorcerer." He gestured around the room. "The magic stored in some of the immoveable objects in the vicinity prevented me from creating a proper portal. It took a few months of reading through Lilith's notes, but I figured out how to scoop out the affected area, place it inside its own realm, and store it for future use." His voice dropped to a near whisper. "Since this place…along with the others…aren't properly tied to any one reality, I've been able to move them from one place to another as it's suited me." Tiredness shone on his face. "Haven't had a need to visit this place since I scooped it out. Shame that it's going to be turned into a prison once more."

It was interesting that a sorcerer had a prison to begin with, but to possess a pre-Quantum Destruction of the Multiverse one was even more so. "Any idea who the sorcerer was?"

His gaze hit the floor. "I do…it was Alfred."

Woah, okay, hadn't considered that. "Why'd he want to use his old…what exactly was this place?"

Henri shook his head. "No idea. This is only part of his complex. I've got the rest tucked away in other places around the house. He was some sort of tinkerer…some of the stuff he taught me to do was centuries beyond my understanding. The lab he created makes mine look like a child's plaything."

Heather stepped forward. "Why don't you use it then?"

He shook his head. "Too dangerous. I attempted to settle into it a long time ago and nearly blew myself up. I go visit as often as I can, read through his notes." He paused and glanced up at Heather. "Remember that angel I made for you one Christmas?"

She gave him a curious look. "The one with the four wings of light?"

"That's the one." He smiled. "I learned how to do that from reading one of his notebooks."

I held up a hand. "Shouldn't that have turned to dust by now? Or does time not work the same way in here."

Henri beamed. "It doesn't work the same, but the books he had were made of the same paper as Lilith's."

How in the hell was that possible? "Weird, but okay. We're getting off track though. But believe me, we'll be revisiting this in the very near future. Especially the part with the angel with wings made of light."

That part had me very curious. Maybe there was something in there that'd help me understand the species. That'd be important when it came to getting a handle on Jade, since she was half angel and half lich lord.

He smiled. "We'll talk soon. And yes, everything is ready. When she arrives, we'll bring her here." Pointing at the chair, he said, "And we'll sit her in this while she's questioned."

Alexander flipped the metal arm clamp. "Not that I'm opposed, but why? Is there something special about the chair?"

"Should force her to answer honestly." I replied. "Truth is something we could all use from her."

Henri gave me a curious look. "Correct…how'd you know?"

I tapped my temple. "Had a little help."

He nodded. "I see."

Alexander frowned. "I don't like this place." He thumbed over his shoulder. "Maybe we should wait outside for our new charge."

Henri gestured toward the exit. "Can't disagree with your assessment."

Out in the hall, Alexander, Isidore, and Talbis stepped into the dining room.

Heather touched my shoulder. "You hungry?"

"Not really." I held the door open for her. "I'll catch up." Putting my hand on Henri's arm, I said, "Got a second?"

Heather grinned. "You two have fun."

He turned to me. "What's on your mind?"

"A shit ton…but I'm curious about a few things. You said you scooped out several sections. Are they all as…unique and or interesting as this one?"

A big smile crossed his lips. "More so…hell there's a massive area I've been unable to access…" His voice trailed off as hope shone in his eyes. "Maybe you could open it. As far as I can tell, the opening repels humans and anyone with an ounce of magical power. And since you're neither, perhaps you'd be the perfect candidate."

The urge to go see the doorway leading to this new zone was strong, but I suppressed it. "I'd love to give it a shot but that'll have to be later." Jade's four golden wings filled my mind's eye. "There's something else that's got my attention. Earlier, you mentioned an angel you made for Heather...the one with the wings made of light."

A confused smile worked its way across Henri's lips. "Uh, yeah...what about it?"

Anxious, I leaned forward a bit. "You mentioned finding the idea in Alfred's lab...was it in a book? Something you saw?"

"Oh, uh...it's nothing really."

Tensing, I said, "It's something to me. Please, if you remember, tell me."

His cheeks burned. "Fine...okay...but it's not exactly going to paint me in a good light." He grabbed my arm, pulled me further down the hall, and lowered his voice. "At the turn of the twentieth century, I locked myself away for several months in Alfred's old lab, determined to figure it out once and for all." His shoulders slumped forward. "All that drive and motivation lasted about three weeks before I gave up, grabbed a book off the shelf, and started reading."

I blinked. "How's that explain the angel?"

"Give me a second." Henri shifted his stance. "The book I picked up was book three in a set of four."

"Weird place to start."

"It was...but it was super interesting...told the story of the Withering God." His eyes lost focus and his voice sounded far away. "It spoke of a beautiful woman with the ability to give and take life. Her parents were the personification of life and death...With little more than a touch she could lay waste to entire worlds to have them reborn as vibrant living things later. Never got to the others...they were simply labeled War, Pestilence, and Death." He shook free of the memory. "When Heather was a child, she loved the glossy version of angels marketed to the public...took a little doing, but I took the idea of the wings of light and created something she'd like."

Smiling, I said, "That's super nice of you." I ground my heel into the floor. "Any chance you still have those books? Specifically, the one about the withering god?"

He beamed. "Absolutely. Would you like to read them?" His excitement dimmed a bit. "I mean, it just sounds like an old take on the four horsemen of the apocalypse."

My gut twisted in on itself. "Any idea how old the stories are?"

Henri was quiet for a moment. "Okay, maybe old was a bad choice of words…given that they're written on the same type of paper as the book on pocket realities from Lilith, they may likely be the source of the legend itself."

The wind left me, and I leaned against the nearest wall for support. My voice came out barely above a whisper. "Could be, yeah."

Every instinct in my being said he was right.

He eyed me. "You okay?"

"Yeah…fine. Tired is all." Clearing my throat, I pushed myself upright. "The next time you're able, would you get them for me? I'd very much like to read them."

Henri's smile faltered. "Sure thing…want me to grab them now or wait till we conclude our business with Ms. Dodd."

"Let's wait. I can always delve into those later…for fun of course."

He nodded. "Of course."

"Right now, my only focus is our soon to be guest of honor."

"Shame that." He sighed. "She's a royal bitch."

How very kind of him. I would've gone with racist cunt myself. "Even so, she might know something."

Henri grimaced. "If she does, we'll figure it out."

Hope he was right. I didn't want the mysterious Mr. Smith to be our only way forward. While my gut said to trust him, my head kept bringing up things like, 'He's lying.' 'In all likelihood, he's setting us up to be ambushed…again.' Etcetera. Yep, I'd come full circle to not trusting the man again. Which was probably good for my health. Still, though, if he was on the level and his information paid off, we'd be able to strike back and actually hurt the Black Circle…possibly the Courts as well. Of course, the latter had problems of its own in the form of Cain and his vendetta against them.

The one thing that bugged me about the dissension in my brain was this...If he'd wanted me dead, he could've easily managed to make that happen over the last thirty years. In addition, he'd gone out of his way to ensure others didn't happily put a bullet through my skull.

Thing was, he'd fucked with my head even if he hadn't meant to. And I was having difficulty getting past that.

A knock at the door broke the awkward moment between Henri and me.

Alexander pounded out of the kitchen to answer it. He pulled the door open to reveal Sam with Ms. Dodd thrown over her shoulder and Dean right behind her.

Guess she'd mouthed off one too many times.

Sam stepped around Alexander and glared at me. "Where do you want this sack of shit?"

"Follow me." I turned to Henri, who opened the way to Alfred's holding cells under the stairs. "We've got just the spot for her."

She paused. "I don't recall there being a door there."

"Long story." Alexander moved up beside her. "It's the safest place for Ms. Dodd, especially since she's been uncooperative."

Dean snickered. "She said one stupid thing too many, is all."

Alexander offered to take Ms. Dodd. "Oh, care to fill us in?"

Sam shook her head. "Nah, I got the bitch." She paused. "I smacked her because she pointed at the ASPCA truck and said she'd have me put down when this was all over with." Shrugging, she frowned. "She's had it coming for a long time. She's lucky I didn't finish the job."

"I'm happy as well. She may yet know something we can use." Gesturing for her to follow, I said, "Let's get her properly situated before she wakes up."

Alexander went first, followed by Sam and Dean, then I closed the door behind us. Halfway down the hall, Ms. Dodd squirmed out of Sam's arms and bolted ahead.

I tapped Dean on the shoulder. "You and Sam stay here. It's my turn to deal with her."

He nodded.

Sam grinned. "She's all yours. Glad to be done with her."

Slowly, I strode ahead to find Ms. Dodd frantically looking for an escape route.

Hate, anger, and disgust war across her face. "Of course, it's you."

"Were you expecting someone else?"

"Fuck you." She sped across to the far side of the room. "What is this place?"

I gestured at the silver seat in the middle. "Take a seat and we'll talk."

She shook her head. "I don't think so."

"Ms. Dodd, please don't force me to get physical with you." Inhaling deeply, I stood there for a long moment. "I ask this for your safety. You see, the last day and a half has sucked. The Black Circle decided to play demolition derby with Heather's car, while I was in it. Deheune did her best to put me in the ground, and people have been generally disrespectful." I sighed. "In short, my patience is at an end. Now, do was I've asked and sit."

Her fangs elongated as she sprinted toward me. The low wail of the demon choir echoed throughout the chamber as my armor slammed into place. Ms. Dodd paused mid step, not moving as I ran to intercept her. I slowed, grabbed hold of her shoulders, lifted, placed her in the chair, and put the restraints in place. A half second later, terror etched itself across her face and she screamed. One of the armored ribbons of my new gear hovered above her face.

I placed a finger to my facemask. "Shh."

"W…what are you?" She stammered. "No, it's not possible…they were right."

Did Sam give her a concussion?

I pried open her eyelids to check her pupils…fine. "Care to start making sense, or do I need to sedate you?"

Weird, my voice came out modulated, slightly raspy, and deeper than normal.

Sweat beaded on her forehead and the restraints glowed slightly. "They said you'd be the death of us all…that you'd killed Namisia and, by extension, the strigoi as a whole." She gulped in air. "I'm starting to believe it's true."

Fantastic, the Courts were giving me credit for the strigoi's extinction. I'd have to deal with that later.

"Tell me what happened two nights ago and why you're the only vampire working with the Archive that's still alive."

Ms. Dodd let out a blood curdling scream as blood ran freely from her eyes and her exposed flesh next to the restraints began to burn. "Not sure...they came for me the same night, but I wasn't home."

There was obviously more to the story. "Where were you?"

She grimaced. "I'd gone out hunting...a human angered me, so I tracked him down and ripped his throat open." Gulping in air, she steadied her voice. "On my way back, the silent alarm from my home went off and I got an alert on my phone...thought it was you or one of the centurions."

"Thought?"

Ms. Dodd struggled against the restraints. "Got a call from my maker asking me where I was...when I questioned him...he made it clear that he was the one who'd sent them. I ditched my phone and ran." She glared at me. "Then that fucking animal found me and drug me here."

"That wasn't so hard." My armor dissipated. "Why did your maker send people to kill you?"

She glared at me. "You'd have to ask him. I have no idea."

I could think of at least a dozen reasons right off the top of my head. "Were you aware that the Courts and the Black Circle were in bed together?"

Ms. Dodd's expression faltered. "Didn't know their name until recently, but I knew we were working closely with the necromancers. I hadn't a clue their plans ran so deep. Not that it would've mattered to me. I hate the Archive and everyone in it."

"Then why join?"

The corners of her lips twitched downward. "Because my maker forced me to take up the position." She fixed her gaze on mine. "Before you ask, it's standard practice. No vampire, other than fucking Alfred Monet, wants to be a member of your shitty club. But we had a job to do and we did it."

Probably already knew the answer, but I had to be sure.

"What was that job?"

She sneered. "To keep tabs on the happenings inside the Archive, report back to our handler, and when the day came, help expunge you all from this world."

"Lofty goal." She was more psychotic than I believed. "Do you know where I can find the Courts or the Black Circle's main office?"

She beamed. "Nope."

Fucking hell, that made her all too happy. "What about your maker? Where's he?"

Her smile faded, replaced by hurt and sorrow. "Don't know. We've only spoken via the phone in the last fifty years." Her voice cracked. "Went to his home a few years ago only to find out he hadn't lived there in decades. Using the Archive's resources, I did my best to find him, but he's in the wind. Got a message a few days later from him, ordering me to stop digging."

Even her own maker hated her. "Did you?"

She squirmed. "Yes…you don't go against the Courts for any reason or you wind up dead."

Damn, she wasn't going to be much use.

"Fine." I gestured at her shackles. "I'm going to release you now. If you try anything stupid, I will kill you. Do you understand?"

"Are you going to stick me in one of those cages?" She growled. "I don't like being locked up."

She could eat a dick.

"Where exactly do you think traitors and murderers go?" I shook my head. "You've admitted to killing at least one human for sport and to betraying the Archive…without you offering me something I can use, it's unlikely you'll ever be free again." Undoing her legs, I sighed. "Think about it, maybe we could work something out…I mean going free is too much to ask, but there might be a place that'd be less… crude for you to go."

After undoing the last one, I jerked her to her feet and force marched her toward the cells. We were about halfway when she whirled around, grabbed my arm, and bared her fangs as she tried to take a chunk out of my arm.

Shadows coalesced around my forearm, shot forward to fill her mouth, then turned indigo. The flames consumed her in an instant, turning her to ash.

Did that bitch try to turn me?

Kur whispered in my mind. *"Perhaps. But it's not possible to infect you with the parasite. You're immune."*

That was good to know. "Thanks."

Alexander sped down the hall and suddenly stopped. "You okay?"

"Yeah."

8

August 18th

While I'd like more sleep, it wasn't in the cards. Between it being three thirty and the vivid dreams of me being turned into a vampire, I was more than ready to get up. Not sure why my mind chose to delve into that particular nightmare when it wasn't possible. Kur assured me that the nanites in my blood wouldn't play nice with the parasite that caused vampirism. Then there was the fact I was biologically incapable of being turned due to my genetic makeup...or so Kur surmised, anyway.

Worst part of the evening, I kept waking Heather. She needed her rest if she were going to heal properly. While she didn't say anything, I had to assume me finally getting my ass out of bed made her super happy.

After my shower, I strolled into the office, hit the power button on the computer, and circled the desk. Before I could sit, my phone rang.

Picking it up, the screen read, Paul Koenig.

"Hello."

Heavy panting came across the line. "Thank god...I'm in trouble. How long would it take you to make it to the Paris Gate?" Incoherent yelling sounded in the background then a small explosion. "Necromancers found me."

During my time overseas, I'd been to Paris more than a few times. "Where are you now? I might be able to get to you faster than meeting at the gate."

Static sounded. "Not far from the main entrance to the catacombs...Alfred's home is a few blocks away."

"Can you meet me in front of the building in two minutes?"

He paused. "Maybe. There's a lot of ground to cover."

Kur whispered. *"Once we're there, we can track him via the coin."*

Damn, I'd forgotten. *"Thanks."*

"Paul, stay safe. If you need to hole up, I'll find you." I put my ID in my pocket. "I'm on my way."

He puffed out a breath. "You sure?"

"Yeah. See you in a few."

I ended the call and let indigo flames envelope me.

When they vanished, I was standing behind a flagstone single story building. From this angle, surrounded by bushes, it wasn't much to look at. I pushed my way through the shrubbery and bumped into one of the tourists waiting in line.

The overweight older American sneered. "Watch it, buddy." He thumbed over his shoulder. "Back is that way...I suggest you move it."

Really? This asshole was going to get testy over being chaperoned through one of the biggest tourist traps in the city. "Easy, fella...save all that vim and vigor for the stairs."

He gave me the finger as I strode to the street. "Fuck you, asshole."

If only I had more time, I'd gladly insult the geezer from here till next week. However, Paul was in trouble and I needed to find him.

Bright sunlight poured through the trees between me and the street. While I found it cool, it was sweltering for Paris. Stopping at the sidewalk, I glanced up and down the street.

Okay, where the hell was Paul?

Kur whispered, *"He's southeast of us and moving in short bursts."*

"Got it, thanks." Uh...hmm. "Which way is southeast from here?"

I could feel him smile. *"Follow your instincts. Allow them and me to guide you."*

Damn it. *"Sure thing."*

Over the last year, Kur had done his best to help me refine the more delicate bits of my newfound abilities. In this case, he was referring to the tracking sense. Unfortunately, given the incomplete state of Kur's network, we were limited to roughly one hundred and twenty miles and they had to still be amongst the living for everything to work properly. By clearing away the clutter in my head then focusing on the person in question…all I needed to do was follow the slight tug emanating from the center of my chest.

I did, and took off at a run parallel to the train tracks across the street. Suddenly, there was a sideways and down sensation. I skidded to a halt next to an overgrown patch of land with a single stone hut behind a metal fence that'd been heavily graffitied.

Pausing, I hurried over to read the plaque there, Medici Aqueduct. I glanced up and didn't see anything remotely Roman in architecture.

Kur swam through my mind. *"He's underground."*

That'd make sense…guess the hut contained a set of stairs.

Grabbing hold of the top of the metal railing, I jumped the fence and jogged over to the structure. A burned-out hole dominated the spot where the locking mechanism should be, and the door was nearly torn off its hinges. Honestly, it was a lot more subtle than I would've been if people were trying to kill me. Had to give Paul credit for not leveling the structure behind him as he went.

I hurried down the narrow passage carved out of limestone that looked suspiciously like Alfred's dungeon. Shouldn't be surprised; most of Paris was built atop this stuff. The further down the steps I went, the darker it became. At the bottom, I found myself in a twenty by thirty room. Down the center they'd cut a six-foot-wide channel into the limestone and it was filled with water.

Ah, yes, the Aqueduct.

Hanging a U-turn, I sprinted to the far end of the room before being forced to slow and angle my shoulders to fit through the opening there. Nine feet later, I found myself in a longer version of the previous room. I kept clear of the duct itself and pounded to the far end, pausing long enough to make sure no one was on the other side.

The passage here was narrower than the last. Meaning, I had to sidestep my way through the next nine feet of stone. Slow going, but eventually, I made it. Faint grunting and shattered rock echoed in the distance.

Good, I was getting close.

Two rooms later, I caught a flash of necromancy speeding through the dark in the next room. Getting through the passage here without being seen was improbable. Still, I needed to do something.

On the far side of the next room, two men were pressed against the wall on the left side and one on the right. They took turns rotating in front of the opening to toss a bit of power through the passage, hoping to score a hit.

Wasn't going to happen for them. Thanks to the readings provided by Kur, I found Paul. He was kneeling next to the entrance several feet away from the opening on this side.

All three necromancers were dressed in street clothes. I guess wearing hooded robes or matching uniforms that said Necro's-R-Us would be too much to ask.

The two on the left side wore jeans, work boots, and printed t-shirts...one white with a faded unicorn and the other red with a griffon on it. Their companion on the right wore a three-piece suit and looked like a model for some men's magazine.

Paul had to be wiped out by this point. No idea how long he'd been running prior to calling me, but it'd taken me a solid fifteen minutes to catch up. That was like a half dozen lifetimes when someone was trying to kill you.

My armor slipped around me with that godawful screech. Considering it didn't echo off the walls in here, it was all in my head.

Slipping into the water, I dove underneath and swam the length of the corridor before easing up to get a better look at things. They hadn't moved much since before...only difference now was Unicorn-man had switched places with the Griffon.

Ducking beneath the surface, I came up even with the next passage. There, I allowed the chains made of shadows to crawl out of the water on either side of the duct till I touched the walls then I curled the ends and retracted as I sprung out of the water to hover there.

All three men hit the floor in quick succession as their legs came out from underneath them. I whipped the chains around to catch GQ in the face, carving a gash through his cheek. Two of the tendrils I shoved through the unicorn's chest. The last caught the griffon across his torso, slicing through his shirt and deep into his ribcage.

Griffon's eyes were wide with fear as he panicked and hurled a bolt of necromancy at me. The impact caused me to sway on the spot and GQ pulled out a pistol and fired several rounds into my chest. I didn't even feel them as they bounced off me and made the slightest plop as they hit the water below.

Unicorn grunted as he hurled fire in my direction, which continued to pour out of him for several seconds. Then they stopped. With his body drained of power, it began to cave in on itself as it disintegrated. The two tendrils whipped back to drive themselves through the griffon's skull, killing him instantly.

GQ dropped his weapon, grabbed something out of his jacket, and vanished in a cloud of darkness.

Goddamn it, I hated those talismans.

Griffon's corpse dusted itself a moment later.

While it wasn't exactly new, it still piqued my curiosity as to why they were doing so. That could wait, though.

Touching down on the non-corpse filled side, I said, "It's clear now. You can come out."

"Gavin?" He hurried through the stone archway and skidded to a halt. "Holy shit."

I blinked. "Huh?"

He paled and stumbled back. "What are you?"

Oh, that. Even those who'd seen me go full Grim in the past were taking issue with the new form. Gone were the flowing shadowy robes. They'd been replaced on my left side by a futuristic matte black armor made of shadows of the souls I'd absorbed. My hand there still burned with indigo flames, but it was more of a gauntlet than talons. My right mirrored the living smoke of my left, only here it was highly polished onyx. My breastplate was an off grayish white made to look like my ribcage with a burning indigo sun threatening to burn through.

Covering this otherworldly fashion was a tattered coat that hung well past my knees and a hood covered my head. Beneath its folds was a mask made of hardened onyx and shadow with a slit showing my eyes that burned crimson.

With a thought, the new armor faded and I held out my hands for calm. "Sorry about that. Things have changed recently. I'm not quite used to it myself."

"I...I hadn't expected the stories to be true." Paul straightened himself. "But apparently, they are."

Rumors about me had obviously gotten out of control over the last year.

"Not sure what you mean."

Slumping against the wall, he slid down onto his heels. "I'm sure you're aware that people have been talking about you since you took over."

"No one's said any of it to my face, so I have no idea what's been circulating."

A bitter laugh escaped his lips. "At first it wasn't anything new... You were incompetent...untrustworthy...some sort of fluke who'd get himself killed within the month." He wiped sweat off his forehead. "Then came the hate for releasing the weres...all easy stuff to ignore." He glanced up at me. "Then details came out about your meeting at your uncle's...you'd removed someone from their office and killed them. Burned another man to death and left his charred corpse on display as a warning to others." Reaching into the duct, he scooped out some water and washed his face. "Then...the video from New Mexico surfaced...that's when the fear settled into the naysayers."

That goddamn video would be the death of me if I wasn't careful.

"Okay...I could've guessed this much...what is it that you suddenly think is true?"

A grim smile crossed his lips. "You're more than you appear to be for starters. Then there are those who believe you're actually the physical incarnation of death." He gestured at me. "Maybe you are, maybe you're not, but with armor like that...I can see how people have drawn that conclusion."

Great, yet one more thing to live up to...or was that down? "I'm just a guy trying to make a difference."

"Rest assured, you're doing that." Paul blew out a long breath and placed his head against the wall. "Without you, the weres would still be enslaved. The rampant corruption in the Archive would only get worse. As it is now, many of the biggest offenders are doing their best to hide their actions. That's something new and different. Especially after you tossed Carlos out on his ass."

I wanted to delve into that a bit more but there simply wasn't time. "Thanks." Pausing, I said, "Look, I hate to bring us back on topic, but mind telling me how this happened? I thought you were going to pack up Alfred's."

"I was." He gritted his teeth. "Got to his place shortly after dawn. Didn't know where to start really...so I went to his office." Pulling a note pad out of his pocket, he handed it to me. "Found this and got a bit distracted."

I glanced down at the paper.

There were several strange markings that seemed familiar, but I couldn't place their meaning...quickly followed by my name, Andrew Gavin Randall, and more of the unusual text.

Showing it to him, I asked, "Know what this means?"

"Sorry, I don't." He shrugged. "I was going to call you a little later and let you know about it."

It was weird that Kur didn't instantly translate the text for me. Maybe he was unfamiliar with it.

"You found this in his office?"

"Yeah." He pushed himself up to his feet. "There were several pages of it laying on his desk with your name in that as well." Shaking his head, he sighed. "I doubt it's anything harmful...Alfred was a good guy...I'm guessing he coded his reports prior to making them official and mailing them to you."

Unfortunately, Alfred didn't care for computers...at all. It'd taken a direct order from Lazarus for him to use the smart phone he'd been issued. All his field reports were either handwritten or typed on an ancient typewriter created before electricity then sent out.

"Okay...the necromancers found you at his place?"

He nodded. "I'd just finished carrying a box of files to my car when they walked up. They had a bad vibe about them but before I could say anything, they drew in power and I ran."

What a bunch of pricks...not even letting us burry our dead before trying to murder more of us. "Any chance you'd be willing to take me to his place?" I held up the pad. "I'd like to see what else is lying around...like a key to this code."

As I lowered it, the letters changed themselves to English.

According to Janus, it's the new vigil, Gavin Randall.

Maybe Kur was sleeping. Who the hell was Janus and what am I supposed to be?

Kur wriggled around in my skull. *"That note is written in Ekerilar. Other than Cain, I'm unsure how anyone else on this world could possibly know it."*

Just what I needed, another mystery on my plate. "Me neither, but it'd probably be in our best interest to figure it out."

Paul shrugged. "Hey, if it'll help get us back in the fight, I'm all about giving you the guided tour."

Didn't mean it to be a group thing, but he knew the address. More importantly, he had a set of keys...which would speed things along. "Sounds good." I pointed up. "Let's get above ground and you can show me the way."

He glanced down at the two bodies that'd turned to dust. "Let me sift through the remains to see if they've got any ID on them."

It didn't take long, since there wasn't anything of value to find. Shame. We could use a few leads right now. The trip back to the surface seemed a lot longer than I remembered. Amazing how that happens when you're not motivated by murderers.

I wasn't above ground for two seconds before my phone began to ping with messages.

Heather.

Honey? Where are you?

Alexander.

Please call...can't find you in the house.

Gabriel.

Not sure what's going on, but you've freaked everyone out. Might want to call someone.

Damn it.

I dialed Heather's number and she answered on the first ring. "Hey, honey."

Irritation coated her tone. "Don't pull that shit, where are you?"

Great, she wasn't pleased. "Paris. Paul had a crisis that required my immediate attention."

"Wait...what? You're in Paris?" She let out a small growl. "On your way back?"

This wasn't going to end well. "Not yet. I've got a few things to tend to first."

Her voice had a hard edge to it. "Fine...fine...where can I send Alexander and Gabriel? I'm sure they wouldn't mind a trip to the city of lights."

"I'm fine." Pausing, I patted Paul on the shoulder. "Paul's with me and giving me the grand tour. When I'm finished, I'll be straight home. Sound good?"

She cleared her throat. "No, it doesn't."

"Sorry, but duty calls."

I glanced over at Paul for some support.

He clamped his mouth shut and shook his head.

Smart man, or smarter than me, anyway.

Heather sighed. "If you're going to be a while, could you check in regularly, so we know you're okay?"

"I'll do my best." If it were up to her, I'd be home being babysat by the centurions until all this passed…which it wouldn't. "Hopefully, it won't be much longer."

She paused. "I'll let the others know you're okay. Talk soon."

As soon as the call ended, I smacked the back of my hand against Paul's arm and chuckled. "Thanks for the support."

He grinned. "I find it safest not to involve myself when a couple isn't seeing eye to eye."

"Wise." I gestured in front of us. "How far away is Alfred's?"

Paul rolled his shoulders. "Not sure since I was running flat out earlier, but maybe five or ten minutes."

It was closer to twenty. Guess Paul was a bit more motivated to get away from people trying to kill him than he believed.

Finally, he paused and gestured across the street. "We're here."

I stood there for a moment puzzled. A nine-foot brick wall ran the length of the block in both directions. A massive solid steel gate on rollers blocked most of the cobblestone drive that lead into a greenspace that easily took up a quarter block. Dominating the property was a U shaped six-story building straight out of the Renaissance.

"Great. Which floor was he on?"

He shook his head. "No, you misunderstand. The entire property is his."

Ooohhhh shit. This was going to take a minute. "Maybe you could show me where you found the notes."

"His office is in the center." He looked at his phone. "Mind if I check my messages after I show you the way?"

I held up a finger. "Hold off on that. I'll call the local Warden Global office and get you a secure line. I've got a feeling our communications have been hacked."

He glanced at the phone and it turned to slag as he dropped it. "That'd explain how they found me."

"Give me a second."

I tapped out a quick text to Lt. Baptist.

Would it be all right if I sent Gabriel over to pick up a new sat phone for Paul Koenig here in Europe?

He replied almost instantly.

No problem. I'll set a few aside to distribute to those in need.

That was fantastic news.

Thanks.

I brought up Gabriel's number.

Would you mind picking up some things from Captain Baptist and bringing them to the Paris Gate? Paul will meet you and bring you to me. Please leave the entourage at home.

A few seconds later, he sent back a reply.

Alexander will murder me…any chance he can come along?

Grr.

Sure.

My phone beeped a moment later.

Great, on my way.

I lifted my gaze to Paul. "Would you mind meeting Alexander and Gabriel at the gate? They'll have your new phone and a few extras for anyone else who might need one."

He nodded. "Sure. Let me get you settled, and I'll head out."

9

I'd underestimated the scope of the place from the street. Save for the section at the front corner of the property that was used as living quarters, every section I passed through was given the museum treatment. Rare books lay behind glass. Roped off sections protected artifacts. Paintings worth more than my house lined the walls like wallpaper. Brass plaques were attached to everything explaining what they were. I could spend the next fifty years in this place and probably not get through the first wing. In addition to the six floors above ground, there were an additional three below. According to Paul, it was just more of the same.

Given the real-estate market in Paris, this place was worth several dozen fortunes in property value alone. Everything else made the home priceless.

On the third floor in the center of the U, we came upon a thick wooden door with an odd glow to it. I blinked and it came into focus. There were literally thousands of glyphs inlayed into the wood.

Since when could I see enchantments?

Kur paused. *"No idea, but it is a useful talent to have."*

Paul gestured at the door. "Alfred's office is on the other side." He pulled out a key and unlocked it. "Come on, I think you're going to enjoy this."

"Why?"

He grinned. "Because I've never met anyone who's seen the place that didn't."

Odd, but okay.

Inside, the ceiling stretched a good thirty feet before stopping to create an oval that went up to the sixth floor and down to the ground. It spread out from the front of the building all the way to the back, a total of nearly half a football field. The display cases here were filled with weapons, armor, books, maps, globes, gems, and so much more. It was so vast that it took my brain several seconds to kick back into gear and start cataloging the items around me.

Paul nudged me with his elbow. "Impressive isn't it?"

"Overwhelming might be a better choice of words."

He laughed. "Take it in small chunks, otherwise, you'll get lost in here."

I believed it. "Where's his desk?"

"Over here." He gestured for me to follow him. "It's a bit of a trek but well worth it."

Along the way, I stopped at an empty case. "Hey, was this missing earlier?"

Paul glanced over and nodded. "Yeah, there's a couple of empty ones throughout." He pointed at the tag. "Says an onyx gladius is supposed to be there." Moving over three cases, he pointed again. "That one is for a silver wakizashi."

I blinked. "Really?"

"Yeah…they're both supposed to have special properties." Tapping the glass of the wakizashi case, he said, "This one is supposed to cut through specters and other aethereal spirits not of this world." He shrugged. "I've forgotten what the other's supposed to do…but it's got some sort of intellect to it to boot…that much I remember."

As it happened, I had two swords that matched both descriptions laying in a go bag next to my desk. "Is there some sort of book or something that lists the items in here and what they're supposed to do?"

Paul hesitated for a moment. "Somewhere in that shelf over there." He pointed past a massive desk. "But we're here now...and this is what I mean...you can lose yourself in here very easily."

"I'm beginning to see that."

He gestured at the desk. "That's where I found the papers and the notepad."

"Thanks."

"No problem." He checked his watch. "I'll need to hurry if I'm going to meet your friends at the gate."

"Drive carefully."

"I can do that." Paul waved. "Take care...see you in a few."

The moment he was out of the room, I pulled my phone out and texted Alexander.

Before you come through the gate, please bring my go bag that's next to my desk. Also, reach out to the local weres and centurions in Paris to see if they could set up a perimeter around Alfred's house immediately. The latter part being of most importance.

I strode over to Alfred's desk, which glowed even more brightly than the door had, to find several sheets of paper laying in the very center written in Ekerilar. Suddenly nervous, I sat in the chair, reached out and picked up the first page.

Gavin Randall,
    It saddens me that after all this time...this is how we'll meet. Ink on paper. Can't say it's not for the best because it is. There's a plan in motion and I've played my part. In doing so, my memories of what came before aren't wholly intact—that'll be cleared up shortly.
    I've spent eons waiting for your arrival...not specifically you...but

someone like you anyway. There's so much I want to tell you. Such as the location of the Courts and the Black Circle. However, I've been forbidden from doing so.

My home is a living museum that should help guide you in future endeavors. Please don't remove anything unless specified otherwise. If you're wondering about my intentions, you passed two cases on your way here that are empty. One of the blades was forged by Takemikazuchi...a legendary smith and a person of significant power prior to the QDM.

The gladius was a prototype created on Eden by Lilith and Adam. My understanding is you know who they are at this point. Please be kind to Cain...he's had it the hardest of any of us up until this point. I don't have many memories of him, but the few that remain said he was a good kid who'd been fucked over far too often.

Anyway, back to the swords. It took a lot of work to slip them past Martha and Gabriel ten years ago, but I managed it with a little help from Janus. Speaking of which, he's the one that's been paving the way for your arrival. Over the last thirty years, he's pushed hard to make sure all the pieces are in place to ensure our...your survival. Then last year, you took up your coin and it heralded a new era. That was when he reached out and asked me to put my affairs in order. With all the chess pieces on the board, my time on this earth was coming to an end.

It was a kindness that he didn't have to offer me. On the upside, it allowed me to work my way through my notes and items to ensure what was asked of me would play out as it should.

After all these millennia, I have but one regret; we will never meet face to face. I didn't get the chance to shake your hand and apologize for the burden that is being placed on your shoulders. There were times I thought my job was difficult...having to give up my powers, memories, and become infected with the parasite...it sucked, granted, but my burden would pass, and I knew it.

You, on the other hand, aren't so lucky. If you fail, all life throughout the universe dies with you. For that I cannot express how very sorry I am. From what Janus has said, you're a good man and don't deserve the obligation that's being placed on you. Even though he won't say it, I think he regrets doing this to you as well.

On to business, I suppose.

There are files in the bottom drawer that'll lead you to a safety deposit box. The information inside should go to Cain to help aid him in the search for his half-siblings. Be aware that the only person capable of killing one of the kings or queens...his half-siblings...is Cain. You can hack them up, burn them, even vaporize the bastards, and they won't stay dead. The most you'll get is a few days reprieve before they regenerate, either in front of you or elsewhere.

This is the only reason Eve, Cain's psychotic stepmother, hasn't killed off the others herself. Not that she didn't give it a good try. She spent nearly four years trying to destroy Namisia before banishing and binding her to what eventually became Romania.

Eve tried again with Vetalas, the man who turned me, for nearly a decade...to no avail. So, if you're thinking of trying to off them yourself or believe that you can somehow bargain with them, you can't. The vampire situation is far worse than you think and is Cain's sole responsibility.

In case you missed the memo, Eve is a psychotic bitch who loves to hurt people. She has two weaknesses and they're both based on her hate of two individuals: Cain, and Viktor Warden. She hates Cain for being born. As for Viktor, I have no idea what happened there, but if she's ever going to be drawn out of her personal realm into this one, it'll be to kill the man. Or try to, anyway.

As far as I know, she has no idea who you are. Trust me, that's a good thing.

Now, to the reason you've been brought here.

Janus and I prepared a special gift for you and hid it inside the desktop in front of you.

Please use it...him, to win the war against the Black Circle and the Courts.

Good luck and again, I'm sorry.

Alfred Monet

. . .

Setting the papers aside, I focused on the desk and it vibrated with energy. Dozens of glyphs swam into view.

Kur whispered. *"They're meant to conceal."*

They were doing a damn good job of it.

In the center of the desktop, a thin line of weird blue energy encircled a dot of swirling shadows. A smart man would've been afraid of the chaos there, but I wasn't. Indigo flames wrapped themselves around my hand as I stretched it out to hold it over the tiny storm. Thin strands of black and blue formed a tiny tornado below and a twisting dagger of indigo pushed downward until they finally met.

Involuntarily, I pushed downward. The blue and black energy shot through my hand and up my arm to vanish somewhere in my chest. A loud thud echoed throughout the room as the doors locked and the windows blacked themselves out. The fire faded. Pulling my hand back, a small figure made of cobalt light flickered into existence. Then it turned into a miniature man, wearing black armor with three blue scratches across his chest.

The cobalt faded to become a tiny glowing replica of Alfred. Holding up a finger in my direction, he stretched, yawned, and craned his neck from side to side. Finally, he stood there, his gaze sweeping me up and down. "So...you're the one we've been waiting for." He glanced around the room and sadness crept into his voice. "That means I'm dead...physically at least."

No way. Really? I tried to poke him with my finger, but he danced out of the way.

Glaring at me, he said, "Watch it."

Oh shit. "Wait, you're...sentient?"

"Of course I am." He shook his head. "I wouldn't be of much use if I weren't." Mini-Alfred created a comfortable but advanced looking seat before sitting. "Where to begin?" He sighed. "What's your name?"

"Gavin Randall." What the hell was I doing? "Who or what are you?"

He puffed out his chest. "I'm Alfred or a part of him. As to what I am...that's complicated."

I leaned back in my chair. "Try me."

Alfred didn't respond for several seconds. "You won't believe me. Hell, I barely do."

"Only one way to find out."

Rubbing his forehead, he shifted in his chair. "This version of me was scooped out of the physical version's consciousness by the hand of a god...perhaps the god...no idea to be honest. Anyway, to keep me from breaking down into useless data, I was bonded to a blank AI created by Lilith then infused with enough magic to make me a proper living being...just way smarter and intellectually quicker than anyone else."

Was that all? "Who exactly created you?"

"His name was or is Janus." Alfred gestured and a set of eyes made up of swirling galaxies appeared next to him. "Only saw his eyes when he gave me the spark of life."

This Janus person kept coming up. "So...'god' gave you life and sentenced you to live in a desk?"

Getting to his feet, he meandered over to the center and gestured at it. "That'd be moronic." A second later, a silver ball bearing rose to the surface and sat there. "This is my home."

"Kur, are you there? Is this really happening or am I hallucinating?"

He tsked. *"I am, and no you're not. I'm still trying to wrap my mind around the situation. The being in front of you is truly unique. It's bound by magic, technology and something else."*

Even in my own head, my tone came out far more sarcastic than I'd intended. *"The breath of god?"*

"For all I know...maybe. I've never witnessed anything like it before." Kur hesitated. *"I'm just as stunned as you are...but I don't think he's lying."*

That wasn't at all unsettling.

I turned my attention back to Mini-Alfred. "How would you like me to address you?"

Without missing a beat, he said, "Alfred...sadly, the other version of me isn't using the name any longer."

"How do you know?"

Alfred turned away from me as he reached out to touch the silver marble. "Because, that was part of the deal..."

"What deal is that?"

Alfred leaned against the silver sphere. "Alfred...the physical version...was meant to set things in place. Once that happened, his usefulness would cease." He pointed at himself. "After which, it'd be my turn." Gesturing at me, he said, "At some point after that," —his voice changed to someone else's— "you'll sleep until the one who will be arrives to wake you. You are to serve him as you've served others. Help them become who they need to be, show them the way so that they won't get lost. Don't let them lose hope, for all life depends on their will to survive." He paused and his voice returned to normal. "In this case, that'd be you."

Fantastic...second time today a version of Alfred has made me out to be some sort of savior. Bad news guys—that wasn't me.

Changing the subject, I asked, "What am I supposed to do with you?"

"Think of me as a database with a personality." Gesturing at the desk, he frowned. "It'd be my preference not to get locked up again for all eternity, so if you could find a comfy spot to park me with some regular company, I'd appreciate it."

I rubbed my hands over my face. "Yeah, uh...not sure how to manage that." Removing my hands, I looked at him. "Not sure where you're from, but holographic men aren't exactly common here."

Panic swam through his eyes. "I've got a lot to offer. Everything I know from before...mostly...is tucked away up here...plus whatever the AI had and what Janus stuck in my head."

"Hey, don't worry, I'm not locking you away...wait...before what exactly? Are you talking about the Quantum Destruction of the Multiverse?"

He arched an eyebrow. "How do you know about the QDM?"

I shook my head. "Not yet. First, tell me where you were and what your job was."

Alfred jumped to his feet. "I was stationed on an outpost on the Rim called Eden. As to my job, I was the commander of the Varangian Guard." His voice hardened. "I answered directly to Hayden and

Prince Muninn." He stared at me. "Now how do you know about the QDM?"

My brain hurt. "Cain told me. He also said that most of the Varangian Guards vanished prior to the QDM."

Relief spread across his face. "He's alive. Thank god."

Not exactly the response I was expecting.

"As to our disappearance, there's a reason for that." His shoulders slumped forward. "We were under orders…all of us…Lilith included. She injected my people with a mutagen given to her by Prince Muninn to create a great army to stop the coming darkness."

I blinked. "What type of mutagen and why weren't you given it?"

"I had to monitor their condition while they were in stasis aboard Skíðblaðnir." He suddenly looked tired. "The transformation was difficult…it stripped them of their abilities before transforming them into something new."

Not sure I really wanted to know but I needed to. "What was that?"

Alfred waved his hand again to show a video file of a man transforming into a werewolf. Another showed a woman becoming a werebear. "They gave up who they were to become something new." Sadness coated his tone. "They knew what was being asked of them."

"And you?"

"I had to watch, maintain, and wait. Once we made it through the rift, I ejected the stasis pods before running to the escape shuttle. I'd barely made it before Skíðblaðnir winked out of existence." Sniffing, he folded his arms. "My ship crashed…things got dicey at that point." His form pixelated. "Someone walked through the fire and plucked my body out of the wreckage. My sentinel uniform was removed…not sure how that was even possible." He pointed at himself. "Then I was plucked out and placed inside the sphere here and Alfred was left to guard me."

Holy mother of god—Lilith created the weres…Alfred was a Varangian Guard commander, and now there was a little holographic version of the man in front of me. "Okay, I'm going to need a few minutes to wrap my head around this. Mind if I stick you in my pocket before my people get here?" I checked my watch—thirty minutes had passed. "I really don't want anyone knowing about you just yet."

He nodded. "I can see that. Just don't keep me cooped up for too long."

"Promise." I placed my hand over my heart. "You'll be out and about soon. Like I said…it'll take the others some getting used to."

Alfred nodded. "Fair."

He vanished on the spot.

I picked up the sphere and placed it in my front pant pocket. The windows brightened and the doors unlocked. Voices echoed down the hall. It took me a minute to make them out…Gabriel, Alexander, and Paul approached. There were others…I had to assume those were the local weres being given their marching orders to protect the place.

10

Much to everyone's displeasure, I'd spent the last several hours alone roaming the halls at Alfred's. Unfortunately, I hadn't learned anything new. Climbing the stairs, I strode over to the desk, sat down, and opened the bottom drawer. In which lay a file, two keys, an empty manila envelope, and a thumb drive with Cain written on it.

I pulled the silver sphere out of my pocket and sat it atop the desk.

Alfred stuck his head out slowly and glanced around. "We alone?"

"Yep." I gestured at the open drawer. "Any idea what this is?"

Pushing himself out of the thing fully, he walked to the edge of the wood and looked down. "If it's got Cain's name attached to it, I suspect it has something to do with the vampires."

I leaned back in the chair. "You've been stuck in a marble all this time…can you be sure?"

"It's bigger on the inside…but that's a different story." Alfred glanced over at the ball then to me. "If you're thinking about not giving it to Cain, I beg you to reconsider."

"Why?"

The sensation of stepping into a pocket reality washed over me as the room vanished, save for a bit of the floor and desk.

A disembodied male voice cut through the silence. "Because it's the one thing that's nonnegotiable." It paused. "For reasons I cannot go into, forcing me to pop in on you to repeat myself is a terrible idea."

I blinked. "You're Janus?"

"I am...please do as you're asked.... if the others figure out what's going on, they'll stop me...trust me when I tell you this...what's been devised is the only course that has a chance of success."

Irritated, I got to my feet. "Why don't you just fix...whatever is broken? You seem to have the power."

Not far away, a frail looking elderly man with eyes made of swirling universes appeared. "I've tried." He sighed. "At first, I forced things to happen, but the end results were weak and unable to do what was needed." A well-used silver metallic chair with clean lines, black cushioned seat, and violet light pouring out of every seam appeared behind him as he sat. "For all my power, there are some things you have to work out for yourself." Sadness shone in his eyes. "Learned that the hard way with the others." He lifted his gaze to mine. "Out of all my attempts, only my son has stayed the course."

My anger evaporated to be replaced with concern for Janus. "I'm sorry...may I ask who your son is?"

"Sadly, that's one of the things I cannot answer." Suddenly looking tired, he slumped in his seat. "I can only point you in the right direction...you and the others have to do this on your own." He gestured at the desk. "Part of that is giving *that* information to Cain no questions asked."

It wouldn't be the first time I followed orders I didn't like. "I can do that."

Janus smiled. "Good." Slowly, he got to his feet. "We'll meet again one day, and that'll be a whole different conversation. In the meantime, there's a lot for you to do and even more to learn. This isn't a sprint but a marathon. If you play it right...and I hope you will... something new will evolve out of the old and I can take my place beyond the veil knowing all is in good hands."

"That's a lot to expect out of anyone...especially me. I'm not exactly what you'd call morally correct."

Grinning, he said, "Oh, I'd disagree. You've done hard things, but you've always done your best to do what was right." He paused. "That's the most I can hope for."

I hung my head and my voice dropped. "What if I screw up?"

Janus laughed. "We all do. It's how you handle yourself afterwards." He sighed. "Our time is up and I've got to go."

As fast it'd wrapped around me, the pocket reality was gone.

Alfred looked up at me. "So, what are you going to do?"

"Exactly what I've been asked to."

He nodded. "Excellent choice."

"Time for you to go back in."

Alfred vanished and I tucked the sphere into my pocket. I pulled the items out of the drawer and stuffed them into the oversized envelope.

Sighing, I cupped my face in my hands before pushing back and yelling, "Alexander."

A few seconds later, he walked in with a tall, dark complected, wiry man I hadn't met.

He gestured at the man. "Gavin, this is Yanis...he's second in command for the local weres. Camille sends her apologies as she's in London today."

I got to my feet and held out my hand. "Pleasure to meet you, Yanis."

"And you." His thick accent made the words flow together oddly. "I've been looking forward to meeting you for some time...seen you, of course, during the mass induction at the centurion ceremony six months ago but...you were wiped out."

That was an understatement...I'd all but fainted.

"Hope I don't disappoint."

He shook his head. "Not possible." Thumbing over his shoulder, he said, "We've taken control of the entire complex...what exactly do you want us to do?"

"Preserve it...don't move anything and under no circumstances is anyone allowed here without proper clearance." I grabbed the envelope and handed it to Alexander. "I need you to personally deliver this to Gabriella within the hour."

He eyed it. "Mind if I ask what it is?"

"You can ask all you want. Truth is, I don't know…but according to Alfred's notes, it belongs to her."

Alexander tucked it under his arm. "I'll handle it." He paused. "Need to talk with Henri afterward…he's a lot more familiar with France than any of the rest of us…hoping he'll come help arrange things."

"That'd be great." I smiled. "About to head home…after you're finished at Henri's, call me and we'll go from there."

He nodded. "Sounds good."

Pivoting on the spot, he strode toward the exit.

Glancing over at Yanis, I asked, "Anything you need from me?"

"No, I think we're good." He beamed. "Have a safe trip home."

Grabbing my bag, I waved as indigo flames enveloped me.

In my office, I set the bag down and placed the sphere next to the computer. Alfred stuck his head out and I waved him off. "Give me a few minutes, okay?"

He frowned. "Seriously?"

"Yes." I pointed. "Now back in…I'll be back shortly."

He ducked inside.

Satisfied he'd stay put, I strode out into the hall to find Heather. It took a few minutes, but I finally found her in the carbon copy of my office on the second floor.

She glanced up from the computer and smiled. "Good, you're home. Now I can murder you for leaving like that."

"Hey, I was helping Paul out of a tough situation."

Getting to her feet, she walked over, hugged me, then punched me in the shoulder. "So I heard…three necromancers had him cornered in the underground aqueducts."

"Exactly." I rubbed the spot she'd hit me. "Wasting time to ask for permission to go out and play would've gotten him killed. This way, we're all alive and well."

Heather huffed out a laugh. "Hope it bruises." She pointed at the chair in front of her desk. "With Baptist's help, we've been able to piece together the events leading up to the attacks."

"Oh?"

She nodded. "Yes, and it's not pretty."

Over the course of the next hour, she explained how we'd been ambushed so thoroughly. It started a few hours before the whole demolition derby contest when necromancers and vampires alike strode through multiple gates in unison. We were fortunate enough to get actual footage from a few of them thanks to the Ulfr…they started monitoring several of them after a team was attacked here in New Orleans last year.

Unfortunately, everyone we had a clear picture of could be counted among the dead save for Deheune…only problem there, she was wearing some sort of veil on her headpiece that kept us from getting a good image of her face. With the use of traffic cameras in the different cities, we tracked each group to their final destinations. There were some obvious blanks, but nothing major.

They'd never wavered from their objective…meaning we didn't have any leads to go on locally in any of the attack locations. Smart on their part. Finally, we traced a ping through the UCD's system to everyone's phone, giving the Black Circle and the Courts our exact locations. From there it was just a matter of waiting for the appointed hour.

I ran my hand over the top of my head. "You're right, that wasn't pretty. But you have to give them credit. They were efficient."

Heather blinked. "Don't tell me you admire them."

"Not at all." I shrugged. "But it's good to recognize the strengths of your enemy. It prevents us from underestimating them in the future."

She grimaced. "Still don't like it. They're assholes who need to die."

"No disagreement here." I held my hands up in surrender. "But if we approach this like they're incompetent shit goblins, we'll be the only ones to pay the price."

She folded her arms, placed them against the desk, and lowered her head. "I know…but I hate them."

Unable to stop myself, I smiled. "For good reason too." I got to my feet and walked over to pat her on the back. "We'll make it right…just have to figure out how to do that while keeping those we trust above ground."

She raised her head. "Does Paul fit into that category?"

Kur whispered, *"He's safe. Being that close to the man moved him up to the priority list to be scanned."*

"He is."

Her voice dropped to a near whisper. "You sure?"

I tapped the side of my head. "Absolutely…Been working with Kur to sort through the vigils to ensure they're all above board."

"Anyone come back as less than desirable?"

Kur shifted inside my head. *"Yes…still putting names to them though."*

"Sadly…but we're still sorting out the who." I held out my hand to stop the inevitable question. "Paul, Vasile, Cole, myself, and a few others are cleared…the rest will take time."

Heather sat up. "Fine…just wish this was over already." She shook her head. "This whole afraid to go outside because someone might kill you sucks."

That was a feeling I'd gotten used to a long time ago.

"Sorry, honey…I'm working on fixing things…I really am."

She leaned against me. "I know…and I get it…this shit takes time." Lifting her gaze to mine, wetness formed in the corners of her eyes. "Being at war with a faceless enemy is terrifying. I'm trying to hold it together…but…it's a lot harder than I thought it'd be."

I kissed the top of her head. "You'll be fine. Keep doing what you're doing…information helps."

She gestured at the computer screen. "This sure as hell didn't."

"But it did." I clicked the mouse and brought up the ping trace. "With this, we've verified that the computers were compromised prior to the attack. It also has a point of origin…Rome. Give Baptist a few days to look into the IP address and we might have a location for the asshole who started this shit. From there, it's about following the leads to see where they take us."

Her voice hardened. "I'd like to give whoever it turns out to be a piece of my mind."

"They don't deserve it." I moved around to the front of the desk.

"But when we're done with them, you're welcome to show them the way to the afterlife if you wish."

Heather frowned. "That's an option?"

"It is." I pointed up. "Going back to my office to see what the weres have for us...as well as anyone else."

She nodded. "See you shortly."

Trekking up the stairs, I pulled out my phone to text Alexander.

Were you able to drop off that envelope to Gabriella?

A few steps later, he responded.

Yes...been talking to Felipe, the werepanther's first, ensuring her safety. On my way back now. Need me?

At the top of the landing, I typed out.

No, I'm good. I'll drop by later. I need to speak with Henri.

His reply came nearly instantly.

I'll let him know. Take care.

Tucking the phone away, I stepped into my office to find the computer on. I paused, unable to remember hitting the power switch. I stepped around to see the screen flashing through websites so quickly it gave off a strobe effect.

What the hell was going on? I thought the Warden Global computers were safe.

Kur wriggled to the side. *"They are...that's Alfred's doing."*

"You sure?"

"I am." He hesitated a second. *"His signal is coming from inside the processor there...and that's about to burn up if he keeps pushing it that hard."*

"Thanks."

I tapped my finger against the computer's outer casing. "Alfred... can you stop that before you break something? Please."

The screen froze, displaying the UCD landing page.

A half dozen others popped up. The first one to open was Amelia's personnel file.

Amelia Eckerd
1 Summit Circle
Montreal Canada
DOB December 12, 1558 Occupation: Vigil for North America

Position Acquired: January 22, 1602
Loads of personal information zipped by then stopped.
Net Worth: $15,000,000 US.

The file jumped again to show personal bank records that weren't a part of the Archive or the UCD files. These listed her current identity as Amelia Eckerd and her previous ones; Amelia Stewart, Amelia Banks, and Amelia Thomas.

Guess she liked her first name.

Several highlighted dates appeared on the screen to show large deposits over the course of the last one hundred and fifty years. A deposit from the late eighteen hundreds caught my attention as it was traced back to John Grant. Dozens of others traced back to different incidents around the country…the latest deposit came a month ago to the tune of one point five million dollars.

While I couldn't prove she was dirty…all roads ran in that direction. It would appear that Amelia and I would need to have a sit down sooner than anticipated. She had a few more days and there were a lot of other irons in the fire, but she was quickly making the top of my list.

Alfred stepped out of the computer dusting his hands. "Couldn't help but overhear the issue downstairs—"

"—Wait…you heard Heather's conversation with me?"

He shifted. "Yes…you were gone. I got bored and decided to investigate this crude tech. It leaves a lot to be desired in processing power, efficiency…well you get the picture…it sucks. Thing was, once I was in, I zipped through the lines to the nearest terminal…Heather's." Puffing out his chest, he grinned. "She did a great job assembling the information…probably took her hours. So, when you two finished, I popped up here to see if I could help. Started with the nearest vigil and I'll work my way out as I move forward."

I really wanted to chastise him for walking around unsupervised… but he'd managed to track down a solid lead in a matter of a minute… so it was difficult to be pissed off.

"For future reference, try not to eavesdrop. I'll happily fill you in on the situation."

Alfred propped himself against the keyboard and nodded. "I wasn't trying to snoop…hadn't exactly figured things out at that point. Since then, I've gotten a much better handle on things…including you."

I blinked. "What's that supposed to mean."

"Did you know you've got a ton of nanites swimming around in your bloodstream?"

Not sure I'd ever thought about it in those terms. "Yes."

"Good." He rubbed his hands together. "They're broadcasting a weak signal to more nanites in the other vigiles if Paul is any indication."

Where was he going? "So far, you're right on the money with this."

He chewed on his lip. "If I had access to some of my old equipment, I could boost the signal, giving you the ability to communicate with me and possibly the others without the need of that crude device in your pocket."

Someone was a tech snob…but considering how far back in time he traveled, I could see why. "Okay, but I have no way of getting you any of that."

Alfred tapped his foot. "Too bad…it would help us get an upper hand in your current situation." He grimaced. "There's no way the physical me would've destroyed what was left of our escape shuttle."

I blinked. "Wait…he had access to that tech?"

"Doubtful." Shifting his feet, he said, "Janus was very specific about him not touching any sort of tech, but I still don't see him destroying anything. It could be useful after all. The one thing I can assure you is…I've always been practical and anything that'd give me or my allies an edge…I'd find a way to preserve."

Henri said that there were sections he couldn't access…could it really be that simple? "There's a chance I might know where he hid it…but that'll take me a day or two to figure out."

His expression brightened. "That'd be fantastic."

"In the meantime, what am I to do with you?"

Alfred pointed at the sphere. "No idea. I'm just glad to be out of that thing."

"Understandable." I leaned back in my seat. "Just don't go walking around and exposing yourself to people…I'm not ready to share you with anyone yet. Not till I figure out how to protect you."

Glancing back at the computer, he said, "Why not let me hang out in there…it'd give me a chance to review this world's network and learn what's going on."

It wasn't like I could stop him.

"Sure, why not."

He grinned, rubbed his hands together, and ran through the casing at top speed.

Dear God, what had I unleashed on the world?

11

Dusk painted the sky in brilliant shades of red, orange, and purple. Day three was coming to a close and I'd gotten exactly nowhere in terms of finding the Black Circle or the Courts. I'd bet good money the envelope Alexander handed off to Gabriella likely had something in there that could've helped me with the vampires...but going against Janus didn't seem like a good idea.

I made it sound like nothing was going my way...not true. Alfred would likely be an amazing resource once he pulled himself out of the net. Leaning my head back against the chair, I blew out a long breath. Heather's fear of being at war, or possibly getting killed, probably wasn't the real problem—or it wouldn't be for long. It'd take her a while, but she'd eventually piece things together.

A massive portion of the Archive had lived long enough to witness war firsthand, be they human or not. They'd lived through the witch trials, Inquisition, and many other purges throughout history. Everyone I spoke to said this was different...and it'd somehow wounded them deeper than anything they'd lived through prior. Even Henri, who'd spent the last three decades at war in Muspelheim, felt that this was one of the most dangerous periods he'd ever experienced.

I begged to differ.

As an outsider, or perhaps, newcomer...I had a different perspective. The key issue bothering them this time was simple; they were seeing their friends and people they trusted in an entirely new light.

The Archive was fracturing before my eyes between those who wanted to do the right thing—or at least not make waves—and those who liked things the way they were before I arrived. Meaning, they didn't mind the corruption, double dealings, and uneven power distribution. What they did mind was the weres being freed and having to face the consequences of their actions.

For them, the problem was change...the fear of something new scared the shit out of them. With the attacks the other night, the Black Circle and the Courts assured the Archive's death in its current form. At this point, it was just a matter of time.

Personally, I thought the inception of the Archive was flawed from the start...especially considering Naevius's route to power. Obviously, the coins believed Lazarus wasn't trustworthy and sent all the unused ones to me.

Reaching out, I picked up a gold coin and flipped it over in my fingers. I had plans for this particular one...if it took...there'd be more than a few angry people within my circle. Thing was, it couldn't be helped. These positions needed to be filled by people I trusted.

My phone rang and I jumped.

Glancing over, John Smith's name came across the screen.

"Hello."

He blew out a sigh of relief. "Glad you answered."

"Happy to be of service." I placed the coin back on my desk. "I take it you have everything in order."

Clearing his throat, he said, "I do."

Coldness crept into my soul. While I didn't know why or how, I knew my life was about to change. "You ready to meet?"

His voice trembled slightly. "I am." He blew out a long breath. "Looking forward to the meeting...it's been a long time coming."

He wasn't wrong about that. "Will you be at this number in five minutes?"

He let out a nervous laugh. "Yes."

"Call you back shortly."

I hung up the phone and dialed Gabriel.

He answered on the first ring. "Hello."

I got to my feet. "Need you and Alexander to meet me outside Henri's in two minutes. Not a word to anyone."

There was a screech of wood against wood. "See you shortly."

I punched in Gabriella's number.

She answered. "Hey, I was just about to call you and thank you for the delivery earlier." Pausing, she said, "How are things?"

Stressed, nervous, and generally weirded out.

"You're welcome." I grabbed my bag and set it on the desk. "Sorry about this, but I was calling to ask a favor."

"Oh?" Her tone turned serious. "How can I help?"

Pushing the bag to the side, I decided not to take it. "How fast can you get to the Gate in Brasilia?" I hesitated. "I mean that literally…forget cars, obeying the law…anything of the sort…how fast can you be there?"

She sniffed. "Maybe a minute…possibly two. Why?"

"Okay, I need you to get there and keep an eye on the gate. There'll be a man coming through shortly…he should be alone. If he isn't, let me know."

Her tone hardened. "Any fall back plan if I'm spotted?"

"First off, don't be…but if you are…and there's more than just the one…kill everyone." I sighed. "Better safe than sorry."

There was dead silence for several seconds. "Got it. Be in touch shortly."

I waited sixty seconds then redialed John's number. "Mr. Smith."

His voice shook slightly. "Yes?"

"Go through the nearest gate to Brasilia, find a spot to sit, and wait. I'll be there in a few minutes."

Papers rustled in the background. "Got it."

Ending the call, indigo flames enveloped me. Sixty seconds after that, Gabriel, Alexander, and I were in Brasilia about a quarter mile from the gate.

Ten seconds later, my phone chimed with a text notification.

A rather interesting looking individual just came through the gate...alone. He's seated on a bench looking at the waterfall. For the record, he looks scared to death and extremely familiar.

What the hell was that supposed to mean?

Can you snap a photo? We're almost there.

Her reply came with a blacked-out picture.

Already tried that. For some reason, this guy doesn't show up.

Shit. Guess I'd figure it out shortly.

Fine, about a minute away. If something happens, we can be there faster.

I glanced over at the other two. "Need you guys to circle around to the gate. I want to arrive on my own."

Gabriel frowned. "Sure that's a good idea?"

"Not at all." I shrugged. "Thing is, Gabriella's already got eyes on the man. If he does something stupid, it'll be a contest who kills him first, Gabriella, you, Alexander, or me."

Alexander's voice hardened. "You sure Gabriella can be trusted?"

That was a fair question. If it weren't for Cain, Nid, Kur, and myself coming to an agreement, I wouldn't be. "Yeah, she's fine."

He pulled air in through his teeth. "Okay, give me a few seconds head start."

Gabriel unfurled his wings. "Want a lift?"

"Damn...guess I'll need one if I want to be there when the party starts."

A second later, they took flight and quickly vanished from sight.

Guess it was time to meet Mr. Smith. Nerves caused my stomach to churn as I took my first step. I paused, took a deep breath, and put one foot in front of the other. A minute later, the waterfall came into view then the back of a powerfully built man sitting on the bench held my attention.

Something about him felt familiar. He had closely cropped gray hair...he turned his head slightly at the sound of my footsteps.

"Evening, Gavin." He stood, brushed his hands down the front of his shirt, and pivoted. "I've waited your entire life for this moment."

I froze on the spot.

Gooseflesh erupted across my body and my breath caught in my chest. Mr. Smith's hazel eyes held me transfixed for a moment longer. He reminded me of a larger version of my father. Heavily muscled, thick, well-trimmed beard, and calloused hands. His jeans fit him well, obviously custom made given he was only a few inches shorter than me. Same could be said for the white button up shirt he wore.

He stepped forward and held out his hand in greeting. "Time we were formally introduced." He gestured at himself. "I'm Harold Randall." A big smile broke across his face. "God, it feels good to say it out loud again. I haven't uttered those words in several decades."

Before I could stop myself, I asked, "Why?"

He waved at the bench. "Sit, we've got much to talk about."

I shook my head. "I'm really going to need an answer."

"Short version...Lazarus." He pointed at the bench. "Long version requires you to sit."

How in the fuck did Lazarus factor into this? I moved over and took a seat. "Okay...I'm sitting."

Harold sat next to me. "Want your friends to come out and join us or you going to leave them sitting out there?"

I held up my hand and waved them in. "How'd you know?"

"Because I know you...with Anubis's help, I guided your training from afar."

Gabriel landed next to the bench. "You sure about this?"

I nodded. "Yeah."

Harold looked out into the distance. "Come on out, vampire. I'm going to need to see you before I say anything else."

Gabriella appeared in front of him and reached for his throat. "Careful, old man."

Harold slapped her hand aside and looked her in the eyes. "It's true...you're a child of the Plague Bearer." He glanced over at me. "You understand the magnitude of what's happening then." Gabriella snarled and lunged at him again, only to be pinned to a nearby tree with a flick of his wrist. "Calm. I wish you no harm. I had to know you weren't one of Eve's children."

She stopped struggling. "Should've asked."

"Call me crazy, but I don't trust any of them." He released her. "They'd lie then try to kill me."

Her fangs retracted. "What makes you so sure I won't."

The muscles in his jaw tightened. "Because you have no reason to."

Interesting. "But the Children of Eve do?"

He turned to me. "Yes. As do all the others. I know their secret."

"What's that?"

His voice hardened. "That they've always been in league with the Black Circle. Not all of them know, but their masters do."

Goddamn it, my head hurt. "Before we delve into that…you were about to tell me how Lazarus figured into you vanishing and losing your name all those years ago."

His expression faltered. "Ah, yes, that." He collapsed into the seat next to me. "What do you know of me?"

I shrugged. "Not much…your wife died then you left my father and Andrew to fend for themselves."

His shoulders slumped forward. "I can see how that doesn't paint me in a good light." He cleared his throat. "It's a lot more complicated than that." Looking up at Gabriel, he asked, "Would you be so kind as to create a sphere of light and show the others one of my memories?" Sadness filled his eyes. "This way, you'll know I'm not lying."

Gabriel blinked. "I've never done it before, but I can try." He waved Gabriella over. "I'll need everyone to stand close."

A moment later, we were encased in a golden light then a few seconds after that, the scene changed to my home in Saint Mary, Montana. Thanks to Gabriel's abilities, it was as if we were actually there.

Harold sighed. "This takes place a few days after Andrew's fifth birthday."

The sky outside was dark. A deep cold seeped in through every surface and the fire in the old cast iron stove burned low. Harold glanced over at Ethel, my grandmother, who slept on her side next to him with her hands tucked under her cheek. Until this moment, all I'd ever seen of her was a painting made by my father not long before she passed away. That woman and this one was very different. Here, her beauty shone through, even in her sleep. Clean jawline, nice cheekbones, blonde hair that reached down to her shoulders.

Harold leaned over and kissed her cheek. "Need to stoke the fire. Be back in a few."

Her eyes fluttered open and she smiled. "Nearly time to get up?"

He checked his watch, 3:10 a.m. "Twenty minutes...but there's a chill in the air and I can't let you catch cold."

"Fine." She pushed him out of bed. "Hurry up and warm us up a bit then come back...the boys are sleeping, and we could use the alone time."

Harold slipped his pants over his long johns before stepping into a pair of boots. "I'll hurry."

In the next room, he picked up a couple pieces of split wood, placed it inside the stove, and stirred it with a poker. The fire bloomed to life. He closed the door, stood, held out his hands as they began to glow slightly, and the air inside the house instantly warmed.

Smiling, he strode toward the bedroom as he tugged off his shirt.

Thud, thud, thud.

Harold stopped and his happiness faded, replaced with concern as he turned toward the door.

Thud, thud, thud.

Ethel hurried into the main room, whispering, "Who's at the door this time of the morning?"

Harold held his finger to his lips. Whispering, he said, "Go to the boys and keep them quiet."

Her expression hardened as she hurried to the back.

Thud, thud, thud.

He strode over to the door. "Hello?"

A voice I recognized, Lazarus, cut through the quiet.

"Open up, it's freezing out here."

Instantly, he placed his hand on the door and a white light flashed across the walls then faded. "Don't recognize the voice. Care to put a name with it?"

"Lazarus." Something hit the door hard. "Open up."

Harold glanced back to find Ethel standing there and he shook his head. "Be out shortly." He pointed toward the kids' room. "Go stay with them. I'll be back shortly." Taking a deep breath, he phased through the front wall and out into the cold to face Lazarus. "It's really you." He gestured toward the barn. "I was just about to tend to the cows. Care to join me."

Lazarus scrunched up his nose. "I would not. I want to go inside your home, now."

Harold shook his head. "Not possible. Andrew, my five-year-old, accidently enchanted the place in such a way that none of us can come and go through the normal exits." He gestured at himself. "I can only phase immediate family in and out. Your best bet is the barn if you want to stay warm."

"So, they're stuck inside?" A malevolent smile crossed Lazarus's lips. "That'll make things much easier."

Harold blinked. "What's that supposed to mean?"

Lazarus spread his hands wide to create a black vortex. "Everyone inside needs to die."

Before Harold could move, the malignant energy slammed into the house, but it remained upright.

In an instant, Harold punched him in the face, knocking him to the ground. Then he summoned fire from the sky. A column of flames dropped down then spread out across a shield protecting Lazarus. An oval shaped ring of earth around Lazarus turned molten. Then the inferno died out.

The shield around Lazarus dissipated and he threw a bolt of black energy that slammed into Harold's chest. It lifted him off his feet and pinned him against the house. Energy coursed through his veins and darkness tinged his vision. He had difficulty breathing. Not because of the damage, but due to the immense influx of power to his system. A moment later, the power vanished to drop him to his knees.

Shock registered on Lazarus's face for a moment then arrogance took its place. "You live because I allow it." He pointed at the house. "Go in and make sure the children are dead."

"Fuck you." Harold dusted himself off and got to his feet. "I'm going to murder you."

Lazarus wrapped necromancy around him as he glared at my grandfather. "Fine, I'll kill you and they can starve to death inside."

A sphere of violet flames appeared a few feet away and Anubis strode toward Lazarus. "You shouldn't have come here." He snatched Lazarus up by the neck then tossed him to the ground with enough force to leave a divot. "Go, now. You will not get a second chance."

Lazarus sneered at Anubis before vanishing.

Anubis helped steady my grandfather. "Are you all right?"

Harold nodded. "I am, but my family..."

Anubis's gaze hit the floor. "Your boys are okay...but your wife...she's human and will waste away in the next few years." He sighed. "Stay with her until she passes. Once that happens, you must leave this place. I'll protect the boys until such time they're able to fend for themselves."

Harold blinked. "Who are you and why would I leave them?"

Anubis puffed out his chest. "My name is Anubis. I'm the first Reaper. As to why you must leave...it's the only way to protect them. In time, Lazarus will return with help when he discovers they're still alive. If you wander off into the sunset, no one will check on them and they'll have time to develop into adults. Stay, and he'll kill you all...that's something that I cannot allow."

The truth of his words washed over Harold and he hung his head. "I see... nothing can be done?"

Anubis averted his gaze. "No...it's the only way to keep them amongst the living."

"Not sure I believe that." Harold's jaw tightened. "But I'll do as you ask on one condition."

Anubis arched an eyebrow. "The lives of your sons aren't enough?"

"Of course it is, but I've got a feeling there's more to it and I want to know what that is."

Anubis pondered the request for several seconds. "Then I have a caveat as well. Once you leave, you'll renounce your name until the time is right to reveal yourself. Is that clear?"

Harold nodded. "Done and done."

Anubis's shoulders slumped forward. "What will be asked of you will be hard...nearly impossible in fact, but you must keep this secret until the day Lazarus reveals himself for who he really is."

"I can handle it." Harold grimaced. "That's my hope, anyway."

Anubis shook his head. "There is no option...I'll bind you to your word, *making you incapable of even saying your own name...are you sure you want to do that?"*

Harold paused for a half second. "I am."

Anubis reached out and tapped Harold's forehead. "Then the bargain is struck."

Holy shit. Harold was working for Anubis all these years. "I see...question is, why come to me instead of Andrew with this?"

Sadness shone in Harold's eyes. "I'm hoping he's our next stop. He deserves an explanation that your father never got."

An old anger flared in my chest. "Speaking of which, where was Anubis when Walter killed my parents?"

He hesitated. "I'm not entirely sure you want an answer to that."

On that he was wrong. "Oh, but I do."

His gaze hit the floor. "Tending to you and Isapo Muxika...it's my understanding that your grandfather didn't heed his first warning well enough."

"What the hell does that mean?"

His voice dropped to a near whisper. "It means he intended to kill you...or tried to. Seeing how your powers were bound at birth...you were defenseless."

Gabriella chimed in. "Bound? What's that mean?"

Harold shrugged. "To keep Gavin hidden from the Archive, Anubis did something to prevent him from accessing his power until the time was right."

This was getting a bit too personal with too many people. "How about we go back home and find a way to break this to Andrew so that he doesn't lose his shit."

Gabriel snickered. "Good luck with that."

Gabriella thumbed over at Gabriel. "I'm with the nephilim on this."

Alexander winced. "I'm with them."

So was I, but saying so wouldn't make things any better. "Thank you, Gabriella, for your help. I do appreciate it."

She brushed her nails against her shirt. "No problem. Maybe next time, you'll actually need it."

"Needed it this time...only it didn't require violence." I grinned. "Go take care of things...I've got it from here."

Gabriella nodded. "I'll be out of pocket tomorrow."

"Understood."

She looked up and took flight, vanishing into the night a second later.

I patted Harold on the shoulder. "You're not going to like what's coming next...but I assure you, it's the fastest, safest way to travel."

Alexander frowned. "That's still to be determined."

Gabriel nodded. "Hope you like being a popsicle."

Confusion worked its way across Harold's face. "What?"

Gabriel grabbed hold of Alexander's arm. I grabbed his then Harold's as indigo flames wrapped themselves around us. A moment later, we appeared in my office and I grabbed Harold's shirt, hefted him off the ground, ducked, and waited several seconds.

"Care to put me down?" Harold patted my hand. "My head isn't going to explode."

Alexander opened an eye and nodded.

Gabriel stood up straight, and I lowered Harold to the floor.

"Sorry, but I had to know."

He shrugged. "I get that."

I walked over, closed the door, and locked it. "We've got to figure out how to do this." I checked my watch...9:35 p.m. "Showing up this late at night could put Andrew in the wrong mood...if you know what I mean."

Dusting off the front of his shirt, he grinned. "He always had a bit of a temper...so, yeah, it might be a bad idea...however, delay my arrival too long and he'll be equally pissed."

Walking over to the storeroom, I pushed open the door, pulled out a third chair, and placed it in front of my desk next to the others. "Sit, we've got a lot to talk about."

A knock sounded at the door as Heather called out. "Gavin? You in there?"

Oh no.

"Yes…give me a second."

She laughed. "Yeah, okay."

I glanced over at Harold. "Mind stepping back. The fewer people who know you're alive, let alone here, the better."

Without a word, he faded from sight. I reached over to see if he was still there and accidently poked him in the eye. "Sorry." Nodding at Alexander, I said, "Let her in."

He pulled open the door and waved Heather through.

She glanced around the room and tsked. "What's the big secret?"

"Would you believe me if I told you I had a mistress?"

Laughing, she shook her head. "No." She glanced over at the three chairs and paused. "Who's the extra chair for?"

Blushing, I said, "The mistress?"

A sphere hardened around the chairs as she narrowed her eyes. The one with Harold turned orange and highlighted his form then dissipated. She placed her hand on Harold's shoulder and he rematerialized.

Heather blinked and stumbled back to steady herself against the desk. "Who…who are you?"

He clamped his mouth shut as he struggled to find words. "Perhaps Gavin should introduce us."

That was one hell of a way to pass the buck.

"Okay, yeah…uh…honey, I need you to not freak out." I gestured at Harold. "Damn…this is a lot harder than it should be."

She shook her head. "Why does he look like a cross between you and Andrew?" Her gazed tracked up and down him. "You're an only child, right?"

Which name did I go with? I mean, either one was going to mess her up.

Taking a deep breath, I said, "Heather, I'd like you to meet Harold Randall, my grandfather."

The corner of her eye twitched and she was quiet for several seconds. "You sure?"

"I am."

She pushed off the desk, leaned over, and hugged him. "Pleasure to meet you...seems a lot of family members we thought were gone are making a comeback lately." Giving me a curious look, she asked, "Why did you think I'd freak out?"

I patted her back and pulled her back slightly. "Because, while that's his real name, he's been using another for the last several decades."

"Huh?"

Harold got to his feet and held out his hand. "Until today, I've been using John Smith."

She slapped him. "You're who?"

Had to give her credit for not trying to kill him.

"It's okay, I promise." I gestured around the room. "If he meant me harm, his head would've redecorated my office."

Never taking her gaze off him, she pointed at the chair. "Sit, you've got some explaining to do."

Oh, goddamn it, this was going to be a long night.

Two excruciating hours later, we were outside Andrew's.

His house was brightly lit. Weres roamed the grounds and generally were on edge. Heather and Alexander preceded us onto the grounds to speak with Isidore, leaving Harold, Gabriel, and myself out here on the corner of Coliseum like three lost hookers in the wrong neighborhood.

Harold glanced over at me. "You really think this is going to work?"

"Honestly, I'm not sure." I gestured up at the second floor where lights sprang to life. "So far, everything's going according to plan."

Gabriel snickered. "Isidore woke the man up...not sure that's a positive yet."

Unfortunately, he had a point. We'd worked it out so Heather and Alexander would speak with Isidore, tell him we needed to speak with Andrew without giving him a reason why before making a hasty retreat out the drive. They'd come back in a few, but they didn't want Andrew reading their thoughts before we got up the stairs ourselves.

I bumped Harold's chest. "Okay, let's move."

We weren't fully across the street before Isidore stepped out the front gate. His expression darkened as he stepped back, gesturing for us to come through. While Harold survived the enchantments at my house, Andrew's were much more complex; a big reason why I wanted to walk him up the stairs and not simply pop in.

The moment we passed through, Isidore hung his head and let out a few choice curse words before looking up at me. "You're kidding me, right?"

In the year plus since I'd met the man, this was the first time he'd ever looked truly unhappy.

"I'm guessing you know our guest?"

His gaze landed on Harold. "I do." He shook his head. "Are you sure about this? I mean his identity and intentions."

Irritation flickered in Harold's eyes. "I'm standing right here."

"I can see that." Isidore sighed. "The question still remains."

Rubbing my forehead, I said, "Positive…I've gone through it with him. Heather, Alexander, and Gabriel all had a go. To top it off, he's survived my home and now he's passed through the gate without incident."

He didn't look convinced. "Andrew is going to freak. You understand that, right?"

"I do."

Isidore glanced over at Harold and his tone turned dangerous. "Look, I don't know what happened to make you bail on your family and I don't want to know…right now. But understand, if you fuck over Andrew again, I'll kill you regardless of your intentions." He thumbed back at the house. "You stay behind me and do your best to look small. If he catches sight of you too quickly, this whole situation will go straight to hell."

Harold nodded. "Understood."

I'd hate for Isidore to try to carry through on his threat. Harold manhandled Gabriella, one of the strongest vampires I'd met, with ease. Not only that, Heather made the man strip down to his skivvies before coming here to make sure he wasn't wired for sound or to go boom and all we'd found were scars. As he dressed, he'd explained that he'd received most of them while sparring with Anubis over the years. The fact he'd survived those skirmishes said he wasn't a man to be trifled with. Then there was the bit where he'd gotten bitch slapped by Lazarus, only to have that power added to his own.

If I had to guess, the only thing that outpaced his power was his lethality. He'd been kind enough to humor us so far, but the moment he tired of playing games, things would get far worse than complicated. There would be blood, death, and general carnage. That was something I was keen on avoiding.

We passed through the doors in a single file line with Isidore and I leading the way. Near the top of the stairs, the wood creaked loudly as everyone took a turn stepping on it. Walking into the apartment, Isidore stopped a few feet in and I stepped out to the right of him, doing my best to obstruct his view.

Andrew sat at his desk with a serious case of bedhead. "It's two in the morning…what's so important it couldn't wait till a decent hour?"

Isidore blew out a long breath. "Please remain calm." He stepped to his left, leaving Harold standing in the open.

No one spoke for several seconds.

Kimberly shook her head. "You look like—"

"—Father?" Andrew cut in. "Is that you?"

Harold nodded slightly. "It is."

Andrew glanced over at me. "Is this for real?"

"Yes."

He got to his feet then walked over and slowly made his way around us till he was face to face with Harold again. "You know I'm going to have to check for myself."

Harold frowned. "Yeah, I do."

Gabriel stepped forward. "I could show him the same memory you showed us earlier."

Andrew hesitated. "You'd do that?"

"If it means no one gets hurt here." Gabriel waved his hand between them. "Neither of you seem like you're in the right frame of mind for a proper scan."

Harold placed his hand on Gabriel's shoulder. "No offense, but it's probably better for him to check for himself."

I blinked. "But…this could settle everything."

"It wouldn't." He kept his gaze locked on his son. "All it'd do is prolong the inevitable. If we're going to survive these next few months, we're all going to need to be on the same page. No one can hold back…especially not Andrew."

"Why?" Andrew stepped closer. "What makes me special."

Harold smiled. "For starters, you're my son…second, the Archive needs a strong leader they can trust and I'm sorry to say…that's you."

Andrew shrugged. "There's Lazarus."

"The key word there was trust." Harold reached for Andrew but stopped himself. "You need to know what's happening…see it for yourself so you can be the man you're meant to be."

Tears welled up in the corners of Andrew's eyes. "I'm not sure I can control myself…I could hurt you."

Harold braced himself. "It's a risk I'm willing to take."

"Are you sure?"

Harold straightened his shirt and nodded. "Yes…let's do this so we can move on to the whole I'm glad your alive portion of the conversation."

Power rolled through the room. Chairs toppled to the floor, paintings fell, and glasses broke. Harold, however, stood his ground. A large amber bubble surrounded him and Andrew.

Harold's voice trembled. "Be wary, my boy. There are things you're about to see that you'll soon wish you hadn't."

A half second later, Andrew held Harold's mind in his grasp. Tears ran down his cheeks as horror etched its way across his face. Several minutes passed and his breathing became labored. Finally, he released him and both men collapsed to the floor, unconscious.

12

August 19th

Things hadn't gone as planned with the meeting between Andrew and Harold. That wasn't entirely true. Andrew hadn't tried to kill his father, but there was still a chance we'd lose both of them anyway. Needless to say, that put me on everyone's shit list. Currently they were both in a coma, lying in Andrew's bed being monitored by Kimberly and Heather.

We originally wanted to give them some space...Andrew in his room and Harold at my place, but the moment we put more than three feet between them, their vitals began to crash. Like it or not, they were bonded for the time being. Again, this made me super unpopular with everyone.

Before I screwed up anything else, I decided to head home with Alexander in tow. Gabriel wanted to stick around in an attempt to help speed their recovery by using his Nephilim abilities.

Sitting at my desk, Alfred poked his head out of the computer. "Hey there, how'd things go with your grandfather?"

"Poorly."

He sighed. "Figured as much by the look on your face."

"Please tell me you've got something." I clasped my hands over my face and rubbed. "I could use some sort of news that isn't utter shit."

Alfred danced to the side. "Then you're seriously not going to enjoy the phone call you're about to get."

"Huh?"

His voice dropped a bit. "I didn't want to duplicate anyone's work, so I reached out through the network and found someone digging into the same things I was and helped them along."

"Who?"

He scratched the back of his neck. "A man named Baptist…I suspect he'll be phoning you any minute."

I nodded. "Thanks."

Before I could say another word, my phone rang.

Sure enough, it was Baptist.

"Hello."

He sounded tired. "How are things?"

"Everyone's pissed at me." I sighed. "On top of that, I'm sort of sitting here in limbo hoping and praying that some sort of lead drops into my lap."

Papers shuffled in the background. "Can't help with the first part…the latter though…I might have something for you." He sniffed. "I've been working with the tech guys from Warden Global and we've found several back doors into our system. Apparently, they've been there since the beginning."

If I had the energy, I'd feign shock or some sort of outrage, but I didn't. "We have any names attached to their design?"

His voice tweaked up an octave. "You're really not going to like it."

Didn't doubt it. "Still need to know."

He blew out a long breath. "Amelia and Lazarus personally signed off on all the tech upgrades over the years. They've always been very specific that everything should pass through them and no one else."

Color me shocked and dismayed. "All righty then. Guess I'll visit Amelia this morning…I'll have to deal with Lazarus in a few days."

Baptist cleared his throat. "Uh…about that. She's one of the few people who's refused to pick up their new phone. On top of that…she hasn't been in her office or spoken to anyone since I was at your place."

"Guess someone is throwing a temper tantrum." Leaning back in my chair, I yawned. "When I see her in a bit, I'll have a frank discussion about her continued employment."

His voice hardened. "Maybe she's with Chala because she's in the same MIA boat."

Again, not exactly shocking news. "Anyone else?"

"Chione is absolutely refusing to acknowledge me or anyone else in the Archive." Something creaked in the background. "The moment the weres showed up at her house, she dismissed them. When they refused to leave...she lobbed a few warning shots at them. They've taken up a wide perimeter around her home...but she's somehow managed to give them the slip and hasn't returned."

Great, just what I needed. A freaking runaway. "Just so I'm clear, we're missing Lazarus, a governor, and two high ranking vigiles? About right?"

He made a meh sound. "At the moment, those are the highlights."

"All right, do me a favor."

Pausing, he asked, "What's that?"

"If any of them decide to bubble to the surface, don't loop them into the new system." I placed my forearms against the desk. "On top of that, lock down the new system to only those who've been thoroughly vetted. Have the tech guys move all the data they can off our old servers then shut them down till such time we can retrieve any lingering information."

Baptist groaned. "No offense or anything, but if you wouldn't mind sending that to me in writing, I'd be eternally grateful. There are those who think that, due to their status in the Archive, they can tell me what to do. A note would make implementing your request tons simpler."

No matter how this turned out, Lazarus, Chione, Chala, Amelia and all their douche nugget supporters would go out of their way to make Baptist's life a living hell.

"Not a problem. I'll send it over shortly." Getting to my feet, I asked, "Anything else you need from me?"

He hesitated. "Maybe inform people you're leaving the house so they're not up my ass?"

"Ha…sure, I can do that…In fact, Alexander and I will be visiting Amelia together. From there, I'll see about tracking down Chala, and while I'm on the same continent maybe give Chione a piece of my mind."

His voice tensed. "Same frank conversation about their employment that you're having with Amelia?"

"Chala for sure…technically Chione is out of my scope…we'll have to see how that turns out, to be honest."

Baptist clucked. "I don't see that going so well." He blew out a breath. "And with South America already down a vigil…that'll likely leave three open spots. Any idea who you might have to take their place?"

"For two of them…yes." I hesitated. "But I could use a few names of some good people on my desk by the end of the week. Anyone you trust with the bureaucracy of being a governor as well…I'd like to nominate some candidates instead of letting Lazarus go willy-nilly with it."

He let out a pained grunt. "That's going to go poorly but sure, I'll have a dozen names on your desk in the very near future."

"Thanks, I greatly appreciate it." I pulled up my email to find a prewritten note about locking everyone out courtesy of Alfred. "Hitting send on that email now."

Baptist snickered. "Cool…be safe…and if possible, try to keep the body count to zero. If that's not an option, could you minimize the number of witnesses? This whole worldwide killing spree by the Black Circle has everyone on edge."

"I'll see what I can do."

He sighed. "Guess that's the best I can hope for. Take care."

The call ended and I tucked the phone in my pocket as I headed downstairs to collect Alexander.

Amelia lived in one of the few countries I hadn't visited. Seriously, it was Canada of all places...one of the few locations on the earth that rarely needed the likes of someone like me. That being said, Alexander took the gate to Montreal to secure a rental car and find an out of the way spot for me to teleport to.

My phone beeped, alerting me to a text.

Ready.

Indigo flames wrapped around me and I appeared in a dark corner of a parking structure next to a blue SUV.

Alexander gave me a curt nod. "Ready for this?"

"Absolutely." Stepping towards the car, I grumbled. "This needed to happen a long time ago." I gestured at the vehicle. "You want to drive?"

A crooked grin crossed his face. "Worried they'll play crash test dummy with you again?"

"Hadn't crossed my mind till just now." I shrugged. "Thought you said you were familiar with the city."

His lips formed an O. "I am...sorry for the reminder."

You'd think given the time, rush hour traffic would've died off at this point. It hadn't. Thankfully, Alexander understated his knowledge of the island. He ditched the major streets in favor of side roads and neighborhoods in order to keep us moving upwards to the center to reach Summit Woods—the expensive part of town.

The moment we hit Summit Circle, city blocks were replaced with dense forest that butted up to the Mount Royal park/peak the city was named after.

Alexander pointed. "To the right up here is a famous lookout where lots of the tourist photos are snapped." Motioning ahead, he continued, "Not far on the other side of that bunch of trees up there are two massive graveyards." He shivered. "Both of which give me the creeps...they're pretty and all...but there's something off about them."

"Good to know."

We rounded a bend to find Amelia's house. From this vantage point, the three-story triangular home with beige stucco walls and an aged copper roof didn't make much of an impression. Okay, it was ugly as sin. The aerial views provided by the internet, however, showed a bit more of what made this place an interesting bit of real estate. The roof was mostly glassed in with an Olympic sized pool. Outside, there was a well-maintained garden with two chairs around a small table and a single bench.

Obviously, someone wasn't big on visitors. Too bad for her.

Alexander slowed to a stop a few car lengths away from the two-car drive made of a light and dark gray flagstone where a black Mercedes sedan was parked. The closer we got, the less attractive it became. Two gaudy, carved stone lions sat on either side of the walkway leading up to the two bronze doors.

"Pull in next to the new black Mercedes."

Alexander hesitated. "You sure? She'll know you're here."

"She'll know she has guests, nothing more." I tapped my knuckles against the glass. "We're in a rental, remember?"

His eyes widened in realization. "Good point." He eased the vehicle into the spot next to the car then threw it in park. "Want me to wait out here?"

I blinked. "Uh, no." Laughing, I said, "Christ, you guys crawl up my ass about crossing the road on my own...but we get here and you ask about staying in the car...what the hell is wrong with you?"

"Well...uh...how do I put this?" He sighed. "I despise Amelia and if she gets too mouthy, I might kill her."

I bumped his arm with my elbow. "Might be a race to that...so, come on in and let's see if she survives the morning."

I popped the door open, stepped out, and walked around to meet Alexander at the stairs leading up to the walkway and those hideous lions. Turning toward the house, Alexander gagged, practically doubled over, and started hacking.

Steadying the man, I patted him on the back. "You okay?"

"No." His tone hardened as he placed his hand on the stone statue for support. "Two strange scents." He turned to the car and glared at it. "It's coming from the car too."

Exceptionally unspecific. "Strange how?"

He shook his head. "Hard to explain...it's like when Gabriel flares on the angelic half of his personality on steroids. The other thing... that's...more wraith in nature."

That couldn't be good.

"You're telling me you smell an angel and a wraith?" I pointed at the shiny black sedan. "And they drive a luxury car?"

Alexander didn't look well. "Never met an actual angel so, I've got no idea. As for the wraith...I've met and fought a few...this is something different but definitely related."

I rubbed my forehead. "Awesome...out of curiosity, what kills a wraith?"

"For you...fire." He brushed his slightly elongated nails against his chest. "I'll use these."

"That works?"

He nodded. "Like a charm."

News to me, but these days, little surprised me. "Guess we should knock and see who answers."

We topped the steps and stopped short. The doors had already been forced opened and hastily closed behind them. Whoever the guests were, they hadn't been invited.

I glanced over at Alexander "Anything new?"

"Not really." He paused. "There's a faint trace of blood and there's more fresh air coming through the front door here than you'd expect."

Time to see who the mysterious callers were. "Let's clear this level then work our way up."

Slowly pushing open the door, I took point. Hardwood floors ran the length of the overly large hall, spilling into the adjoining rooms. Sage green colored the walls and highly varnished wood planks lined the ceiling. A few steps in and to the side was a beautiful matching staircase with an antique rug running up the stairs. Other than the trashed entry, you'd think this place was straight out of one of those architectural magazines on how to style your home...if you had a few hundred grand to spare.

I hated leaving the stairs open, but with just the two of us, there simply wasn't a lot of options. The first room was a formal dining room. Even though it was spotless, I doubted seriously it'd been used in a very long time. I circled through the back entrance into the overly large kitchen fit for a celebrity chef on one of those food channels. On the counter was an old pot of coffee that'd turned off.

The next room was huge, stretching the better part of the house. A wall of windows in the front gave a great view of the wooded area across the street. Finally, we came to what had to be her office. She'd forgone sheetrock and paint in favor of hardwood, built in bookshelves, and a stone fireplace. It'd been a nice place and probably would be again once it was cleaned up.

The desk on the far side of the room was splintered, most of the books on the wall behind it were on the floor, and the nearby bay window was shattered. Blood covered a spot outside on the ground.

"Hear or smell anyone in the house?"

Alexander frowned. "No."

I sighed. "Guess it's time to go sightseeing."

A couple of awkward moments later and we were out the window. Okay, Alexander was graceful as hell. I, on the other hand, wasn't. Didn't need a weres's sense of smell to follow the blood trail across the road and into the woods. I cut through the trees at a hurried pace with Alexander at my heels. Whoever was bleeding—likely Amelia—was losing a lot of blood and wouldn't get far. It took another two minutes to find the three of them.

Amelia was propped up against a tree. A tall, shapely, dark haired woman stood with her back to us. A well-built man with shoulder length black hair and a highly advanced cybernetic arm stood next to her.

The woman spoke. "Where is he?"

Amelia coughed up blood. "Fuck you."

"Such loyalty in the face of death." The tall woman's voice softened. "You realize that Dvalinn and his pet Seth despise Lazarus, right? If you tell me where he is and swear loyalty to me, I'll let you live. You might even be able to maintain your charade within the Archive for a bit longer."

Amelia snorted. "Your offer is hollow." She sucked in a breath. "Lazarus will deal with you soon enough and I'll be rewarded with eternal life at his right hand."

The tall woman threw back her head and laughed. "Oh dear...what sort of crap has he been feeding you?" She knelt. "Lazarus lacks the power to bring back the dead. Hell, it took Seth and a dozen of the most powerful followers he could find to breathe life into Lazarus's broken form." She stood and dusted off her pants. "That was a costly mistake...crippling Seth and angering Dvalinn."

Who the fuck was Dvalinn...and how does he relate to Seth?

Kur squirmed. *"Dvalinn is the king of the Svartálfar...and the one who made it possible for the lich lords to be created."*

Oh...uh...okay.

Amelia glared at the woman. "Why should I believe you? You're no one important—"

Golden light flared around the woman. "I am the light...life itself. I'm Heidr, Queen of the Álfheimr."

"Not possible." Fear shone in Amelia's eyes. "Y...you're lying."

Heidr touched the man's shoulder. "Ethan, be a dear and go back to the house for a shovel."

He snorted. "We could use a new wraith."

"That wouldn't be an issue had you not screwed up so badly." Heidr sighed. "But you're correct. Replacements are needed after that fiasco in New Orleans."

Holy shit...this was that Ethan. The one Viktor was looking for and did his very best to kill a few months back. I glanced over at Alexander, who seemed to understand just how bad things were.

Heidr leaned forward to eye Amelia closely. "Oh, you've been inscribed. Clever. Too bad for you, I'm not interested in your soul." She tapped her finger against Amelia's forehead. "Everything I need is in there. Ethan, fetch me one of the containers out of the car. Her cortex will make a nice start to what I'm sure will be a large collection."

All right, time for this to stop.

Moving into the open, I said, "Excuse me, but I'm not about to let you lobotomize one of my employees." I glanced over at Amelia. "Even though I'm about to fire her."

Heidr turned to me and my brain screeched to a halt. A black scar ran from her forehead down the side of her face and another cut across her eye...which was totally black. The face however, I recognized. "Kira?"

Heidr grabbed hold of Ethan, stopping him from lunging at us. "Not sure why you're all so fixated on the previous host of this body but it's no matter. Care to introduce yourself."

I held out my palm. "My name is Gavin Randall."

Relief spread across her face. "You should be thanking me. I'm removing a problem from your house...given a chance, I'll make a clean sweep of the place for you." She thumbed back at Amelia. "She works for Lazarus, who in turn works for the lich lords and Dvalinn...you do know who that is, right?"

"I'm aware." Pointing at Amelia, I frowned. "She's got a lot to answer for, but you're not going to be the one making her talk."

There was a gurgling sound and we all glanced over at Amelia, who'd slit her own throat with a shard of glass.

Heidr sighed. "Pity." She folded her arms. "Since you're here, I've got an offer for you."

By the tone of her voice, I knew what came next was going to be good.

"I'm listening."

A tad bit of psycho tinged her voice. "Swear fealty to me and I'll allow you to live." Her ingratiating gaze tracked up and down me as a sneer crossed her lips. "You have no idea what's coming...this is your only chance." She snorted. "From what I can tell, you've got no power...how you've risen to your current position eludes me." Narrowing her eyes, she said, "You're lucky it's me you met first...Seth or one of his minions would simply kill you out of hand. I on the other hand, offer you power...the type that'll allow you to not only fight back, but win."

Good to know she was out of her damned mind. "And all I have to do is bind myself to you—becoming your servant—and all will be well...about right?"

She grinned. "Better to serve than die."

Her arrogance...no, her presence...angered me on a fundamental level. She shouldn't be here. Fury coursed through me as my armor slammed around me unbidden and my voice shook the ground. "No."

Ethan stumbled back.

Heidr got to her feet, concern etched across her features. "Who are you?"

I stepped toward her. "You should've stayed where you were…it was safe there."

She glanced at Ethan. "Kill his friend."

Heidr leapt off the ground and threw a bolt of golden light at me. I took flight, easily avoiding the projectile. Closing the distance between us, shadowy chains leapt out of my hand, clipping her across the temple. Blood ran freely from the wound. She created a sword of gold and I called forth the scythe and blocked the attack meant to remove my head.

I kicked her in the side, putting her through a thick pine tree. A roar cut through the ensuing silence and Ethan went flying after her.

Heidr grabbed hold of Ethan's unconscious form and vanished on the spot.

"Goddamn it." I turned to find Alexander returning to his human form. "You all right?"

He shivered. "Yeah, you?"

A black shadow showed in my periphery and I glanced over to see nothing less than wings. Shaped like a bat but made of smoke. "Uh…is this as weird looking to you as it is to me?"

"Considering you haven't shit your pants, I'd have to say my view is weirder." He took his phone out and snapped a photo as I touched down. "I'll text it to you."

Not sure I wanted to see it but sure, okay. "Thanks." I turned to Amelia's corpse. "We need to contact the UCD and have them pick up the body."

Alexander nodded. "What are you about to do?"

"Call Viktor." I blew out a long breath. "He should know about Kira—Heidr, and what she's doing."

My armor vanished and my pocket suddenly got heavier. "What

the hell?" I stuck my hand in and pulled out a denarius coin. Damn, yeah, that.

Alexander gave me a weird look. "What's up?"

I showed him the coin. "Received Amelia's official resignation."

"Guess we're back to the old-fashioned way vigils retired."

Before I came along, the only way to lose your position within the Archive was to die. "Yep." I sighed. "Let's hope that our next few stops are less exciting."

Holding up his finger, he said, "Good morning, Baptist...yeah, we're in Montreal. I need you to send a UCD team to my current location while I have the local weres secure Amelia's...no, it wasn't our doing and there weren't any witnesses...who did it..." He glanced over at me and I shook my head. "Uh...I'll let Gavin fill you in when we get back to the city...thanks."

He ended the call.

I chewed on my cheek. "Contacting the local weres next?"

"Yeah, a buddy of mine has a clan of werebears nearby...they'll be able to secure the house quickly."

I gave him a thumbs up. "Sounds good."

Took half an hour for the UCD team to recover Amelia's corpse. Alexander's friend, Logan Sanders, took another twenty to secure the house and begin repairs, using their construction company as cover as to why they were there.

With that taken care of, we were off to visit Chala Tren. Hopefully, her fate would turn out less terminal.

With the seven-hour time difference between Montreal and Cape Town, the sun was in the process of setting and the temperature was somewhere in the mid-sixties. Unlike Canada, I'd traveled Africa and South Africa several times over the years. That, however, was a different story all together.

We picked up a rental car and it was my turn to drive. Chala lived in an uber expensive part of town called Llandudno. Her house sat up on the side of a hill off Ty Gwyn Road and the drive leading up to her place was marked private in large white letters on the asphalt. I chose to ignore her wish for privacy...what was she going to do, call the cops? The tricky part was figuring out which of the two carbon copy residents she lived in.

As far as I could tell, neither were marked and she hadn't been kind enough to say *hey, I live in the one nearest or furthest from the main road*. Thankfully, the lights were on in the one at the end of the drive. Worst that could happen…someone other than Chala was home.

I killed the lights and pulled over to the side of the road. "We've reached our final destination."

Alexander sighed. "Let's hope she chooses to come in peacefully instead of slitting her own throat."

"That'd be nice."

We were about halfway to the house when Heidr stepped out the front door carrying a metallic cylinder, gave me the finger, and vanished.

I put my hand out to stop Alexander. "Hold."

A half second later, the house bloomed orange as the shockwave knocked us over the side of the railing. I hit hard on the grassy hill, bounced, and came to a sudden halt with the help of a very large tree.

I scrambled over to find Alexander still alive and more than a little unhappy.

Growling, he asked, "What the hell happened?"

"The house blew up."

He pushed himself into a sitting position and cocked his head to the side. "I know that much."

"Great, we're on the same page." I got to my feet. "Let's go put out the fire and see what we find."

Alexander gestured ahead. "After you."

I scrambled up the hill and onto the drive. Raising my hand, I brought down a thick coating of ice, snuffing out the fire in an instant. Sirens sounded in the distance.

I sighed. "Get on the phone and get us jurisdiction before anyone fucks up our crime scene."

"Already on it." He placed the phone against his ear. "I'll walk down and stop them while I chat."

"Thanks."

Taking my time, I walked through what used to be the front door. All the debris made it difficult to tell, but this was likely some sort of living room. The fire had charred the area but hadn't had time to burn away the blood evidence, thanks to my intervention. A large black pool of wet covered the floor in front of what was left of the wall.

Pushing aside the wreckage, I found part of a leg, a hand, an arm, then her head…what was left of it anyway. What'd taken place here wasn't due to the explosion…well, her missing jaw, burned flesh, and hair sure…but the surgical incision used to slice away the top of her skull was too clean to be an accident. Another weird bit…not one piece of her brain remained. From the looks of things, Heidr scooped it out cleanly.

Was that what she was carrying? What in the hell did she want with Chala's brain? Was this what she'd intended to do to Amelia?

The deeper into this I got, the more questions I had.

I heard a jingling of metal inside my shirt pocket. Reaching in, I found Chala's coin and another golden one for the governors.

Fuck.

If I had to guess, Chione was dead as well. It wasn't Andrew, as Heather hadn't called.

Pulling out my phone, I dialed Baptist, asking him to send people back to Chione's place. Maybe they'd find her in one piece…but I sort of doubted it. If I had to guess, Ethan murdered her.

Fantastic. Now all I need to do is fill the open positions while tracking down Lazarus. Apparently, we needed to discuss a hostile takeover of the Archive. It was time for a change.

Kur writhed in my head. *"A new name wouldn't hurt either."*

"Why bother?"

His tone turned cold. *"Think about it, what does the Archive mean?"*

"To file or catalog…" Holy shit. "Wait, you think it was created just to track those with power?"

He writhed in my mind. *"I do. If you're serious about making a change, you should turn it into something more meaningful."*

"Any suggestions?"

Kur was silent for a long moment. *"Long before the contagion took hold, we were governed by a council of equals called, Witenagemot."* His tone turned soft. *"That was a time of peace, cooperation, and great progress."*

The name felt right. *"It sounds better to me than a cataloging system meant to line folks up for the slaughter."* Nodding, I said, *"When it comes time, we'll go with that. Thank you for sharing."*

"Glad to help."

13

August 20th

My nerves were getting the better of me as I pulled through the gate at Warden Global. As much as I hated to do it, Viktor needed to know about Kira—Heidr. Other than Alexander, no one knew about the incident in the forest with Amelia. People had their assumptions that the official story was bullshit, but on paper, she'd slit her own throat rather than be stripped of her position.

There wasn't any way that I'd discuss the particulars over the phone, so I had Heather call Justine to set the appointment. Told her I had questions about Kira's disappearance and needed to speak with him in person about the details.

Now, here I was, and I didn't know exactly what to say.

"Hey, saw your daughter in Montreal yesterday and she tried to kill me."

Probably not the smoothest of opening lines.

I put the car in park.

It was my hope that something better would come to mind before I reached his office on the third floor. Otherwise, our cozy relationship might come to an abrupt end. While Heidr was an issue, having Viktor turn on me would be so much worse. We were using his tech, people, and resources to prop up what was left of the Archive. Without him, we were dead with no hope of resurrection.

I strode through the front doors into the lobby to be met by Justine, Viktor's significant other.

She smiled and wrapped her arms around me for a big hug...okay, she was five-four, so as big of a hug as she could give. "Good to see you again, Gavin." Releasing me, she stepped back and raised her gaze to mine. "Seems I owe you again for saving my friend."

"You're welcome." It was unusually warm in here as I glanced over at the staircase. "He in his office?"

Justine hesitated. "Yes, I'm to walk you up."

"That isn't necessary, I know the way."

Hooking her arm in mine, she pulled me toward the elevator. "Not exactly an option."

Damn, did he know about what happened in Montreal? "Uh...okay...the conversation though—"

"—Will be had amongst the four of us."

"Four?" I arched an eyebrow. "Not sure an audience is needed."

Reaching out, she pressed the up button. "We think it is." Her voice dropped slightly as we stepped into the car. "There are things you need to know."

That didn't sound positive.

"Sure...but I'd like to have a private discussion with him as well."

Justine sighed, pulled her phone out, and handed it to me as the elevator dinged for the third floor. There on the screen was a picture of me in full armor, scythe in hand, blocking the blow meant to take my head.

"Oh...I can explain."

Justine bumped her shoulder into my arm. "It's you who is owed the explanation." Her voice trembled a bit. "Please don't be angry with us...we were doing our best to handle the situation on our own. Had we known she'd go after the Archive, we would've said something."

Rubbing my temple, I said, "Let's have this conversation with the others. Apparently, we're all missing some important facts."

Viktor's office was huge with a full bar near the windows on the far end of the room. Two sofas facing one another and a few chairs sat on a twelve by fifteen crimson rug. On this side was his desk, a combination of high tech and old-fashioned wood, set facing away from another set of windows. In front of that were three chairs, one of which was taken by an Asian woman.

The stranger was stunning. Thin, defined features, muscular… everything, save for the height, to be a runway model. The combat boots and solid black fatigues looked fashionable on her. Even though I was positive there wasn't any music playing, a faint song hung in the aether. Not that I was able to make it out.

Viktor stood.

From the looks of things, he'd undergone some serious changes since we'd last met. He still sported the three scars that cut through his eyebrow down to his cheek. The solid blue eye was gone, replaced by a golden one with a violet iris with some sort of design I couldn't quite see at this distance. In addition to that, he'd added a considerable amount of muscle mass. He wasn't overly bulky, but if we were boxers, there'd be a good chance we'd be in the same weight class.

Viktor stepped around the desk and held out his hand. "Glad you could come by this morning." He glanced over at the Asian woman. "Saves me the embarrassment of having to reach out to you instead."

The Asian woman jumped to her feet. "Embarr—"

Viktor whirled on her and growled. "Sit."

The single word had power to it, knocking the woman back into her seat and nearly flipping it over.

Justine stepped between them. "Honey, you're being a bit harsh."

"Sorry." He turned to me. "Forgive me. I'm being rude." He gestured at the frightened Asian woman. "Gavin, this is Nora, Kira's wife." His voice dropped slightly when he addressed her. "My apologies…Nora, this is Gavin."

Nora slowly got to her feet and bowed to me. "Pleasure." She turned to Viktor. "No need to apologize, I was out of line."

"Great to meet you…and forgive me, but I've got no idea what's happening." Frustrated, I did my best to contain my concerns. "Have I done something wrong? Why does Justine have a photo of my encounter with Kira, who by the way, is going by Heidr?"

He winced. "Yeah...I know."

"If you'd be so kind as to sit, we'll try to fill in what we know." Justine motioned at the nearest chair. "There's a lot to go over." She paused. "You said that there were some facts we're not currently in possession of."

Sitting, I sighed. "Several."

Viktor held out his hand. "We can get to that in a minute. First, I'd like to show you something." He tapped his desk. "Mir, could you bring up the security vids from the med bay for June seventh." Shifting in his seat, he grimaced. "What you're about to see takes place after we recovered some contaminated wraith samples. Our working theory is the man in the video was hijacked by foreign nanites. Then he proceeded to the ICU, where he injected those same unknown entities into Kira's system." A grave look settled across his features. "This is how my daughter's body was taken hostage by the entity we now know as Heidr."

When he stopped speaking, a hologram appeared atop his desk.

Kira lay unconscious in a hospital bed with Nora sitting next to her, holding her hand. A thick dark-skinned man strode into the room carrying a syringe full of a dark swirling liquid.

Nora cocked her head to the side. "What's that?"

"If we're right, it'll wake her up." He thumbed over his shoulder. "Nicholas and the other doctors will be in shortly. They sent me ahead to start the process." Giving her a big smile, he said, "The sooner she's up and about, the better we'll all feel."

The worry on Nora's face faded. "You have no idea."

He injected the contents into the IV then picked up Kira's arm to check for a pulse. His fingers turned black for an instant then it crawled onto Kira's arm and vanished beneath the skin.

Nora jumped to her feet. "What was that?"

The man stood there, dumbly blinking. "Wh...what am I doing here?"

Kira sat bolt upright in bed then grabbed the man by the face and the back of the head before snapping his neck. With a casual flick of her wrist, the corpse hit the wall, shattering more bones where he crumpled to the floor.

Nora jerked Kira around to face her. "What the hell is wrong with you?"

"Shangyang, remove your hands from me this instant." Hate filled her voice. "You and your master need to be taught a lesson."

Kira got to her feet, snatched Nora off the floor, and slammed her face first into the observation window, sending cracks radiating out from the impact. Viktor pulled open the door, dropped his vest and grabbed Kira as Justine hurried in behind him. He struggled to pry her fingers off Nora's throat and force her back against the wall. Kira brought up her knee to catch him in his ribs. Then she headbutted him, breaking his nose, causing him to stagger back. She slammed her bare foot into his chest. He toppled over onto the broken form of the man she'd killed a minute before.

Viktor stood up. "Kira, honey, you need to relax."

Kira glared at him then her expression changed, a hint of recognition coming into her eyes. "It's you...but it's not." Raising her voice, her tone became dangerous. "What have you done to the Gray Wanderer?"

Viktor moved around the bed, placing himself between Kira and Nora. "You know he's dead. You were there when we confirmed it."

She shook her head. "It isn't possible." Stumbling back, she placed her hand against the wall to steady herself. "What have you done?"

He held out his hands for calm. "Kira—"

Fury and hatred filled her voice. "—Why do you keep calling me that? Don't you recognize me?"

Viktor frowned. "Of course I recognize my own daughter...and your name is Kira."

Her aura flared golden. "My name is Heidr."

"You're Heidr?"

She nodded. "But you're not the Gray Wanderer."

He shook his head. "No, I killed him not that long ago. Why are you looking for him?"

She sped across the room and slammed her forearm into his chest. "Liar. There's no way someone as feeble as you could kill the Mad God."

Viktor's face turned crimson and he was clearly struggling to breathe. Ice wrapped around him, creating armor from the neck down. He delivered a wicked uppercut to her stomach with the newly formed gauntlet, causing her to double over. He hit her again in the face, knocking her to the ground.

"Look, lady, I don't know how you got here, but you need to vacate my daughter's body."

She slowly got to her feet and wiped the blood off her cheek. "You'll pay for that."

Faster than the video could keep up, he crossed the room, slammed his shoulder into her gut, and pinned her against the wall then quickly wrapped ice around her to prevent her from getting away. "Stay."

Heidr growled. "Fool." Amber light filled the room and the ice fell away. "I'm a god, and you're just living inside the carcass of the most powerful being to ever exist."

Nora slowly crawled into a sitting position. "Careful, Viktor. She's lost her mind."

Justine helped Nora to her feet. "We've figured that out for ourselves."

Nora stumbled to the side. "Guess I missed that part."

Justine nodded. "Yeah…things are not going so well."

Viktor held out his hand in their direction. "Ladies, do you mind? I'm trying to handle a rather bad situation here."

Heidr glared at Nora. "You're still alive? That's unfortunate. I really wanted to send your broken corpse to your master."

Nora struggled to free herself from Justine's grip but failed. "I don't know who you are—"

Heidr screeched, "—I'm Heidr, Queen of the Álfheimr."

Nora went rigid. "That's not possible."

Heidr sneered at her. "You'd be surprised what's possible, little one." She cut her eyes at me. "And you, I'll have to find a way to fix whatever it is you've done."

When he spoke, his words rattled the room. "Listen to me when I say this: what you want is not possible."

Tears welled in the corners of her eyes as she screamed, "No! You've ruined everything. You have no idea what you've done."

Annoyance flashed in Viktor's eyes. "Lady, I'm going to ask you once more to vacate my daughter and go home—"

She screamed again and charged him. "I'll kill you."

Lightning arced from his hand into her chest, sending her through the already weakened window. Shattering glass filled the room then there was a nasty crunch when she landed in the hallway. He stepped out the door to grab her, but she wiggled away. This time, when she looked at him, the arrogance was gone, replaced by fear.

She got to her feet and threw a bolt of yellow light at him and it pinned Viktor to the wall. Unable to move, the ice armor melted in an instant. His skin bubbled as he caught fire and let out a howl.

Justine grabbed one of the guns off Viktor's body armor now on the floor, lifted the weapon, and fired. Thunder cut through the silence as a massive black divot appeared in Heidr's forehead. Trails of black settled into the deep gashes across the side of her face, and her eye turned black. She slapped her hand over the wound, turned, and ran toward the wall at top speed. Amber light enveloped her, and she vanished.

The hologram faded and I stood there dumbfounded.

Viktor collapsed into his chair. "Spent the rest of the day in ICU before I was moved over to the rejuvenation chamber." He rubbed his hand over his face. "That's where I spent the following nine."

Damn, his daughter…Heidr, nearly murdered him.

This wasn't going the way I thought it would.

I gestured at Nora. "You're the spouse?"

Nora nodded. "Yes."

Justine gestured at the top of the desk and the picture she'd shown me in the elevator came up. "Nora's been tracking Kira ever since... Montreal was the first time we've spotted her since the day in the med bay."

"Could've used a bit of help out there."

Nora's gaze hit the floor.

Viktor's voice came out hard. "She wasn't particularly worried about you." He leaned forward to put his elbows on the desk. "Tell him what you told me."

Anger burned in her eyes. "I didn't want witnesses...my plan was to let her murder Amelia, you, and your friend. From there, I'd step in, bind her, and bring her in. That way we could contain the situation."

"Glad to know I'm expendable."

She glared at me. "Turns out, you're far more formidable than I anticipated."

Viktor slapped his hand against the desk. "Do you have any idea how lucky you are he didn't kill her?"

"How was I to know the stories about him were true?" She got to her feet and leaned over the desk to glower at him. "When this is over, I want her to have her life back." Gesturing at me, she said, "Can't do that with too many people wagging their tongues now can we?"

I closed my eyes and shook my head. "Lady, you don't have any idea who I am or what I'd say. If you'd given me the opportunity, there was a chance we could've captured her together. But you fucked that up." I locked my gaze onto Viktor's. "I get that she's your daughter, and I'll do everything in my power to help get her back." My heart suddenly felt heavy. "With that said, she's powerful and pulling punches will get everyone killed."

Sadness shone on his face. "I know. Not asking you to risk others' lives...it's enough you're willing to try to help considering how things have gone with you and the Archive."

I got to my feet. "About that…you should know that Amelia, Chala, Chione, and Lazarus have all been compromised."

Nora gave me a questioning look. "How so?"

Glancing over at her, I frowned. "They're connected to the Black Circle, Dvalinn, and a lich lord named Seth."

Viktor let out a groan as he placed his forehead against the desk. "Fuck. You sure about that last name?"

"Absolutely…any idea where to find the guy?"

"No." He looked up. "If it's the same man…and considering he's working with a bunch of necromancers and has a group called the Black Circle…I'm certain it is…you don't want to face off against him on your own."

I blinked. "Why's that?"

"A long time ago…before the pyramids were built…I came across him. He spoke of love, peace, and forgiveness. Yet he taught the opposite. It wasn't until about a decade later I discovered what he was really about…necromancy. At the time, he led a group called the Black Circle. I spent the next century burying them. Seth and I faced off in Egypt and things went south. I was severely injured, but he got the worst of it when his temple caved in on him." He shrugged. "Seriously thought he was dead. These last few years have cast doubt on that for me. Especially after you sent me a copy of those books you found in New Mexico."

Goddamn it.

"Looks like he's still breathing."

Nora glanced between us. "Am I done here?"

Disappointment worked its way across Viktor's face. "I guess… you're still going to do what you're going to do…so yeah, I'm done with you."

She whirled on me and shoved a finger into my chest. "If you hurt her—"

My armor snapped into place in an instant. Indigo flames engulfed us as a choir of demons screamed in the background. Chains of shadow and fire wrapped around her and we lifted off the ground. "Speak to me again in such a fashion and Viktor will be short a daughter-in- law. Endanger me or my people like that once more and I will end you." My voice softened. "I get that you want to save her...but don't do that at the expense of everyone else...that's a road you don't want to go down."

The flames dissipated and Nora's knees nearly gave out as I released her.

Her voice barely above a whisper, she asked, "What are you?"

I leaned in and whispered in her ear. "Death...if you cross me again."

She paled and, without saying a word, staggered out of the office.

Viktor arched an eyebrow. "Normally, I'm not a fan of people creating pocket realities in my office." He glanced over at the door and sighed. "But if you were able to talk some sense into her, it was worth the inconvenience."

"Sorry." I rolled my shoulders. "I couldn't let her continue down that path...trying to save a single life at the expense of everyone else's makes you an asshole."

That probably wasn't the smartest thing I could've said at this moment in time.

Viktor rounded the desk and leaned on it next to Justine. "That's never been my intention."

Justine visibly relaxed. "Oh, thank god. That didn't go nearly as badly as I expected."

A sad smile crossed his lips as he nudged her arm. "I love Kira, and I'd do almost anything for her. That being said, I didn't defeat Kvasir, the mad god, just to burn the world to ash for my daughter." His voice hardened. "Don't get me wrong...if someone harms her just because they can, they're going to answer for it. My goal is to bring her back here and introduce a sequence that will give her a fighting chance." He sniffed. "If that doesn't work...it's my understanding that it will kill her."

Horror shot through Justine's eyes. "You never told me that."

"It's not your burden to carry." He raised his gaze to me. "It's mine and mine alone."

Translation: Don't kill Kira…if she was going to die, it'd be at his hands.

"I understand."

He stepped forward and patted my shoulder. "Good man."

14

It was shortly after lunch when I finally made it upstairs to my office. My meeting with Viktor went—decently, I suppose. He hadn't rescinded his assistance, tried to kill me, or displayed any unhappiness with me at all. On the other hand, he made it crystal clear that we should do our best not to kill Kira but bring her in. That'd make things difficult but not impossible.

Alfred stepped out into the open. "Welcome back."

"Thanks."

He moved over to the silver sphere that'd been his home for…well, a long time. "You should be aware that your new network is under attack. I've been able to fend them off, but it's only a matter of time before someone infiltrates these primitive systems."

That didn't take long for them to come after the new servers. "Are the techs aware of the situation?"

"They are, and they've implemented several failsafes." His tone hardened. "They're implementing advanced techniques that shouldn't be available to them." He grimaced. "Off topic. Thing is, it's not the programming so much as the hardware."

I rubbed my forehead. "Sorry, you're going to have to explain, because I'm not exactly technically adept."

He chuckled. "Fair…here's the breakdown. The hardware currently available to you can only handle so much input without burning up or crashing due to an overload to the system. Eventually, the people attacking you will figure that out and if they can't compromise it, they'll crash it, leaving you and everyone else on your network crippled."

Oh, wonderful news. "My understanding is they're using the best tech available…hell, most of what they're using is decades ahead of what's on the market right now."

Alfred nodded. "That's true, but it's not enough to sustain the kind of attacks you're receiving."

"Not sure how to rectify that."

He stepped closer. "You said that you might have a line on the tech the other me kept hidden."

"Yeah, but…not sure I've got time to go rummaging around for it today."

He sighed. "Make the time soon."

I leaned back in my chair. "What's in there that we can use? I mean…if it's as advanced as you say it is, it wouldn't be compatible with what we have."

"Not sure that's true." He returned to his sphere to lean against it. "There's a chance I could patch the core into one of the terminals here." Thumbing back at the computer, he said, "From there, I could secure the system and maintain it while doing all the other stuff we discussed."

Kur wriggled inside my head. *"The added boost to our systems would make things easier and more streamlined."*

"You're suggesting that I go rummaging through Henri's pocket realities till I hit the right one?" I sighed. "Doesn't seem practical at the moment."

Excitement tinged his tone. "Not all of them…just the one he can't enter. If there was something in the others, he would've used it by now."

"Fine, I'll go talk with Henri." I pointed at the sphere. "Hop in, we're going for a ride."

Alfred hesitated. "Right now?"

"Yep." I got to my feet. "If I do find something, I might need help getting past any locked doors. Plus, I have no idea what it is I'm supposed to pull out."

His expression faltered as he put a leg inside. "Good point. Just tell me when I can come out."

"Absolutely."

Going down the stairs, I stopped on the second floor to talk to Alexander. "Hey, I'm headed to Henri's. Want to come?"

He shook his head. "If it's all the same to you, I'd like to catch up on some paperwork."

"Liar." I laughed. "You just don't want to port over."

A big smile crossed his lips. "Partly." He turned his screen to me. "But there's just a shit ton of stuff to get through due to all the missing vigiles. I'm not sure if they actually handled any of this or if they just buried it. Doesn't matter anymore since they're no longer with us."

While I wanted to ask what he was referring to specifically, I opted to wait. "True. Do the best you can and I'll be in touch."

A few seconds later, I strode through the gate at Henri's and stopped at the front door to press the button for the doorbell.

Gabriel opened the door. "Good to see you. Everything all right?"

Italian herbs, cooked meat, and sauce wafted past me, causing my stomach to growl.

"Fine and dandy." I glanced past him. "Is Henri home?"

He flicked a finger up as he stepped back to let me in. "Yeah, in his office."

"Thanks."

Stepping toward the kitchen, he paused. "Need anything from me?"

"Not right now." Patting my stomach, I said, "When I'm done upstairs though, I could use a bite to eat."

Gabriel snickered. "You can always eat these days."

It was true. While the ravenous hunger that'd driven me for the last several months was gone, my ability to put food away whenever it pleased me astounded everyone, including me.

"Beside the point."

He nodded. "Don't worry, I've made a special pan just for you."

"Thanks."

Gabriel waved and trotted off to the kitchen.

I made my way up the stairs to the office to find Henri reading through one of the books about the Black Circle from Atsidi.

Tapping on the doorframe, I said, "Looking for something in particular?"

"Not really." He closed the tome. "I was trying to find a connection between the Courts and the necromancers."

No one else had any luck so far, but Henri was the best at digging shit up.

"Find anything?"

He shook his head. "Nothing." Sighing, he gestured at the chair in front of his desk. "Anything I can help you with?"

I placed my hands on the back of the chair. "Actually, there is. You said that there was a section of Alfred's that wouldn't allow you entrance."

"I did." He furrowed his brow. "What about it?"

Standing up straight, I pointed at myself. "You invited me to give it a shot, remember?"

Henri slowly got to his feet. "You sure this is a good time to do that?" He shrugged. "With everything going on…maybe we should wait?"

"At this stage of the game, it might be a few centuries before things slow down again." I shook my head. "No, I think today…now is best."

Walking over to the bookshelf, Henri touched the spine of several books in a specific order. "Okay, let's give it a shot."

Huh? "Wait, I've been to your lab…nothing out of the ordinary in there."

He hesitated. "It's not in my laboratory…but it is connected to it."

"Why?"

His expression faltered. "Because, being directly connected to the house causes…issues."

Something about his tone said there was more to that story. "What sort of issues?"

Henri paled. "It violently reacts to everything in my home…and occasionally, me as well. To keep that to a minimum, I've parked it in its own reality so as not to set off a series of explosions that'd level the city."

Awesome...and my dumb ass was about to casually walk into it. Smart.

"Maybe I should rethink this a bit."

He blinked. "What...oh...the reason it has a violent reaction to me and my home is all the magic here...something about this space it doesn't like at all." Gesturing at me, he said, "That's a problem you don't possess. While you have power, you have no magic in your system, which is proven by your inability to access the gates."

Damn it. Okay, so he had a point. That didn't stop the sweat from trickling down my back. I mean...who wants to blow up an entire city?

Hanging my head, I closed my eyes. "You're guessing, aren't you?"

He let out a meh sound. "If it helps, it's an educated guess."

It didn't.

"Fine, let's do this."

Henri walked across the lab, pushed a bookcase out of the way, and chanted something in a language I'd never heard.

Kur whispered, *"Sorry, I really didn't expect anyone in this world to be speaking in Ekerilar, so I hadn't uploaded that to your cortex yet. And... fixed."*

"That's the weird future language, right?"

He slithered in my minds eye. *"It's a dialect that was commonly used before the fall...it's something Cain would be familiar with."*

I rubbed my forehead. "Great, something literally from another time."

"Yes." He paused. *"The big question is, how does Henri know it?"*

A brilliant light filled the room then a section of the wall vanished to reveal a limestone corridor leading off into the darkness.

Henri gestured me ahead. "This is as far as I go."

"Henri." I moved up to the opening. "What language was that and how do you know it?"

He shrugged. "Haven't a clue what it's called. As to how I learned it, that's easy. Alfred taught me." He gave me a dismissive wave. "Parts of Lilith's journal were written in it and without his help, I couldn't have built the safe haven for the vampires."

Made sense. "Speaking of that, how's the key coming?"

He frowned. "Slowly. It's a difficult thing to create but with luck, it'll be ready by the end of the week."

Damn. Was hoping to have it sooner. "Thanks. I appreciate it." Taking a deep breath, I let it out slowly. "What's at the other end of the corridor?"

He rolled his shoulders. "Wish I knew. I've only been able to take about four steps in there before getting tossed out on my ass."

"No incantations, special words, or any such shit for me to say before entering, is there?"

He patted me on the back. "If there were, I'd already been through."

Point taken. "All right, here goes nothing."

Steadying myself, I stepped inside the hollowed-out tunnel. The moment my foot hit the ground, power surged through my being and the opening closed. Shit. Nothing left to do but move forward. Two bends later, I came up to a charred metal wall.

Kur paused. *"That's Tyridium. Not sure how that's possible."*

"We're walking from one pocket dimension to another. We've met Cain and Viktor, who are literally from a dead timeline, and you're questioning how a little Tyridium can be a thing?" I huffed out a laugh. "Really?"

Kur harrumphed. *"Fine...I get it but...people are one thing. What lies before us is something else entirely."*

"How's that?"

His tone turned curious. *"It means there's a possibility that other such objects and not just living matter made it back through the QDM to exist here in this world."*

Hadn't thought about it in those terms. "Could be a serious game changer."

"Indeed."

Slowly, I reached out and placed my hand against the metal. Cold cut through me. A fear not my own danced through my mind. The universe tore itself apart around me. In my mind's eye, sirens blared, telling Alfred it was well past time to go. He ran through the door and up to the cockpit. Grabbing the controls, he accelerated quickly, passing through a set of closing bay doors. Outside, he struggled to maintain control of the ship as a swirling vortex of immense power buffeted his shields. Then everything cleared and he hovered in the emptiness of the abyss.

The memory faded.

A thin blue line appeared in the metal then the opening simply appeared.

I pulled the sphere out of my pocket. "Alfred."

He stuck his head out. "Yes…holy shit, is that my ship?"

"No clue." I glanced around for a place for him to stand. "Damn it. Okay look…we're not going to make this a habit, but if you want to get on my shoulder and guide me through this thing, that'd be great."

His voice dropped as he climbed into place. "We will never speak of this after today."

Even though some of the lights were on, no one was home. The Tyridium floor was painted with a non-slip matte gray substance. The walls were highly polished black with lights, screens, and other important features just below the clearcoat. Ozone and burnt plasma hung in the air. Scorch marks marred the hallway. Cracks ran through the walls. A few sections were missing entirely. I stopped at a set of access panels on the wall beside the doors leading into the cockpit.

Alfred jumped to his feet. "The network core is in there." He pointed to the lockers on the wall. "There's a case in there meant to be used to secure the core once it's out—"

"—You guys made a habit of pulling them?"

His expression soured. "Whenever possible, yes. Allowing the Loki to gain access to anything with current data was bad for the war."

Made sense.

"I see."

He shifted on my shoulder. "Inside, you should find a couple holo-balls, along with several small devices meant to breach data centers and retrieve the information held there."

Cocking my head to the side, I said, "What was that for?"

"What do you think?" When I didn't answer right away, he continued, "We used them to hack the enemy's network and retrieve anything useful inside."

No idea what we needed those for, but sure, why not. "Uh, yeah, okay."

Opening the locker, everything was just as he described. There were six holo-balls, which I only took one of. Then I pocketed a half dozen of the hacking devices. Last, but hardly least, I found an onyx Tyridium case about the size of my cell, pulled it out, and set it on the fold out table. Afterward, I opened the access hatch. Core was written in big red letters just above a marble shaped sphere that looked suspiciously like the one Alfred lived in.

"Did Janus stick you inside of a network core?"

He shook his head. "No…I mean it might've started out as one, but the thing I live in is fundamentally different as it houses me alone." Gesturing at the core in my hand, he beamed. "That transmits, moves, receives, and distributes data. While I can access that, I can't live in it. There's no room in there for anything else." He rolled his shoulders. "My hope is, I can connect my home to the core and it to your network. From there, it'll branch out to secure things in such a way to prevent anyone from accessing it without the proper credentials. Even then, it has an AI that'll add an extra layer of security."

I placed the core inside the case, causing it to light up blue as thousands of tiny circuits suddenly formed across its face. "What makes you think this isn't hackable?"

"It took the Loki a trillion plus years to finally gain access to the cores…and that was toward the end of the war." Sadness sounded in his voice. "As far as I know, no one on this backwater planet is anywhere close to that level of tech at the moment."

"Good point." After tucking the core into my back pocket, I grinned. "I've always wanted to see what the cockpit of a spaceship would look like."

Alfred blushed. "It's nothing special, I assure you."

"Maybe, if you've seen others, but I haven't."

I touched the pad to the door and a static charge hit me and knocked me to the ground. Power wrapped itself around me, hooked itself behind my sternum, yanked me up to my feet... then dissipated.

A tiny holo hovered above the core and a voice came out of the cabin speakers. "Please replace the core so it can be properly accessed."

Alfred shook his head. "Sorry, we need it to secure another network on a primitive world."

The voice sounded again. "Alfred, is that you? As in the Varangian Guard commander?"

"It is." He puffed out his chest. "Again though, I'm sorry to say we cannot comply."

It laughed. "Good god, glad to have you back...though you don't seem yourself." An iris opened above the door and a green light spread across the cabin to scan us. "Uh...you've been digitized...sort of. There are bits to your code I don't understand, but that's beside the point." An arrow appeared over the access panel. "Please replace the core. I'll be able to assist you from here far better than taking a small piece of my cortex out to play."

I cleared my throat. "Excuse me...how can you help? I'm not sure you realize this, but you're stuck inside a pocket reality in the middle of nowhere."

The voice turned pleasant. "Greetings, commander...what is your name and rank?"

"Huh?"

It repeated itself. "Name and rank so I can store your data."

Alfred nodded. "Do it or it'll never stop."

"Gavin Randall, vigil."

The light scanned me again. "Gavin Randall, vigil...unknown rank." Another scan. "Species, Stone Born, Reaper, and...godling." It paused. "That explains a lot."

Was this thing on crack?

"You're two out of three...the last bit is wrong."

Its tone turned serious. "Perhaps, but it's still accurate. Only godlings possess the genetic code that allows me to bond with you in the way that I have. If you'll replace the core, you'll have access to the ship, what's left of it, me…well a different version of me anyway."

"Hold on…what?"

It spoke again. "Alfred, in your digitized state, you'd be able to take over the functions here." A small opening appeared next to the core on the wall. "All you'd have to do is insert your sphere into the adjacent port."

I blinked. "Alfred?"

"I'm thinking." He shifted on my shoulder. "This is either going to go really wrong…or extremely well."

The voice came out of the speakers again. "You've decided to join me?"

He nodded. "I have."

The cabin dimmed. "You need to hurry."

I pulled the case out of my pocket, replaced the core, and the lights came back up. "Better?"

It spoke again. "Yes."

Alfred stepped inside the sphere. "If this goes wrong, I'm sorry."

"Me too."

As soon as he was fully inside, I pushed it into the second port.

The voice came over the speakers. "Initiating the Janus protocol."

Holy shit, Janus was here? How did he know which ship Alfred would take? Let alone that I'd find him before finding the ship? Everything surrounding Janus confused me.

I sat there in silence for several seconds as the lights flickered on and off. Eventually, they stopped, and a life-sized Alfred appeared before me.

He patted his chest and it made a sound. Holding out his hand, he smiled. "I'm Alfred, Commander of the Varangian Guard and survivor of the QDM. It's a pleasure to finally meet you properly."

Shrugging, I reached out and to my surprise grasped it. "Pleasure is all mine." I held his hand, twisting it from side to side. "How's this possible?"

Alfred waved his hand and the cabin doors opened to reveal the cockpit. "Take a seat, there's a lot to explain."

15

Back at home, I sat at my desk with a healthy portion of Gabriel's lasagna. My conversation with Alfred was educational to say the least. One of those enlightening moments was the revelation of the godling comment, which referred to the nanites in my blood provided by Kur. Turns out, not all nanites were created equal.

Through the nanites, the new version of Alfred could reach through the pocket reality that was now attached to my office. It'd pleased Henri to no end to be rid of it. In addition, he gave me access to Alfred's lab, since that was where the reading material was located. I hadn't bothered to poke around in there yet as the network took priority.

While we couldn't actually update the server hardware, we used the ship's core to turn the terminals into drones. They held zero information, yet they could access it through the proper protocols. Meaning they had to be approved by me, the UCD, and finally Alfred. Anyone doing sketchy shit would instantly be locked out of the system and the nearest vigil or centurion alerted.

My phone rang. Heather.

"Hello. Everything all right?"

Relief sounded in her voice. "Yes...it seems they're coming

around. Harold is up…weak but awake. Andrew's vitals are improving steadily. Thought you'd want to know so you could come over."

"On my way."

I ended the call as indigo flames wrapped around me. When they faded, I stood in Andrew's living room.

Heather shook her head as she lowered her phone. "Could've at least said bye."

"Nah." Walking over, I leaned in and kissed her on the cheek. "Hello is a lot more interesting."

Her cheeks darkened as she nudged me with her elbow. "Someone's in a good mood." Taking in a deep breath, she waved for me to follow. "That'll have to wait. Harold is watching over Andrew and I need to check on him."

"Lead the way."

Andrew's bedroom was directly off the living room. Even when I lived here, entering it never crossed my mind. A few steps, a creak of the door, and that was behind me. His room was larger than I thought, being a thirty by twenty thing. The king-sized bed sat against the far wall. Near the center was a sofa and two wing chairs. By the door were bookshelves filled from floor to ceiling.

Kimberly sat next to the bed checking his pulse. Harold sat in one of the wing chairs he'd turned to face the bed. I'd expected him to be weak or pale or something, but he looked the picture of health…if a little worried about his son.

He glanced back at me and walked over. "Hey, glad you're here. You okay?"

"I'm hardly the one to be worried about." I gestured at Andrew. "He going to be all right?"

A pained expression settled across his features. "Yes and no."

"Don't do that. Just tell me what's happening."

His shoulders slumped forward. "Fine…Andrew did a deep dive into the happenings over the last several decades…up to and including the ordeal with Lazarus outside our home." He turned to face his son. "I suspect part of what's going on right now is him working his way through the grief…possibly anger at losing his mother and brother."

Kimberly sidled up next to him. "How can you be sure?"

His gaze never faltered. "I can feel his emotions from here." He waved his hand to reveal a faint golden glow around Andrew that quickly faded from view. "I'm doing what I can to keep them from tearing the house apart."

She sighed. "What can we do to help?"

"Nothing." Tears formed in the corners of his eyes. "He's never been good at listening or taking it slow…now he knows things I wish he didn't." He glanced over at me. "Not because I'm ashamed." Turning his gaze back to Andrew, he said, "There are some things a parent shouldn't burden their children with."

We stood there in silence. Eventually, Kimberly returned to her seat with Heather in tow. I moved the other wing chair around and plopped into it.

Harold lowered his voice. "You know when he wakes up what he's going to want…don't you?"

My heart sank at the thought of what was coming…a trip home. I had questions for Isapo-Muxika as well. Hell, it'd crossed my mind to go speak to him on my own. That, however, wouldn't stop Andrew and Harold. At least this way, I'd be there to keep things moderately peaceful.

"I have a good guess."

He frowned. "Not that I think you will, but protecting Isapo-Muxika from me or your uncle is a bad idea."

"I want to hear what he has to say." I chewed back my anger at the man. "If he's working for the Black Circle, we'll know very quickly. At which point, he'll need to be dealt with… harshly." Shaking my head, I blew out a long breath. "Can't have people thinking family gets a pass."

His voice hardened. "There's another possibility."

True. Isapo-Muxika could be nothing more than a narrow-minded prick that hated me for the exact reason he said he did. "I'm aware."

His jaw went taught. "He's still responsible for Zach's death."

Inadvertently. Not that it made my father, his son, any less dead.

"Yeah...he is."

He clicked his nail against the arm. "Plan on doing anything about that?"

My feelings for my grandfather were muddled, to say the least.

"Me personally? No." I locked my gaze onto his. "However, I'm sure justice will be served."

If I tore into Isapo-Muxika, there was a good chance I wouldn't stop. He wasn't the only one who'd done their best to harm me. Other's took every opportunity to cause me pain. Hell, one of the new tribal elders stabbed me in my sleep. More than a few of them wanted me dead, and with my emotions this close to the surface...I couldn't be trusted.

Harold nodded. "I understand."

"I don't think you do."

Andrew groaned and sat up in bed. "But I do." He looked at his father and nodded. "It's safer for us all if we handle the situation."

Concern shone in Heather's eyes. "Handle what situation?"

I got to my feet. "We're going home to see my grandfather."

Kimberly grabbed Andrew's arm. "Are you sure that's a good idea? You've been out for a day."

"A shower and some good food will help me feel much better." He glanced over at us. "Thing is, we need to handle this situation before Isapo-Muxika finds out my father is alive." Patting her arm, he said, "Honestly, I don't know how this will turn out. There's a chance he'll live to see another day...but he's got a lot to answer for."

Kimberly nodded. "Fine." She turned to us. "Everyone needs to go...make yourself useful and pull leftovers out of the fridge." Turning to Heather, she said, "You should supervise."

What a polite way for her to tell us to get the fuck out.

"Yes, ma'am."

Harold took the time to get clean himself, leaving me and Heather to prep the food. Which was probably for the best.

In the kitchen, Heather pulled out a pan of lasagna. "You really think it's a good idea to visit your grandfather with the mood the three of you are in?"

"Not particularly." I sighed. "But, if he's involved with the Black Circle, we've got to know." Shrugging, I said, "If he's not and just a racist prick...that's entirely different. Fact is though, he's tried to murder me on several occasions throughout my childhood, and it cost my parents their lives. I won't touch him for that...I can't." I paused. "If I allow my rage to flow...there's a chance I wouldn't stop."

Heather turned and hugged me. "I get that...but do you really think those two will give him a fair chance?"

"Can't say, but one thing is certain, I wouldn't." I stepped over and turned on the oven before slipping the pan onto the rack. "Isapo-Muxika needs a reckoning either for working for the enemy or allowing so much harm to come to my family by being a racist."

She nodded. "Just...don't do anything rash, and try to keep them from making a decision they'll regret."

And there was the disconnect. Without witnessing my grandfather's actions or living through the consequences there of...there was no way she'd ever understand how despicable he was. The only people that'd miss his existence for a moment would be the other small-minded assholes he'd infected with his slanted view of the world. None of us would lose a second of sleep over his demise, let alone regret any part we played in his trek beyond the veil.

After we were properly fed, we said our goodbyes as indigo flames enveloped us. The moment they died away, we were standing just beyond the tree line on the reservation in Montana.

Across the grassy clearing sat a log cabin that served as my grandfather's office for the better part of a century. The only thing that'd changed in the last thirty years was the old dirt pathways were now covered in asphalt. A small breeze brought with it the scent of old earth, evergreens, and a sorrowful song sang by some bird out in the distance.

No reason to belabor the issue. I stepped out into the open and the other two quickly fell into step behind me. I reached out with the Grim to see that there was life inside. No need to kick in the door if there wasn't anyone home.

Turning the knob, I snapped the lock and pushed it open to find my grandfather sitting at his desk.

"What are—"

His words died in his throat as his gaze cut past me to find Andrew and Harold standing there.

"Kur, this would be a good time for you to tell me if Isapo-Muxika is compromised or not."

He swam to the forefront of my mind. *"Not in the way that he's been touched by blood magic or necromancy."*

"Thanks."

I plopped into the chair in front of his desk and shook my head. "Hello. Long time no see."

Harold folded his arms. "Not long enough."

Andrew remained mum.

Isapo-Muxika glared at the three of us then sneered at Harold. "Thought you were dead."

"You were meant to."

He stepped forward and I placed my hand on his arm. "Wait. I've got questions."

Isapo-Muxika gave me the finger. "I don't care." He pointed at the door. "All of you need to leave, now."

I pushed my will out to encompass the cabin. Indigo flames crawled across the floor, up the walls, and covered the ceiling.

My grandfather's eyes went wide. "Stop it."

"No, I don't think I will." Slowly, I got to my feet. "As I said, I've got questions."

Andrew glanced over at Harold, who shook his head.

Arrogance painted Isapo-Muxika's face. "This is some sort of trick of your uncle's." He gestured at me. "You don't have any powers of your own."

I appeared directly behind him, jerked him to his feet, and hovered a few feet off the floor. "Believe what you want. I'm not here to correct your misconceptions." Leaning forward, I whispered in his ear. "Tell me about Lazarus."

His body went rigid. "He's an asshole."

"True…but my gut tells me you two have spoken in the past."

He shook his head. "You're wrong."

I glanced over at Andrew and Harold, who'd taken a few steps back. "Is that true, Andrew?'

Isapo-Muxika gritted his teeth. "Stay out of my head, freak."

"It's not." He turned to Harold. "He's the one who sent Lazarus to our home when I was a child."

We lifted several feet into the air…a few more inches and we'd be in the flames. "Why did you contact Lazarus all those years ago." I dug my finger into the top of his shoulder. "Lying is no longer an option."

His body went slack. "Fine…we, the village elders, were given a vision." He glared at Harold. "If Harold, Andrew, and Zachary were allowed to live, it'd be the end of everything…the Archive included." His voice shook with anger. "Yet one more thing the English would murder. So, I reached out to Lazarus, told him what we'd seen. He confirmed it with a vision of his own. He said he'd tend to it. Years later, you wondered off. Then your son stole my daughter and gave birth to this abomination…a half breed." He twisted around to spit in my face. "That's when I took it upon myself to end you."

I wiped the saliva off and sat him on the floor. "You're an idiot."

"Fuck you."

Striding past the desk, I pulled back the flames, stopped, and turned to him. "Because of your need to kill me, you allowed someone to murder your daughter."

He blinked. "What?"

"In your repeated attempts to kill me, you took away the only person watching over my family. While he was preventing you from murdering me, Walter Percy took the opportunity to kill my parents…your daughter. Your hate of me and my existence actually murdered her."

Shaking his head, he glanced over at Andrew with fear in his eyes. "Is this true?"

His voice came out hard and flat. "It is."

"No…that's not possible." He turned to Harold. "It's a lie."

Harold stepped forward and stopped short. "You knew me for

decades prior…I don't lie." He pointed at me and Andrew. "They're both telling you the truth."

Isapo-Muxika fell to his knees as a part of his soul broke. "My Nadie, died because of me?"

My voice rolled across the cabin like a sledgehammer. "Yes." I placed one hand on Harold's shoulder and the other on Andrew's. "Leave him. He isn't worth our time."

Andrew didn't move. "He cost my brother his life."

"His interference cost me my parents' lives. Killing the man would simply alleviate his suffering." I glanced over at Isapo-Muxika and sighed. "Let him live with knowing what he's done." Shrugging, I said, "Besides, I've got enough blood on my hands without adding his."

Andrew hung his head and turned to follow me out the door with Harold taking up the rear. The door had just clicked shut when a gunshot cut through the silence. I didn't need to go back in to know that my grandfather was no longer amongst the living. Hell, I didn't need the coin that'd appeared in my pocket to tell me either. The moment he figured out what he'd done, he checked out.

This was just the final step.

16

August 21st

We'd spent most of yesterday afternoon dealing with Isapo-Muxika's funeral. His death had one of two effects on those that knew him best. One, they were angry and blamed me personally for him taking his own life. Or two, they were relieved. There were far more of the latter than I'd ever suspected. Shame they hadn't the courage to show themselves earlier; my childhood could've been very different.

Sitting up, I placed my feet on the floor and rubbed my face.

Heather's hand touched the small of my back. "You okay?"

"Actually, I am." I turned and patted her arm. "My grandfather finally gave me the gift of clarity, and for that I'm thankful."

She sat up. "How's that?"

"Simple." I got to my feet. "All of our troubles—with the weres, Black Circle, and especially the Gotteskinder—are caused by people who hate others due to them being different."

Cocking her head to the side, she pursed her lips. "I get the weres and Gotteskinder...how do you figure the Black Circle fits?"

"Easy. If you're not part of their little blood cult, you're the enemy."

She frowned. "Doubt it's that straightforward, but I see what you mean."

I thumbed over at the bath. "Got to clean up then delve into paperwork."

"What time are they supposed to get in touch?"

Damn, I'd hoped she forgot about my meeting with Andrew and Harold. "Mid-morning, I think."

She smiled. "Go clean up." Pointing at herself, she said, "I'll get a few more hours of sleep for the both of us."

"Gee thanks."

She shooed me out of the room.

A half hour later, I sat at my desk and waved my hand over the holo sphere Alfred helped me remove from the ship.

A life-sized Alfred appeared in the seat across from me and waved. "Hey there. Good to see you."

"How are things?"

He grimaced. "Bad news first or the good?"

I leaned forward and clasped my hand over my forehead. "Always start with the bad."

"Okay then." He sighed. "Where to start. Multiple terminals were attacked overnight. None of them got through the front door, but the voracity of which they came for us showed a level of technology that shouldn't exist in this world."

Holding up my hand, I frowned. "What's that supposed to mean?"

He shook his head. "It means we're fighting an enemy that's far more advanced than we'd anticipated." Giving me a dismissive wave, he said, "It's nothing we can't handle, but it is surprising. I get how Warden Global is ahead of the game, seeing how they have Prince Muninn running the place."

Huh? "Are you talking about Viktor Warden?"

Alfred paused. "That's the name he goes by, but where I'm from, he was simply known as Prince Muninn or the prince. Would you rather me use his current name?"

I rubbed my temples. "Yes, I would. I'm not from where you are and it's confusing."

"Very well...should I fill you in when there are such incongruities?"

I'd probably regret this. "Yes, but please lead with a name I know first."

He grinned. "I can do that."

Alfred proceeded to walk me through the way we were attacked and the how. Somewhere after the first three or four sentences, I blanked out due to the technobabble. The gist was this... whoever came for us did so through our old servers...multiple terminals, a few of which currently belonged to the dead, such as Amelia and Chione. Our biggest threats came directly out of Waterford Ireland, and Rome.

The latter I expected. My question was, who lived in the Emerald Isle that wanted a piece of us?

"You mentioned something about good news."

Chuckling, he said, "I did. All the data from the old servers has been cleaned, copied, and saved for later use. In addition, subroutines are sorting the information into useful bite-sized pieces. Anything useful should bubble to the surface in the near future." He got to his feet and stretched. "There's quite a bit to get through, and most of it is likely useless thanks to the numerous forms needed to run a bureaucracy."

Not sure how helpful that'd be, but okay. "Anything else?"

His good humor faded. "Yes, but it's neither good nor bad. Mostly, I need Kur's help."

Kur became attentive but remained quiet.

"With?"

"Well, it'll take some doing, but I can reconfigure the ships communications array to boost his signal...but he'd have to allow me access."

Kur wriggled. *"While I'd love to comply, we're short a few vigiles at the moment. Until all of the vacant positions are filled, what he's asking isn't possible."*

"Once that happens, you'll cooperate?"

Even though I couldn't see it, I felt him smile. *"Oh, yes...it'd make organizing and protecting those under our authority easier."*

I frowned. "That'll have to wait...we've got to fill the vacant positions before we can comply."

Nodding, he said, "Not a problem. Just say the word and we'll make it happen."

The door to the office pushed open. Heather stood there looking between me and Alfred.

Eventually, she stopped and stared at him. "Aren't you dead?"

He wobbled his hand back and forth. "Yes and no." Turning to me, he asked, "Want to tell her, or shall I?"

It took a few minutes to bring her up to speed that this Alfred was an AI construct and a hologram. While I didn't lie, there were several bits I chose to leave out, such as anything to do with the QDM, Janus, the escape pod, and everything related to Cain. She made the assumption that the holo-ball came from Warden Global and I didn't correct her.

It wasn't about trust. We had an arrangement to do our best to keep our work and personal life separate. That'd become harder and harder to do over the last few months, but we were still managing it. Then there was how crazy it sounded. I mean, a spaceship, an AI construct from the future, and Cain was a real person who'd been trapped in a hell version of Groundhog Day...I'd witnessed it all firsthand and still had difficulty believing it.

One day soon, I'd start walking her across that bridge, but for all our sakes, it couldn't happen before Cain and Jade revealed themselves.

She sat in the chair next to Alfred with her face in her hands. "My head hurts."

"Sorry."

Raising her gaze to mine, she took in a long breath. "There's more to this than you're saying, isn't there?"

"Yes."

She tapped her nail against the armrest. "Would you tell me if I asked you to?"

"I'd rather not." I shrugged. "Other people's lives are on the line... but if you really wanted to know...probably."

Heather slowly stood and shook her head. "No, I'm good. But one day soon, I might ask."

My heart sank. "I got a feeling we'll have that talk before you're ready. At this point, it's just a matter of time."

Her expression faltered. "Bucharest?"

"Yeah."

What she didn't realize was Bucharest was the final step in a series of events that'd started when I went to Brasilia back at the end of May. That'd been when I met Cain for the first time. From there, things continued to spiral out of control with one of the governors, Eduardo Hernandez, getting himself killed.

By all accounts, he'd been mixed up with the Black Circle for years and brought a couple of necromancers to Gabriella Medina's apartment to reinstate her as a prefect. One thing led to another and we had to cover up the death of three people to hide the fact that Gabriella was now a vampire. She didn't show the typical outward signs...her eyes were brown and she could still use her powers as a sorcerer.

Then last month, Cain went to Romania and killed his half-sister Namisia. Her death heralded the end of the strigoi as a whole. It took a hell of a lot of work, but we arranged it so Cain, Gabriella, and Mitchel were kept out of the limelight. Instead, we focused all the attention on a man named Marius, who assumed control of Strig Enterprises' holdings on paper. Not sure how they managed it, but the digital footprint made it look like Naadir, Namisia's second, was stealing from the company to transfer everything over to a human, Marius. From there, everyone just assumed that Naadir murdered his mother and in doing so, inadvertently killed himself along with every other strig on the planet.

To help sell those events as billed, I stuck to the script. Heather and the others knew there was more to it because I'd told them so, but that was as far as it went. When the events of Bucharest reveal themselves, everything else would as well.

She nodded. "In that case, I'll leave you two in peace."

Alfred smiled. "It was a pleasure to meet you."

"And you." She grinned as she turned to me. "I've got a feeling whatever comes next is going to be very interesting."

"You aren't wrong."

Waving, she closed the door as she stepped out.

Alfred turned to me. "I'm guessing the official report on Bucharest isn't entirely factual."

I shook my head. "No, it's not."

Ten minutes later, he sat there perplexed. "So, Cain is in Romania."

"Yep."

His form pixelated for a second before returning to normal. "That'd likely explain a few things."

Oh, shit. "Care to share? I'm not great at guessing."

With a wave of his hand, a globe appeared in midair. He walked over and touched the Carpathian Mountains and it zoomed into view. "There's a rogue signal emanating from this area. I can't be more specific at the moment because I simply don't know more. What I can tell you is that there's an AI with similar programming as mine and it's not the only one." Placing his hand on the sphere, he turned it and touched New Orleans. "There's another one here in town as well."

I blinked. "How can you be sure?"

"Well for starters, sensors. Secondly, we're all related…not by genetics but by programming."

Kur swam to the forefront of my mind. *"Ask him if his kind have a name."*

"And what are you called?"

His tone hardened. "We are the Húsvættir. To my knowledge, only one was built from the ground up. His name was Tomte. The other was a partial program called Mimir. There were others such as the blank I bonded with, but I've no idea if they're still around."

"Hold on, I met a talking cat called Tomte." A pain shot through my skull at the magnitude of the revelation. "Could something like you bond with a cat somehow?"

Alfred shook his head. "No, only the central core of the Ark Ship, Skíðblaðnir, could handle the complexities of such an entity." Shock registered on his face as he paused. "But...if he was using a companion skin, that'd work."

"Stop...what's a companion skin?"

He shifted in his seat. "They're highly complex biomechanical machines that are meant to serve the commander of Skíðblaðnir and act as a second in command. Thing is, if there's a companion skin walking around Romania, the Ark Ship isn't far off."

"Great...that's just wonderful."

Ignoring me, he continued. "That'd explain the readings of another AI and why it's so strong." He grimaced. "It doesn't tell me why there's another one in town and why it's so much harder to detect."

I think he was missing the obvious. "Maybe it's coming from Viktor's place."

His eyes glowed slightly. "No...it's mobile...but if anyone would have a clue about it the Prince...sorry, Viktor...would."

"I'll add that to my list of things to talk to him about."

That snapped him out of his thoughts. "You have something else? Equally as important?"

"Hazard to guess...more so."

Alfred shook his head. "Not possible."

"I bet everyone involved would disagree." Grimacing, I leaned back in my chair. "It's not every day I get yoked with the responsibility of having to tell someone that they have a son."

His form winked out of sight to reappear next to me. "You're telling me that the prince has a child he doesn't know about?"

I pulled air in through my teeth. "Pretty sure, yes."

He vanished to reappear in his chair. "Okay, yeah, that's huge. Especially after what I've found out about his daughter, Kira."

Exactly. How did one approach a grieving father and tell them such a thing? On top of that, I was betting neither of us needed or wanted an audience for that conversation.

"Hoping to see him alone in a few days so we can discuss it properly."

His entire body slumped slightly in the chair. "Who is it?"

"Vasile Ciocan...one of the vigils." I took in a deep breath. "He's a vampire with golden eyes." Sighing, I said, "Before you ask, his mother is Lilith…which makes Vasile Cain's half-brother as well."

Jumping to his feet, he stood there silent for several seconds. "You're shitting me, right?"

Yeah, that about summed up my feelings on the subject as well.

"Afraid not."

"Oh, God…that discussion has the potential of going rather poorly." He glanced over at me. "Have you thought about what you're going to say?"

Laughing, I said, "No…I've been a bit busy with the whole not getting dead thing." I gestured at him. "Creating a new AI, speaking with Janus—who scares the absolute shit out of me—and dealing with my own family issues."

Alfred sighed. "I can see how that'd keep you occupied, but do everyone a favor and try to be diplomatic about things." He shivered. "The pri—Viktor is powerful. Maybe more so than his adoptive father, which means if he got too upset, he might unmake the world as we know it."

"Awesome, one more thing to worry about." I closed my eyes and took a deep breath. "You should work on your pep talks."

Regaining his composure, he said, "I'll try…in the meantime, maybe start working out how you're going to break the news to the man. Otherwise, all of this planning will go straight to hell."

"You realize continuing to emphasize how careful I should be isn't helping, right?" Leaning my head back, I closed my eyes and sighed. "What exactly did you mean by unmake this world?"

Alfred cleared his throat. "The—Viktor is…was powerful. When he and his brother were little more than toddlers, they had an altercation that brought down a building and killed a bunch of our people." He winced. "It was an accident but the Mad God's—their adoptive father—response was brutal. He strode through the wreckage, pulled them out, and transported them to his command vessel where I was stationed at the time. He set a course deep into enemy territory then teleported them planet side with the instructions to finish their fight." Trembling, his voice shook. "What happened next is hard to explain.

They fought…the enemy found them and the brothers proceeded to kill them by the score. At some point, they returned to their spat, tearing the world apart." He swallowed hard. "We had to pull the ship back as they destroyed the rest of the system, wiped out the star, and tore a hole in the fabric of the universe. Only then did the Mad God tell them to stop."

Every muscle in my body tensed and my bones began to ache. Focusing, I did my best to relax. "Toddlers?"

Alfred slowly nodded. "Yes."

Goddamn it.

"All right, good to know."

It really wasn't.

He took a deep breath. "I'll work on the array so when you're ready it will be too."

"Sounds good."

With a wave, he winked out of existence and the holo-ball stopped glowing. That left me on my own to find a way to kill a few hours till Andrew or Harold called. Opening the drawer, I pulled out the three Denarius coins from Amelia, Carlos, and Chala to pocket them. On my feet, I walked downstairs to Heather's office.

"Hey there…wanted to let you know that Alexander and I are going out for a bit."

She gave me a concerned look. "You don't seem happy. Everything all right?"

With what I was about to do, I wasn't. "It'll work out…I think." I raised my hand to stop her. "Nothing dangerous on my part, just need to visit Cole and Vasile. I should be back by nine or ten at the latest."

She nodded. "See you shortly."

After hammering out a text to Alexander, Cole, Dean, Gabriel, Sam, and Vasile that I was coming, indigo flames wrapped themselves around me.

17

In Montana, the four of us appeared in the same spot I'd arrived the last time we'd come to find Vasile. Meaning we had a fifteen-minute walk in front of us to get to his home. Neither Kur nor I could reason out why we simply didn't appear on his doorstep now that we knew where he lived. There was that weird little push in the pit of my stomach as we came in, but I couldn't tell you what it meant.

Vasile stepped out and arched an eyebrow. "Walking?"

"Apparently." I shrugged. "Mind if we do this inside?"

He gestured at the door. "Come on in."

We moved into the center of the house and everyone sat around the table with Vasile at the head.

Alexander leaned back in his chair. "You finally going to tell us what this is about?"

Sam nodded. "Yeah, I have to say, I'm more than a little curious."

Time to see how this worked out.

I locked my gaze onto Vasile's. "Before we get truly started, how difficult would it be for you to move?" Gesturing around at the place, I frowned. "You've put a lot of effort into this place, but it'd be immensely helpful if you were open to such a thing."

His expression turned blank. "When I arrived in this land it was to hide." He shrugged. "Thanks to the passage of time, that's no longer possible." Blowing out a long breath, he said, "Moving wouldn't be difficult. Why do you ask?"

"Well, it's like this." I placed the three coins on the table. "There have been some job openings come up recently, and they need filling."

Everyone at the table stopped moving.

Vasile glanced at the coins then me. "Why do I get first pick?" He thumbed over at Cole. "He's got a wife, a business…and a lot more reason to stay here than I do."

"True." I grimaced. "But I'm still giving you first choice…think of it as a way of me apologizing in advance for a conversation we'll have in the near future."

He frowned. "Is it really that bad?"

Unable to stop myself, my gaze landed on the painting of Lilith and my voice dropped to a near whisper. "Depends on how you want to look at it."

Drumming his fingers against the table, he said, "With the gates, a move wouldn't be mandatory."

I shook my head. "It wouldn't. Then again, after our talk you may want to either stay put and celebrate or vanish again." Pausing, I said, "The choice is yours."

His fingers came to an abrupt halt. "If the coin will have me, Southern Africa wouldn't be a bad change of scenery for me."

I placed my middle finger atop it and slid it toward him. "Let's find out."

Everyone sat there waiting for him to pick it up. Then he did. It melted into his skin and a smaller version of the coin reappeared in front of me as a jolt of power rocked me back in my seat.

"Excellent." Turning to Cole, I said, "North or South America?"

The skin under his eye twitched. "Danielle would murder me if I didn't take North America and I had the chance to."

Nodding, I slid him his coin. The scene from earlier repeated itself, but this time I was prepared for the incoming wave and held fast.

I took a deep breath. "All that's left is South America." My gaze tracked around the table. "Who's interested."

Silence reigned.

Eventually, Gabriel spoke up. "You realize that everyone else is either a were or a nephilim, right?"

"I do." I placed my index finger over the coin and flicked it toward him. "Thanks for volunteering."

His chair skidded against the hardwood as he pushed back. "Hold up." He pointed at Alexander. "How about you pick it up?"

Alexander shook his head. "No, I've got plenty on my plate with my clan and dealing with the centurions."

Sam and Dean both shook their heads.

I tapped my fingers against the table. "I need someone trustworthy in the position."

"What if it doesn't accept me?"

Grinning, I said, "Then no harm done."

His hand shook as he reached out and slowly picked it up. It sat there for a moment then he winced as the Aquila vanished from his wrist, at which point the coin melted into his hand to disappear beneath his skin. A second later, a flash of golden light pulsed through the room and pushed all of us back slightly.

I pulled my seat back up to the table and smiled. "Welcome aboard." Turning to Sam and Dean, I placed my index and middle finger over the last two coins. "Since Alexander has made it clear he isn't interested in the job, looks like you guys have volunteered by default."

Dean placed his forearms on the table. "We're weres…we can't be vigils."

I flicked a coin at him. "Who says?"

Sam frowned. "Everyone."

"No, they were repeating racist bullshit." I scooted a coin over in front of her. "I for one would like to know if they're wrong." Pointing at either coin, I said, "One of you would take Vasile's position and the other would take Cole's." I gestured at Vasile. "As he said, with the gates, technically it doesn't matter where you live."

Dean glanced over at her then held her hand with one of his own while they both reached out for coins in unison. The coins instantly liquified and vanished beneath their flesh. A flash of dark snapped across the room, knocking us all to the floor.

Alexander, Dean, and Sam vacillated between their human form and the beginning stages of their transformation into werebears. Swirling shadows and multicolored lights encircled us, spinning faster and faster until it slammed into my chest, hammering me into the wall and knocking me unconscious.

Opening my eyes, I found myself lying atop a comfy bed and voices could be heard in the next room. A few seconds later, Vasile strolled in looking a bit concerned. "You okay?"

I sat up and nodded. "How'd you know I was awake?"

"You forget, I'm a vampire?" He touched his ear. "I could hear you."

"How the hell do you hear someone wake up?"

Grinning, he said, "With most people it's simply a change of heartrate and their breathing." He pointed at me. "You had those plus a few additions, such as a few tiny groans that I doubt you even know you make."

Okay, that was new. "Sure, uh...fine...everyone else all right?"

He nodded. "Fine...but now that I've got my coin...did you want to tell me what our future unpleasant conversation is about?"

"Close the door." I sighed. "Neither of us want anyone to overhear this."

He did as I asked. "Okay."

I got to my feet. "There's a chance I know who your father is." Holding up a finger to stop his questions, I said, "No, I'm not telling you who he may be until I know more. Also, I won't be telling him about you either. I simply need to talk to him then you, and if it works out, set up a meeting. Sound fair?"

I expected to see anger or resentment in his eyes but there wasn't...only curiosity reigned.

"You really think so?" He stammered. "Th...the Star Born is a real person?"

"They are...but there's no guarantee that Adam told you the truth. That's the bit I want to find out."

He cocked his head to the side. "You're familiar with Adam?"

My head suddenly started to hurt. "Not personally, but…Christ…okay…here's the thing, you've got a brother as well."

He shook his head. "I did…I mean…technically, I had two half-brothers, but they're long since dead."

"Not exactly." I sighed. "I really didn't mean to have this conversation today but here goes." Sitting on the edge of the bed, I said, "You're speaking of Cain and Abel, right?"

He nodded. "Yeah."

"Hate to break it to you like this, but only one of them is dead…just not really…and the other one just woke up from an extended nap."

Vasile didn't speak for several seconds. "Gabriella…"

Wait, how'd he get there? "I'm sorry?"

He narrowed his eyes. "She's a vampire…and you knew."

"Yes and yes." No point in lying.

He plopped into a chair next to the door. "She's a vampire with power and her eyes are normal…shouldn't be possible. There isn't a strain of vampirism that allows for that."

I gestured at him. "You have golden eyes."

"That's my point." He grimaced. "Even my eyes have a change to them…not that I know why they're gold and not silver."

Kur whispered, *"He has a high concentration of inactive Idunn in his system, which more or less confirms he's Viktor's son."*

"It's because you have a high concentration of a nanite called Idunn in your system. Likely due to your father."

Vasile chewed on his cheek. "And you know this how?"

I tapped my temple. "The nanites in my head belong to a dragon lord named Kur and that's his summation."

He looked at his hands. "So, I've got different types of nanites in my system…this Kur and the Idunn?"

Kur swam to the forefront of my mind. *"He does…I'm not sure what'll happen when the others kick in, but there's a small chance he'll lose his coin."*

It was weird having to relay messages like this. "Yes, but the Idunn are inactive. If they were to turn on, there's a chance you'll lose your coin as the systems may not be compatible."

"Okay, I think that's enough for the day." Breathing out, he said, "Come, we should join the others."

He didn't look well at all, but I followed him into the next room to find Gabriel, Dean, and Sam comparing wrists. Gone were the centurion marks. Instead, their hands were marked with a single sword on the back then in their palms, PAX was spelled out.

On a hunch, I checked mine to see the laurel leaves and double swords were gone, replaced by the single blade. As if to answer my unasked question, Cole and Vasile showed me their hands. Theirs had changed as well.

I blinked. "What the hell?"

Cole shook his head. "No idea."

Kur pushed forward. *"The coins were formed to fit with the culture of the day. I think we can both agree that's changed. You'll notice that the new coins will look different as well. The Archive is in its final moments. What comes next is up to you and those you choose to build the future with."*

"Just like that?" I sighed. *"We and the Archive are instantly changed?"*

He hesitated. *"We both know the Archive is dead. All this does is finalize it. You've already settled on the new name, Witenagemot. Now, all that's left is to let the world know. Perhaps start with your core here and let it spread organically from there. This is your chance to help those around you move forward in a way that wasn't possible sixteen months ago."*

I looked up to find the others looking at me. "What?"

Vasile shook his head. "Was someone talking to you?"

"Uh, yeah." I didn't know where this was going. "Why do you ask?"

Cole frowned. "We could hear something, but I don't think any of us could make out the words."

Alexander grinned. "Glad I'm not involved in this shit."

Sam frowned. "In this case, you're lucky, because that was strange and more than a little uncomfortable."

"Sorry, that's Kur...the nanites that are in your system belong to him."

Dean nodded as he raised his hand to inspect it. "So, we're really vigils?"

"Yeah, you are." While I wanted to delve into the rebirth of the

Archive, something else was on my mind. "What happened earlier?" Gesturing at Alexander, I said, "As you've pointed out, you're not a vigil, yet you were still having more than a few issues."

Everyone froze.

Alexander's gaze hit the floor. "We're not entirely sure." He tapped Dean on the shoulder. "Show him."

Dean's nails elongated and electricity danced between them. "It's not much more than a light show at the moment…it appears we have magic."

"How's that possible?"

He shook his head. "It shouldn't be."

Kur harrumphed. *"Perhaps, by giving them a coin, it's somehow activated their base genetic code. I mean, we both know the original weres were people of power."*

"And you think that's all it took?"

He writhed on the spot. *"Possibly…it's doubtful they'll be sorcerers, but it's possible they might have a fraction of power that'd help give us the edge in the upcoming war."*

The muscles in my jaw tightened. "We'll do some tests when we get back home. For now, I think we've accomplished everything I set out to do this morning." I checked my watch. "Need to get back to the house to talk with Harold to find out how to give the Black Circle a bloody nose."

Vasile nodded. "Let me know when that happens." He suddenly went still. "Hey, I just realized I don't have a governor to report to… and there's no way Lazarus is going to appoint anyone I like."

I flinched. "About that…I've got those coins at home. Don't ask, you don't want to know right now." Shaking my head, I said, "I've got some ideas about the new governor situation, but it'll have to wait till we're a bit further down the road. At the moment, I don't think Lazarus realizes he doesn't have the coins. The moment he finds out I do though, things are going to get shittier than they already are."

Everyone stood there stunned into silence save for Vasile, who started laughing. Slowly, the others turned their gazes to him as he continued hooting. The longer it went, the more out of breath he became. His face reddened and he fell into a nearby chair, doing his best not to pass out.

Eventually, he stopped. "Sorry." He chuckled. "At the moment, I want nothing more than to see his face when he realizes he's lost control of the Archive...and to you, no less. Oh, God...that'll be priceless." Snickering, he said, "Of course, that's when he'll try to kill you... you know that right?"

"I'm thrilled you find my possible demise so amusing."

He shook his head. "No, that part concerns me. The rest though...god that's awesome. To see the end of people like Chione, Amelia, and Chala being given positions they didn't deserve is something I thought would never happen."

Alexander frowned. "What are you going to do about Lazarus?"

"What is there to do?" I shrugged. "He won't leave me any options. When he shows up— and he will—he'll need to go away."

Vasile's expression turned grim. "About that, he's stupid powerful." His voice dropped to a near whisper. "He's versed in necromancy."

"I know...it's the reason why he's got to go and why I have the coins." Leaning against the wall, I took in a deep breath. "It's also why I want to wait until I have a plan to hand out the coins to the governor's office."

Dean nodded. "Good point."

Sam extended her nails and flames wrapped around them. "Oh, please let me be there when he shows up."

I blinked. "Wait...you've got fire and Dean's got electricity...what do you have, Alexander?"

He shrugged. "No idea, haven't bothered to check."

"Would you?"

"Do I have to?" He frowned. "I mean...okay...yeah, I'll check."

His nails were metallic in nature. A faint green glow emanated from them, and power radiated from him, causing us all to take a step back.

I held out my hand. "Okay, we're good and sorry I asked."

Alexander's cheeks turned crimson. "Sorry…didn't know what to expect."

Obviously, neither did the rest of us.

"It's fine…really."

That was only partially true. The reality was, whatever change was happening to him scared the shit out of me, and if the others faces were any indication…them too.

Vasile gestured at the door. "Are you leaving from here or out there?"

I glanced around. "Here, I guess. Need to drop Cole off at home—"

Cole cut in. "Hey, I just realized…do we get a pay raise with the new position?"

Laughing, I said, "Almost certain…have to figure out the finances, but we should be able to manage something."

He high-fived Vasile. "Awesome, new tax bracket."

Vasile looked a little uncomfortable. "Doubt that…I live in the woods and—" He paused. "Fuck it…I'm close to fifteen thousand years old…money hasn't been an issue for me since its inception."

Guess that settled it. He was a lot older than the pyramids.

Alexander's gaze hit the floor. "Mind if I ask a personal question?"

Vasile shrugged. "Not at all."

"Were you the one who stopped the war between the weres and the vampires?"

Suddenly, Vasile looked a little uncomfortable. "Yes. How do you know about that?"

"He's the secret keeper for his clan." I gestured at Alexander. "He told me the story about the necromancers involving themselves and a golden eyed vampire intervening…eventually stopping the war."

Vasile's shoulders slumped. "It might've been better to let them fight it out considering the repercussions."

A grim look crossed Sam's face. "What's that mean?"

Deflated, he sighed. "While open warfare was no longer an option, whispers crept through the land. At first, it wasn't anything big… derogatory remarks about weres. Then came the shunning and outright hostility. Eventually, full segregation. At some point, it became law, turning an entire species into slaves." Tears formed in the corners of his eyes. "I did what I could to stop it…it's why I became a vigil. But until Gavin officially changed the laws, there wasn't a lot I could do."

Anger welled up inside me. "People are assholes."

"No disagreement here." He wiped away the wetness. "Most of what came about was due to one man."

Curious, I asked, "Really? Who?"

Disgust washed over Vasile's face. "Never had the pleasure of meeting the asshole personally, but he was a Stone Born named Eleazar. He traveled with a bunch of other people of power, spreading the seeds of hate as they went. As the story goes, he fell ill, suffered, and eventually died. I'm just sorry it didn't happen sooner."

"What about his companions?"

He shrugged. "No idea. Never heard any names attached to the others. All I know is they were a mixed group…vampire, necromancer, sorcerer, etcetera."

"Probably best they were forgotten to the annals of history." I glanced at my watch. "Fuck, I'm going to be late if we don't hurry."

Sam hugged Vasile. "You're a good man and we're grateful for what you've done." She turned to Dean. "Come on, we've got work to do."

The rest of us linked arms as indigo flames enveloped us.

18

Alexander and I appeared in my office as my phone rang.

Hurrying, I answered it. "Hello."

Andrew's voice came across the line. "Hey, we're ready…I think." He sighed. "Your grandfather keeps adding to the plan."

That probably wasn't as helpful as he thought it'd be. Then again, maybe it was. I hadn't seen it yet. "Okay, I'll need to gather Heather and we'll be right over."

"Sounds good. See you shortly."

The line went dead.

Seems the universe was with me. I'd added to the vigils' ranks and got back in time for my meeting to give the Black Circle a kick in the balls. Yay, me.

I tapped Alexander on the shoulder. "Hey, I've got to get Heather then we can go to Andrew's."

He didn't look well. "Take your time. I'm in no rush to get back inside that damn thing."

I shook my head as Heather walked into the room.

"Good, you're back." She held up her phone. "Mom says they're ready for us."

"So I've heard." Waving her over, I said, "Let's go."

She hesitated. "Uh...mind if we drive?"

Alexander straightened up. "That's not wise given our current situation."

I grinned. "We can take the Tucker 48. It's just as safe as the other form only slower."

"Not exactly, you have to walk to and from it." He argued. "That gives people a chance to do really bad shit."

"I hear you, but—"

Heather cut in. "The trip home nearly killed me the other night."

It hadn't...not really, anyway. She'd gotten sick and it hurt like hell, but she was fine within an hour.

I gestured for them to sit. "You two relax and I'll go move everything to the trunk so there's room for you two."

Over the last year, I'd accidently turned my car into a rolling office in order to skip going to Elmwood, as it was always crowded now. Centurions coming and going for training, inductions...hell, there were even people living there while they were in town. In short, it was too crowded for my tastes.

As to my vehicle, it'd been a slow thing. One night, I was working my way through a bunch of files and the trainees were being rowdy. I packed up and brought the box home with me, except it never made it inside. Over the next few months, I needed my official seal, personal forms, etcetera...and the backseat filled up. Then I started on the passenger side of the front.

It'd turned into a bit of a problem, to be honest.

Grabbing a box, I walked around back, opened the trunk, and tossed it in. Standing upright again, I suddenly had the urge to vomit. Sweat beaded along my hairline, weakness set in, and I felt genuinely unwell from head to toe.

I checked myself for wounds but found none.

Glancing around, I did my best to find the source of the weird pulsating energy that continued to grow in strength. Then about a dozen yards away atop a swath of grass, a circular patch of air turned to liquid gold. It extended out into two forms, one distinctly female and the other a slightly shorter male.

With the liquid stretched to its limits, it began to snap and fall to the ground behind them, each drop turning the grass a brighter shade of green and causing it to grow several inches. The fluid continued to fall away to finally reveal Heidr and Ethan. Flowers bloomed at their feet and the grass shot up to midcalf level then the hole in reality faded, and I felt righted once more.

Heidr smiled. "Glad to see you." She pointed toward the front. "I was about to knock, but this is much more efficient." Pausing, her gaze tracked across my home. "How very interesting." She tapped her finger against her lips. "Looks as if it's of Domovoi construction but seeing how they don't leave the motherland…that's unlikely." Her tone turned curious. "Who in this nasty little city does such wonderful work?"

Even with that dig, this was way too polite for my liking. "Independent contractor." I clucked my tongue. "Doubt they'd work with you though, due to you being out of your mind. Technically, out of your body as well."

Ethan stepped forward. "It'd be in your best interest to watch your tone, son."

"First off, fuck you." I held up a finger. "Second, when I want to hear you speak, I'll let you know."

He lunged forward but Heidr caught him by the shoulder. "Calm, Ethan. We're here to talk, remember?"

Seething, he glared at me but stepped back.

Someone had a change of heart. "Have to ask, what happened to me being worthless?"

As she shrugged a faint smile crossed her lips. "Made a rash judgement." She stopped and a soft golden glow emanated from the bushes, grass, trees…essentially, everything but me. "You have to understand, this is how I see the world." Turning her hand, Ethan was suddenly encased in the yellow light. "Do you see the difference between him and you?"

"Yes."

Heidr frowned. "Technically speaking, you shouldn't exist." She clenched her hand and the spectrum of the light changed to gray around Ethan's hand. When she turned it toward me, black shadows crawled across the pavement and sidewalk. Again, it didn't touch me. She pointed at a glob of darkness in the pavement. "That was once a squirrel...seems someone paved over it."

Arching an eyebrow, I said, "Not sure I get it."

Ethan huffed out a derisive snort. "God, you're stupid." He sighed then said, "The gilded light showed the energetic signature of anything with life. The other is the absence of it."

She considered Ethan's words for several seconds. "Elementary, but mostly accurate." Turning her gaze to me, she said, "Thus making you an anomaly." Her eyes slightly unfocused as she lost herself to a thought. "I didn't bother to check as deeply as this the other day...you didn't seem to have power, yet you do." She cocked her head to the side. "How is that?"

"No idea."

Heidr's dark eye sparkled in the sunlight. "I've come to amend my offer."

This was going to be good. "Doubt that'll change my answer."

"It should." She stepped forward. "Help me win the war against Dvalinn and I'll reward you with a place at my right hand." Excitement tinged her voice. "With you at my side, we could crush our enemies to rule over the nine realms."

Yeah, she was out of her damned mind. "When you say we, you mean you."

She shrugged. "As I said earlier, it's better than the alternative."

"See that's the thing...what happens to me after Dvalinn is no longer an issue?"

Her expression became blank. "What do you mean?"

I pointed at myself. "At the moment you're ready to make a bargain with me." Smiling, I shook my head. "But you don't seem like a woman who'd want to share her power...making me a potential threat you'd need to handle."

She placed her hand over her heart. "That wouldn't happen... you're not a threat to me." Her aura flared gold with red blotches inside. "I'm the very essence of life itself and cannot die or be harmed in any meaningful way."

I tapped my forehead. "Really? Then what's that shit across your face and eye?"

Her haughtiness faltered. "This body is not who I am…it's a vessel for my essence. While it may have its flaws, I assure you, I do not."

"But you do." I gestured at myself. "You thought I was human, or at the very least, someone without power…that isn't the case."

Ethan's voice came out hard and cold. "I'm telling you to mind your manners."

Ignoring him, I kept my gaze locked on Heidr. "While I appreciate the offer, I think I'm going to have to pass for multiple reasons." I flicked up a finger. "First of all, you're riding around in my friend's daughter. Which is all sorts of fucked up." Another popped up. "Two, I don't work for those who'd associate with people like Ethan." A third. "Then there's the whole god complex—"

Heidr cut in. "I assure you, it is not a complex…I. Am. A. God."

"But are you really?" I did my best not to laugh in her face. "Personally, I just believe you to be deluded, so I'll make a counteroffer. Get out of Kira and return to whatever realm you came from to wait your turn, or I'll be forced to deal with you now."

"You've chosen death." Rage burned in her eyes. "Unwise."

My scythe formed in my hand. A chorus of demons sang in the distance as my armor snapped around me and I stepped forward. Golden armor encased Heidr as a massive, matching sword formed in her hand. Her visor sported the same flaw as her face and instinctually, I knew a hit there would end her.

She stepped to one side as Ethan moved to the other. In a flash of fur, green, and pulsating power, Alexander suddenly sprinted into view to take Ethan off his feet. Alexander flexed his legs and they became airborne for a second then landed heavily in the grass across the street. Bringing up his clawed hand, he swiped it against Ethan's mechanical arm.

While I'd love to watch him get his ass kicked, I had my own problems in the form of a wannabe deity trying to murder me.

She sprinted the distance between us. The moment she was in range, she lunched forward, doing her best to skewer me. I sidestepped the attack, knocking the blade clear with the snath of the scythe. Heidr kicked me in the shin then backhanded me across the face, knocking me slightly off balance. She came in again to launch a flurry of attacks, her blade repeatedly ringing off the handle of my weapon.

Heidr slacked for a moment and I punched her in the face, causing her to stagger back. Screaming in frustration, she waved her hand in a wide arc and a wave of yellow energy hit me, rocking me back onto my heels as it passed to crash against the fence behind me, cracking several boards. Lunging for me again, I barely moved out of the way in time. As she overextended herself, I cracked her in the side of the helmet with the butt of the scythe.

Not to be outdone, she planted a boot in my gut that took me off my feet and launched me several yards back to land on my ass. Before I could get up, she was on me, sword raised. On instinct, I took a knee, gripped the handle in both hands, and raised it overhead to keep from being cleaved in two. Her golden blade slammed into indigo flames with such force as to shatter the cement below.

She continued to press downward.

The hairs across my body stood on end as our auras clashed against one another. Shadow and indigo flames poured out of me as light and life flowed out of her, encircling us in a ball of power. Her visor vanished and fear shone in her eyes. Slowly, both of us lost our armor. Neither of us were willing to stop lest we die. Lightning made of darkness and golden light danced around us till they finally struck home. A bolt of golden plasma tore through her shoulder and into my chest. That was quickly followed by a blast of the dark energy tearing through me and into hers.

I screamed out in anguish as the power tore through my body to leave my chest smoldering. The ball around us condensed suddenly, snapping her arm and breaking one of my legs. Breath caught in my throat, but I refused to lesson my grip. The sphere contracted again, increasing the pressure around us several fold. Blood ran freely from every orifice on both of our faces.

Every inch of exposed flesh began to burn. Our clothes began to smolder then the world around us exploded. She flew back out of sight and I was forced backward atop my broken limb, the sudden stop snapping each of my ribs. The bones shot through flesh. Vital fluids poured out of me. Darkness ringed my vision for a moment as the misery was nearly too much for me to bear.

That was when things got so much worse.

Air filled my lungs. My chest suddenly rose, and my bones pulled themselves back into my body to set themselves right. Flashes of bright light and darkness filled my vision. I howled and cried out as tears streamed down my face. If I'd been able, I would've begged whatever god there was to end my torment and let me die. My breathing came in small gasps between waves of agony.

Blood caught in my throat and I choked and gagged on the chunky bits…the liquid too. This had to be what death was like. The world suddenly cooled as frost coated the ground around me. Ice jerked me this way and that to pull me straight, allowing my leg to heal. Then it stopped. Misery moved into my being, sent a change of address, and made itself at home.

Yet somehow, I lived.

The scythe vanished from sight and my armor wasn't coming back. Still though, I needed to get to my feet to see where Heidr was. Maybe it'd killed her. A low groan from somewhere on the other side of the Tucker killed that hope before it took hold.

Rolling to the side, I sluggishly got to my feet. I didn't have any fight left in me. Worst bit, I didn't have a weapon. The gladius was upstairs and there was no way to get it. The thought barely crossed my mind before the gladius appeared in my hand. It hummed as a jolt of energy pulsed into me, dulling the pain.

Not sure how that happened, but I didn't care.

Heidr staggered into view. Scorch marks marred her smart business suit and her flesh; the latter of which was healing before my eyes.

Her gaze fixated on my sword arm and horror shone on her face.

She stumbled back. "How…no…it's not possible." She looked up at me. "Where did you get that?"

Excellent, something scares the woman.

I clenched the hilt and stepped toward her. "Like it?"

A meaty thud sounded. Ethan cried out and flew across the street, bounced across the sidewalk, and skidded to a halt in front of his boss. Smoke poured from four long gashes across his mechanical arm, which was making a nasty grinding noise.

She glanced down at Ethan then over to Alexander, who'd changed into his werebear form—a human bear hybrid with glowing green claws and eyes. Power washed off him in waves, his every step sending small tremors through the earth.

None of us were prepared for what stomped our way.

Heidr reached down, grabbed Ethan, and vanished.

Unable to bear my own weight any longer, I collapsed to my knees.

Alexander returned to his human form and rushed over to check on me. "You okay?"

"I'll live." Curious, I looked up at him. "How about you?"

He pulled off what was left of his ruined shirt. "Fine." Holding out his hand, he helped me to my feet. "Better than that…I'm good. You, however, look like dogshit."

"Feel it too." My shirt was soaked with blood from where my bones tore through my flesh. They were in the process of knitting themselves back together, which just sucked. "Mind if I stand here a minute? Moving isn't on my list of things I want to do."

Alexander frowned. "I'd rather you not since I'm half naked in the middle of the street."

Like anyone would care. The man had the physique that'd give the Olympic gods a complex.

After fishing them out of my pants pocket, I gingerly handed him my keys. "There's a shirt in the trunk that'll probably fit."

"Okay, I don't like the idea of you standing out here in your current state." He pocketed the keys and pointed at the house. "You can either make it in under your own steam or I'll happily carry you."

If he picked me up, there was a chance I'd pass out...that might not be a bad thing.

"Fine."

I hobbled toward the house. Inside, I collapsed onto the couch.

Heather walked in and dropped her purse. "What the fuck happened?" She turned to see Alexander shirtless. "Were you guys fighting?"

He nodded. "Yes, but not with each other. Heidr and Ethan showed up at our doorstep."

Wincing, I placed the gladius on the coffee table. "She's gone now, but I'm going to need a few minutes to heal before we go to Andrew's."

"Not to mention a shower." Alexander dug black gunk out from under his nails. "Me too from the looks of things."

Heather shook her head. "Wait...you can't just say Heidr showed up but left with no other explanation."

I stood, grabbed the sword and hobbled around the table. "In that case, Alexander can fill you in. I'm going for that shower."

Indigo flames wrapped around me and I was in the bath a second later. I cranked the water temp up to as high as I could stand and got in.

Kur was sluggish as he made it to the forefront of my mind. *"That hurt."*

"No shit. What happened?"

He was quiet for several seconds. *"We got hit with pure...well, there's no other way to describe it...life."*

"Is that like the necromancy I got hit with...would that be death?"

Grunting, he shifted to the side of my head. *"Not exactly...it stems from death, but it isn't in its distilled form like this. What we got hit with was feedback between her power and yours. Hers just happens to be the building blocks for life itself in its every form."*

"Great...it sucks, by the way."

"Can't disagree." He cleared his throat. *"However, there may be an upside to it."*

I placed my head against the tile. *"Really? Like what?"*

"Her power is seeping into your bones, much like the necromancy did. You're healing faster than normal, even if it doesn't feel like it." Awe sounded in his voice. "With the kind of power we were hit with, neither of us should've survived."

I glanced down at the tree on my chest to find gold embedded in the trunk and limbs. "Then, how did we?" Frustrated, I asked, "And how did the gladius suddenly appear in my hand?"

"As to your first question, I have no idea." He paused. "The other seems to be more complicated."

Turning in the shower, I let the hot water run down my back. "Dumb it down for me."

"Fine...with the introduction of the weres and Gabriel's power, it's allowed the nanites in your system a greater range." Kur pushed forward. "As you know, the gladius has an intellect to it and given its origins, some technological advancements I'm still trying to work through. Simply put, you called for it and it heard you."

I opened my eyes and sighed. "Great. Me and the sword have a link... okay, more so than I thought."

Kur shrugged. "It is what it is. I suspect there will be other oddities with it and more as time goes on." He sniffed. "In case you missed it, you're totally healed."

"Oh, yeah, thanks."

Still….

While my body was technically fixed, there was something very off. Everything about my being was slightly askew and I felt—uncomfortable. A weird sensation spread throughout my form. No matter how hard I tried, I couldn't quite put my finger on what was happening to me. All I knew for sure was that this would pass…in time.

I turned off the water, dried myself, dressed, and staggered into the bedroom. Everything started to spin. My legs trembled. A choice had to be made, so I leaned to the right as my vision went black. The sensation of falling wrapped around me and I slipped into unconsciousness before hitting the bed.

19

August 22nd

For the first time in I couldn't say when, I felt—good. Mind you, my eyes were still closed, and I was horizontal. On the upside, I was on something soft, so I'd likely hit the bed before passing out. Then again, Heather was more than capable of picking me up...so maybe I hadn't. I ran through my checklist to make sure everything still worked. So far, they did. Slowly, I opened my eyes. Darkness filled the room. Turning my head, I glanced out the window to see it was night.

How long had I been out?

I craned my neck from side to side before sitting up and placing my feet on the floor. The door creaked open to allow the hall light to cut through the darkness. It took me a second to work out the features of the massive silhouette.

"Hey there, Alexander...how long was I down?"

He turned his head and called out. "He's awake." Looking at me, he hesitated. "Mind if I flip on the light?"

"Not at all." I glanced over at the clock...3:45 a.m. Crap. "Please tell me I only slept away the day."

The overhead light blared to life. "You've been out around eighteen hours? Maybe a little less." He lumbered over to inspect me. "The rest seems to have done you good."

"Huh? What's that supposed to mean?"

Alexander beamed as he puffed out his chest. "You've finally grown a proper beard." He tsked. "Not sure you're going to like the length of your hair and nails, but we can tend to those rather quickly."

I glanced down at my hands to find my nails were overly long. My dark hair hung down to my waist as did my whiskers. "What the fuck?" Raising my gaze to Alexander, I asked, "All this in less than a day?"

He nodded. "We were a little freaked out watching it grow…which is why you're alone and I was out here."

"Goddamn it." I grabbed a handful of hair and frowned. "Oh, this isn't going to work…not even a little."

He chuckled. "Not a problem." Thumbing back at himself, he grinned. "I've got sheers, clippers…generally everything needed to clean you up." He paused. "All you have to do is decide if you want me to do it or if you want to call someone else."

"You can handle it?"

Smiling, he stepped into the room. "I'm a licensed cosmetologist, so yeah, I can."

Heather rounded the corner and skidded to a halt outside the door. "Holy shit, I'm dating a wizard."

"Not for long." I laughed. "This isn't for me."

She pulled out her phone and snapped several photos. "Maybe not, but this…this is awesome."

"Hope you enjoy them."

She grinned. "I will…feeling all right?"

I nodded. "Yeah, I'm fine."

Alexander pointed toward the bathroom. "It's probably better if we do it in there. It'll be easier to clean up."

I got to my feet, hiked up my hair and beard so as not to trip, and stopped when Heather wrapped her arms around me.

She whispered, "I'm so glad you're okay. You had us worried." Stepping back, she punched me in the arm. "Don't do that again."

Hadn't meant to do it this time. "I'll do my best."

Alexander already had a chair sitting in the middle of the room. "Sit and tell me how you'd like to look."

This was a first for me. As a child, my grandfather, Isapo-Muxika, made sure my hair remained short. Overseas, I'd kept up the tradition for ease of maintenance. Now, I could do whatever I wanted…but that wasn't an easy answer.

"How about we start with shoulder length first and work our way up from there."

It took the better part of an hour to finish but when we did, I looked pretty much the same as I had yesterday. The main difference being I didn't have any gray…like at all. Another oddity, the moment the hair was cut off it turned into a golden dust-like substance before vanishing. Same with my nails and beard, which I'd opted to turn into a goatee, again.

Alexander patted me on the shoulder. "Okay, so, yeah, I'm done here." He looked at the floor. "Since there isn't any clean up, I'll leave you to it."

I held up a finger. "Does Andrew or Harold know about what happened?"

"No…we told them there'd been an emergency and we'd have to reschedule." He checked his watch. "Probably something you should do in a few hours."

"Yeah, I can do that." I sighed. "Thanks."

He packed up his kit. "I'm going to let you clean up. Hungry?"

Oddly enough, I wasn't. I mean, I could eat, but it wasn't a thing. "Not particularly, but I'm guessing everyone else is." I grabbed my towel. "Meet you guys downstairs in the kitchen."

Fifteen minutes later, I strolled into the dining room to find Alexander and Heather waiting on me with a plateful of food.

She smiled. "You look better."

"I am."

Hugging me, she said, "Have a bite to eat then call Andrew to let him know we'll be over shortly."

"Sure thing." I fixed myself a modest plate of eggs, bacon, and toast. "Did you tell him or the others anything?"

She glanced over at Alexander and shook her head. "No, we decided it was in everyone's best interest to go into detail once you woke up."

"You mean if I woke up." I took a bite of the bacon and frowned. It didn't taste right. "What's wrong with this, did it go off or something?"

Alexander stuffed a second piece in, chewed, and swallowed. "Nothing as far as I can tell. Why do you ask?"

I took another bite only to be met with disappointment. Picking up another, I tried it to the same end. It wasn't bad, it just wasn't good.

Indigo flames wrapped around my hand and tinged my vision as Kur surged forward. *"Oh, sorry."* They died out instantly. *"We're both resetting ourselves to a new normal."*

"Not sure I like it if bacon is now shit."

He laughed. *"Not to worry. Your taste buds will right themselves in a few days."*

"What the hell is going on?"

His amusement faded. "Can't be sure, but that surge of power that hit us during our encounter with Heidr set off a series of growth spurts as shone in your hair, beard, and nails. It rejuvenated you in other ways as well. Check your hands."

Since the day I'd picked up my stone, my left hand looked as if it'd been melted in God's furnace. Today however, things changed. Sure, there were scars, but they were few and far between. I wanted to rip my shirt off to see my chest and back but that'd be rude. I'd gone into the shower and mechanically cleaned myself up without bothering to look, something I'd have to rectify shortly.

"Holy shit."

Heather arched an eyebrow. "What?"

Damn it, I'd said that out loud. Holding up my hand, I turned it for them to see. "The scars, they're fading."

Heather got up and grabbed my wrist to look at it. "It is."

Alexander gestured at me. "Stand up."

I reluctantly got to my feet. "Why?"

"Heather, if you wouldn't mind." She reached out and undid the buttons on my shirt to open it up. She stumbled back as she put her hand to her mouth. "Oh…my…that's…different."

I glanced down at the scars gifted to me by Lewis Grant's blood magic last year. At the time, it'd taken the form of a tree if you squinted your eyes just so. Now, however, it'd changed into the tree of life I'd been shown as a boy. Thick roots delved down to disappear into my pants. The trunk had veins of crimson and blue snaking up the bark and out through the limbs where tiny bursts of energy seemed to bloom. To make it all the more surreal, actual power coursed through the thing with each beat of my heart.

Pulling my shirt closed, I hurriedly buttoned it. "I'm not ready for that right now. Let's all pretend we didn't see it."

Heather reluctantly sat back in her chair. "You sure you don't want to talk about it?"

"I am."

Alexander took a bite of his food. "Then you're going to need a darker shirt before we leave."

Pushing my plate to the side, I said, "Back in a few." I pulled out my phone. "I'll call Andrew to let him know we're on our way."

It didn't take me long to get changed into a black t-shirt and a black button up to go over it. From there, it was a simple matter of setting things up with Andrew and taking the indigo express to his place.

Andrew met us in the living room. "Glad you could make it…even if it is a day late."

"Long story."

He nodded. "It can wait. Follow me."

We worked our way through the halls to the meeting room. All the seats along the lengthy table were filled with techs hammering away at their keyboards. At the far end of the room, next to the charred remains of Brad, were two portable workstations with a half dozen monitors each. Against the far wall were a dozen large screen TV's. Each had a different scene; a map of Waterford Ireland, blueprints for several businesses, pictures of houses, and what amounted to surveillance style mugshots of thirty people.

While I hadn't seen one in a while, this was a situation room where you'd plan out a coordinated attack on the enemy.

The photo in the center of an attractive redhead with pale skin and baby blue eyes struck me. Though I'd never seen her before, I had an idea who she was…Chandra Raghnailt.

I tapped the photo. "Is this Chandra?"

Harold popped up beside me. "Know the woman?"

"No, but I know the name. Is that her?"

He frowned. "We weren't sure…there were rumors about her name, but we haven't been able to verify."

I smacked my gut. "Do you know if she has a scar right around here?"

"Uh…hmm." He thumbed through some notes on his tablet then stopped. "Yes, she does. Is that important?"

"Yeah, it is." Viktor wasn't going to be thrilled. "Are you familiar with Viktor Warden?"

He wobbled his hand back and forth. "Not personally. I met with his brother, Nicholas, not long ago."

"According to Viktor, he tried to gut her back in the day. He'd hoped she died of her wounds." I sighed. "Apparently, that didn't happen."

Harold tapped out a few things on the tablet and her name appeared on the screen. "No, no it didn't."

"How'd you find her?"

His gaze darted around the room. "Had some help." He gestured at the workers throughout. "All these men and women are members of the Pacis Gladius." His voice dropped. "Over the last few decades, I recruited those who'd become discontent with the Archive and its decrepit system. While they weren't fans, they weren't exactly on board with becoming a weapon to be wielded by other factions…even ones as noble as Warden Global or the Ulfr." He shifted. "So, I offered them a chance at something different."

"The Pacis Gladius...sword of peace. Isn't that a bit of an oxymoron?"

Harold lifted my hand. "You have the word Pax on one side of your hand and...a...a single sword on the other?"

Slowly, I winced. "About that, the Archive is going through some changes. To be more accurate, it's dying, and the coins are choosing a different path."

Andrew blinked. "What's that even supposed to mean?"

I blew out a long breath. "It's difficult to explain."

"Try." Harold frowned. "Because I'm with Andrew on this."

I leaned against the wall. "The coins are living beings made up of nanites. They did their best to adapt to those in positions of power... meaning they adopted the whole Roman Empire coinage and look. Now that things are changing—thanks to some safety protocols being activated—they're able to fight back." Not knowing what else to do, I went with the truth. "I have the coins for the missing governors. Same for the prefects and triumvirates. Whoever is in charge of those coins has decided that Lazarus has been compromised and is making changes to ensure they're no longer used inappropriately. In short, the Archive is dying and it's up to us to create something better."

Andrew blinked. "But if the Archive dies...won't they go with it?"

"No, the Archive isn't a living entity so much as beings, such as Kur." My head began to ache. "This is a lot harder to put into words than I thought it'd be."

Kur pushed forward. *"Would you like me to help?"*

"Could you?"

Indigo flames wrapped around me as a blue dragon the size of a Great Dane glided out of my torso to hover there. Electricity danced along his scales and flames flickered behind his dark eyes.

Everyone in the room got to their feet and put some distance between them and us.

Kur gave everyone a big toothy smile.

It wasn't as comforting as he'd meant it to be.

He bowed slightly. "I am Kur, the eldest of the Dragon Lords." His gaze tracked across the room. "I mean you no harm." He turned his attention to Andrew and Harold. "As Gavin was saying, the other coins house the essence of another being such as myself."

Andrew cocked his head to the side. "Other Dragon Lords?"

Kur's body went slightly slack for a moment. "I do not know...but it's possible. Then again, it could be one of the other notable powers from before the Great War. Honestly, we won't know until someone worthy in both spirit and power takes up Lazarus's coin."

"I've got nanites inside me?" Andrew suddenly looked uncomfortable. "Will they hurt me?"

Kur's gravelly voice cut through the silence. "No, not at all. Once they're properly activated, they'll add to your powers." He turned to me. "Much like what's happened to the centurions now that the weres and a Nephilim have picked up one of my coins."

"Wait." Andrew's mouth fell open. "Weres and Gabriel are vigiles now?"

Damn it. "Yes, they are. Seems to be working out for the best." I paused. "Cole took over North America, Gabriel has South, and Vasile has Southern Africa. That meant I had two openings here in North America, so those went to Sam and Dean."

Andrew frowned. "Goddamn it."

"What?"

His gaze locked onto mine. "Why couldn't you have left Ms. Dodd alive long enough to see this?" He burst out laughing. "I would've paid good money to watch her have a fucking coronary."

Oh, thank God that didn't go where it could've. Then the thought of Ms. Dodd's head exploding from the realization that her new vigil was a were flashed through my mind and I laughed. "Watching her stroke out would've been glorious."

Kur cleared his voice. "Sorry to cut in, but I don't have a lot of time."

Harold stepped forward. "So, you're saying when someone picks up Lazarus's coin, it'll change things as a whole?'

He nodded. "It will. Simply put, we're here to help you survive what's coming. We're an unseen ally that will add to your strength and help you tap into your full potential." Leaning against me, he said,

"Gavin's right, the Archive itself isn't a living creature, but we are…it doesn't matter what name you give the umbrella so much as who is wielding the handle. Until recently, the coins have been used to give the Archive power that didn't belong to it. That's changing now."

Harold's voice sounded far away. "How do we get his coin from him?"

Kur hesitated. "Other than killing him? I'm not entirely sure. There's the off chance that someone who met all the criteria and wielded enough power could simply shake his hand and take it. But do you seriously think for one second that's going to happen?"

Andrew shook his head. "Lazarus is stupid powerful so, no I don't."

Kur glanced between my uncle and grandfather. "Now do you understand?"

They nodded.

"Good." He turned to me. "Time to return home."

Flames enveloped me once more as he vanished inside.

Harold gave me a pained expression. "Does that hurt?"

"No." I shrugged. "It tingles a little at times, but other than that… nothing really."

He huffed out a laugh. "That's some weird shit. No way to say this so that it doesn't come out wrong. If you are thinking about trying to bring me on board with whatever you're wanting to change the Archive into…I'll pass." Tapping his forehead, he said, "After the deal I made with Anubis all those years ago, I don't want anyone else in my mind ever again."

I could see that being a problem. "Speaking of Anubis, any chance you've got his number?"

He shook his head. "Nope…I heard from him just before emailing you."

"What did he say?"

His gaze hit the floor. "That he couldn't be involved in what we're planning." He looked up at me. "And that he'll be in touch with you when he's ready."

What a sack of shit. "Did he really just pull a *don't call me I'll call you* by proxy?"

Harold shrugged. "Sort of." He sighed. "For what it's worth, I'm sorry."

Me too. Anubis promised to help me when I needed it. Hell, he'd said something about training me, but as far as I could tell, he was doing everything in his power to avoid me. Not entirely true...he and the Loki saved my ass in New Mexico. But since then, getting in touch with the man had proved impossible.

I gestured around the room. "What do we have?"

Andrew gestured at Harold. "Why don't you walk him through it."

"With pleasure." He stepped up and tapped the nearest screen to bring up Chandra's photo. "Until just now, we didn't have a name that stuck, so we've been simply referring to her as the woman in charge."

"Catchy."

He shrugged. "Not particularly, but it is accurate." Touching the screen again, it changed to a new set of photos I hadn't seen before of twelve men. One of which, I recognized. "These are the Twelve."

Stepping over, I tapped James Matherne's image. "What's he doing there?"

"I don't know." Harold sighed. "He seems to be a new recruit for the Twelve."

The skin under my eye twitched. "His name is James Brody Matherne and he's a cop here in town." Unclenching my jaw, I asked, "What is the Twelve?"

Harold shrugged. "All we know is mostly through rumor and hearsay but simply put, they're some sort of cabal doing their best to mirror the Archive." His voice hardened. "One of the few facts we know is that they're led by twelve individuals." Pointing at the screen, he grimaced. "That's Andrew, Bartholomew, John, Levi, Luke, Mathew, Peter, Philip, Thaddeus, Thomas, your buddy James, and their leader, Paul...who's an utter douchebag from what I understand."

My head hurt. "Not sure I get this...these twelve lead some sort of organization separate from the Black Circle?"

"Not exactly." He paused. "They don't advertise their affiliation but from what I can tell, they're another offshoot that doesn't require a blood ritual to join."

The screen changed again to reveal a twelve-headed dragon.

Kur pushed forward again, anger burning inside him. *"No...it can't be."*

"What?"

He twitched. *"The similarities between that symbol and Zmey Gorynych are too great to be a coincidence."*

"As in the Dragon Lord that betrayed you?"

Seething, he said, *"The very same."*

On a hunch, I turned to Harold. "Does the name Zmey Gorynych mean anything to you?"

"It does." He frowned. "We haven't been able to put a picture with the man yet, but we're working on it."

"No need." I shook my head and touched the symbol. "This is Zmey...or a representation of him." Sighing, I said, "He's a Dragon Lord much like Kur." Only issue was, he had a full set of hosts. "Please tell me we're not dealing with them."

Harold shrugged. "No idea. This photo was taken June of last year."

Baptist's email came back to haunt me.

From what I've been told, he's on vacation somewhere in Ireland for the next few weeks.

This was where he'd gone, and we'd been none the wiser.

Fantastic. "So, he's not human."

"No...he's a Stone Born...why do you ask?"

I frowned. "You can officially change his name as well...or add on to it anyway...his father is or was Walter Percy."

Fury burned in Andrew's eyes. "Are you sure?"

"Ninety-nine percent." Hanging my head, I rubbed my temple. "We checked him out thoroughly at the time...everything pointed to him being some random adopted kid. My gut, however, said otherwise." I gestured at the screen. "This only seems to verify that."

Harold scribbled down a few notes. "I'll have my people look into it." He clicked the thing in his hand and the screen changed again to show a thin, pale woman with dark hair. "This is Monica Balfour, a powerful sorcerer and Chandra's second." Another photo popped up of a powerfully built man. "Finally, to the reason for this whole dog and pony show." He pointed. "That's Stephan Morrigan. He's an ancient Stone Born who is incredibly powerful."

I frowned. "Thought Chandra would be the target."

He shook his head. "No…I mean she could be a secondary, but he's the main objective."

"Why?"

Harold sighed. "He acts as a trainer there in Waterford, but on his off time, he's been building something. It's our understanding he's been working on some sort of gate for the last three or four thousand years…and he's supposedly close to completing it."

"Like a transport gate?"

The screen changed again to show a room carved with ancient symbols so old that even Kur didn't know their origin. A large stone and steel circle lay in the center of the room with other symbols carved into it.

These however, Kur recognized. *"Those are glyphs meant to open a door between our realm and the Svartálfar."*

"I'm guessing that's bad."

Rage sounded in his voice. *"It'd give Dvalinn and his ilk a foothold in this realm."*

Well fuck.

"We need to trash that. It's meant to create a foothold for the Svartálfar."

Andrew grimaced. "Isn't that one of the horrific realms Henri described?"

"It is, and their leader, Dvalinn, would love to get into our world. Especially since Heidr's here."

Harold's shoulders slumped forward. "Then we need to hurry. I've been told he's a week, maybe two, away from completing the thing."

Andrew held up his hand. "So what? Won't he just remake it somewhere else?"

Kur's knowledge poured into my mind and I simply repeated it.

"A gate of this type requires a lot of very specific things…location being one due to the Ley lines. Even if he could find a similar situation elsewhere in the world, it'd open a portal to a different location—if not realm—altogether. On top of that, they're not easy to build. They take a lot of time, power, and patience to create. Each glyph has to be powered slowly in order to ensure the whole thing doesn't blow up. I could keep going why it's unlikely he'll just make another, but simply put, they're difficult to create, taking centuries of dedication to get right."

Andrew nodded. "Fine…then let's destroy this one and kill him before he takes another few thousand years to try again."

Harold walked us through a virtual version of a small compound outside Waterford run by a bunch of necromancers. Turned out that the small unassuming city was the training ground for the Black Circle and its members. Somewhere along the line, they'd become so comfortable that they stopped trying to hide who they were and what they were doing.

20

My meeting with Harold had been educational. As soon as I got home, I reached out to Baptist about James Matherne-Percy, but he was out of the office for a few hours. At a guess, he'd be just as thrilled as I'd been at the revelation. In addition, I'd sent an email to Viktor about the situation as well.

Since then, I'd spent three hours constructing an email to Jade.

Good day to you Ms. Baker,

I wanted to thank you again for saving my life the other night. Normally, I'm doing the saving, so this is a weird place for me to be. Still, I appreciate it a great deal. There have been several developments you should be aware of.

First, there seems to be another offshoot of the Black Circle called the Twelve. Not sure if you've heard of it or not, but they're supposed to be some sort of mirror image of the Archive. They target those disgruntled with the laws of our community and bring them into their fold. They do this while keeping clear of the whole necromancy blood ritual thing.

It's my understanding they've really stepped up the recruitment process since Andrew became governor, and I've only made them more appealing to certain factions. I guess any chance they get to say they're better than someone else, they'll take it.

Second, Heidr, Queen of the Álfheimr, has taken possession of Kira Warden, Viktor's daughter. She's currently running around the globe offing people who work for the Black Circle by proxy. To make things worse, she has a lot of power behind her, so if you run into her, be very careful.

Third, we've got plans to attack one of the Black Circle's strongholds in Ireland. It's come to my attention that a man named Stephan Morrigan has been working on a gate between our realm and that of the Svartálfar in the hopes of bringing Dvalinn and his ilk to this world.

Seeing how that'd be a bad thing and I want to stop him...would you consider lending us a hand?

Please.

Hope to hear from you soon,
Gavin Randall

We had less than twenty-four hours before we made our move on Waterford, and there was a lot to do in the meantime.

I dialed Hayden's number.

She picked up on the first ring. "Hello."

"Hey there, how are things?"

Laughing, she said, "Skip the niceties and tell me what's on your mind."

It took me a few minutes to run through the morning's events.

Hayden paused. "Dvalinn would be very bad news."

"It ranks right up there with Heidr, who I might add, I've run into twice in the last week."

She groaned. "Heard about the one but not the second."

"She tried to kill me in front of my house. Afterwards I spent the better part of a day unconscious." I gritted my teeth. "I know it's Viktor's daughter and all, but she's making herself a dangerous nuisance."

Sighing, she said, "Just do what you can. No one expects you to lay down and die."

"That's not true." A bitter smile crossed my lips. "Nora wouldn't mind that one bit."

Anger coated her tone. "She's blinded by desperation. She'd let anyone—including Viktor—die to save Kira."

"Got that feeling. Is there any chance you could lend us a hand with Stephan's madness?"

Her voice softened. "Maybe…but I can't promise. We've got a couple uprisings in Southern Africa and Europe we're trying to contain." She blew out a long breath. "It'd be best to make a plan that didn't involve us. If we show up then great…if we don't, then no harm done."

"Fair…hey look…we need to speak in person for like five minutes…can you spare me that?"

Hayden was quiet for a moment. "Is it important?"

"I'll give you three letters and you decide…QDM."

The line went dead and, before I could lay the phone down, a brilliant orange sphere appeared in front of me. The flames dissipated and Hayden stepped forward. "How do you know about that?"

I got up and closed the door to my office. "That's a long story but one you need to hear."

She folded her arms. "I'm listening."

Gesturing at the seat, I smiled. "Sit. This is going to take a minute."

She did. "Better?"

Damn, someone was upset…or perhaps scared. "First, I need you to promise not to run out of here looking for the source. They don't know you're still alive and them seeing you again might not go over so well."

She blinked. "What do you mean, still?" Waving a hand at herself, she said, "Other than you and Cole, no one else even knows who I really am."

I shook my head. "That's not true, there is another. They knew you and Prince Muninn prior to the QDM."

Hayden froze. "Do you know who Prince Muninn is?"

This was going to get complicated. "Viktor."

"Good, then I can spare you that shock." She hung her head. "Look, if you're right about someone else knowing who I am, then you've got to make doubly sure Viktor doesn't find out about me."

Weird. "I can do my best…care to tell me why?" I sighed. "What's the issue there, anyway?"

Her voice trembled. "Everything hinges on him not discovering who I am until the time is right." She sniffed. "Viktor." Tears rolled down her cheek. "I don't have all my memories…just a few. But I know who he was…is. There's a plan in motion to help stop all this craziness." Not looking at me, she slumped in her chair. "This will sound crazy…well, probably not since you know about the QDM and you've spoken to Viktor…but, we're stuck in a time loop. It's my understanding that things—scenery, worlds, events—change from one to the next but it doesn't negate the whole stuck bit."

Well, this was going to blow her mind. "I know…someone else recently told me the same thing." I pointed at her. "He knew your name, what you looked like…everything."

She finally looked up at me. "Who?"

There wasn't any easy way to reveal it to her, so I just went for it. "Cain. He's alive, and he's been busy."

Her eyes went wide. "The strigoi?"

I nodded. "That was him."

A big smile crossed her face. "He made it. That's wonderful."

"Oh, but there's more." I held out a hand. "Please remain seated. Do not scream or jump or blow anything up…okay?"

Smirking, she shrugged. "I'm a big girl and know how to contain myself."

While I didn't doubt that under normal circumstances, what was about to happen was anything but. "Please, just keep calm."

She rolled her eyes. "Fine."

I waved my hand over the holo-ball and Alfred sprang to life a few feet behind her. "Okay, slowly turn around."

Hayden gave me a curious look but did as I asked. She didn't move.

Alfred stood there with a mixture of joy and sadness on his face. "Hello, old friend."

Her voice cracked as she spoke. "Is that really you?"

"It is."

She blinked. "I cannot believe it…how's this possible?"

While I'd never seen it, a glamor covered Alfred's physical form from the time this version of him was plucked out of his brain till his death. They'd gone through a lot of trouble to ensure that no one recognized him as the commander of the Varangian Guards prior to the QDM. In a sense, Alfred sacrificed everything about who he was to make sure the plan worked. That was a level of commitment and dedication not many people possessed…including me.

It took them several minutes to catch up.

She stood, walked over, and tried to touch him…but to no avail.

Alfred smiled. "I've missed you as well."

"I'm sorry for getting you involved in this." She hung her head. "But you and your people were the only ones I could trust."

Pride filled his eyes. "It was and is my pleasure to serve." His gaze darted over to me. "Can I tell her?"

"About the stasis chambers?"

He nodded.

"Absolutely."

Beaming, he stood at attention. "I'm happy to report the mutagens worked to create a species unable to be harmed by necromancy or life magic."

She gestured at herself then to me. "We don't count."

"Wasn't talking about you." Excitement tinged his voice. "The weres…"

Realization washed over her. "They're the origins?"

He grinned. "Yes."

Anger burned in her eyes. "I'd been furious at their enslavement before but now…now I want to fucking murder Lazarus for allowing it to happen in the first place."

"Get in line." I popped my knuckles. "He and I need to have a long conversation about a lot of things…including the weres."

She nodded. "If I see him first, should I let him live that long?"

"Honestly, I'm not sure." I sighed. "He's dangerous and it may be best to just put him down…but we'll cross that bridge when we come to it."

Hayden sat back in her chair. "Goddamn, I can't believe Cain is here." She beamed at Alfred. "And you, my old friend…God, it's good to see you." Her smile faltered when she turned to me. "You know we're on a dangerous path."

"I do." A part of me wanted to tell her about Janus, but Alfred had gone to great pains to avoid the name, so it was probably best I did too. "One last change of subject…and yet another thing you can't tell anyone, especially Viktor."

She snorted. "I'll just add it to my list."

"I think Viktor has another child."

That wiped the amusement off her face. "I'm sorry, what?"

"You heard me." I fidgeted with my hands. "But I need to know something before I can be sure."

She folded her arms. "Such as?"

"Were he and Lilith an item at some point?"

Her composure crumpled. "Oh, yeah, that…they were together for a while after his arrival…before he lost himself to the madness." Wetness formed in the corners of her eyes. "Adam drugged her and tried to have her murder him in his sleep. It didn't work out well and she vanished that night. No one has seen her since."

"Was this around fifteen thousand years ago?"

She did some quick calculations. "Something like that, yeah."

"Viktor, Nicholas, and Kira are the only three you know with the Idunn running around in their system…right?"

Frowning, she said, "Other than vampires with that parasite attached to them…yes."

"Okay, then yes, I'm ninety-five percent sure he has a son."

She held out her hands. "Don't tell me anymore. I don't want to know." A sad smile crossed her lips. "He's always wanted kids and he was thrilled when Kira was born. It might kill him to find out about a son after fifteen thousand years." Shaking her head, she sighed. "I don't want to be the one who slips and tells him. That's strictly on you."

"Gee, thanks."

Getting to her feet, she waved at Alfred before turning to me. "Hey, if I'd been the one to find out, it'd be on me to tell him. Instead, it's fallen to you."

Plus, she was in love with the man. "Not a problem. One thing... when are you going to tell him your secret?"

She glanced down at herself. "That I'm a woman?"

"That...and...you're in love with him."

Hayden went unnaturally still and for a moment, I was concerned she was plotting to kill me. Eventually, she found her voice. "I suspect both will come out at roughly the same time."

"And Justine?"

She grinned. "I'm willing to share if she is. But just because I still love him doesn't mean he'll love me back. His memories were wiped, and he was set on a different course to ensure things would go in a new direction." Her voice cracked again. "If it leads us to a place of safety, a broken heart is a small price to pay."

Holy shit. Just how bad were things? Alfred gave up everything and now she was watching the love of her life—a man who'd likely once loved her back—become someone new without any memory of her.

"I've got to ask...were things bad enough to justify the price you, Alfred, and Cain have paid?"

She stiffened. "Do you really want to know?"

Every brain cell in my head screamed no. Kur and the Grim objected. Hell, even my gut wanted nothing to do with it. Thing was, if I was going to see this to the end, I had to understand what we were avoiding.

"No, but I need to."

Nodding, she stepped over to me and place her hand against my forehead.

We were suddenly aboard a badly damaged battle cruiser in the depths of space. Everyone save for Hayden was wearing black armor with their helmets in place. A whistling sound filled the room. Turning, I found a gaping hole in the side of the hull.

A Jörmungandr the size of the moon opened its maw, ready to swallow the ship whole. Hayden called forth an orange scythe and leapt through the opening into the beast's mouth. She swung her weapon with all her might, catching the corner of its mouth as she took off running, slicing a gash a mile long down its side.

Suddenly, another ship appeared to open fire on the Jörmungandr, punching holes through its body. Hayden kept hacking away at the thing, but it wouldn't die. Thirty-five more ships came out of wormholes all around them to open fire, finally obliterating the world eater.

Exhausted, Hayden stepped back inside her ship, sounded the alarm, and spoke. "While the calvary is here, our ship is doomed, but our mission remains the same." She glanced through the tear in the hull. "We'll be boarding the Prince's ship for the remainder of our trip."

A voice I recognized, Alfred, cut through the helmet of the man at the helm. "We need to hurry. The engines are going critical."

Hayden nodded. "How much time do we have?"

"Six, maybe seven minutes." Alfred shrugged. "Not much more."

Hayden sighed. "You heard the man. Move your ass."

Three minutes later fifteen thousand men and women were beamed aboard Prince Muninn's ship. A wormhole opened in front of each of the ships and they left the area, leaving the cruiser to die where it lay gutted.

Hayden stepped onto the bridge where Viktor hurried over to hug her. No one uttered a word when he kissed her. After several long seconds, he pulled back. "Got your call."

She grinned. "Damn near late."

"Not possible." He pulled a square stone onyx box with gilded lines pulsing through it out of a nearby cabinet and smiled. "It guides our way now. I showed up as soon as it'd let me."

Hayden frowned. "You've really let it take over the controls?"

"I have." He sighed. "There isn't much choice. Between the Loki and my grandfather doing their best to lay waste to the universe before the other can, it's the only safe way to travel."

She winced. "How's the war going?"

"About as well as you'd think." He tapped a monitor. "See for yourself."

A casualty list appeared. It didn't list names of people, but entire systems. People were dying by the trillions. Entire solar systems, stars and all, were being devoured by the Loki or burned to ash by the Gray Wanderer.

Sadness filled Viktor's tone. "We've got three hundred and sixty-seven days to put the last few pieces in motion before it ends."

Her expression hardened. "I know...but—"

"—There's no but. We know what needs to be done." Pointing at the monitor, he said, "What's being asked of us to save all those lives is miniscule." He winced. "Out of all of us, you'll have it the hardest though. Having some of your memories to ensure the rest of us do what's needed. For that, I'm sorry."

A sniffle escaped her. "As you say, a small price to pay to save the universe."

Kissing her forehead, he held her in his arms and whispered, "I'm sorry...if I could, I'd take this burden from you."

Refusing to cry, she nodded. "I know." She pushed back and looked up at him. "It's just hard knowing you won't remember me, and I won't be able to say anything...literally. Achelous and Xiwangmu will personally see to that."

His shoulders slumped forward. "I've been told."

"Until certain things fall into place, I won't even be able to be myself around you."

Viktor's voice trembled. "I know...and I'm sorry. There's nothing that can be done."

Hurt, anger, and regret etched itself across her features. "I know...I was there...but it doesn't mean I like it. We've all agreed to see this through, but none of us enjoy the prospect."

"Neither do I." Fury burned in his eyes. "But I won't let that man use me to burn down the universe again...and this is the only way that won't happen and me still live to see it."

She kissed him. "And that's the only reason we agreed. We love you...me most of all."

Tears welled up in his eyes. "I love you too. You're the only reason I'm willing to go through this…without you, none of this means anything to me. It'd be simpler to pass beyond the veil and let something new come from the ashes."

Hayden hugged him tight. "I know."

Viktor kissed the top of her head. "We'll pass through the field shortly then it's less than a day to Eden. You should get some rest."

She smiled. "Join me."

"I will, soon."

The memory faded and the reality of what we were fighting for hit me. Everything would burn. Not just this world—the entire universe would go down in flames if we failed. It was clear she didn't have all the answers, but she knew far more than she wanted to. Cain was in a similar boat…being burdened with too many memories. The only thing was, he hadn't a clue as to the overall plan other than he needed to wipe out all of his father's children. Would he need to amend his mission when he found out about Vasile?

Not long after she left, I got an email from Jade letting me know that she wouldn't be participating in our raid on Waterford to stop Stephan as she had something else more pressing to handle.

Of course she did.

21

August 23rd

    We'd arrived outside the necromancer village near Grannagh Castle a few miles away from Waterford, Ireland a little after two in the morning local time. Would've gotten here sooner had it not been raining its ass off. Between Pacis Gladius and the Centurions, we had roughly a thousand people ready to storm the small village the necromancers claimed as their own. Still, we were sorely outnumbered as they possessed twice our number on their home turf. Sadly, it was the best we could manage on such short notice without calling attention to ourselves.

    Given our numbers, we opted to put four groups in play in the hopes of breaking through their defenses quickly. A lot easier said than done considering they'd spent centuries building up a nine-foot stone wall that measured a meter across at its narrowest point. Armed sentries patrolled the inner compound, which spanned roughly two kilometers in total.

    It was my understanding that Stephan set up shop first and everything else grew up around him. Anyway, the compound turned into a training ground and a hub for the Black Circle as a whole. That'd been why Chandra moved into a pseudo castle furthest away from Stephan's modest house.

Over the last century, they'd really gone all out to make it a fully functional city to keep the trainees in and everyone else out. Apartment buildings dotted the landscape, a couple of grocery stores…but mostly, there was a plethora of office buildings and two outdoor arenas that would look at home in any gladiator movie.

Vasile and Gabriella, along with a healthy number of centurions, were on the southern side of the County Waterford. They'd have to cross the water and enter the refurbished Grannagh Castle.

Henri, Keto, and Kimberly were set up in the east with a mixture of weres and Pacis Gladius troops. Heather and Cole held the western front. That left Harold and Andrew behind me to coordinate the attack and control the northern wall.

Alexander, Gabriel, and I were with them as we were the point team. Stephan's humble little stone home stood behind a three-story apartment complex straight out of the eighties and an even taller newly built office building. Unfortunately, the latter was always abuzz with activity. Tonight, however, they were moving stuff out of Stephan's into the other building, so getting in quietly would prove tough if not impossible.

Still, we had to try.

Once we were in place, we were to alert the others so they could rush in from all sides to give us time to destroy the gate without too much interference from the guards. If we didn't notify anyone within a reasonable amount of time…God only knew what the fuck that was…they'd attack the place anyway.

So, win win…I guess.

If we were fortunate, we'd wipe out any resistance, take prisoners, and call it a day by sunset. Let's face it, that wasn't my kind of luck. The reality would likely be a lot less glorious. If we succeeded in destroying the gate, I'd call that a victory. A lot of people would die here and there wasn't anything I could do to stop that. Sacrifices had to be made to prevent Dvalinn and his horde from entering this realm.

Andrew stepped forward and clapped me on the shoulder. "You ready, son?"

"No, but that doesn't matter." I sighed. "It has to be done."

He nodded. "That it does."

Gabriel looked down at us. "We'll be fine."

It wasn't us I was worried about. The others; Heather, Kim, even Andrew, had very little field experience.

"Let's hope so."

Alexander nudged me. "The guard just turned out of sight. Time to go."

"Right." I nodded at my uncle. "See you in a bit."

He smiled. "Be safe."

Alexander, Gabriel, and I set off at a trot. We had about a hundred and fifty yards to cover before we'd have to worry about scaling the wall. Thankfully, the pouring rain and pervasive darkness allowed us to cross the meadow without being seen. Gabriel pressed his side against the wall, bent at the knees, and cupped his hands. Alexander stepped forward, put his foot into Gabriel's hands, and was propelled to the top of the wall with enormous grace. I followed Alexander's example, only to land stomach first. Which I absolutely planned—not —but I covered by helping Gabriel up and over.

By the looks on their faces, neither of them was buying it. A wide patch of rich green grass kept the sounds of our feet hitting the ground to a minimum. Now, to cross the street, avoid the guards, the people next door, and somehow manage to get into the cottage without setting off every alarm known to man.

We hurried across the lawn to hide in the shadows of a multilevel treatment center that was closed for the evening. Our target was cattycorner, one and a half buildings down. The old apartment complex took up a lot more room than the clinic.

According to the information Harold provided, Stephan's workshop was on the third sublevel. Reports, satellite images, and rumors said the first was mostly an oversized storage room with a set of stairs leading down. On the second, it got cut up into rooms where the tech guys set up monitoring equipment and dampeners for the floor below. The third was little more than a bedrock floor, solid stone walls, and the gate Stephan was creating.

To date, other than the two photos I'd seen, no one knew what else lay there. There was talk that he'd forbidden Chandra and Monica from impeding into his territory. Either he had the clout and power to make sure they listened or people higher up the food chain ensured they obeyed.

Either way, we were pretty much blind at that point.

Alexander whispered, "What's our move here?"

All the people coming and going were wearing gray coveralls and lugging shit from one building to the other. "Fit in." I pointed at the building with all the activity. "We need to find something that'll fit. Grab a box or three and see how far we can get before anyone has to die."

Gabriel looked down at himself. "You really think that's an option?"

"Maybe." The likelihood of them having anything that'd fit him and his seven foot plus height was unlikely. "Still seems like a better idea than trying to kill…" I paused and counted off nine people. "There's nine, plus the ones already downstairs, and the ones inside." Shrugging, I said, "If there's nothing there…we'll do it the hard way. Until then, let's see what we can figure out."

We crept across the street then circled behind the apartments and into the opposite door in the new building. Took us a minute to find the lockers and another ten to find something that didn't look absolutely stupid on us…okay there wasn't any helping Gabriel and his several inches of high-water pants. Still, we tried by slicing off someone else's pant legs to duct tape to the inside of his. It wasn't perfect or long lasting, but I hoped it'd be enough to get us in.

I took point and stepped through a set of swinging double doors into a storage room. A rather portly man with a nametag that read, Tolan, stood at the far end of the room holding a clipboard. His hand was heavily scarred, and he had a slight limp as he moved around a pallet to check off something on the papers.

He glared at us and waved us over. "Come on, this shit won't move itself."

On the bottom side of his wrist was a red tattoo of a three headed dragon.

Kur whispered, *"Careful, he's one of Zmey's enforcers."*

"He's got a three headed dragon on his arm, not twelve."

He squirmed in my mind. *"Zmey is a complicated entity…think of it this way. He's got four modes. Red is enforcer, green is for his assassins, metallic gray for his soldiers, and a rusty brown for command. They answer to the twelve directly."*

"Great. Thanks for the heads up."

I smiled and moved over to Tolan. "What's next?"

"These." He frowned as he glanced over at Gabriel and Alexander. "Where did they dig the three of you up? Christ, you're huge."

My gaze hit the floor and I dropped my voice to a near whisper. "Uh…we just got here a few hours ago…they've been bouncing us around since New Mexico."

Tolan's eyes widened. "Oh shit, you worked with the Grants?"

"We did."

He shook his head. "Damn shame what happened to John and his brothers. They were good people." Pointing at three rather large crates, he said, "If you guys would grab those, take them down to the second level, and deliver them to a man named Jared, I'd appreciate it."

Each of us picked one up and we followed him over to the door, where he pulled out three green lanyards and tied them around the handles.

"Make sure those stay on or you won't get past the first floor."

I smiled. "Thanks."

"Anytime." He paused. "Hey look, if you guys want a fulltime gig here, come talk to me and I'll get you settled. If you were good enough for John, you're good enough for me."

What the actual fuck? John Grant was a psychotic, sadistic, arrogant ass. "Appreciate it." I hefted the crate. "Once we're done, we'll look you up. Can't tell you how grateful we are. A lot of folks consider us failures after what happened."

The skin under Tolan's eye twitched. "What was allowed to transpire there wasn't your doing. That's entirely Lazarus's fault...but we can discuss that later." He pointed at the door. "They'll be needing those soon."

With that, we were out the door, only to have to stand in cue at the entrance to Stephan's shack. The guard paused long enough to point us to the far side of the room. "Down to the second level, make a left, last room on the right."

"Got it, thanks."

The stairs in question barely qualified considering the stones were worn smooth from centuries of use. It was more of a slanted slope with a trip hazard involved where the steps used to be. On the next level, another guard simply pointed to the other side of the room where we found a second stairwell. These steps were in slightly better shape if a little uneven in height.

At the bottom there wasn't anyone to greet us.

Gabriel frowned. "Can I put this shit down now? It's heavy as fuck."

"Not yet." I turned left. "Let's see who Jared is first then we can find the hole that leads down to Stephan's place."

Alexander repositioned the crate. "If he's a hassle, I'll squish him with this goddamn thing."

"Let's see if he can help us first. then you can quash the man. Deal?"

He shrugged. "We'll see."

The last room on the left had floor to ceiling glass walls and contained a server room. An overly thin man with greasy black hair, brown eyes, and more than a few stains on his shirt appeared in the door. He glanced between the three of us then looked down at the string and nodded.

His hand shook as he pressed his finger against something on the other side of the metal frame. Then a speaker blared to life. "Okay, I'm going to unlock the door. Come in single file, shortest to tallest." It clicked off then back on. "Don't touch or say anything...just bring them in and put the crates where I tell you. Understood?"

Moving up front, I nodded.

"Good."

The door buzzed then slowly swung open as Jared skittered away from the entrance. I stepped in first, followed by Alexander then Gabriel.

Jared pointed toward the back. "You'll need to set them to the right of the stairs there."

So this was where the third set of stairs were. Good to know.

"Gabriel, handle the situation, please." I hesitated a fraction of a second. "Just don't kill him."

A meaty thwap sounded then Jared hit the floor. I knelt and opened the crate to find it filled with a weird techno steampunk contraption. Alexander and Gabriel both had something similar.

"Restrain the man and gag him. Last thing we need is someone to hear the asshole."

Gabriel complied. "Killing him would ensure he didn't raise a ruckus."

"I'm with Gabriel on this." Alexander pointed at the unconscious Jared. "He's a liability."

I walked over to the nearest terminal and saw a retinal scanner. "Lift him up and open his eye."

They did and the computer unlocked. The screen revealed several cameras aimed at a massive contraption that matched the items in the crates we carried. In the center of the room was a circular basin about the size of a manhole filled with a glassy black substance. On the far edge of the machine, Stephan was working to fit another piece into the circular device.

He was a big man. His file said he came in at six-foot-nine and two fifty of nothing but solid muscle. His physique said he worked out, but I still wasn't sure where he packed in all that weight as he didn't look much bigger than me and definitely smaller than Alexander. Everyone's best guess...he was around eight thousand years old and a Stone Born. To date, no one knew exactly what his powers were, but if I had to guess, that's because anyone who faced off against the man didn't live to tell the tale.

Not sure why, other than the look in his green eyes. They said he just didn't care to impress anyone. If you crossed him, you'd die, simple as that. The long black hair and permanent tan sold the whole evil mastermind bit. He was good looking but not overly so. Given his size, demeanor, and looks, you'd remember seeing the guy, even if it was for a few seconds.

I collapsed into Jared's chair and sighed. "Those machines must control the gate." Shivering, I said, "And that shit in the floor is creepy as hell."

Stephan stood, walked over to the machine, and flipped a switch. It clanked and clattered as it stuttered to life. The liquid in the pool bubbled up to create a horrific skeletal face then it broke apart and faded from sight. He frowned and turned it off then knelt and took the back off to make some adjustments I couldn't see.

My gaze tracked back to the pool. Something about the visage chilled my soul and it was my greatest hope that I'd never see it again. I tapped through the old tapes to see that this wasn't the first time he'd conjured the thing.

Jared came to, grumbling and writhing on the floor.

Turning around in my chair, I held my finger to my mouth. "Jared, I'm going to need you to keep quiet." I pointed at the crates. "Are these the last three pieces needed to complete the gate below?"

He stopped moving and narrowed his eyes as he mumbled a fuck you in my direction.

My armor snapped around me and one of the shadowy chains wrapped around his chest to drag him toward me. Horror filled his eyes and he futilely scrambled to keep distance between us.

When he was a few inches away, I growled. "I hate to repeat myself. Now answer the question."

Quickly nodding his head, he looked away.

"Now, is he expecting you or us to bring them down?"

Jared jerked his gaze up to mine and stared at me for several seconds before making a muffled sound of *you*.

A dozen chains whipped around and tore through his head and chest, killing the man instantly as we devoured his soul.

Gabriel flinched. "Goddamn. You should've just let me end him earlier…that's fucked up."

"Then we wouldn't have gotten a free pass downstairs." I gestured at the open crates. "Find something inside your box and break it. Make sure it isn't obvious."

I knelt next to mine, removed the backing, and paused to find a weird glowing ruby powering the machine. "Uh, guys."

Alexander leaned over. "What the fuck is that?"

"No idea. Either of you have something similar?"

Two minutes later, we figured out they did. Alexander's was a bit of supercharged onyx and Gabriel had a lot of power wrapped around what looked to be a diamond. Taking them out would be way too obvious but switching them around…that might work. I looked around to find an insulated glove under Jared's desk.

Reaching inside, I grabbed hold of the ruby. It didn't want to budge. I repositioned myself, took hold, twisted, and pulled for all I was worth. There was a tiny bit of give as it twisted to the side and slowly came my way. Easing up, I pushed it forward and it snapped out. I set the gemstone to the side and repeated the process on the other two.

I moved the diamond over to replace the ruby and the machine instantly began to overheat so it got switched out for the onyx. With the stones changed, I grabbed a pair of cutters out of the toolbox and snipped the wires going to the switch, then a few others for good measure.

We closed them up then checked the screen to find Stephan working on another section.

"Okay, guess this is where it all goes to hell."

I pulled out my phone and texted Andrew.

We'll be in place in two minutes. Feel free to start blowing shit up in three.

He responded instantly.

. . .

Glad to hear it We were starting to worry. We'll be moving in four minutes. Sorry for the delay but the southern faction needs time to cross the Waterford.

"Lock'em up boys. Time to visit the creepy uncle they keep hidden in the basement."

Each of us grabbed a crate and lined up to head downstairs.

22

With me at the front of the line due to being the shortest—a situation I never thought I'd be in considering I stood six-foot-six—we trekked down the stairs. These were the nicest of the bunch as they were evenly spaced, in good condition, and carved out of bedrock.

Stephan glanced over the top of a brass and copper contraption with a computer screen built into it. He paused, got to his feet, and wiped his hands on a work towel he tucked into his waistband. Pointing at the empty space to our right, he said, "You can put those over there."

I set mine down and moved out of the way so the others could do the same.

Stephan strode into the center. "Did you kill him?"

"I'm sorry?" Had this asshole figured us out already? "Kill who?"

He grinned. "Gavin, right?"

Well shit.

I pointed at myself. "Mind if I get out of this getup?"

"Not at all." He rubbed his fingers across the top of his watch and the face glowed slightly. "I mean, you're not getting out of here alive, so you might as well be comfortable."

Gabriel stepped forward and I put my arm out to stop him. "Slow down."

He glanced over at me. "Why?"

The floor had a slight glow to it, and I pointed. "Because, I get a feeling that's not exactly safe."

Stephan clapped. "Impressive. Not everyone can see glyphs. Something you inherited from your family, or is that the coin's doing?"

Why lie when the truth worked better? "No idea. What makes you ask?"

"Like I say, it's rare." He shrugged. "A skill that none of the twelve seem to possess." Smiling, he strolled around the circular bit of black liquid on the floor. "You can't come in here without blowing us up, and I'm not coming out there after what you did in New Mexico." Admiration shone on his face. "Hell, you held your own in Rome as well. I'm not foolish enough to give you the opportunity to destroy over nine thousand years of work to settle a score."

Alexander frowned. "He's stalling."

"I know…just trying to figure out how to get to him without killing the three of us."

Stephan stepped up to the edge of the ring of power. "Oh, don't lie to them."

"What's that supposed to mean?"

He gestured at the circle. "I'm betting you could get in here and survive the blast." Pointing at the others, he said, "They, however, would be very dead."

"There's a chance we could all get in there…then what?"

Stephan shook his head. "I don't think so."

Alexander glanced up. "We've got company."

"Damn." We were out of time. "Last chance Stephan. Come out, or things will go poorly."

A lilting laugh from a female floated down the stairs.

Stephan swelled to his full height. "Oh, this is going to be fun. Give me a second and I'll be right out." He waved his hand, the glyphs vanished, and the floor stopped glowing. "Come on down, it's safe."

Good thing we didn't try to escape. It appeared that he had the stairs rigged to go boom as well.

Soft-sole combat boots appeared at the top of the stairs. Slowly, an attractive redhead about five-foot-nine wearing tactical gear made her way down the stairs. Her gaze tracked from Stephan to the three of us. A hint of recognition shone in her pale blue eyes.

She moved around to stand next to Stephan. "Is that the vigil... what's his name?"

"Gavin." He grinned and patted her back. "Glad to see you've been keeping up with your studies."

She beamed with pride. "Thanks."

Christ, these two were fucking annoying.

"Hello, Chandra. Nice to properly meet you." I eased forward a step. "Viktor's going to be sad he missed the opportunity to finish the job he started."

Fury burned in her voice as she reflexively touched her stomach. "Don't worry, I'll be seeing him soon enough."

Alexander and Gabriel fanned out to either side but kept their distance.

"How about this. I'll put a new offer on the table." Chandra started to speak but I held out my hand to stop her. "Wait, I think you're going to like this."

Her voice hardened. "Fine, then hurry up."

Grinning, I checked my watch...roughly thirty seconds to go. "Surrender now, or I kill everyone above us."

They both looked at me like I was stupid before laughing.

Chandra stopped laughing and shook her head. "That's your offer?"

"It is."

She snickered. "No."

I lifted my hand as blue flames wrapped around it. "Too bad."

Within the space of a heartbeat, four massive explosions tore through the silence and the aftershocks shook the room.

Their amusement died in an instant.

I allowed the flames to die out. "Last chance to surrender." Shrugging, I said, "Or you can die with the rest."

Stephan gave her a nervous glance. "He's lying about the others."

"Am I?" My armor snapped around me in an instant. "You've heard the stories about New Mexico and Rome." My voice came out hard and cold. "Hell, I'm guessing you've seen the videos. I'm sure you passed it off as creative editing, but now that you both know that Deheune came for me and wound up in a coma because of it…you're having doubts." I cupped my hand against my ear. "If they were still alive…wouldn't they be here by now?"

Beads of sweat appeared on Chandra's forehead. "What are you?"

"Not an answer."

Stephan stepped forward and threw a bolt of lightning at my chest as he rolled out of the way of Alexander who had launched himself at the man. Instead, he took down Chandra, snapping her out of her stupor. Stephan was up again and barreled into Gabriel, taking him off his feet with ease. They hit the floor hard. An armored gauntlet wrapped itself around Stephan's hand then he slammed it into Gabriel's face, knocking him unconscious.

He stood and turned to face me. "Let's dance."

"I'm leading."

A dozen chains snapped out to wrap themselves around his arms and chest to pull him toward me. He dug his heels in. Black metallic armor wrapped itself around him, giving him the look of a cyborg Nazi. The SS helmet and face guard had a long narrow band of red across his eyes. The moment it fully formed, he shrugged off my attempts to move him further. The chains simply banged against the metal. Shadows snaked across the floor to leap up and slam into my chest, causing me to stumble backwards.

Kur whispered, "*Svartálfar armor…death magic in its purest form. Be very careful.*"

"Thanks, but I'm trying to stay alive here." I gritted my teeth. "Any suggestions?"

He paused. "*Not really, no.*"

More shadows scurried across the floor, only to stop dead in their tracks as a flash of lightning filled the room. Guessing the fight between Alexander and Chandra wasn't going well. Too bad I didn't have time to look for myself, but now I knew why Stephan took out Gabriel first. Light and shadow magic didn't mix.

Still, I had a few cards to play. Indigo flames crawled up my arm to burn brightly. While it wouldn't stop the attacks, it'd lesson their impact and allow me to dispel it at will. As if he knew what I had in mind, he rushed me then stopped short, dropped low, and swept my legs out from under me.

I landed on my ass and he was on top of me in a second. His mailed fists hammered against my facemask. The first snapped my nose. I felt the skin along my cheek bone slice open with the next. Another caused me to see stars. I grabbed hold of his arm and turned up the heat. He screamed and jumped off me, waving his arm around as the metal vanished. Sluggishly, I got to my feet, and let my facemask vanish so I could set my nose.

Stephan looked at his arm with my handprint burned into it. "That was rude."

"Seriously?" I flung the blood on my fingers onto the floor. "That's all you've got to say?"

Our armor reappeared then he charged me. He speared me in the gut with his shoulder, lifted, and slammed me into the machine he'd worked on earlier. He flung me to the floor. "Thought you'd be—more, somehow."

He raised his boot to squash my skull, but I rolled to the side to kick him between his ribs and pelvis. He lost his balance and hit the stone. I spun around to put my boot into the back of his head. I held out my hand and the onyx gladius appeared in my hand.

Stephan rolled to his feet and laughed as a round shield formed on one arm and a long silver blade in the other. "Thank you for making this entertaining. You'd be surprised how few people wish to have a good sword fight these days. It's becoming a lost art."

Goddamn it. This was supposed to intimidate the guy. But no, the dude was getting off on it. Where in the fuck did he come from, anyway?

"Really?"

He grinned. "Yes."

Stephan brought up his shield arm and slowly advanced. Concerned, I stepped back and walked counterclockwise. He simply pivoted with each step, steadily closing the distance between us. Since my chains hadn't bothered the man in the slightest, I wasn't sure what the sword was going to do. There wasn't any place to run and by the sounds of things, Chandra and Alexander were tearing shit up. Only problem there, I couldn't spare a moment to look around to make sure he was okay.

Stephan rushed the last few steps with his sword out in an attempt to skewer me. I batted the blade aside and sent a chunk of ice into his back foot, causing him to stumble. Taking advantage of the opening, I brought the gladius down, but he blocked it with his shield. Odd thing happened in that moment...my blade dug into the metal and Stephan cried out in pain.

He dropped then rolled to the side to put distance between us before getting to his feet. Obviously, he'd been just as stunned by the gladius as I'd been. Good news...I could hurt the guy. The bad...my sword skills, while not too shabby, wouldn't keep me above ground with someone who had several thousand years of expertise behind them. I wasn't about to roll over and die here, but this was going to be tough.

His facemask vanished as he inspected the shield then gave me a worried look. "Where'd you get that blade?"

"Does it matter?"

He shook his head. "Not really."

Slowly, he stalked toward me. The moment he was within range, he brought his blade up at an angle. I blocked with the gladius. A brilliant light blinded me as the impact of the resounding shockwave lifted me off my feet and slammed me into the far wall. At nearly the same moment, a meaty metallic thud hit across the room. I groaned as I slid to the floor. My vision cleared in record time and I got to my feet before he did.

Sparing a moment, I glanced over to see a bloody Chandra and an equally messed up Alexander. While he was holding his own, I was about to get my ass handed to me. By the time I turned back to

Stephan, he was on his feet. Shadows danced around him, skidded around the walls and across the floor and ceiling.

Guess he was finished playing games.

I coated the floor, ceiling, and walls with a sheet of flaming ice about three feet around me in every direction. The darkness hovered just beyond the light. Stephan growled and hurled a bolt of malignant energy my way. It slammed into my chest, lifting me off my feet, pushing my back into the wall and shattering the ice and stone there. Still, the flames held the shadows at bay.

He stomped my way with his sword at the ready.

I hurled several balls of ice at his ankles in the hope of tripping him, but he simply danced out of the way. Stepping forward, I brought the gladius up under his shield arm to slice through the armor there, causing the shield to vanish. I shuffled forward a bit to kick out to the side, catching him in the knee. While it didn't snap it, his leg did bend weirdly as he hobbled back. Black blood dripped onto the stone floor from the wound just past his wrist.

He lowered his hand. The blood covered his metal glove and he hurled flames at me. I'd dealt with enough blood magic to know that shit wasn't good for my health, and I dove to the side. Thankfully, the intensity of the inferno caused the shadow magic to dissipate. It also burned away every last scrap of ice, destroying my safety zone.

New shadows reached out of the floor to pull me flat. Stephan stalked over to stand over me.

His armor vanished and he smiled. "Time to die."

No way I was going out like this. Indigo flames laced with gold wrapped around me to burn through the darkness in an instant. With a thought, the flames shot up to catch him in the chest, lifting him off his feet and knocking him halfway across the room. I rolled to my feet in an instant. Hurrying after him, I coated the floor with burning ice as he skidded to a halt near the black gooey material in the open manhole in the floor.

Fear registered in his eyes as he glanced between me and the machine just out of reach. He stretched out his hand and a shadow flicked it on. The moment the creepy face appeared, he dove headfirst into the ichor and vanished along with the entity that'd been there. He was gone and there wasn't anything I could do about it.

Alexander, however, could use a hand. Hopefully, Gabriel would wake up from his nap in the near future and jump in to let us put an end to this madness. Until then, it was time for me to wade into the fray.

Chandra was wrapped in malignant gray shadows. Fire bathed her one hand and electricity the other. There were several claw marks across her face, arm, and abdomen. Sadly, none of them appeared to be lethal. Even worse news came in the form that they were healing at an accelerated rate. Alexander, however, wasn't.

That was a bullshit move on her part.

She threw a bolt of lightning at Alexander, forcing him to dive to the side while putting distance between them. Her gaze tracked around the room, bypassing me once as she continued to search for Stephan. Not finding him, she took a couple steps back, trying to angle herself toward the stairs while keeping the two of us in her view.

Circling around, I cut off her means of escape as she hurled a ball of flame my way. I brought up a wall of ice between us. The moment the flames hit it, pain shot through me as it tried to tear through the barrier. It barely held. The hag was using blood magic. That crap was bad on a good day and this wasn't anywhere near close to being a decent one.

Alexander took the opportunity to rush her, only to be met with a torrent of lightning to the chest. It lifted him off the floor and slammed him into the stone wall with a nasty crunch. Were's were tough by nature, but I wasn't sure how much more he could take. Hell, if I'd been hit with that much blood magic, it might kill me outright. Still, Alexander pushed himself to his feet as his chest smoldered. The scent of charred meat hung in the air.

Taking a page out of Heather's book, I formed a thin sheet of ice stretching from ceiling to floor then exploded it toward the woman. The flame tornado she created destroyed most of the slivers of ice, but there were a few that got through, slicing through her face, forearm, and leg. She cried out as she hobbled back against the stone for support.

I was starting to see why Viktor failed to kill the woman on their last meeting. Lifting my left hand, I sent a column of indigo fire hurtling for her chest as I snaked a few shadowy chains around to either side, hoping to catch her if she was able to evade the blast.

She stumbled to the right. The chains wrapped around her legs and arm, tugging her to the ground. She screamed in frustration as her whole body lit up in a crimson glow. Pain surged through the chains and I was forced to remove them.

Chandra righted herself to hurl a solid crimson beam toward my skull and another at Alexander's chest. I dove to the side, barely avoiding the thing as it tore a basketball sized hole through the bedrock behind me. I glanced into the depths to see that she'd dug out a channel at least a dozen meters deep. By the time I turned back to her, it was too late to stop the woman from flipping the machine on.

To my great relief, the skeletal face didn't reappear. Then a cold dread struck me as the SS helmet formed. Slowly, the cyborg Nazi armor Stephan wore reappeared. This time, though, there was something more to him. His rather plain looking facemask broke into a toothy smile and the crimson visor split into two demonic eyes. It lasted for all of maybe a millisecond before it vanished.

The sword in my hand was replaced by the scythe as I darted toward him. Stephan fell back as I brought it down, missing him by a fraction of an inch. Unfortunately, the blade plunged into the still active pool.

I knew something was wrong when it dug into the liquid there. Power rushed through me. Stephan darted toward Chandra. Gabriel picked up Alexander, half helping, half carrying the man toward me.

"No—"

The word wasn't fully out of my mouth when the room tore itself apart and the shockwave took us all off our feet. Screams of terror, thunder, and even what might be the voice of God cut through the area. The scythe vanished and the world of unconsciousness took me in that instant.

23

I couldn't see. The stench of charred meat filled my nostrils. A horrible ringing noise filled my ears. All I could taste was blood. The tinging in my ears began to fade, replaced with rolling thunder that shook the world around me. Cold stabbed through my flesh and bones as rain pounded down on my broken form. My body refused to move as bones began to right themselves and fuse back together. I screamed. Eventually, my sight returned. Not that it mattered as I was face down in something meaty and cold.

Blood continued to pour out of my nose and mouth to coat the thing below me.

More explosions, thunder, and fighting filtered through the haze. There was still a lot of fighting going on and here I was, laying down on the job. Chandra and Stephan were likely close by. Hopefully, the same could be said for Alexander and Gabriel.

"Gavin." Gabriel's voice trembled. "You okay?"

Turning my head to the side, I coughed and spat out blood. "I think I'll live. Where's Alexander."

Silence reigned for several seconds as a belt buckle came into focus. I was lying atop someone very dead.

Gabriel grabbed hold of my shoulders. "Everything's fine...you'll be okay."

He didn't answer my question. As he lifted me, I got a good look at the broken form I'd been laying on...it was Alexander. A circular hole was punched through his chest...he hadn't dodged Chandra's blast. His face was scorched, and his limbs lay at weird angles.

No. This wasn't right. Fuck that.

Indigo flames tinged with gold wrapped around me, forcing Gabriel to release me. A drop of blood fell, caught on fire, then hit Alexander. The gore there flared to life and a brilliant column of fire dropped out of the sky to slam into the corpse, obscuring it from sight for several seconds. The flames flashed out from the center to travel across the open ground then vanished. Shadows coalesced on the spot where Alexander lay then there was a blood curdling scream, quickly followed by a roar that shook the bedrock.

Kur swam to the forefront of my mind. *"Oh, God. What have you done?"*

"Huh?" I didn't understand the accusation. *"What's wrong?"*

He shivered. *"You've lost yourself in your grief."*

"Could you please make some sort of sense."

Then his words from New Mexico echoed through my mind. *'Such is the power of a Reaper's blood...it is able to give or take life depending on the intent.'*

Long claws coated in green energy tore through the shadows to reveal Alexander in full werebear transition, but he was bigger than normal, and power rolled off him in waves. He jumped to his feet, looked through me and Gabriel, then sniffed the air. Lifting his muzzle to the sky, he let out a deafening roar and the night went still.

All the fighting ceased, the rain stopped falling, and even the thunder fell quiet. A half second later, several roars sounded throughout the night. None were as fearsome, or voluminous, or in any way comparatively the same, yet to him, it meant something, and he bounded off into the night.

Gabriel yanked me to my feet. "What the hell was that?"

"Honestly, I don't know."

His gaze tracked over me. "You able to walk?"

I tested my legs to see that they'd hold my weight and nodded. "Yeah… I think so."

"Good." He pointed in the direction Alexander ran and where the screaming was now coming from. "We should catch up and maybe see if he's in his right mind, since I'm almost certain he was dead a few minutes ago."

If I had to guess, he wasn't. "Not sure how fast I'll be, but go on and I'll catch up."

Gabriel glanced around and frowned. "You do realize this is more or less a free for all, right?"

"Yes, but I can handle myself." I shrugged. "Not entirely sure I can catch up with Alexander in his current state. You, however, can."

Golden light blazed to life as his wings unfolded. "Fine…when I catch up, I'll try to calm him down, but you'll need to be right behind in case I fail."

"Yeah, I'm coming."

With that, he took to the air and sped out into the darkness. It didn't take long before I lost him behind the next building. I took a tentative step and nearly fell but steadied myself on a nearby broken wall outside Stephan's shack. Moving closer, I looked down to find a gaping hole inside where the floor should be. The third level looked mostly intact, but everything above was simply gone.

I had no idea where Stephan and Chandra were off to. A horrified scream cut through the night and the rain began to pour once more. While the water made me feel slightly better, it also left me drenched. Even without the random screaming, following Alexander wouldn't be difficult. Massive claw marks were dug into the pavement, grass, and walls where he'd passed through in what looked to be quite a hurry.

Where the hell was he going and why? You'd think being dead would slow you down a bit. Hell, I was plenty alive and moving like an old man who'd forgotten his walker. Everything from the soles of my feet to the actual hair on my head hurt. While this wasn't the worst thing I'd experienced, it was up there.

I made my way around the first corner and came to an abrupt halt. In front of me was a pair of boots. Beyond that, blood, guts, and flesh covered the ground. Whoever this'd been was hit so hard that their body simply exploded from the impact. There were bits of gray coveralls in the mix, which meant it'd been one of the necromancers, but at the speed Alexander was traveling, I wasn't sure he'd be able to tell the difference between enemy and friend.

Giving the area a wide berth, I continued on my way. On the next street I found four more dead. One had her rib cage torn open and her internal organs were missing. The next, a male, had a hole that went through his sternum and out his back. Another had a massive portion of their face and skull missing. I'd love to say it was due to a swipe of one of Alexander's clawed hands, but it wasn't. Judging by the teeth marks, he'd simply bitten off the side of the man's face. The last victim had been ripped apart. His arms and legs were removed, the latter of which had been used to beat the man into a near paste-like substance.

All right, it was official. Alexander wasn't in his right mind and I wasn't sure we could stop him in his current state.

What in the name of God had I done?

Kur wriggled in my mind. *"I'm not sure, but it's upset the natural balance."*

"What do you mean?"

"Look for yourself." He sighed. *"Were's have always been an anomaly but this...this is insanity."*

As much as I wanted to argue with him, he was right. *"Perhaps...let's just find him and stop him before he hurts himself or someone that isn't a necromancer."*

Panic sounded in his voice. *"Then move."*

Great...my invisible dragon was having an anxiety attack.

Picking up the pace, I rounded the corner onto the main thoroughfare and came to an abrupt halt. Across the street staring at me was Chandra's second, Monica, with a dozen of her nearest and dearest friends right behind her. She made a gesture and her people fanned out to either side.

Narrowing her eyes, she slowly stepped forward. "Gavin Randall." She shook her head and sighed. "I'm guessing this is your doing."

Oh shit.

I wobbled my hand back and forth. "More or less." Thumbing over my shoulder, I said, "Look, can we skip the whole trying to kill me thing and go straight to the part where you surrender?"

Shock and amusement crossed Monica's expression. "Are you fucking kidding me?" She glanced around her. "Are you so fucking arrogant you think you can take us all on your own?"

"See, this is where you've got to get a clue." Maybe this bluff would work better than my last. "I made a similar offer to Stephan and Chandra. They turned me down and are no longer in the picture. Understand?"

Monica wasn't fazed, but those standing with her were visibly shaken.

She snorted. "That's what you're going with?" Waving a hand up and down at me, she sniggered. "Look at you…you're a fucking mess. Covered in blood, barely able to walk…I mean, that was what you were trying to do with that weird mismatched hobble you were doing, right?"

I didn't answer.

"My guess is you've somehow escaped the death blow and are running to your friends in the hopes that'll save your ass." She shook her head. "News flash, you're never going to make it."

I tried to summon my armor, but it didn't quite come in as intended. The older black and blue version appeared from the neck down. Indigo flames wrapped around my left hand and the gladius appeared in the other.

"Want to test that theory?"

Monica stepped forward. "Actually, I do."

The others were a little less convinced. Nevertheless, they readied themselves for battle. A man on the far end hurled a bolt of lightning at me as Monica stalked toward me, her own cyborg Nazi armor forming around her. What the man intended to be a single attack wouldn't stop. His power seeped into my bones at an accelerated rate.

Monica took two more steps then the first of her people died as I pulled the last of the life energy out of him.

She tugged a gun off her hip and fired. I stepped to the side. The bullet grazed my shoulder, cutting through my armor as something dark and malevolent coated the outside of the projectile.

What the actual fuck? How were they able to fuse magic—likely blood magic—with standard weaponry? This little wrinkle made things significantly more dangerous.

With a thought, ice formed in the barrel of the weapon. She pulled the trigger again, causing the slide to catch as the barrel exploded. Monica screamed as she tossed the ruined piece of metal aside and shook away the pain.

Her followers stepped forward as they sported the same cyborg Nazi armor.

Just where in the fuck were they getting this shit from?

The boost I'd gotten from the first guy wasn't going far. Now, with Monica and her eleven douchey friends, this was going to turn into a very long night. Worst part, Alexander was still running around out there on his own, killing folks as he went. I needed to end this quickly and get back to what was important.

I lifted my hand and called down a column of fire atop the three men grouped together on the side. With a flick of my wrist, two large jagged pieces of ice cut through the woman to the left of Monica. When the flames died, the three were little more than charcoal statues of themselves. The exertion left me winded and my knees weak. Thing was, she still had seven more flunkies to throw at me and I was running out of gas.

Monica gave me space to tend to her injured hand. Two of the larger males stomped past her with their swords out. I stepped to the side, trying to angle them so that one was behind the other. Pushing forward, I struck out with the gladius, piercing the man's arm at the elbow and into his gut. His friend yanked him free as he lunged forward, his blade aimed for my heart. I deflected the blow and brought my sword around to lop off his forearm.

A massive fireball exploded at my feet. The grass charred black and the ground itself turned to magma. With a thought, a dome of ice formed beneath me just as a torrent of wind slapped me across the face. I lost my balance, hit the ice, and skidded several feet before coming to a stop on the pavement.

A monolithic stone shot through the asphalt, clipping me in the shoulder. The impact lifted me into the air as I spun about helplessly. Another gust slammed me into the pavement. Multiple ribs broke. My leg and arm were shattered. In short, they were whipping my ass and I couldn't even get a word in edgewise. On the plus side, my healing ability was out of this world for some weird reason. The only negative came in the form of the pain of everything righting itself.

A low rumble came from the earth below me. I shuffled back just as another giant spike came out of the pavement meant to skewer me. Rolling to the side, I got to my feet, created a thin sheet of ice, and hurled it toward the man manipulating the earth. He never saw it coming as it sliced through the bridge of his nose, then his eyes, and out the back of his skull, bisecting it in an instant and stopping the madness.

Focusing on the woman who stood next to him, I clenched my fist and froze her lungs solid. A massive wall of fire erupted between me and those that remained upright. Indigo flames wrapped around me. I appeared behind the man conjuring fire and slipped my blade through the back of his neck. With a nasty yank, I removed his head from his shoulders. I spared a glance to the side to see the man I'd given the gut wound was also on the ground. He wasn't dead but he wasn't long for this world. His friend that was missing part of his arm was in slightly better shape but didn't have any fight left in him.

That left two plus Monica.

A soggy footstep pulled me out of my thoughts. I turned and barely blocked the sword strike meant to decapitate me. The woman pressed forward with all her strength and grinned. That was when a boot caught me in the back of the knee, sending me to the ground. As I fell, indigo flames wrapped around me and I appeared a few feet away and stood. Creating three massive icicles, I forced them forward.

One skewered the woman and the other two the man. They both dropped to the ground quite dead.

Breathing heavily, I dropped to my knees. All the power I'd used to heal and defend myself made my bones ache.

"Goddamn it." Monica stepped into view, pulled a second gun, and aimed it at me. "You're a real piece of shit." She gestured at the dead. "Do you have any idea how long it took me to train those assholes?"

I pointed at her. "What's with the getup?"

She puffed out her chest and grinned. "Like it?"

"No, not at all." I shivered. "Seems like a throwback to an era best forgotten."

Monica beamed. "It's a gift from Dvalinn. Those of us who serve at his right hand have been blessed with the armor of the chosen."

The woman was insane, but I let her keep yapping because I needed to catch my breath. "Ever stopped to think it looks a bit like Nazi armor?"

She shrugged. "Where do you think they got the idea?"

Well fuck.

"Wait, Hitler was one of yours?"

Rolling her eyes, she sneered. "No...but one of the architects of the Reich was a big fan of Stephan's and chose to honor him by fashioning the Nazi uniforms after this." She waved her injured hand at herself. "Not like it'll matter to you in a few seconds."

I held up a finger. "Don't do anything hasty. I mean, my offer still stands. You can surrender and you might live through this."

"Are you a special type of stupid?" She cocked her head to the side. "You're dead and you're still trying to negotiate?"

Slowly, I got to my feet. "Lady, I've had about enough of your shi—"

In that instant, several things happened.

Alexander dropped out of the night sky, landing with a massive thud behind her. Monica squeezed the trigger as he slapped the side of her head, his claws digging into her face and tearing through her forehead, cheek, and mouth, killing her instantly. The bullet, while off track, still hurtled through the air as I brought up a wall of ice and lurched to the side. The slug ripped through the weakened structure, tumbled, and tore through my shoulder.

My entire being became a holy shrine that worshiped anguish and agony. My muscles seized. I couldn't breathe, scream, or even whimper. Time slowed to a near stop as I pirouetted from the impact. Unable to correct myself, I lost my balance and fell. The rain kept pace with me as I collapsed to the ground. Water, mud, and blood splashed underneath my shoulder as I bounced off the manicured lawn.

Pain leeched through me as my eyes fluttered of their own accord. My heart slowed and cold seeped into my bones.

Thunk, thunk. Thunk…thunk.

I was dying from what should've been a flesh wound.

Thunk.

How was this possible?

Thunk.

What was happening to me? Why wasn't I healing?

Thunk.

A massive roar from Alexander deafened me as he rolled me onto my side. He took one of his clawed fingers and shoved it through the wound. Pain and agony coursed through me, starting my heart again.

Thunk.

Alexander rummaged around inside me for several more seconds then the pain began to subside as he pulled his finger out. He slapped his nails together and held something in front of me. It was a small sliver of black metal… a fragment of the bullet Monica hit me with.

He swayed and fell forward, landing hard atop me. My vision darkened and I joined him in the realm of blissful unconsciousness.

24

August 28th

Gasping for air, I woke with a start. I glanced around the room to find myself in my own bed. The closed drapes cloaked the room in darkness. Shivering, I sat up and placed my feet on the hardwood. I expected the door to open but it didn't.

Weird.

It took me a moment to realize the horrid stench was coming from me. How long had I been here? I reached over and picked up my mobile. August 28th, 4:30 a.m. Apparently, five days and some change. Had we won? How many casualties had we suffered? I could get the answers to those questions and many others after getting cleaned up.

Tentatively, I stood. My muscles were weak, tired, or both. Taking a deep breath, I bent my knee, slid my foot forward a few inches, and stopped. Then I did the other. After what seemed like a small eternity, I made it into the bath and turned on the water. Not waiting for it to warm up, I shuffled into the shower.

Each droplet cascaded over my flesh, sending a tiny charge of energy through my body. My heart thudded against my chest and the memory of Alexander coming out of nowhere to save my life swam into the forefront of my mind.

I reached out to Kur. *"Hey, you all right?"*

A ragged voice came out of the depths of my mind. *"No, but I'll survive. Much like you, I have some healing to do."*

"Blood magic can harm you?"

He let out a low growl. *"That wasn't blood magic."*

"Then what?"

"Those bullets were created from an alloy from the Svartálfar realm." Anger coursed through him. *"I'm not sure how long they've been importing it, but they couldn't have gotten that much given the gate could only stay open for maybe thirty seconds."*

I leaned my forehead against the tile. *"Well, we closed it, so they won't be getting any more through there."*

Kur relaxed. *"That's true...but there's a possibility they could open another gate somewhere else within the realm and start over again."*

"Wonderful." I paused. *"Hey, I hate to be an asshole, but do you know if Alexander and the other centurions survived?"*

He was quiet for a second. *"Alexander is alive and close by...as for the rest of that question...I don't know. Given our current condition, we're a bit on the fritz here."*

Damn. *"Anything specific causing problems or just being hurt?"*

"Our injuries aren't helping, but most of the interference is coming from Alexander." He grunted in pain. *"And before you ask, I don't know why."*

"We'll figure it out shortly."

After cleaning up, I turned off the faucet and proceeded to dry myself. The hole in my shoulder was fully healed. Other than a bright red patch of skin, you wouldn't even know anything had happened. Interesting. It seems this alloy could kill me, but it didn't leave a mark after it was gone. Good to know, I guess.

Unfortunately, I hadn't been bright enough to bring clean clothes with me, so I hobbled into the bedroom. I grabbed a pair of jeans and button up shirt as lifting my hands over my head wasn't going to happen.

I was tying my boot when the door pushed open to reveal Andrew and Harold standing there.

Leaning to the side, I looked for Heather. "Morning, gentlemen."

Harold stepped in. "Morning. You all right?"

"Been better." I shrugged. "But you know that I've been worse as well."

That'd come out a bit harsher than intended.

Harold winced. "Yeah...I know...but—"

"—Sorry, didn't mean it that way." I sighed. "Just tired."

Andrew stepped in and gave me a mechanical smile. "You able to make it to your office?"

That didn't bode well. "I think so." Standing up, I gestured them ahead. "Everything all right?"

Harold produced an onyx stone about the size of a golf ball. "Not even a little bit."

"What's that?"

Andrew grumbled. "Let's take a seat first. There's a lot to go over."

A few seconds later, I plopped into my chair while Andrew and Harold sat across from me. "Okay, what's with the stone?"

Harold's body tensed as he pointed at a box on the floor next to his seat. "Last year when you confronted Walter Percy, I've been told you acquired a literal horde of stones from deceased Stone Borns."

"True, but those were confiscated...and are sort of dead now."

He nodded as he leaned over and pushed back the lid. "Right." There were a number of glass-like clicks as he rummaged around in the box. Eventually, he sat up and placed several glowing stones in front of me. "Do you know what these are?"

They looked like the things powering Stephan's freaky gate machine. "Some type of enchanted gemstone?"

Andrew wobbled his hand back and forth. "Close." He gestured at the stones. "These used to belong to living Stone Borns."

I blinked. "Wait...like the creepy collection Walter had?"

Harold glanced over at Andrew, who nodded.

"We think." Harold hesitated. "What you found wasn't a trophy room so much as a storage center meant to be utilized later by the Black Circle. For what purpose, we have no idea."

A sharp pain shot through my skull. "I think I do." I slammed my fist against the desktop. "We...Gabriel, Alexander, and I, saw stones like this being used to power the machine they were using to create the gate for Dvalinn."

They both froze.

Andrew leaned forward and placed his elbows on his knees. "You're sure about that?"

"I am."

Harold sighed. "That's truly unfortunate. Sort of blows my theory."

"And what was that?"

He picked up a large diamond. "There are glyphs here used to resurrect." Grabbing another, he pointed. "This has ones that heal." Disappointment sounded in his voice. "The others have different types of enchantments on them…none of them say to open a gate, though."

Kur whispered, *"Perhaps the stones have multiple uses."*

"Ever stop to think that they could be used for that too? I mean, there were maybe a dozen machines down there. Meaning they probably used the same amount of stones. You'd think they'd have other uses if they had a vault full of those things."

Andrew nodded. "Could be." He stole a cautious glance over at Harold. "Maybe that'd explain what Gabriel said about Alexander."

I flinched. "Uh…no."

"What's that supposed to mean?"

My cheeks burned. "We were below ground fighting Stephan and Chandra. She created these weird beams that cut through the wall. It narrowly missed me but caught Alexander. She turned on the machine and Stephan came through…to prevent anything else from escaping, I sank the scythe into it. That's when things blew up." Not knowing what else to say, I went with the truth as I knew it. "A little while later, I woke up atop Alexander's corpse. Somehow, my blood triggered something that brought him back to life."

Harold blinked. "Didn't know that was possible."

Kur swam to the forefront of my mind. *"It's rare but not impossible. The conditions have to be right and the person being revived has to be able to survive the resurrection. It's also left you weakened, temporarily unable to repeat the act for years or centuries or possibly, never again."*

"It is...just hard on me. Not something I can repeat for a while, if ever." I shook my head. "I hadn't meant to do it this time...it was an accident and one that I hope Alexander can forgive me for."

Andrew gave me a sad smile. "He's recovering...slowly. We found the two of you as we were securing the village."

"So, we accomplished our goal?"

Harold nodded. "We did. A lot of good people died along the way, but we were able to secure the facility." Sighing, he said, "We're sifting through the records to figure out what they were doing there...but that'll take some time."

"I see."

Andrew took a deep breath and slowly let it out. "It's been a rough week since the attack."

"How so?"

He leaned back in his seat. "You and Alexander being unconscious...we had to charter a plane to fly you back since you can't use the gates."

Harold frowned. "A fact we'd all forgotten about until we got there."

Andrew grimaced. "Then there's Vasile. He's been chomping at the bit wanting to see you, but every time he gets to town, he passes out due to some sort of massive headache."

"So that's caused some issues in the park." Harold picked up. "Then there's the whole Lazarus problem. He's been losing his shit for the last several days, threatening everyone he talks to with summary execution if we don't bring you to him."

"Fuck that asshole." I leaned forward in my seat. "He and I need a long overdue conversation about how things are going to work from here on out." My voice turned hard. "It doesn't bode well for him in the slightest." Glancing around the room, I asked, "Where is everyone else?"

Andrew grinned. "If you mean Heather and Kim, they're at Henri's house tending to his and Gabriel's wounds." He glanced at his watch. "They should be here shortly. I called them when Alexander woke."

Harold smiled. "They'll be thrilled you're awake."

"I'm fairly happy about it myself." A sinking feeling festered in the pit of my stomach. "How long ago did Alexander wake?"

Harold shrugged. "Maybe forty-five minutes ago?"

Henri's place was maybe a five-minute drive from here. "Shouldn't they be here by now?"

Andrew blinked. "Well…yeah…maybe they're downstairs checking on Alexander."

That didn't feel right.

I picked up my phone and hit Heather's number. It went straight to voicemail. "Uh…Andrew, try Kim."

He did then looked at me. "It went to voicemail."

Scrolling through, I hit Henri's number.

He picked up on the first ring. "Gavin?"

"Yeah—"

"—Holy shit, you're alive." He yelled out. "Gabriel, Gavin's awake!"

Aggravated, I said, "Hey, I'm fine…where's Heather and Kim?"

"Huh?" He stammered. "What do you mean? They're at you're place."

Harold jumped to his feet. "Be right back."

He bolted out the door and his footsteps hammered down the stairs.

"Would you mind checking the driveway?"

"Sure." Henri grunted and a few footfalls later, he spoke. "Kim's car is gone."

"Thanks. I'll call you back."

I ended the call and got to my feet.

Harold called up the stairs. "They're not here."

Glancing over at Andrew, I said, "Sit tight."

The thought of being where Heather was filled my mind, but the indigo flames didn't come. I tried again with Kim as the target. Indigo flames enveloped me. I found myself a few blocks away. Kim's car was trashed. The middle of her bumper was where the engine should be. The windshield was in the middle of the street and Kimberly was unconscious but alive in the grass at the side of the road. She was bloody and banged up, but she'd live. Taking her in my arms, I returned to my office.

Glaring at Harold, I said, "Call Baptist and ask him to pick up Kim's car...it's on the corner of Pitt." I turned my attention to Andrew. "Is Keto here?"

He blinked. "Uh...yes...I think so...we called him—"

"—Don't care, get him up here now." I nodded out the door. "We'll be in my bedroom."

I hurried through the hall and laid her on the bed.

My phone rang.

Henri.

I answered. "Found Kim. There's been an accident or maybe retaliation. Heather is missing. Get over here but be careful about it."

Not waiting for an answer, I hung up.

Keto burst into the room. "Good to see you, Mr. Randall. Now, if you'll step aside, I've got a job to do."

So did I.

"You've got this, right?"

"I do." He opened her eyes with his fingers and shined a light in. "Please, let me work. I'll be in touch as soon as I know something."

"Okay." I stepped out into the hall and stopped Andrew from going in. "Keto's in there. I'm going back to the car to see if there's something there that'll tell me what happened to Heather."

Harold hurried out of my office. "Baptist is on the way."

"Tell him I'll meet him there."

Indigo flames wrapped around me again and I stood on the corner of Pitt as sirens cut through the early morning. Kim's car door was open, her seatbelt cut, and the airbags were deployed. The part that had my attention was the seatbelt. I doubted seriously that she'd cut it herself. I checked the passenger side to find a similar scenario. Save for the fact Heather wasn't anywhere to be found.

What the fuck was going on?

On the driver's side, I popped the trunk. Nothing but medical supplies and Triumvirate files. Thankfully, no dead body.

Circling around to the front of the vehicle, I knelt in front of the bumper. The divot there was angular...something hit them with significant force. If we were somewhere up north, I'd say a snowplow. This being New Orleans, that wasn't possible. Plus, anything metallic would've rubbed off onto the paint. That hadn't happened.

A cruiser screeched to a halt and Baptist stepped out of the passenger side. The driver's side opened to reveal an entirely unpleasant looking man whose nametag read J. Riggs.

Baptist hurried over. "What'd you find?"

"Other than an unconscious Kimberly Broussard?" I bit back my anger. "Nothing." Pointing at the bumper, I said, "Magic did this."

Riggs lumbered up beside us but didn't say anything.

Baptist sighed. "Where's Heather?"

"Can't find her." I glanced around the street, looking for a camera. "Any chance you've got this area under surveillance?"

Riggs snorted. "Not a chance." He gestured around at the houses. "Rich folks don't like us watching out for their best interest."

Baptist frowned. "He's not wrong."

"Goddamn it."

He gestured at me. "Can't you do your thing where you just appear next to her?"

"Tried, didn't work."

His mouth dropped open slightly. "Didn't realize that was possible."

"Neither did I."

Kur wriggled in my head. *"It's unlikely...but with the proper technology, she could be shielded. As you know, enchantments don't work on us, but if she's somewhere that's technologically advanced enough, that could do the trick. At least, that's my working theory concerning Vasile's home."*

"What do you mean?"

He cleared his throat. *"It's my guess that Vasile has something from his mother that prevents us from appearing next to him."*

"Damn it." I pushed down the despair growing in my soul. "Thanks."

Riggs leaned over. "He okay?"

Baptist nodded. "Probably just thinking."

"I am." I pointed at the trunk. "Nothing back there of importance. I need to get Vasile down here."

Baptist shook his head. "No, don't do that. Every time he shows up, he passes out." He sighed. "The only cure is getting him out of the city. If you're needing someone to track Heather, maybe try Dean."

"Could you call him?" I grimaced. "I want to get back to Kim… when she wakes up, maybe she can tell me what the fuck is happening."

"We've got this." He tapped my arm. "Call me when she wakes up."

"I will." I held out my hand toward Riggs. "Pleasure to meet you. Thanks for helping out."

He hesitated for a moment then took my hand. "You're welcome."

I let go, stepped back, and allowed the indigo flames to envelope me.

Thirty long minutes later, Kim came to…screaming. "No. Leave her—" She glanced around the room, realizing she wasn't in the car any longer. "Where's Heather?"

I shook my head. "No idea. I was hoping you could tell us."

Fury burned in her eyes and hate coated her tone. "Then Lazarus has her."

"I'm sorry?"

It took her a minute to recount what happened. They'd left Henri's about ten minutes after the call telling them Alexander was awake. They'd cut over to St. Charles to pick up a burger for him before heading our way. Then, out of nowhere, Lazarus appeared in the middle of the street. Kimberly slammed on her brakes then he threw something at them. The airbags deployed, causing her to see stars. Then he punched through Heather's window to drag her out of the passenger side. Kimberly tried to stop him, but he hit her with something to knock her out.

"What in the hell is wrong with that man?" Rage filled me and everyone took a step back. "I'm going to kill him…I was going to do it anyway, but now…it's going to hurt."

Harold held out his hands. "Could you please turn that down a bit. The rest of us want to see the sunrise."

Alexander burst into the room looking like hell. "What's going on?"

Forcing calm, I said, "Lazarus has Heather."

His knees gave out, but Andrew caught him. "Easy there. You're still healing."

"I'll be fine."

I put a hand on his shoulder. "Heal up first, then you can help. Right now, you look—"

"—Like warmed over death?" He grinned. "It's okay…I'll be fine." Wincing, he staggered back to sit in the chair at Heather's vanity. "Just need some time…I guess."

"Take all you need." I hesitated then asked the question I wasn't sure I wanted the answer to. "Why are you up here?"

His gaze hit the floor. "I…could feel you were upset and well, you needed help."

Goddamn it. "I'll be fine. You just need to relax and heal."

"Sure thing."

I glanced over at Andrew and Harold. They helped him to his feet and walked him back down the stairs to his room.

I turned to Kimberly. "I'll find Lazarus then Heather, since the other option isn't open to me."

"What do you mean?"

I shook my head. "Long story."

Keto gently pushed her into a horizonal position. "Rest now. We'll handle things from here." He handed her a glass of water. "Drink this and take those two aspirin." He looked up at me and pointed at the door. "You need to leave now."

25

Someone, not sure who, had been kind enough to bring me lunch. I wasn't hungry but ate it anyway as to not be rude. Hayden once pointed out I didn't need to eat as my body would tend to itself. Thing was, it made the others feel better. I tried to teleport to Lazarus earlier but that turned out to be an abysmal failure. The flames came but I didn't go anywhere due to being pulled in multiple directions at once. I wasn't sure what that was about. Perhaps someone beat me to him and hacked the bastard into several pieces.

Didn't feel right but one could hope.

My phone dinged. Text message from Alfred.

Mind if we talk?

I got up and closed the door.

"Come on out. Maybe you can help me find this piece of shit."

Alfred appeared in the chair in front of my desk. "That's my hope."

I moved around and plopped into my seat. "Please tell me you've got something."

"Maybe." He chewed on his lip. "I need some additional data to narrow things down."

The way he said that made me uncomfortable. "What can I tell you that you can't get from the files?"

Getting to his feet, he pointed at me. "Tell me about the teleportation bubble you use. Is it mechanical or biological?"

"I can't see how that's relevant."

He shrugged. "Because it tells me how you're targeting your destination. If it's mechanical, it'd have to be programmed in and it'd help me exclude certain frequencies."

"Frequencies? What in the hell are you talking about?"

Alfred waved his hand and a large indigo ball appeared on the desk. It sat there for several seconds as it tried to move in multiple directions at once. "What you're seeing here is you…the sphere that's containing your form is trying to move in thirteen different directions at once." He grimaced. "That shouldn't be possible. Thus, the reason I need to know if the teleporter is mechanical or biological."

Honestly, I didn't know.

Kur tsked. *"It's neither, but biological will likely suffice as an answer."*

"If it's neither, then what is it?"

He shifted from one side of my skull to the other. *"No idea. It's almost as if your consciousness is tapped into something beyond this realm. You think of something and you're there. Simple as that. Distance—even other realms—wouldn't be a problem for you to traverse in an instant. I've only seen one other instance like it and that was controlled by the Mad God and Viktor toward the end…hell, it may've controlled them. I have no idea."*

"Let's say biological…sort of."

Alfred sighed. "I'm going to need you to be as specific as possible."

"I am." Shrugging, I said, "It's rather difficult to explain. I don't have any machinery in me that'd make that possible. And while I have nanites in my system, none of them are capable of teleporting me from place to place. That being said, I'm not sure that it's entirely genetic either."

He closed his eyes and slowly shook his head. "I can eliminate the mechanical…that'll help." Easing in closer, he touched the image of the indigo sphere. "Next, how do you target your destination?"

"That I can answer." I grinned. "As long as I've been to a location at some point in my life, it's accessible to me." Frowning, I said, "The one addendum to that requirement is if there's someone there that I have a strong bond with, either through the coins or personal relationship." I gestured at the image. "In this case, I was trying to find Lazarus."

Alfred paused. "Can you teleport across the room?"

I stood and crossed the room with a thought. "Does that help?"

"Sadly, no." His eyes glowed blue for a moment. "I mean, that gave me some readings but nothing that'll help me narrow things down, yet."

That sucked. "Sorry."

"Don't be. It was a long shot at best." Scratching the back of his head, he grimaced. "Maybe, if I had more information about Lazarus, I could work on the equation while compiling other data in the meantime that'll actually help."

At least he had a plan. "Okay, sure. What do you need to know?"

"Tell me about him."

I blinked. "Not sure I get what you mean."

"Well, everything I've read says he was brought back from the dead. Do you have any idea how that happened?"

I snorted. "Not specifically, no." Wait, what'd Dermot said. "I've got some general ideas but they're not fact."

Alfred gestured for me to continue. "At this point, I'm more than willing to take conjecture to help fill in the missing data."

"Fine…I recently found out that the man who had my position before me—"

He cut in. "Naevius Sutorius Marco."

"Right, him." I grimaced. "He'd been conditioned through blood magic and imbued with powers that weren't his own in order to have the strength to take up the coin." Shrugging, I said, "In theory, the same thing could've been done to Lazarus, only they went one step further by killing the man then bringing him back from the dead a few days later."

Alfred narrowed his eyes. "You sure he died?"

Kur's memory of the event flashed to the forefront of my mind. "Absolutely."

"If that's right then…you're saying that he was resurrected by the use of some sort of cosmic glitch perpetrated by what exactly?"

"Twelve followers of a powerful necromancer."

His eyes glowed again. "Could the necromancer in question have actually been one of the nine lich lords?"

"Maybe…I guess…it's possible. Why?"

He grinned. "That'd explain his massive bump in power, the necromancy and all the other shit too. Do you have any idea what species he was and what the twelve were?"

"Well, necromancer…possibly lich lord, vampire, sorcerer, witch, elemental, shaman, Stone Born, monk, possibly an angel…maybe multiples of the others." I rubbed my forehead. "As to what he was… Stone Born."

"Are you sure he was a Stone Born?"

Given the fact Talbis got his stone after I'd hit him with the scythe, yeah. "Without a doubt. Why?"

Alfred reached out and turned the image, studying it for several seconds. "Okay, I'll do my best to figure out the equations that'll help track him. In the meantime, I have other news."

"What's that?"

Another wave of his hand caused the sphere to vanish and a set of ancient blueprints to appear. "Apparently, someone's turned on the lights at Lazarus's place." He touched the drawings to create a three-dimensional rendering with several underground areas that glowed. "According to the satellite imaging, power consumption, and other boring shit…someone is on the fourth sublevel. Not entirely sure what they're doing, but it's sucking up a ton of electricity from the grid. It's caused a few brownouts in the area."

"Unbelievable." I clenched my fist. "That bastard went home."

Alfred shrugged. "Can't be one hundred percent sure, but it does look that way."

"Anything else?"

"A few things." He returned to his seat as the blueprints vanished. "The records from Waterford are encrypted with a cypher I'm not familiar with. Meaning, that'll take some time." His voice hardened. "Your people recovered thirteen bodies from the area you and Alexander were found in."

"That'd be Monica and her people."

He nodded. "Right. Anyway, they've been quarantined due to them having unusual qualities even after death."

Images of the dead appeared before me, each still armored, or partially so, with the cyborg Nazi gear. Their flesh was quickly deteriorating, and the armor had fused to the bones.

An uneasy feeling crept into my soul. "Where are they being held?"

"At an offline storage unit outside of Waterford." He winced. "They've taken the precaution of installing an old analog camera to watch over them."

I leaned in to get a better look. "Is it spreading?"

"It is."

Goddamn it. "Burn them...find a fire elemental and have them turn those things to ash." Leaning back, I said, "Then have the remains scooped up into a container and kept in a secure facility...without computer access."

"I'm on it." He shifted in his seat. "And to the weaponry they were using. It seems that the bullets in their guns are made from an unknown alloy not of this world. If I had to guess, it's not even of this realm."

"After being shot with one of those rounds I'm going to agree with you as I think it's from Svartálfar." I shivered. "That's some bad shit and we've got no idea how much the Black Circle has in reserve."

He grimaced. "Not sure if this is good or bad, but so far, no one has cataloged a cache of ammunition."

Not sure why they hadn't found it but hey, the less of that shit out there the better.

"Anything else?"

Alfred shook his head. "Nothing useful yet."

"If that changes, reach out." I got to my feet. "As for me, I think a trip to Rome is in order."

He gestured out the door. "You going to tell the others?"

"More or less." I sighed. "They'll know I'm out and that I'm looking for Lazarus, but I need to keep the rest close to the vest to find Heather."

Alfred's gaze hit the floor. "Has it occurred to you that she may not be amongst the living?"

"It has." Anger and sorrow fought for supremacy within my soul. "But if there's even a slight chance she's alive, I've got to do whatever it takes to get her back."

He gave me a sad smile. "I understand, I do. But I'd be remis if I didn't remind you that the very fabric of reality rests in the choices you make."

"Not sure that's entirely true." I shrugged. "Here's the thing about that logic. Let's say you're right and everything I do has a ripple effect on the future. Maybe my not going in search of Heather means that it all goes to shit. Ever think about that?"

Leaning back in his chair, he said, "It has occurred to me, yes."

"This grand design that's been put into motion cannot remain so if I'm inactive."

He pulled air in through his teeth. "That's also true…but doing anything terribly foolish and getting dead will fuck shit up too."

I rubbed my forehead. "True. Thing is, I've got to do what I think is best. Second guessing every move isn't something I'll do." Doing my best, I tried to keep my tone even. "This isn't meant the way it's going to sound." I locked my gaze onto his. "Your advice, knowledge, and everything that you are is super helpful. Thing is, this is my life and I need to live it. I've heard what you have to say, I get it, but there will be times, like this one, where I have to go on my gut. Does that make sense?"

He snickered. "It does. Doesn't mean I have to be comfortable with it. We've all sacrificed so much to get to this point." Holding out a hand, he said, "My comfort isn't that important. If we took the safe way, all those sacrifices wouldn't have been necessary." His tone softened. "My job is to advise. Yours is to do the best you can."

Alexander pushed the door open and hobbled over to a chair. "What he's trying to say is don't get dead, we need you."

I smiled. "Good to see you."

"And you." He readjusted himself in an attempt to get comfortable.

"Got a minute before you go do whatever madness you're about to attempt?"

Not sure I was ready for this conversation but sure, why not. "Absolutely, what's on your mind?"

"Where to start?" He gestured at himself. "Any idea why I'm here instead of laying in my bed downstairs?"

"Not a clue."

Alexander glanced over at Alfred. "You?"

He shifted on the spot. "Got an idea."

"Excellent." Alexander turned his attention to me. "Not sure what happened the other night. We were downstairs dealing with Chandra and Stephan. I got hit then everything blew up."

"Right…I got that much."

His voice dropped to a near whisper. "I died…There wasn't a bright light or any such bullshit. Just moving on beyond the veil. Then something pulled me back. My body healed. I transformed into my were form and we went for a jaunt." He sighed. "Even in that delirious state, I felt…you and that you were in trouble. On instinct, I stopped what I was doing and found you within seconds."

Oh, shit. "And earlier, I got angry and you came up stairs."

He nodded. "You're angry and afraid but you're still going to do something a little unwise…thus, I'm here."

"Yeah, but you're in no condition to help."

A bitter chuckle escaped his lips. "Tell me something I don't know." He gestured at himself. "I'm healing quicker than I should but even so, it'll be a few days before I'm back to normal, whatever that's going to be like."

"Sorry."

He shook his head. "Don't be. I wasn't done with this life yet."

Alfred winced. "About that."

Curious, I asked, "What?"

He glanced between us. "I've been going over his medical…bloodwork etcetera. While the others are going to tell you that everything is fine, and it is, there's more to it that they're not realizing."

Alexander leaned forward. "Such as?"

"For starters, that new healing factor you have. That's not going away if I had to guess." His tone turned professorial. "It's my theory that your normal lifespan has been altered significantly and that Gavin's blood has created a strange bond between you that'll go until he dies."

"You mean until I die." Alexander snorted. "He's a Stone Born after all, which is like saying he's immortal unless he's killed somehow."

My heart sank.

Alfred hesitated. "No, I mean until he dies. I need to conduct some further tests to be sure, but that immortality thing is now something you'll have to deal with. If the simple blood tests they've run so far are any indicator, you've stopped aging. Your healing ability is off the chart and there's an empath type bond between you. In short, you're both forever linked to one another."

Alexander's eyes widened. "You're saying that I'll still be here in a thousand years."

Alfred pointed at me. "If he is, yes."

"What about my children?"

Alfred's gaze hit the floor. "Your friends, children, loved ones, etcetera will age normally, passing beyond the veil before you. It's a curse that the Stone Borns have always lived with."

Alexander's shoulders slumped forward and a deep sadness settled into his eyes. "I'll have to watch them die?"

Neither of us said anything.

Tears ran down his face. "My people will leave me." He glanced up at me. "How do you cope with that?"

"One day at a time." I walked around and took a knee in front of him. "I'm truly sorry."

He sniffed. "It's okay. We'll meet the future together." Getting to his feet, he said, "I've got a lot to think about. Don't get dead in the meantime...I'll cover for you with the others."

"Thanks."

Alexander shuffled to the door and closed it behind him.

26

It was shortly after sunset by the time I arrived in Rome. Surprisingly, the only thing left of Lazarus's home, on the surface anyway, was a pile of bricks. Since the last set of photos were taken, someone had demolished three of the still standing walls to more or less level the place. It may've been the city for safety reasons but, no matter how you sliced it, the roads were open and a lot of people were standing around gawking at the rubble.

Getting into the property through the main entrance without being spotted in the first three seconds was going to be difficult. So, plan B it was. According to Andrew, they'd escaped via a tunnel a few blocks over that lead to a basement where the gate was located. Most of the floor had caved in, sealing off the rest of the house. Thing was, it'd get me closer to my objective than waiting out here.

I crossed over two blocks, found an old Roman sewer gate, and slipped inside. Thankfully, the city no longer used these tunnels for the local residents' waste. Unfortunately, the corridor was still full of trash, dirt, and general debris, making the cramped quarters even tighter. About a half block in, the tunnel dropped into a cistern filled with stagnant water. Turning around, I climbed down the ladder built into the stonework centuries earlier.

There was a plop. Rings of water spread out from the side nearest me maybe a dozen feet away. A chill ran up my spine and I came to an abrupt halt.

It was just some stale, stagnant water…wasn't it?

Another plop sounded, followed quickly by another set of rings, this time at the far side. I was standing on a three-foot section of stone nine feet down and needed to circle the pool to go up the ladder on the other side.

Taking a deep breath, I took another step and a large, greasy, grayish tentacle slammed into the wall in front of me. I stumbled back when another whipped out of the water to slap me into the stone. A half second later, a massive creature with the flesh of a crocodile, vaguely humanoid with the appendages of a squid, surfaced. Where the head should be was a faceless blob. It leaned closer as its face bloomed like a flower to show a massive beak. Everything about this…thing, reeked of death.

Suddenly, it lunged for my face. I dove to the side and nearly wound up in the water. Another appendage slammed into the rock in front of me, drilling a hole through the wall. Scrambling to my feet, I called forth the scythe and drove it into the side of the beast's neck. It screamed out in pain but didn't drop dead.

Kur sounded panicked. *"It's already beyond the veil. All that's left is a mishmash of parts."*

"Thanks."

The scythe vanished to be replaced by the gladius.

It dove at me again. I stepped to the side, brought the blade down, and lopped off its creepy mouth head thing. The beast went nuts but still somehow managed to grab hold of the beak and lift it back to its neck hole.

Fuck this, I was out.

Indigo flames wrapped around me and I appeared at the top of the cistern on the other side. The mutant undead beast set its head back in place. Tar like strands of black ichor formed around the cut, reattaching itself. I hurled a spear of ice through its mouth and scrambled up into the next tunnel, trying to put distance between me and it.

A long tentacle stretched out but didn't quite reach me. Still, I wasn't taking any chances. Turning, I scurried down the corridor as fast as possible. This one was much cleaner than the previous, but it was a bit narrower, so give with one hand and take with the other. Three turns later, I found myself in a square stone room with an ancient looking wooden door partially off the hinges.

Slowly, I pulled it open to find the place much like Andrew described it. Full of brick, stone, and lumber. It'd once been a massive thirty by thirty area with the gate located on the far wall. While I was sure the gate was still there, it was useless until we were able to dig it out.

Time to play hopscotch through the wreckage. I climbed through about ten feet before it turned impassible. Forming a blade of ice, I chiseled through a layer of downed floor to see an opening a few feet away. I focused on the spot as indigo flames wrapped around me. When they faded, I found fresh prints in the dust leading downstairs. Curious, I followed them back to the gate. Someone…okay, Lazarus, blasted their way through the broken room then cut a trail to the same opening I'd found.

Dick.

Sadly, there was only one set of tracks and they didn't imply he was carrying anyone, so it was doubtful he'd brought Heather with him. The likelihood of her remaining alive became slimmer and slimmer with each hour that passed. At this point, I was just waiting for her coin to suddenly appear in my pocket to seal the deal. Thankfully, that hadn't happened.

With an abundance of caution, I crept down the stairs to the second level. It was the same size as above but cut up into rooms. The damage here wasn't as noticeable save for one of the storage closets that was currently holding part of the floor above. Given the creaks and groans coming from the ceiling, it wouldn't be long before the first level and this one was one and the same.

Delving deeper into the darkness, the third floor was a combination alchemy lab straight out of the middle ages, Frankenstein's mortuary, and server room. To add a bit of ambiance to the creep factor, he'd used a mashup of the steampunk tech I'd seen in Waterford tied into a computer system straight out of Buck Rogers.

One of the tables had the parts and pieces of a man's body sewn into a weird fleshy material filled with circuitry. Everything about it made my skin crawl. Just what in the fuck was Lazarus doing? As much as it pained me, I strode over to the nearest sever tower.

I tapped out a message to Alfred.

Found a mad scientist laboratory and need you to secure the data there, if possible.

His response was almost instantaneous.

Please attach the transmitter from the ship to the nearest terminal and I'll see what I can do.

Pulling the tiny square out of my pocket, I stared at it for several seconds.

Exactly how am I supposed to do that? There isn't a port or wire or anything to make that happen.

Alfred messaged me back.

Just set it on the machine I'll handle the rest.

I sat it atop the case and waited. The box turned gray, then orange, then blue.

My phone vibrated again.

Done.

After thanking him, I pocketed the transmitter and my phone.

Backtracking to the stairs, I proceeded down to the main event.

Unlike the other levels, this one was comprised of a multitude of tunnels that lead to different open spaces; some connected, some not. Finally, I took the only path left to me. A half mile later, the sound of steel grinding stone drowned out everything else. I stepped into a gigantic chamber to find Lazarus hurriedly throwing gold bars into a crate. Across the room was a massive drill—the type used to dig out subways or cut through a mountain so cars could drive through.

Lazarus froze. Then he dropped the bar in his hand to the floor. With a simple gesture, the big machine died and the room got quiet.

He turned to me with fear and anger in his eyes. "Of course, it's you."

"Why'd you attack Kimberly and where's Heather?"

His expression faltered as he stepped back. "Look, that whole situation wasn't supposed to go down like that." He grimaced. "But after what you've done by attacking Waterford, I needed to protect myself."

The chorus of demons sounded in the distance as my armor wrapped around me. "Where's Heather?"

"It...it was an accident." Panic sounded in his voice. "I didn't know."

The flames around my left arm intensified. "Lazarus, you should know that this is your only chance to live through the night." I held out my right hand and the scythe appeared. "Tell me what I want to know, and we can discuss your retirement."

He stumbled and fell onto his ass. "Wait...I went to collect Heather and Kim to keep you and your fucking uncle off my back."

I stepped forward as fire dripped onto the floor. "And?"

"And...for some reason I couldn't bring both of them...or either of them." His voice cracked. "I mean...Kim stayed where she was, but Heather came through the aether with me...then she was gone."

My voice turned hard and gravelly as it wasn't entirely my own. "What do you mean, gone?"

He rolled onto his feet, backpedaling away from me. "I mean she was in my arms one second and gone the next." Holding out his hands, he pointed at the gold bars. "Look, we can make a deal. I've got lots of gold...take it. Just leave me be, that's all I ask."

"You lost her?" Was he fucking kidding me? "Find her, now."

His gaze hit the floor. "I've tried...I mean, a missing hostage isn't exactly useful."

"Lazarus." I stepped closer as more fire burned through the stone. "You're testing my patience." Moving forward, more flames hit the floor to vanish below the surface. "Where exactly did you lose her?"

He moved to the side, trying to distance himself from me. "I'm not sure what it's called." Pausing, he lifted his hands. "Think of my right hand as our world and my left as another realm. That empty space there is the in-between." His voice dropped. "That's what I call it, anyway. Not sure if that's what it is or not."

Kur wriggled in my mind's eye. *"That's a forbidden zone. No one is allowed there. Reality as we know it doesn't work in the space he's describing."*

Goddamn it.

"Lazarus, why are you running?"

He blinked. "Because you intend to kill me."

"What makes you think that?"

Snorting, he said, "Because I'm not stupid."

"But you are." I allowed the armor to fade. "Take me to the in-between and I'll find her myself."

A massive groan sounded overhead. That was quickly followed by a crack. Then, the tunnel I'd exited shot dust and dirt into the room, making it impossible to see for several seconds. Once it cleared, Lazarus was nowhere to be found.

Goddamn it.

27

August 30th

The last two days were a serious pain in the ass. A ton of centurions secured Lazarus's abode. Henri was looking into how to enter the in-between and generally, things were more or less fucked on a royal scale.

I asked the remaining governors and vigiles to meet me at Alfred's home in France. In addition, I'd invited Henri, Keto Baba, and Baptist to join us. Given how enormous the place was, you'd think he'd have a conference room. But that wasn't the case, so we settled around the massive table in the formal dining area.

I cleared my throat. "Thank you for joining me today."

The others quieted down.

Henri frowned. "I'd like to get back to finding my granddaughter if you don't mind."

"I'm getting to that." I gestured around the room. "Just give me a second."

He sat back and glanced over at his friend, Keto, who sat next to him. "Fine, let's get on with whatever this is."

I reached into my pocket and palmed two gold coins. "As everyone knows, we've lost a few people recently. Alfred Monet and Chione to name but two."

There were murmurs of agreement.

"Then there's that scumbag, Lazarus, who's been playing us all for a long time."

Keto growled. "And with him gone, there's no way to fix the Archive...we'll be short governors going forward...meaning we're crippled." He slammed his hand against the table. "The Black Circle will pick us off easy as you please now."

"About that." I leaned between Keto and Henri, placing a gold coin in front of each of them. "The coins no longer acknowledge Lazarus as their master." Pointing at them, I said, "As you can see, they've changed. The Latin is gone...replaced by Runes and glyphs I'm not familiar with. The Archive is in the past. Going forward, it's my suggestion that we change our name to Witenagemot. Think of it as a council managed by the governors...sages if you will." Taking a deep breath, I continued, "Gone are the days that didn't give you voice. It's our job to create an environment that'll make everyone feel welcome, not just the elite." I paused for a moment to let that sink in. "You are the future." I gestured at Harold. "My grandfather has built a new organization that has zero ties to the Black Circle. I've gained access to a new computer system that'll help keep us safe. Let the Archive die as the archaic piece of shit that it was and let's move forward together." Placing a hand on either of their shoulders, I smiled. "I'd like to ask you both to take up the coins. One of you for the governor of Europe and the other of Southern Africa."

Henri blinked. "What about Heather?"

"You need to be close to Lazarus's freaky lab and catacomb system, right?" I shrugged. "So why not live there while you figure shit out? We can rebuild the house and secure that gate to make sure you don't have any unwelcome visitors."

"Uh..."

I patted his back. "Think about it...you'll have everything you need at your fingertips to find her."

Keto reached out and picked his up. "I'm all too happy to make the change." He turned to Henri. "I'll be right here to help you. You'll have the resources of two continents at your disposal."

Henri hesitantly reached out for his coin. The moment he picked it up, his centurion mark faded then the gold melted in his hand and delved under his flesh. "Fine…fine…I'll do it."

I blew out a long breath. "Baptist has several names of folks who might be useful in filling the spaces that are currently vacant around the world."

Attila stood. "As to your proposal for us to fold the Archive into the Witenagemot…who will rule the council?"

An excellent question and one I'd given a lot of thought to. "Until such time as we can recover his coin, I'd suggest that you guys work together and make decisions that'll benefit us as a whole." I gestured at Gabriel and Vasile. "That's what we're working on." Sighing, I said, "I don't want this to turn into a dictatorship again. And if you're looking at me, don't. I've got my hands full trying to quash all the bullshit that's springing up around the globe. You guys are some of the most powerful people in the world. Some of you have centuries of experience to share with others." I pointed at Attila. "You actually ruled an empire at one point in your life. I'm sure you can help us set something up that'll work for the general good."

He chuckled. "You're not at all the man we were told."

"If you heard anything about me from Lazarus or his flunkies, then I'm happy about that."

Mirth laced its way into his tone. "Rumors, none of them flattering. Most painted you as a power-hungry wannabe dictator. Glad to see that isn't the case."

"You're welcome."

He grinned. "What's next?"

I pointed at Harold. "Talk to him. See how we can get this rebranding going. I'm sure there'll be more than a few of the old guard who won't want to change. Honestly, I'm not sure what we'll do about them, but they can't be left to their own devices."

Gabriella nodded. "Agreed."

Henri nudged me. "Got a second?"

"Sure." I looked out at the others. "I'm going to steal Henri for a moment."

Outside in the hallway, Henri reached into his coat pocket and pulled out a small box. "I finished the key."

"Key?"

He blinked. "For the vampires under Notre Dame."

For fucks sake, I'd totally forgotten about them. "Oh, right, thanks."

"Not sure what you're going to do with it since you're not a vampire."

I smiled. "You're right, I'm not." Pulling out my phone, I began to type out a message. "One second."

Vasile pushed open the door a moment later. "Yes?"

"I've got a job for you." I gestured at Henri then handed Vasile the box. "He'll explain."

Henri glanced over at me. "I will?"

"Hey, do you really want me saying pocket reality thingy and weird key that requires a vampire to enter the portal?"

Henri's eyes bulged. "Absolutely not."

"See, I occasionally make sense." I tapped Vasile on the shoulder. "Once he gets through the technical aspect, the short version is we need allies. The more the better."

"O…okay…whatever that means."

A remorseful chuckle escaped Henri's lips. "Oh, you're in for a treat, my boy." He gestured over at a couple of wing chairs. "Come, let's talk about the underground railroad for vampires."

Vasile went unnaturally still. "That's a real thing?"

"It is." Henri's voice turned professorial. "It's been going on for a long time now."

I left them to their discussion.

Everything was handled here. Now, I had to tend to another issue in New Orleans.

Turning, I smiled. "Vasile."

"Yes?"

I hesitated for a second. "While you tend to this matter, I'm going to handle the other…if you're still okay with it."

He didn't say anything for several seconds then he nodded. "I am. You got that photo I sent?"

"I did."

It'd take the governors a few days to sort things out with Harold, and I simply didn't have that kind of time. With that in mind, I went back into the dining room, said my goodbyes, and returned to New Orleans.

28

Not wanting to invade Viktor's privacy any more than I was about to, I opted to take the Tucker. I pulled into the lot and parked. Sitting there for a second, I took a deep breath, pushed open the door, and walked toward the entrance.

Inside, Justine met me with a tag. Her smile was missing. "How are you holding up?"

"About as well as anyone else, I'd expect."

She nodded. "Henri will find her."

I clipped my pass onto my belt. "I know."

Heather and Justine had been best friends since college. Justine had gone off to do her duty in the service, while Heather went to New York.

Justine hugged me. "She's going to be fine…her coin still hasn't showed, right?"

"Right."

She wiped away a tear. "He's expecting you." Pointing up, she asked, "You sure you don't want me to come with you?"

"No, but it's probably for the best."

She hugged me again. "Go on up."

I walked over to the elevator and hit the up button.

On the third floor, I took my time getting to the door at the end of the hall. To be frank, I wasn't thrilled about having to relay this information, but someone needed to, and for some reason, the universe elected me.

Joy.

I stepped into his office and Viktor got to his feet. "Afternoon, Gavin. What can I do for you today?" He frowned. "Damn."

"What?"

He shook his head. "That look on your face says you have a whole bunch of bad news for me."

"Actually, I don't." How in the hell did I break this to the man? "I'm just stressed."

His tone softened. "Right, Heather."

"That's part of it." I gestured at the sofa. "Mind if we sit over there and maybe get us both a stiff drink?"

He blinked. "Thought you said it wasn't bad news."

"It's really not, but yeah, can I have a scotch…double?"

Snickering, he walked over to the bar and grabbed a bottle of eighteen-year-old scotch and two tumblers. He filled them both three fingers deep. "That enough?"

"No, but it's a hell of a good start." I took a long draught of the amber fluid and sighed. "Okay, you might want to down that and pour yourself another."

He smiled and did as I asked. "Okay, what's got you so worked up?"

I pulled out a printed photo of the painting of Lilith in Vasile's home. "Did you know this woman at one point?"

Without looking at it, he took it out of my hand and sipped his whiskey. His gaze fell on the picture and he froze then he downed his drink, grabbed the bottle, and poured another. "I did, but that was a very long time ago." He strained to keep his voice even. "Why do you ask?"

I downed the amber fluid. My throat, chest, and stomach burned. "Okay, so you know who that is…right?"

"Lilith."

Christ. "Okay, and you two were…a couple?"

Viktor shifted in his seat. "Like I said, that was a long time ago." His tone hardened. "Why do you ask?"

I held out my hands for patience. "I'm working on it, man. This isn't what you'd call easy."

He leaned forward and placed his elbows on his knees. "I get that, but I haven't seen her in—"

"—About fifteen thousand years. I'm aware."

He blinked. "Wait, that's some awfully specific math."

"It is, isn't it." Suddenly uncomfortable, I shifted in my chair. "Have you had any headaches recently…like in the last two weeks?"

He glanced around the room and lowered his voice. "How do you know about those?"

"I need you to remain calm and don't push, okay?"

Viktor wiped his nose. "I can't tell if you're trying to piss me off or gently break something to me. Either way though, I suggest you get to a point, soon."

"I think you have a son."

His expression blanked then his cheeks turned crimson as he got to his feet, fury in his tone. "That's not funny." He pointed out the window. "Especially since you know what's happened to Kira."

I pulled out a vial of blood. "I'm not joking."

"What's that?"

Handing it to him, I said, "Proof? Or not…but I need to be sure. You're the only one I'd trust with this sample. The man who gave it to me wants to know his father. For centuries, Adam claimed to be that person, but that turned out to be a lie. After he was confronted, he told this person that the Star Born was his father." I gestured at him. "Unless there's another one of you walking around that slept with Lilith, I'm ninety-nine percent sure you have a fifteen-thousand-year-old son."

His eyes unfocused as he took the vial. "Are…are you sure?"

"No." I pointed at his hand. "That's why I got that. Test it. Let's figure this shit out and if he is your son, I'll see about arranging a meeting. Which could be problematic."

He waved for me to follow. "Why's that?"

"Every time he steps through the gate here in New Orleans...close proximity to you, his head feels like it's going to explode then he faints."

Viktor grunted. "We'll figure it out."

We made our way over to the north wing and up to lab eighteen. The doors slid open to reveal a large man who looked remarkably like Viktor standing on the far side of the room.

He pointed at an automated conveyer belt. "Place the sample there. I'll handle everything else."

Viktor nodded and did as he was asked. Once he was finished, he gestured at the large man. "Mir, this is Gavin." He turned to me. "Gavin, Mir."

I stepped toward him and held out my hand. "Pleasure to meet you."

He grinned. "Viktor, if you wouldn't mind."

"Oh, yeah." He closed his eyes and a pulse of power rippled through the room. "Should be good."

Mir stepped forward and took my hand. "Pleasure is all mine."

I shook it then my hand slipped through his thumb and fingers. Stepping back a bit, I asked, "What the fuck was that?"

Mir frowned. "Someone being stingy."

Viktor sighed. "Sorry, I'm...well, stunned at the moment."

Mir sighed. "I'm mostly a super advanced AI/hologram/fraction of Viktor's consciousness." He leaned toward Viktor and smiled. "See the resemblance."

No way this was real. "You're joking, right?"

Viktor shook his head. "Not even a little bit."

"Oh fuck...your full name is Mimir, isn't it?"

They both stopped moving.

Viktor nodded. "Yes, but the number of people who know that is super small and you're not among them. Care to tell me how you know it?"

Open mouth and insert foot.

"It's a long story that involves an escape pod and a blank Húsvættir." Judging by the confusion on their faces, they had no idea what that was. "That's a super advanced AI that can be imprinted with a personality." I rubbed the top of my head. "Lilith created them…don't ask me how, because I don't know."

The screen behind Mir lit up and the printer came to life, pushing out papers.

Viktor sighed. "We'll revisit this conversation." He turned to Mir. "Verdict?"

Mir beamed. "You're the proud father of…a vampire?" He glanced over at me. "Is that right?"

"It is." I bit my lip. "How much do you know about Lilith and Adam from before the whole universe reset itself?"

Viktor leaned against the counter. "Guess that's as accurate as any other way of putting it…nothing, why?"

Taking a deep breath, I delved into what I knew. That being, Adam and Lilith were carriers of the parasite that caused vampirism. While neither of them was affected by the parasite themselves, their children were.

Viktor sounded lost in thought. "That'd make Cain and Abel the first Vampires."

"It would."

Mir folded his arms. "How do you know so much about them?"

Time to put my cards on the table. "You know what happened to the strigoi last month?"

"They were wiped out." Viktor frowned. "What's that got to do with anything?"

Well, here went nothing. "It means, your son's half-brother, Cain, is awake." I held up a finger. "You've got to understand, he has a job to do…wipe out his father's children to fix whatever cosmic glitch that has him stuck in this fucking nightmare reset scenario."

Mir cocked his head to the side. "What's that supposed to mean?"

"It means, he remembers everything." I tapped the side of my head. "Like perfect recall. Thanks to some weird shit with the nanites in his system and mine, he shared some truly unpleasant memories with me not long ago. So, before you go looking for him, you should know he wants to meet you. In fact, that's one of his big to do things. When he resurfaces in the next few weeks, I'll happily do a number swap for you two then you guys can sit down and talk to your hearts content. Sound good?"

Viktor closed his eyes, laughed, and shook his head. "Fuck, this has been a messed up few months. And yes, it sounds great." He sighed. "I'd like to meet my son first, though."

Mir's expression turned serious. "I've got an idea, but no one is going to like it."

Viktor shrugged. "What else is new?"

"Hey, like he said, it's been a fucked up few months." I rubbed my forehead. "I doubt whatever you have in mind is going to make things that much worse."

Mir pointed at Viktor. "When the time comes, you'll need to give Gavin a vial of your blood." He turned to me. "And you'll need to give it to his son and have him drink it."

Okay, I was wrong, it could get worse. "That sounds like a poor idea. What's it going to do?"

Mir shrugged. "Not entirely sure, but I'm hoping it'll push him onto the Nexus so he'll stop causing a feedback loop…meaning, he'll stop passing out and Viktor will stop being bedridden."

"Fine…but it can't be today…he's out of touch for a bit." I hung my head. "When he comes back, I'll see how he wants to proceed. Fair?"

Viktor nodded. "Works for me."

29

It was nearly sunset by the time I got on the road home. About three blocks from Viktor's, a cop turned on his lights and I pulled over and put the car in park.

An officer in plain clothes got out of the vehicle and strode toward the car. "Step out of the vehicle, sir."

Goddamn it, I didn't have time for this shit. Still, I undid my seatbelt and got out to find myself face to face with James Matherne.

"Evening, Randall." He sneered at me. "Still got that blog?"

I resisted the urge to roll my eyes. "We both know that wasn't a thing. So, what do you want, James?"

Fury swam through his eyes as he reached into his jacket to pull out a thick envelope. "Against my better judgement, Dermot has ordered me to offer you a truce." He handed it to me. "The terms are spelled out in there."

"Uh-huh."

He flinched forward as hatred coated his tone. "If it was up to me, we'd wipe you out, but this came from higher up the food chain." Seething, he said, "The were's are yours. Anyone who wants to stay with whatever you're working with these days can go with our consent. Those who wish to stay with the Archive…the chosen…can do so with the blessing of the twelve—you do know who we are, right?"

"I'm familiar, yes."

James spat on the ground. "Good. Read over the documents…once you're finished, email the address at the bottom of the page and we'll make it public." He tugged off his gun and badge to hand them to me. "Give these to the NOPD with my sympathies. I quit."

"Happy to."

He handed me a set of keys. "The car too. I'm done here. You have ninety days to respond." Reaching into his pant pocket, he produced a small piece of bone. "If I see you again, treaty be damned, I'll take your head."

James clasped the thing to his chest and vanished.

30

September 8th

The Archive wasn't as dead as I'd hoped it'd be. The Twelve resurrected the name and was openly recruiting folks. To my surprise, not as many were jumping at the chance as I'd thought. Again, it would seem the masses were only too happy to go along for the ride, even if it was something they found distasteful.

I'd turned the treaty over to the governors the day I got it. Problem was, they were still working through it, making changes to have me email Dermot to approve. So far, all of our adjustments were taken without argument.

Our hope for additional allies from the vampires in the pocket reality wasn't looking good. According to Vasile, they were discussing their options, but he didn't sound confident. He'd resurfaced late last night and I'd collected a vile of Viktor's blood this morning. All that was left to do was to deliver it to his son. From there, they'd hopefully have a lovely reunion. I still wasn't sure how that'd turn out.

Much to my displeasure, Heather was still missing. The upside, her coin hadn't shown up on my desk, so that was a positive…she still lived. In my desperation, I'd reached out to Dermot to see if he knew anything. He assured me he didn't and would do everything he could to help.

Part of that came with a bounty on Lazarus's head. For the first time in history, the Black Circle and the rest of us had a common goal—bringing the fugitive back alive. I had no idea what they wanted to do to him but if I had my way, Andrew would tear his mind apart until he told us where Heather was.

Worry set in. She wasn't the kind of person who'd do well as a prisoner...no one did...something I was intimately familiar with. Wherever she may be, it was my hope that she knew she was loved and that we were coming for her.

Alexander rummaged through her things to have trackers from around the globe get a scent they could use. One way or another, she would be found.

In the meantime, Henri continued to search for a way to access the in-between. As for me, I tried to teleport to her several times a day. Something had to give...it was just a matter of when.

What made things worse was how quiet the world had become. No one, especially me, knew quite how to deal with that. On top of everything else, the necromancers were moving into the open in their new incarnation of the Archive. At this point, it was only a matter of time before something blew up in our faces.

One crises at a time I suppose...first we needed to find Heather, then we could deal with whatever came next.

ACKNOWLEDGMENTS

A big thank you to all of you for supporting the books. Without you, I wouldn't get to do this.

ABOUT THE AUTHOR

Ken Lange is a current resident of the "Big Easy," along with his partner and evil, yet loving, cats. Any delay, typo, or missed edit can and will be blamed on the latter's interference.

He arrived at this career a little later in life, and his work reflects it. Most of his characters won't be in their twenties, and they aren't always warm and fuzzy. He is of the opinion that middle-aged adults are woefully underrepresented in fiction, and has made it his mission to plug that gap.

Translation: he's middle aged and crotchety.

ALSO BY KEN LANGE

Warden Global

The Wanderer Awakens
Sleipnir's Heart
Rise of the Storm Bringer
Children of the Storm

Vigiles Urbani

Accession of the Stone Born
Dust Walkers
Shades of Fire & Ash

Plague Bearer

Dawning

Coming soon:

Fall of Eleazer, Withering, Book 1